Eden's Flesh

'How gorgeous!' Eden exclaimed as she laid her eyes on the shining, curved metal form of the small bronze sculpture which rested in the middle of the polished table. It *was* gorgeous. But the sculpture wasn't at the crux of Eden's interest. Rather, what grabbed her attention was the physical presence of the tall, hunky man with the shock of thick, curly red hair. The man who had created the sculpture. Eden felt a flush travelling up her body. She knew then, how difficult it would be to hide the sexual arousal she was feeling.

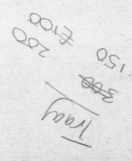

Eden's Flesh
Robyn Russell

BLACK Lace

Black Lace books contain sexual fantasies.
In real life, always practise safe sex.

This edition published 2004 by
Black Lace
Thames Wharf Studios
Rainville Road
London W6 9HA

Originally published 1997 as *Ginger Root*

Printed and bound by Mackays of Chatham PLC

ISBN 0 352 33923 3

Contents

to all the bears

Chapter One
Hot Photographs

During a slow afternoon, Eden Sinclair, Director of the exclusive Galerie Raton in Atlanta's prestigious Midtown district, sat alone in her office. A shaft of warm summer sun shone through the skylight above her head, falling across her shoulders and chestnut hair, to lie shimmering upon the smooth maple surface of her desk. Bouncing off the highlights of a group of black-and-white photographs arranged before the young woman, the ray of afternoon light spilled off the desk and spread, diffusing in intensity, across the Persian carpet on her office floor.

The sun was like Zeus' famed 'golden shower' in Greek mythology, Eden Sinclair thought idly, as she looked up from her intense study of the images and watched the sunlight dance its dappled pattern at her feet. She considered the erotic implications of the god, Zeus, sprinkling his 'golden shower' of seed over the unknowing Danaë, impregnating the girl with his immortal come so that she gave birth to the hero Perseus.

Eden, who wore her thick and shiny, chestnut-brown hair close against her head, emphasising the oval shape of her face, sighed impatiently at the thought of a sexy ejaculation. She uncrossed her legs, kicked off her high-heeled sandals and stood up.

Tall and graceful, Eden stretched and smoothed down the hips of the snug skirt hugging her figure. Her brilliantly coloured linen suit was a deep blue that matched her big dark eyes. Eden picked up a handful of photos and walked to the low teak balustrade that formed the edge of the mezzanine eyrie that was her office.

From this perch above the main floor of Galerie Raton, Eden could survey most of the tall exhibition spaces below, normally inhabited by the highly priced art so admired by the gallery's clients. But this afternoon, the walls and the floor were empty; the space silent. Her gaze lingered on the stark white walls and polished maple floors, and on the fine lines of the spiral stair that curled upward to bring visitors to her sanctum. Except there was no visitor. No art and no artist, when there should have been both.

Perusing once again the large format photographs fanned out in her hand, Eden admired the anatomical details of the cast bronze male and female figures. In reality, the nude sculptures were maquettes, though they looked monumental in scale, so life-like were their details. Some of the polished beauties stood or reclined alone, while others, in couples or larger groups, touched or bonded in a variety of poses. Some of the lovingly modelled, smooth metal figures were clearly engaged in sexual activities, while others were more contemplative.

Every member of this sculptural cast radiated sensual power just from the black and white 8×10 inch reproductions, and Eden was impatient to see them in their bronze 'flesh', filling the hollow receptacle of the gallery with their erotic energy. But the floor space in the room below was still empty. For at least the tenth time since lunch, Eden wondered impatiently, where were those sculptures?

Having cleared out the gallery in readiness to hang the new group show that would launch the summer's exhibition season, Eden had yesterday dispatched one of the art gallery's delivery vans with a crew to pick up the new work from Savannah, only four and a half hours away on the Georgia sea coast. And the sculptures' creator, Michael MacKenzie, a Scottish artist new to Atlanta and to Galerie Raton, was supposed to have called her today to set up a meeting.

Eden needed to see these new bronzes before selecting several complementary works by the gallery's other artists. Her boss, Alexander Raton, had decreed just two days ago that MacKenzie's sculptures would be the centrepieces of this imminent show.

From the photographs in her hand, Eden recognised that this new work of MacKenzie was certainly good, but having to include it this late had completely messed up her original plans, forcing her to rethink the whole exhibition. The opening reception was now only nine days away, and Eden was still undecided how to curate the show. At the last minute, she had been forced to cancel the original announcements at the printers, and instead had hurriedly sent out invitations to gallery clients in the form of a generic postcard, with no illustration and few details. This was not at all the way she liked to do business! Eden paced the floor in annoyance, growing tense with worry. She started to call the gallery's receptionist, Angela St John, at her desk below, but paused as a movement caught her eye.

Looking down towards the foyer of the gallery, Eden saw that honey-blonde Angela was otherwise engaged. The focus of the young gallery assistant's excitement was not, however, the imminent arrival of the new statues, but instead a local artist, Winston Fineman, who doubled as the part-time critic for the *Atlanta Democrat*. As Eden watched from above, the tall angular Fineman walked through the gallery foyer and approached Angela's desk.

3

The receptionist was leaning against the desktop, one cheek of her trim bottom firmly wedged on one corner, her skirt hiked up high on her thighs, and today she wore heels that almost qualified as stilettos!

As they talked and laughed, the tall, urbane and dark-haired Fineman loomed over Angela's shoulder from behind as she proffered a sketchbook for his attention. But from where Eden was standing, undetected above, she saw that the man's interest was not on the artwork Angela held but rather on the trim receptionist's pert breasts which he deliberately and languidly absorbed as he looked down her low-cut blouse.

Only recently, Eden had discovered that Angela, like many workers in the art business, nurtured ideas of her own career as an artist. A week or so ago Angela had brought in her sketchbook for Fineman, a frequent visitor to Galerie Raton, to critique, and she had been hanging around him at every opportunity since.

At Angela's suggestion, Eden had leafed through Angela's sketches and, to her surprise, had been quite impressed. Most of the figurative drawings from life or from copies of classical statues were nudes, and Angela's technique for rendering the muscles and bone structure of the human body was very accomplished for a young artist. Eden had recognised several classical poses from her own art education, when she herself had nurtured ambitions of becoming a practising artist.

She had been pretty good, too, thought Eden, allowing herself a smile of remembrance, although it had been several years since she had painted seriously. Like many artists setting out on their careers, Eden had taken a series of part-time jobs in the art business to make ends meet. Eventually, she had forged a career in gallery management, handling other people's art instead of making her own. Eden continued to use her trained painter's eye to assess talent, and her commercial judg-

4

ment had improved over the years to match her critical opinion.

Skimming through the pages of Angela's work, it was obvious to Eden which drawings had been made from real-life models and which were from plaster statues. About half of the pencil sketches vibrated with a special energy which the others lacked, despite their crisp technique. These better drawings were all of the same young man, and several of them depicted him in states of evident sexual arousal. One sketch in particular had made Eden pause in her brisk perusal and stare with critical approval and a tingling enjoyment: the young man, reclining on a covered couch, was fondling his very erect penis with obvious pleasure, gazing straight at the viewer, tense, as he stroked the long shaft of his member with one hand and cradled his balls in the other, but still with a lazy half smile on his lips.

Angela's drawing technique had captured both the physical details of her model's anatomy, and a sense of sexual energy barely held in check, as if a great burst of semen was about to erupt from the young man's cock. This sketch was looser than the others, a quick study with brisk and confident pencil strokes. Eden had imagined Angela working fast and furious to capture the moment before she gave in, threw her pencil and sketchbook aside, and knelt in front of her lover (for surely this was he!) and took that delicious-looking flesh in her mouth, sucking her lover's cream, tasting his essence and his lust. Or perhaps Angela had just pulled off her clothes and impaled herself on that impressive member, riding her man for the last few moments before he inevitably came with a flood inside her!

But after only a few more drawings, the young man had disappeared from Angela's pages, to be replaced by more conscientious but dull studies of standard statues. Eden had felt a sense of disappointment, both as a critic, sensing that something had been lost from the work; and

5

as a woman, for the only reasonable interpretation seemed to be that Angela's affair with the handsome young man had come to an untimely end.

Bringing her sketchbook to Galerie Raton had been only a prelude for bigger things. Today, Angela had carried in an actual painting for Winston Fineman to see. Eden observed it now, propped against the reception desk below her. It featured the same young man who appeared so often and so aroused in the pages of Angela's sketchbook, although in the larger oil painting the man's sexual prowess was held in check. Although naked, his pose was more demure, his penis politely flaccid and his hands occupied with a book as he lay on the same couch, his attention apparently focused on his reading.

As she watched them from above, Eden saw Fineman lead Angela by the arm around to her painting, gesturing between it and the sketchbook's open pages.

'This captures the spirit of some of your best sketches,' Eden heard Fineman say. 'It's obvious you do your best work from life rather than classical copies. You clearly respond to your subject in an immediate and sensual way, capturing all that sexual energy, whether he's turned on or not.'

Not bad, mused Eden, poised unseen on her balcony above the pair, and thinking that Fineman's comments, while ostensibly about Angela's art, were a pretty good opening for a more personal agenda. She nearly laughed outright when her intuition was borne out by Fineman's next little speech.

'It is easy for me to critique your work from an academic perspective, and from my experience as a painter myself, Angela,' he began. 'I could remark on your quality of line, on your brushstroke and handling of paint. I can see some problems of composition, of difficult negative space on the canvas. But your colour mixing is

6

good; it's very clear that you don't just use colours straight from the tube.'

Angela was absorbed, a rapt expression on her face.

Fineman smiled and continued. 'But I could really be of more help to you if I could observe you at work, visit you in your studio, perhaps. It's evident that there's a strong sensual component in your painting that I could analyse much better by being there with you and watching you work. If you're going for coffee soon, we can talk more about it then.'

Men are so transparent, reflected Eden, as she observed Fineman's none-too-subtle moves on Angela. But she supposed Angela, too, had some ulterior motives of a sexual nature. Now that Eden paid attention, it was evident that Angela had discarded her bra after returning from lunch, and the cotton fabric of her blouse allowed a clear outline of perky nipples and the contours of high rounded breasts.

Eden understood her assistant's intentions as she watched Angela turn to face Fineman, flip her long, honey-blonde hair over her shoulders and laugh prettily. Standing on tiptoe to brush his lips with hers, Angela whispered something in Fineman's ear that Eden did not catch. As they turned to go, the art critic's hand delicately cradled Angela's right breast, brushing her inviting nipple with a thumb. Then they were gone, taking the painting with them.

The couple's departure deepened Eden's sense of solitude in the empty spaces of the gallery. A glance from the single window of her office revealed the soulless cacophony of glass and polished stone façades that comprised Atlanta's business and cultural Midtown district. The cold reflective surfaces of the new edifices stole the beauty of the few historic structures that remained in the cityscape, hugging the refracted images of the old buildings to their shiny new walls.

Galerie Raton was housed in one such older property, sharing its spaces with some attorneys and accountants on the lower floors. It was an idiosyncratic building, originally a town mini-mansion for a wealthy industrialist. Now it sat wedged between skyscrapers that tried desperately to look like 1930s art deco, resembling, Eden thought, second-rate rejects from Gotham City in a Batman movie.

Although dwarfed by its neighbours, the building which the gallery inhabited was large on a domestic scale, having five storeys rising straight up from the pavement. The top three floors sat above a two-storey plinth of local granite, which disappeared into the steep slope of the site as it rose towards the rear. The attorneys and accountants occupied the floors in the stone base, while the gallery filled the upper three spaces, which had been extensively remodelled to provide tall, light and airy volumes, ideal for the display of fine art.

But tired now of these empty rooms below her, Eden strode across to her single, sloping skylight. This afforded her a southerly view towards downtown where, framed between adjacent towers, Eden could see the larger multitude of skyscrapers that marked Atlanta's commercial heart, two miles away. The teeming activity implied by all these gleaming commercial hives, each with their thousands of workers, contrasted starkly with her own seclusion.

Irritated by her introspection, Eden snatched a plump cushion from her chaise longue and tossed it on the floor. She gathered up all the remaining photographs from her desk, and rearranged them around her as she knelt on the sun-flecked carpet. In the absence of the sculptures themselves, perhaps she should just run through potential exhibition strategies in her mind one more time.

But as she studied the sensual imagery before her, composed of bronze heads and hands, handsome torsos of athletic hips and muscular thighs, buttocks, breasts and genitalia, Eden's thoughts drifted. The heat of the summer afternoon, with its sun-laden silence broken only by the gentle whisper of the air-conditioning, deflected her intentions. She found herself pondering not the logic of sculptural selection for the space below, but rather the erotic nature of the statues themselves, which seemed to celebrate physical intimacy and the tenderness of sex.

Most of the MacKenzie sculptures were neoclassically inspired by masterpieces such as Giorgione's famous painting, the nude *Sleeping Venus*, an opulent odalisque, whose left hand gently played with her pubic hair as her fingertips seemed to explore the very opening of her vulva. As Eden examined the sculptor's reinterpretation of this elegant lady daintily fondling herself, she found her own hand wandering between her thighs, raising the hem of her skirt and stroking her own pubic mound through the thin silk of her panties. Sinking back into the cushion, she stroked the flesh of her inner thigh as she gazed next at a pair of lovers whose mingled limbs recalled the sensual foreplay captured by Jacques-Louis David in his canvas *Venus Disrobing Mars*.

In MacKenzie's sculpture, a nude woman undressed her lover as he lay back, unresisting to her ministrations. The woman's nipples were erect and a bulge was rising from the male figure's groin, still partially covered by clothing. As if in sympathy, Eden felt her nipples stir beneath her blouse. But her admiration for the work transcended superficial eroticism. These sculptures were more than just clever elaborations of sensual paintings by old masters. Whereas the motions and passions of love-making were timeless, the figures in the sculptures seemed utterly contemporary.

A young lady lawyer from the high-rise office tower next door could have been the model for MacKenzie's rendition of Venus. His Mars could be an investment analyst from the Magnolia National Bank skyscraper down the street. Or, with their trim bodies, they could be instructors at Eden's local health club, a couple blocks over by the commuter train station.

Eden's attention returned to the solitary female figure who daintily fondled herself. Whether her small caresses were in preparation for her lover, or as a solo substitute for the attentions of an absent partner, was unclear, but Eden's sympathies lay with the latter interpretation; there was no man in her own life at present, and she wondered if MacKenzie's Venus was also without a man to fondle and caress her.

Having spent more than a year without a man close to her, Eden allowed the erotic charge of these bronze images to lead her mind down an increasingly familiar path. She transferred the sensual daydreams of her reveries to her co-workers and gallery artists, while the figures in the photographs of the cast bronzes, mythical beings and goddesses, danced in her mind.

While Eden enjoyed these fantasies, they were ultimately unfulfilling. But they must remain fictitious, she reminded herself, for over the years she had developed an inflexible rule never to become romantically involved with her clients or her artists. She had seen too many instances where reputations had been unravelled because professional boundaries had been erased and integrity compromised. Having sex with her artists was definitely out of bounds, but fantasising about it didn't do any harm!

And though she didn't really like the man who was her boss, Eden couldn't help speculating about Alexander Raton's sexual attributes and appetites. His tall, slim grey-haired figure was always clothed in what appeared to be exactly the same fitted Italian suit. He must have dozens of identical outfits, mused Eden, to look so immaculate day after day. Even in the harsh heat and humidity of Atlanta's summers, he never seemed to sweat; he always smelled of lavender.

Conjuring up an erotic daydream, Eden pictured

Alexander Raton as one of MacKenzie's neoclassical satyrs, naked to her gaze at last, his long fingers grazing her skin as he undressed her, his solemn countenance changed into a grimace of lust as he buried his face between her thighs, his long tongue probing her swollen flesh, seeking her clitoris.

As Eden imagined being ravished by insatiable desire, she transformed Raton into the similarly tall and elegant figure of Winston Fineman, last seen playing with Angela's nipples. Eden formed an image of Fineman re-clining naked on a large bed with Angela, who lay with her legs apart, the golden curls of her pubic hair matching her blonde tresses. Both lovers turned towards her, invit-ing her to join their revels; Fineman's hand moved from stroking Angela's clitoris to his own cock, as he raised its full length between his fingers in silent invitation.

And to one side of the lovers, Eden's imagination placed Justin and Paul, the gallery delivery men, now posing as a pair of attendant young cupids, their nude bodies rippling with muscles while both their cocks responded directly to Eden's gaze, rising straight out from their flat bellies and tight pubic curls.

In her mental picture, Justin and Paul walked towards Eden, deftly masturbating as they offered her the deli-cacy of their dicks, by now glistening with the first beads of pre-come. As Eden took first one and then the other of their cocks in her hands, she knelt and licked them with her tongue.

In her imagination, Eden now felt her own body the focus of attention, as Fineman and Angela stroked her buttocks and teased her clitoris with their tongues and hands. Her love bud pulsed with pleasure as clever fingers found their way to her very core, one set reaching into her vagina, the other teasing her clitoris, goading her forward to the edge of climax.

Her fantasy dissolved in an instant to the jangling of the telephone.

Chapter Two
Coup de Foudre

*E*den could just reach the ringing telephone, and as the instrument throbbed, one ring, two, she sat with parted legs, with one hand inside her panties, where she curled a finger around her clitoris.

As she rose to her knees, Eden withdrew her hand from its arousing activity and picked up the telephone. Her momentary sense of unreality was compounded by Angela's voice on the other end talking about sex, as the receptionist said, 'He thinks it's very sexy!'

Eden slowly realised that Angela was talking about Fineman's opinion of MacKenzie's work, and not giving a description of her own amorous adventures with the art critic. As she listened to Angela's excited tone impart other, more important news as well, Eden came back to reality.

Angela explained, 'Eden, the guys called from a quick stop. Their cellular phone needs recharging, or something, so they couldn't call earlier. Traffic delays on Interstate 16 held them up, but they've just passed the Beltway, and the sculptures should be at the gallery soon.' Pausing, she added, 'Oh, and Winston will be coming up to your office to get some quotes for his article. He's going to review the show.'

After she had put the phone back in the cradle, Eden swiftly gathered the sensual images of the bronze sculptures in her hand, stood up, smoothed down her skirt, and put the cushion back on the chaise. Stooping to retrieve the jacket she had discarded in her lusty fantasies, she tossed the brilliant blue garment across the back of the couch. Her simple lime silk blouse gave her a less formal appearance, and set off the pleasant tones of her lightly tanned skin. As she sat down on the buttery smooth leather of the chaise, her skirt rose high on her thighs.

Glancing down towards the gallery's main floor, Eden saw Winston Fineman staring up at her, and she felt a strong erotic pull in her groin as his eyes raked over her body. Instinctively, she started to adjust her short skirt lower as he slowly mounted the steps to her mezzanine office. But as the tall, dark man ascended, his eyes hovering around her legs and hips, Eden left her skirt where it was and subtly rotated her body so that the hem rode even higher, showing off her trim thighs further. Young Angela may have a few years on her, decided Eden, but she could still show off her legs if she felt like it.

And, she realised, she did feel like it.

Seconds later, as Fineman stood beside her, his scent, or maybe his and Angela's combined, came to her nostrils. As his eyes explored her body, Eden crossed her legs to show Fineman even more of her thigh, barely concealing her pubic mound beneath her shortened skirt. Eden again felt an erotic impulse as Fineman stared down at her. She felt like squirming on the chaise, imagined opening her legs and masturbating in front of him. But although she was hot with a wild sexual drive, Eden projected a businesslike countenance towards Fineman, rather at odds with her pose on the couch.

The critic's voice faltered as he dragged his eyes away from Eden's provocative display and asked, 'S-s-so just who is this new artist Angela keeps telling me about? His work certainly looks very hot in reproductions.'

Eden stalled, finding it enjoyable to turn on this man. She stood up and invited him to sit on the couch while she herself returned to her desk, nestled deeply into her office under its sloping ceiling. Aware of his hooded, black-lashed eyes following her, she consciously swayed her hips provocatively as she moved away from him, and coiled herself sensuously into her stylishly ergonomic chair. The shafts of sun had moved on, leaving her work area in deeper shadow.

'I haven't met him yet myself,' Eden admitted.

Fineman's eyebrows arched in surprise. The Eden Sinclair he knew from his visits to the gallery was competent, efficient and always in charge. He knew that Alexander Raton normally left the day-to-day running of the gallery in the hands of his director, ever since she had assumed the post nearly a year ago. Fineman knew that Eden also influenced most of the artistic policy, with Raton only turning up at just the right moment to seal a sale with the sort of unctuous charm that fed the appetites of Atlanta's bourgeoisie.

'So, how is it that this exciting new artist is unknown to the gallery's director?' Fineman asked, somewhat coyly, noticing that she was radiating sexual energy and heat in waves that seemed to raise the room's temperature by several degrees. He glanced at her curiously but Eden merely shrugged, deflecting his enquiry. This was the same question that had been bothering her. Getting no response, save Eden's unusually smouldering attitude, Fineman turned his attention to a folder of slides on the glass-topped coffee table in front of him.

From her side of the room, Eden tried to concentrate her thoughts on the new artist's work, but with half her mind she continued to see Fineman as the subject of her recent erotic fantasies. She found him vaguely attractive, even though he was so shameless in his pursuit of Angela

– or perhaps because of it; he was so obviously horny. She wondered how he and Angela would make love; how their bodies would meld together in the heat of their lust. Fineman himself could be Peleus, in naked pursuit of his lover Thetis, the subject of one of the new sculptures laid out in the photographs before her. All the male bronzes had finely modelled genitals, with most of the male members in states of mild or extended arousal. Peleus' proud manhood was no exception, and Eden grazed Fineman's crotch with her eyes, imagining the size and shape of his penis, and the weight of it in her hand, feeling as she did so slightly envious of Thetis, or Angela, as the case may be.

The object of her erotic fantasy was silent. Sitting across from her on the chaise, he flipped through the magazines and artists' slide albums on the glass-topped coffee table. Over there, Fineman seemed miles away, too far to know that Eden was surreptitiously fingering herself beneath her desk, affecting nonchalance as she contemplated the photographs of the sensual bronzes. Slouching slightly in her rotating chair, she spread her legs and reached her hand between her thighs, and asked, 'Did you want to ask me some questions about the art?'

'Yes,' he responded, 'I want to get some quotes for my article on your new group show. The first show you did after arriving at the gallery set the artistic tone and direction for the year. What do you plan this year, and how does the work of this new guy, MacKenzie, fit into it? For example, do you think these sculptures are truly sensual or just pornographic? And how do you think they'll be accepted by Atlanta art patrons?' He had taken out a small pad of paper and was marking off points with the tip of his pencil.

Good questions, mused Eden, who didn't answer at first, appearing to weigh the matters carefully. Behind her desk, she secretly slid her forefinger across her thin panties, and caressed the inside of one thigh. Seconds of silence ticked by as she pulled aside her panties and masturbated softly, slowly circling her clitoris until she felt the tiny nub stand up rigidly.

He was staring at her but said nothing.

Reddening slightly at her own arousal, Eden finally replied, 'I think there's no doubt that these works demonstrate very clearly the difference between truly erotic art and simple pictures of fucking. They're in a different class than, say, Jeff Koons' explicitly sexual sculptures from the 1990s.' She looked up at him and saw that he was shocked by her blunt language. 'From what I can tell,' Eden continued, 'MacKenzie's works capture erotic emotion and the details of sexuality as well as anyone since Rodin.'

Fineman stood up, his sudden movement putting Eden's sexual wanderings on hold. She slipped her hand out from between her thighs and sat up, alert to Fineman's approach and to noises below in the gallery.

At that moment, Angela came halfway up the stairs, to say, 'Eden, the delivery van is here!'

Almost disappointed, Eden pressed her knees together, stood up and straightened her attire while Fineman's attention focused on the movement below them. Perhaps she would have been daring enough to coax Fineman's long hands under her skirt, inviting him to repeat what he was probably doing earlier with Angela. As Fineman and Angela descended the stairs, Eden saw him caress the receptionist's hips and lean buttocks, his fingers hesitating just long enough to press between the cheeks of her bottom, lingering in the shadow of the deep cleft outlined by her tight skirt. Eden shivered.

Already aroused from Fineman's lusty stares, her own masturbation, and the increasingly sexual displays of the budding couple below, Eden was hot, moist and frustrated, her labia throbbing with the desire to be touched. With one finger, she felt her rigid clitoris through the material of her skirt. Before descending to check on the arrival of the sculptures, she wanted to masturbate to a satisfying climax, but as she looked down from the balcony office, toward the main gallery floor, Justin and Paul appeared, manœuvering in the first of the bronzes.

As she watched the two young delivery men strutting their stuff below her, Eden felt herself gather even more heat; unconsciously she unfastened the top two buttons of her silken blouse. Justin was good-looking in a bad boy sort of way and Eden thought of him as a sexy jungle cat, like a jaguar. Paul was stockier, but with good muscle tone and posture. She enjoyed watching them move as they deftly positioned a bronze sculpture. Justin was newly decorated with one small gold earring, Eden noticed, and was also now sporting what looked like some form of tattoo that peeked above the waistband of his Levis.

Eden feasted her eyes on them for several minutes, for each boy was sexy, well muscled and tanned, naked from the waist up, and with a macho appeal in his work-hardened body that really turned her on. Closing her eyes for a few seconds, Eden imagined lying between the two of them, nuzzling her lips in their hair and along the line of their necks and shoulders.

In her mind, their sun-tanned bodies contrasted with her lighter flesh as, with bronzed hands and fingers, they fondled her breasts and teased her vagina. She imagined her pale forearms between their legs, her hands reaching to massage their hard cocks and fondle their balls. For one luscious moment, Eden caught in her mind's eye the contrast of white semen spurting over brown bodies as she masturbated one of them to his climax. Suddenly, she wondered if they were tanned all over.

Still enshrined behind the balustrade of her eyrie, Eden stared frankly down from her office perch as Justin and Paul moved another wrapped bronze sculpture slowly across the foyer of the gallery. Lustfully, Eden devoured the sight of the young men's muscles playing in rippling

17

rhythm across their torsos. Justin's long brown hair was gathered in a clip at the nape of his neck, that nape she had fantasised about licking and kissing just moments before.

But Eden noticed that another man, too, had come in from the loading dock – a tall, ruggedly handsome man with vivid auburn hair. Eden speculated that perhaps he was a specially hired helper, for he was dressed in working jeans and tool belt with a Charlotte Hornets' T-shirt stretched across his chest, and hefting another smaller sculpture. That bronze looked familiar!

As the sexy stranger carried the smaller bronze out of sight, Eden retrieved the sheaf of photographs from her desk top, and selected one. There it was!

In this maquette, a three-dimensional version of an image from the wall paintings at Pompeii, a nude Dionysus lay across the naked breasts of his beloved Ariadne. Eden could just see the contours of the god's penis as he positioned himself between his lover's open thighs, his hand reaching between her legs to guide his rampant rod into her vagina.

Moving from sensual foreplay to rampant coupling, the twentieth century counterparts in MacKenzie's *Dionysus and Ariadne* had taken lessons from their classical progenitors, making a frankly explicit erotic piece of sculpture. Eden wondered again how the Atlanta public would respond to this. The city was very contemporary in matters of style and commerce, but its attitude towards the arts was still parochial. Eden knew this well, having already battled fiercely against political conservatives and religious fundamentalists in the twelve months she had lived in the city. Both groups liked nothing better than to force their narrow-mindedness upon others, and artists were most often the targets of their invective. In particular, mulled Eden, anything to do with sex brought these morons crawling out of the woodwork!

At that moment, Alexander Raton himself whisked up

the stairs, and Eden jerked back to the present as she once again admired the figure her employer cut in his habitual grey suit. As always, its colour was an uncanny match for the shimmer of his hair. Eden wondered if his mane of silver hair would be mirrored by furry grey curls around his dick. Pale blue eyes blinked at her from behind thick eye glasses.

Unaware of his employee's sexual speculation concerning his genitals, Raton smiled as he handed Eden a second sheaf of photographs. These seemed to be detail shots of the work arriving downstairs, but Eden only gave them the briefest of glances. Although she usually paid close attention to her boss, this time Eden hardly heard what Raton was saying. Distracted, she peered around his tall figure as Justin and Paul slid the next sculpture carefully on to its pedestal; again, the third man assisting them garnered Eden's attention, but Raton was blocking her view. When Raton stopped chattering for a few seconds, she detected a Scottish accent below. Could this be the mysterious MacKenzie, whose work had spawned so many erotic fantasies for her this afternoon?

Raton floated back down the stairs and greeted the man who left Justin and Paul to their task and followed Raton into the conference room. Moments later Eden's telephone rang. It was Raton, asking her please to hurry up: they were waiting for her!

Scolding herself for not paying closer attention to the business at hand Eden made the move downstairs, tucking her lime green top into her blue skirt, pulling on her high-heeled sandals, slipping back into her blue jacket and readjusting her short skirt. She scooped up the collection of photographs and smoothed her hair into place as she circled down to the exhibition floor.

Still feeling sexually charged by her afternoon fantasies about the men in her vicinity, she moved though the gallery with a provocative gait to her walk, emphasised by the heels she wore. Prancing by in her sandals, Eden stopped to allow space for Justin and Paul to navigate another precious object. As they worked this next sculpture past her and into the corner of the room, Eden's eyes frankly appraised their muscular forms.

'Whoa,' said Justin, 'Pretty lady, you're going to make us drop this, you looking like that.' He and Paul, having placed the somewhat larger, wrapped object upon a sturdy pedestal, paused in their movements and stared in open admiration at Eden, ranging their eyes over her figure, from her face and hair, all the way down to her toes. Paul took a slug from the Evian water bottle he wore on his belt, and Eden felt Justin's eyes lingering on her breasts, the outlines of which were visible through the unbuttoned top section of her blouse.

She teased him in her newly polished French, which she had recently studied for her last visit to Parisian galleries, '*Aimez-vous cettes sculptures, Justin? Les trouvez-vous excitant?*'

The young man looked at her blankly for a few seconds, but slowly retorted, 'I don't know much about art, honey, but I reckon I could copy a few of them moves with you on that big old table . . .'

Paul guffawed softly but did not speak.

Although it was comical to think of Justin and Paul abandoning the sculpture to make love with her on the table in the conference room, Eden couldn't help picturing a reclining scene for all three: herself mounting both these men on that large mahogany table, her juices and their semen joining in rivulets across its polished surface. The intensity of the vision brought a bright flush to her cheeks, and with a half-embarrassed smile she turned away.

Eden didn't look back as she turned the knob of the heavy oak door. As the workmen watched her figure disappear into the room, Justin nodded to his friend, touching the evident bulge at his own crotch with a knowing wink, but Paul hissed in a low voice, 'You'd be wasting your time. I hear our Eden prefers girls to play with!'

'No way! She's too much a woman!' retorted Justin, 'What I heard was she wasn't getting any!'

Paul said, 'She's got to be getting it somewhere; maybe she really is a lesbian . . .'

'Oh, yeah? Maybe we can convert her to dickdom!' suggested Justin, demonstrating by grabbing the crotch of his jeans and rubbing the outline of his erection.

'You and me, both!' said Paul, who pretended to unzip his jeans. The men sniggered.

Having slipped inside the darkened chamber, Eden was unaware of this locker room repartée. As her eyes gradually adjusted to the room's more subdued light, she saw two men loading twin slide carousels; one figure stood to offer her a chair. As he moved into the light Eden recognised him as the red-headed stranger who must be Michael MacKenzie. The small bronze sculpture that recalled Ariadne and her lover rested in the middle of the polished table like a centrepiece.

'How gorgeous!' Eden exclaimed spontaneously, as she laid her eyes on the shining, curving metal forms of the reclining figures. It *was* gorgeous. But the sculpture wasn't at the crux of Eden's interest. Rather, what really grabbed her attention was the physical presence of the tall, husky man with the shock of thick, curly red hair.

Eden caught her breath when their eyes met, and felt herself colouring more deeply. To her alarm, she simultaneously dropped the sheaf of photographs and blurted out 'You're the Scotsman!'

MacKenzie smiled his assent, drawing nearer. Alexander Raton began to introduce them, but got no further than, 'Eden Sinclair . . . this is . . .' before he broke off in silence, halted by the intensity of his two companions' mutual appraisal. As Eden and MacKenzie gazed into one another's eyes, the visitor completed the sentence. '. . . Michael MacKenzie.'

Although they hadn't touched, her body responded as though held tightly in his muscular arms, or with his large hands spread across her breasts. Eden muttered, 'Hello,' and then lost her ability to speak. As she looked into the sculptor's dark, liquid brown eyes, she experienced a decidedly erotic ripple and roll, a jolt and charge deep in the pit of her vagina. As her inner lips moistened, her excitement was much more immediate, much deeper than the feelings elicited by her fantasies, or by the physical presence of either Fineman or Raton, other gallery artists, or even Justin and Paul when they looked at her so suggestively.

As Michael MacKenzie's eyes remained locked with hers, Eden felt a flush travelling up her body and a throbbing intensity as her nipples hardened, all in the space of a few seconds. Speechless, her gaze clung spellbound to his gorgeously fringed mahogany dark eyes and she thought, *Mon Dieu, c'est un coup de foudre*, a thunder clap!

As MacKenzie stepped forward, he broke the spell. He extended a large, well-shaped hand towards her, and she grasped him back, receiving a firm and friendly handshake. He said in a lilting baritone, 'I've been looking forward to meeting you, Miss Sinclair!'

Chapter Three
Cocktails

'Yes, yes, I've wanted to meet you, too,' Eden said, as she stood beside the tall sculptor who now offered her his chair. Feeling flustered and foolish from the erotic sensations spreading throughout her body, Eden struggled to regain her poise. For a moment she thought he was going to kiss her fingers, and reluctantly she released the Scotsman's hand, realising she had been grasping it for a full minute.

Raton started to speak again, but the taller man glanced down at the clutch of images scattered on the carpet, and blocked the gallery owner's words, saying to Eden, 'Let me help you.' With an agile motion, MacKenzie bent to his knees before Eden to retrieve the spilled photographs, and said, 'Ah, I see that these are mine.'

Eden stared down at the top of the man's head, feeling an almost irresistible impulse to run her fingers through his flame-coloured hair as he carefully stacked the images. She clenched her fists at her sides, rather than allow herself such a display in front of Raton. She was both amused and embarrassed by the thought.

From his position on bended knee, MacKenzie looked

up at her, grinning broadly into her eyes as he grasped the photographs in one hand. 'These are the newest . . .' he began, his thumb unconsciously tapping an image of a woman's breast as he spoke.

Eden swallowed hard and a small smile touched her lips; mistaking him for a delivery man seemed suddenly amusing. She told him simply, 'Your sculptures are very beautiful.' She couldn't help batting her eyelashes uncharacteristically as she gazed down into his eyes that reminded her of melted chocolate. She felt herself inching closer to him, and the hem of her short skirt fluttered near his face. She was extremely aware of her moist panties, and she wondered if he could smell her sex, as the lips of her vagina grew even more warm and liquid at his nearness.

Tilting her head back as he stood up again, Eden felt her heart beating wildly as heat radiated from his close proximity. She was breathless. She wanted to touch him, to run her hands along the thick muscles in his arms.

From nearby, Raton cleared his throat and spoke, 'Ms Sinclair, we need to choose some sculptures for the show.'

Returning with some difficulty to the situation at hand, Eden put on her 'cool' face and moved to the table. She regained her equilibrium and was utterly businesslike. Looking at the artist, she said, 'It's really a pleasure to meet you, Mr MacKenzie. Have you been in the States long?'

MacKenzie muttered only a vague reply that didn't tell Eden much and before he had time to elaborate, the three had settled down at the large table, while two young part-time gallery assistants, Lola and Claire, art students from Georgia Tech doing their summer internships, brought in refreshments. The two young women wore cotton dresses as thin as gauze.

As Eden, MacKenzie and Raton sorted the photographs the two students, one blonde and one brunette, busied themselves serving. As they carried around trays of cool drinks and light snacks, their loose breasts bobbed free and clear beneath their thin cotton shifts. Eden considered how comfortable the women looked in their loose, soft clothing. From the low cut of her dress, it was evident that the lush blonde Lola wore no bra. And was it Eden's imagination that curly dark-haired Claire, the younger and thinner of the two, wore no panties? She couldn't tell whether the shifting faint triangle of shadow discernible through her skirt of layered voile was a tiny bikini bottom, or the outline of her pubic hair. Intrigued by the young women's sensual spectacle of flesh, Eden wondered if the girls were intent upon some star-fucking.

The two men in the room were momentarily transfixed by their display. As Lola bent to fill MacKenzie's glass, Eden almost giggled as the curvaceous student brushed her gauze-covered tits against the sculptor's upper arm. Who did Lola think she was fooling, wondered Eden, her own covert gaze detecting that MacKenzie *was* affected, his erection unmistakenly blooming inside his jeans.

Eden's appraising glance was intercepted by the warm brown eyes of the sexy sculptor himself, who contrived to look embarrassed and accepting of his priapic state all in one fleeting expression. Correctly interpreting Eden's gaze, MacKenzie gave her a slow, meaningful look that reignited her desire and which would smoulder in her mind for many hours and days afterwards. To her surprise his eyes skipped over the two nubile younger women and sought out her own body. As he smiled he frankly absorbed her form, rather than attending to the increasingly visible attractions of the two art groupies competing for his attention. He seemed to want to keep them at arm's length, like a pair of appealing but overly attentive puppies.

The girls' unwilling departure was eventually orchestrated by Raton, who himself seemed to be having trouble concentrating. But the cut of his suit and his position behind the table, defeated Eden's surreptitious attempt to ascertain her boss's bodily reaction to the two nymphets. In the sexual vacuum created by the departure of the lissom harlots, Eden was professional enough to quell her imagination for the moment and said, 'I've made a preliminary selection of three.' Holding up the relevant black-and-white photographs, she added, 'But let's look at them in the flesh, so to speak.'

At Eden's suggestion, all three moved into the gallery where Justin and Paul had deposited a total of six separate sculptures. As the trio toured the exhibition area where the bronzes now reposed, Eden paused first beside the odalisque entitled *Stephanie*. Every bit as erotic in its reality as Eden had expected, the bronze woman stretched out languidly, fingers curled at the opening of her vulva as she leant in a half-reclining pose on her elbow. As Eden gazed at the piece, her own sexual desires welled up once more. Was this MacKenzie's lover? she wondered, with a surprising pang of jealousy. She pushed these mixed feelings half-heartedly to one side of her mind and continued doggedly with her selection.

With Raton and MacKenzie in her wake, she moved to another sculpture and stroked the body of Peleus, still in naked pursuit of the luscious but fleeing form of his lover, Thetis. Eden's voice was strong as she said, 'Peleus gets my second vote.' And, although the men were watching her every move, she couldn't resist running her finger over the tumescent penis of the handsome bronze figure. She caught MacKenzie's brief smile as he watched her touch his creation, and she moved quickly on to the third compelling work that she had decided would complete MacKenzie's contribution to the show: a group of Bacchanalian revellers, their bodies intertwined in a variety of suggestive activities.

'All these sculptures excite me . . .' Eden began, but stopped speechless as MacKenzie caught her eye. He was

26

grinning at her with a distinctly lustful twinkle in his eyes. Bravely, she continued.

'They, um, excite me in their skill and technique. I think they will make great focal points in the new show.' She paused, and suddenly gushed, 'I really do look forward to working closely with you, Mr MacKenzie!' She looked over at Raton, who was smiling in a particularly smarmy manner. Damn him, thought Eden; he knew she was turned on. She could see by the smug grin on his face. And MacKenzie was just as bad! But, speaking clearly, she persevered, saying, 'I find that even in their casual state of unstudied exhibition, this group of three, in particular, charges the air with erotic tension!'

In the ensuing silence of this heightened atmosphere, Eden imagined she saw the men exchange glances. She discovered within herself a burgeoning annoyance at not being involved in formulating this arrangement. She wanted to ask where and how Raton had found MacKenzie and his work. And how would the gallery market respond to this unabashedly sexual material? She realised this situation was unlike her previous working relationship with Raton, who had deferred to her in decisions regarding art policy. She had managed to stay current on the art scene while putting together a successful stable of artists who met the expectations of more conservative clients. As wonderful as this Scotsman and his work had turned out to be, she didn't understand why Alexander Raton had completely ignored her regarding MacKenzie's work!

Eden's angry feelings brought a sharp tone to her voice as she confirmed the selected trio to Raton. MacKenzie looked up, shocked by the change in Eden's demeanour, and clearly at a loss. Raton, too, was momentarily startled, but became all smoothness and charm as he studiously agreed with Eden's selection, complimenting her on her choices. With polished ease Raton led his companions back to the conference room where he defused Eden's anger by suggesting they review slides together of MacKenzie's new work.

In spite of her feelings, Eden found she was as impressed by the quality of these newer works in progress as by the completed pieces next door in the gallery. She was particularly taken with the images of the interior of MacKenzie's studio, which contained a lot of well-lit space, filled with partially completed sculptures and maquettes of various sizes.

While MacKenzie's sculptures were modestly scaled, none being over half life-size, Eden knew their production costs would still be considerable. She wondered how MacKenzie afforded the expense. But putting these questions aside for the moment, Eden concentrated on the celluloid images projected on the screen. The sculptor's fine technique was evident in several of the preliminary clay models, where sensuous curves, apertures and protrusions of naked bodies had been captured by MacKenzie's skilful hands. One slide showed a female studio assistant polishing a bronze figure. As she ran her hands carefully between the naked buttocks, she rubbed the testicles of the nearly completed statue. No doubt the pretty assistant was smoothing the surfaces for entirely technical purposes, but the image was exciting none the less. Eden imagined touching MacKenzie's balls, and his penis too, reaching between his legs to grab the sturdy member, the shape of which was so recently visible before her eyes in its denim outline.

As enticing as these images and thoughts were, Eden reminded herself that the gallery's forthcoming group show was still her responsibility to compose properly; for all the allure and potency of MacKenzie's work, there were many other artists to consider. Standing quickly, Eden said, 'Excuse me, but I must select the accompanying pieces from the inventory of our other gallery artists.' She was still angry at Raton for his obscure manipulation of the situation, but was anxious not to transfer this emotion to MacKenzie. Besides wanting to ask him all sorts of questions about his work, Eden frankly wanted to spend more time in this man's formidable physical company, to be touching him, lying next to him, even riding him astride his naked body.

But Eden was forestalled in her intention to seek a private meeting with MacKenzie by Raton, who remarked, 'I see you have more work to do, Ms Sinclair. Let us meet again at 6.30 for a little celebration I've arranged in the conference room to toast Michael's arrival in Atlanta.'

Eden felt her irritation rise again at Raton's exclusion of her from her normal take-charge role. What was going on here, she pondered. Raton was up to something! But what? In her confusion, all she managed as she left the room was a shy smile at MacKenzie and a vague 'See you later, then.'

In the 48 hours since she had handled the photographs of MacKenzie's work, Eden had mulled over possible themes for the new show. Now, having seen the real sculptures, so obviously generated from life, Eden decided that the most powerful theme for the exhibit would be the relationship between love and sex.

As the topic crystallised in her mind, Eden set about selecting works from her stock that addressed romance and lust from a variety of viewpoints. She always maintained that curating a show should be a very creative act in itself, expressing a particular point of view as well as laying out a visual spectacle. To surround MacKenzie's sculptures, plainly products of a male artist, with a selection of drawings and paintings by several of her recently recruited women painters, appealed greatly to Eden's feminist instincts.

After two hours of concentrated effort, Eden felt confident that she had made all the major decisions, and retired to her office to complete the details of the exhibition sketches. It would take another day or so to refine the selection of paintings, but with a satisfied air Eden returned to the conference room for a hard-earned glass of wine, looking forward to MacKenzie's company, even if she had to share it with several others.

Lola and Claire were back again, all but falling out of their bogus peasant smocks, tending bar and flirting with the half-dozen men present at the small gathering. Justin and Paul were there, dressed up in clean shirts and Levis but just as sexy as when they were semi-naked. Fineman was engaged in conversation with Martin Bulgaria and Roscoe Ball, two of the gallery's most prolific and successful painters, and also occasional subjects of Eden's sexy fantasies. Two other men whom Eden didn't know were clearly enjoying the girls' charms.

Michael MacKenzie stood slightly apart, listening politely and absently fending off the renewed attentions of the two young art groupies. Angela was nowhere in sight, and in her sweep of the company, Eden registered that Raton, too, was absent; but any speculations she had about this were cut short by MacKenzie's gaze as it connected with hers from across the room. Unlike Justin and Paul, he hadn't changed from his work clothes, but despite this he still looked to Eden the most poised and attractive man in the room.

When his eyes locked with hers, MacKenzie untangled himself from the amorous attentions of Lola and Claire, and turned towards Eden. He moved closer to greet her, but was overtaken by Raton who materialised out of nowhere and said, 'Ms Sinclair, we have an important client with a problem which he says requires your immediate attention! I promised him that you would be there within the hour.'

Eden, finding herself profoundly irritated by Raton's behaviour, snapped, 'Why did you do that?'

Raton countered, 'Well, my dear, it's work! Work! Chop, chop!'

Blushing furiously and stunned into silence, Eden glared at her boss.

Unfazed, Raton continued, 'It's J J Ritchie, and you know that he might be buying that huge abstract expressionist piece, the one that we've had for ages! I nearly sold it to that German bank, but they said it had too much angst for them. Poor dears! Please go and take care of Jay Jay right away! Humour him, even if all he needs is to change a light bulb or something! He has some important lunch tomorrow. He said he has a new client, someone special from Magnolia Bank.'

As Eden opened her mouth to speak, Raton rattled on, 'Whatever his problem is, resolve it. It could be worth thousands of dollars!'

Eden's heart sank as she listened to her boss. Much as she adored Jay Jay, as all his friends and associates called him, listening to his problems was the last thing she wanted to do now that MacKenzie was so close. He stood there, just out of reach, only a step away.

But at Raton's insistence Eden had to go, reluctantly, having only a brief chance to catch MacKenzie's crest-fallen look and to murmur another goodbye to him, with a hope for another meeting soon. However, as Eden turned to go MacKenzie took a sudden initiative. Taking her arm and speaking softly in his Scottish brogue, he declared, 'I'm sorry you have to go. I'll be sure to call you at the gallery later in the week.' He then hugged her, if somewhat formally.

As Raton fussed noisily on the periphery of her vision, Eden drew closer into MacKenzie's arms, and looking up at him, responded with an ironic smile, 'I'd like that. Damn Jay Jay! But I'll talk to you soon.' Then she pulled away, her mind awash with conflicting emotions. She looked back from the doorway and saw Lola and Claire fill the space around MacKenzie like gas in a vacuum.

They were offering him drinks and canapés, garnished with plentiful opportunities to appreciate their breasts and youthful bodies.

Caught with the room's lighting behind them, the two students were visible in sexy silhouette through their thin cotton dresses. Even in her growing bad mood, Eden had to admit that they were both very attractive women, seemingly enjoying their own company as much as that of the men around them.

Walking grumpily towards her office, Eden wondered if one of the two girls would become MacKenzie's lover that night, or perhaps both in some exotic troilism. Away from the room and the party, Eden's mind wandered to encompass a range of three-way possibilities, with both girls performing for MacKenzie's delectation, before she snapped her imaginings closed in a mixture of annoyance, frustration and envy.

Chapter Four
A Very Long Day

*A*s she fumed over this unwanted errand, Eden wondered what on earth the matter could be with Jay Jay's design scheme this time. Galerie Raton, in collaboration with a team of interior designers and architects, had recently refitted the man's entire house.

Jay Jay, who now waited for her in his mansion in Buckhead, a chic suburb just a few miles to the north, was an old school chum of Eden's. Indeed, Jay Jay Ritchie *was* a very important client of the gallery, having spent thousands of dollars in the gallery over the past year. But his investment in art was incidental to the close personal friendship he enjoyed with Galerie Raton's director, Eden Sinclair.

Eden had known the elegant southerner since college when they were Tulane undergraduates together in New Orleans. During those youthful years, Jay Jay had made the difficult decision to come out of the closet and be openly gay. Eden had admired him and supported his sexual struggle with advice and companionship; in return, Jay Jay had always welcomed Eden to his home and, over the years, they had forged a deep friendship.

Thoughts of her friend soothed Eden's annoyance, but

she rested for a moment before gearing up to attend to Jay Jay. It had already been a long and frustrating day. But not without its excitements, she reminded herself.

Despite the lack of walls around her mezzanine office, its height above the now darkened gallery floor gave her privacy at the rear of the space under the skylight. All was quiet, the sounds of the cocktail party effectively muffled by the thick oak doors and the solid brick walls that defined the conference room below. To polish her appearance for this unexpected early evening meeting, Eden chose a fresh outfit from the two or three selections she kept in the closet at the back of her office for such emergencies.

Undressing herself, she imagined MacKenzie's body stripped of his workman's clothes. She recalled his scent, his body, the curl of his hair still smelling of some apple shampoo despite his day's exertions, allowing all these recent memories to wash away her earlier sexy thoughts about Justin, Raton, Fineman and the others.

As she stood before the mirror she pondered again Raton's selection of MacKenzie. The owner of the gallery had recruited the talented sculptor without any warning or discussion, making the decision without seeking any advice from her. Why? Her boss's action piqued Eden mightily, especially as it was a potentially brilliant move! MacKenzie's joining Galerie Raton seemed very significant for the firm, and the overt sexuality of his work marked a departure from previous policies and artistic emphasis. So why had Alexander Raton not consulted her in advance?

Succumbing to an irresistible desire to take off all her clothes, Eden stepped into her tiny, private bathroom, shivering for a moment in her bikini panties and lacy bra. She unhooked her bra, letting her breasts swing freely, her nipples starting to stand straight out from her rounded flesh. Then slowly, deliciously, she rolled her panties down, and stepped out of them. Reaching into

34

her bag for a moisturiser, she rubbed the fragrant potion over her breasts and felt her nipples ripen like cherries, erect at further thoughts of MacKenzie.

Did Raton think her such an ardent feminist that she would reject a new male artist on the grounds of some sexism, or his 'white male perspective'? Eden considered Raton's position as she caressed her breasts, belly and thighs with the delicately scented moisturiser. Certainly she had expanded the number of women artists on the gallery's books, and there had been some initial opposition by Raton to these ideas, but surely that was in the past now. The work of her new women artists had been a critical and commercial success, and sales were ultimately what mattered to Raton.

Standing nude in front of her reflection, Eden assessed her career and her figure. At 32 she enjoyed a well-paid, creative position, and peak health was mirrored in her well-shaped body. Tall and slender, she worked hard to maintain her trim figure, with its high rounded breasts and slender waist. Her hips and thighs were sleekly muscled from exercise. Within this elegant exterior, however, Eden felt torn between her career worries resulting from Raton's selection of the new artist without her knowledge or involvement, and her unbridled lust for this newest stable member! Studying her unusually celibate body, she felt her inner lips moisten with her daydreams about MacKenzie. She parted her pubic hair and gently pushed a finger into her vagina with a moan of temporary satisfaction.

She dimmed the light and tuned her little waterproof radio to her favorite rock-and-roll radio station. The increasingly restless feelings the tall red-haired stranger stirred in her body were disquieting, and as her fingers moved between her legs, softly playing with herself, her clitoris stood up like a tiny ridge through the triangle of her pubic hair. The sensitive little bud was a carmine red that matched her nipples.

While Eden's love life had often been characterised by major swings in desire, she had rarely been without a warm body in her bed. Having been without a man in her life for over a year now, Eden found herself unremittently turned on by MacKenzie's easy manner and sexy masculinity. She studied her reflection as she danced naked to the low music. Enjoying her sensual display, Eden recalled MacKenzie's brief but exciting hug only minutes before. She tossed her thick, bright, chestnut-brown hair around her. Her blue eyes were dark tonight and as she recalled the feel of his sinewy arms around her, she stopped dancing and hugged herself; squeezing her breasts together until her nipples jutted, she imagined the sculptor's hands upon them.

Eden's private world was interrupted by the sounds of conversation and laughter followed by doors opening and closing in the still-dark space below her. Naked, but secure in her lofty privacy, Eden turned off the radio, opened the bathroom door and tiptoed silently to the edge of the balcony, only to see the figures of Angela and Winston Fineman slink quietly towards the rear exit, their figures briefly silhouetted in the light of the passageway leading past the gallery storeroom.

Mindful now of her appointment with Jay Jay, Eden quickly pulled on fresh underwear, a new silk blouse, this time in simple white, and a mid-length charcoal linen skirt and matching jacket. Not what she'd have worn for MacKenzie, she thought, with another pang of regret for missing his company.

After brushing her hair and applying fresh make-up, Eden hurried down the spiral stair, her soft loafers making little sound on the treads, and headed for the back door. The corridor was dark now, but she could see her way adequately enough with scraps of light leaking in from the parking lot outside and, surprisingly, from the partly opened storeroom door. Not wanting to be any later for her appointment, she wasn't going to bother switching it off, but as she passed the door she detected a motion and a murmur. Wondering who it could be, she glanced inside the room. From the darkened doorway she saw Winston Fineman standing beside the filing cabinet under the single meagre bulb that burnt overhead.

As she focused on Fineman's figure, Eden realised that his trousers were pulled down, bunched around his ankles. And Angela, bare-breasted, sat on a low packing crate, looking up at him smiling, and holding his loaded phallus in her hands. Suppressing a startled giggle Eden watched wide-eyed. As if hypnotised she could not pull herself away from the provocative tableau of Angela, her clothing falling around her waist, lovingly handling Fineman's long narrow penis, which extended straight out from his crotch, perpendicular to his tall skinny body.

As the young woman played with his virile member, bobbing it up and down and fondling his balls, Fineman moaned luxuriously, and the honey blonde rubbed the pulsing length of his cock against her breasts, sighing, purring and giving out little squeals. The couple rocked together in rhythm, and Eden watched Angela slide her tongue over the engorged rod. While he ran his hands through Angela's copious hair, the woman took his long member between her lips and Fineman looked like he was going to come there and then!

From the shrouded doorway, Eden was captivated as Fineman drew his glistening phallus from Angela's mouth and pulled his partner to her feet, slowly and sensuously rubbing the length of her body against his. They stood breast to breast for a lingering moment, swaying, as Angela's hands encircled Fineman's buttocks, pressing his penis against her.

Slowly, Fineman turned his partner around and pulled up her short skirt. Angela bent over, sweeping the floor with her long blonde hair. Eden knew that her assistant had trained as a dancer and practised yoga, but she was still amazed to see her flex all the way over and push her bottom upward against Fineman's thrusting phallus. As Angela swayed her hips back and forth, enticing her lover with the sight of her beautiful bottom, the cleft between her cheeks was barely concealed by minuscule panties.

Fineman fondled Angela's rounded bottom, toying with her tiny panties, and laid his hardened shaft along her cleft. Eden caught her breath as she heard Fineman moan audibly with desire. She grew moist herself as she watched him pull the bikini panties down from Angela's buttocks, past mid-thigh, until the scrap of silk fell around her ankles.

As he bent over, Fineman used his tongue to lick Angela's cleft thoroughly from clitoris to anus, pleasuring himself especially around the open lips of her vagina, before straightening and pushing his throbbing dick straight into Angela's lush channel. The woman moaned with pleasure as Fineman pounded into her.

Spellbound, Eden watched as the wiggling Angela reached back between her legs to grab her lover's balls, squeezing them as if to milk every drop of semen from the pendulous sacs as they slapped against her with every thrust that Fineman made. But, feeling suddenly guilty at her voyeuristic pleasure, Eden slipped silently away before Fineman or Angela came. Escaping out the door, the imprint of the writhing, bucking, copulating couple was emblazoned on her mind as she climbed into her car. As she reached to start the engine she heard what could only be the moans of orgasm riding on the warm night air.

As he enjoyed another glass of Raton's hearty Liberty School Cabernet in the Galerie Raton conference room, MacKenzie thought again about the pretty gallery director. The physical rush of desire he had felt when he had first looked into her eyes had been unusually strong. He recalled trying to cover his disappointment with a stupid smile when Eden had to leave.

Although he knew many beautiful and intelligent women and had made love to several of them, the Scotsman had rarely responded with such profound initial emotions when meeting a woman. His mind kept returning to thoughts of Eden, rather than to Lola and Claire who were still busily flaunting their charms at him right this minute. The love nymphs from art school *were* quite sexy, and he liked to watch them fluttering around him. They would take off those dresses in a heartbeat, MacKenzie knew, and spread their legs for him. He imagined the pair naked before him, sex-ripe for his pleasure. If it wasn't for Eden Sinclair, he mused, he would probably follow that line of lustful thinking and take them both to bed tonight; they obviously wanted him to. He wondered wryly what the director would think of her newest artist if he fucked the hired help on his first night at the gallery!

Not the impression he wanted to make! He recognised that he was becoming quite love-struck with Eden Sinclair, who was every bit as sexy as these two nymphets and probably a lot more serious as well. He loved intelligent women.

Having made up his mind, MacKenzie quickly accepted a lift to his hotel from Raton. The two art school girls looked crestfallen, but as he left the room, he noticed they promptly transferred their sexy spirits to the two delivery men, who suddenly looked as if they'd won the jackpot!

In spite of her initial reluctance to leave the Galerie Raton scene starring the sexy Michael MacKenzie, Eden's frustration nevertheless turned to pleasure when she arrived at her destination. Her old friend Jay Jay greeted her in the vestibule with hugs and kisses. She admired his newly renovated original marble floor and stone staircase, lit by zinc lanterns from Morocco. He guided her to his study, and by the time Eden had settled into her favourite plush settee, Jay Jay had brought her a tall goblet of crisp Chardonnay from her preferred Californian vineyard.

As he set a plate of green grapes, water biscuits and fresh brie sparked with cracked black pepper on the low table in front of her, Jay Jay said, 'You're looking well Eden. Thank you so much for coming over at this late hour. But I do need your advice desperately! Have you had dinner? Please join us; I have just two other guests.'

Eden realised how hungry she was; all this sexual tension had left her feeling weak now that she allowed herself to relax in pleasant surroundings with attractive company. She looked around the exquisite study, admiring the familiar sight of a 1930s desk and chair lit by a Tiffany lamp, the pleasantly faded warm tones of a floral Aubusson carpet. She nibbled the grapes.

An ornate library ladder in the background gave access to regimented shelves of books, including many rare and expensive editions, reflecting her client's omnivorous reading habits. She knew these books were the accumulation of Jay Jay's own researches and purchases in book fairs from across the States, a luxury afforded him by his uncanny skill in playing the stock market, personally and professionally.

Before dinner the gentle stockbroker-cum-art collector showed Eden to the next room where he displayed his latest acquisitions from a Parisian gallery. This set of small bronze sculptures depicted dancing figures, both male and female, modelled after the Impressionist Degas.

'God, Jay Jay,' lectured Eden sternly, 'These are kitsch! You've got to see the work of Michael MacKenzie: it's much better than this!' Eden surprised herself by invoking the man's name, now firmly lodged on the tip of her tongue after only a few hours' acquaintance, but it was glaringly conspicuous to her that his sculpture would be infinitely more appropriate for Jay Jay's posh setting. She elaborated, 'The work from Paris is just plain tacky!'

If Jay Jay was hurt by Eden's bluntness he didn't show it. 'Who is this Michael MacKenzie?' he asked, sinking into an elegant little chair covered in plush, charcoal velvet.

Eden, sitting beside him on a matching tuffet, found she relished the opportunity of talking about the man who had filled her thoughts all afternoon. 'He's our newest gallery artist,' she blurted. 'He's Scottish, about six feet tall with red hair, and . . .' She stopped, suddenly shy at her rush of words.

Jay Jay smiled and said quietly, 'But what's his *art* like, Eden? If it's made the same impression on you as his physique obviously has, it must be something really special!'

Eden grinned in return, and admitted, 'Yes, it is. And so is he! Oh, Jay Jay, I just think he's gorgeous. I wanted to go to bed with him right this very evening!'

'And instead here you are, having to help me out of one of my dilemmas!' cried Jay Jay ruefully. 'Eden, I'm sorry if I messed up your plans!'

Seeing the genuine remorse in her friend's eyes, Eden burst into a laugh that released the tension in her, and reassured Jay Jay with a hug. She said, 'Oh, you sweet man! He'll still be there tomorrow, and the next day! I don't know why I'm acting like a sex-starved teenager! Let's have dinner and then we'll solve your problem, whatever it is!'

As they moved to the dining room, Jay Jay's other guests showed themselves, a handsome pair of young men, who looked to Eden as though they had just stepped out of the shower and massage parlour. Their tanned skin positively glowed with health and their matching blue and green silk shirts set off the colours of their eyes that held clear signs of affection for each other, visible in every glance.

'Eden, I'd like you to meet Greg and Jerry, dear friends of mine!' introduced Jay Jay. One of the men hurried over with a captivating smile.

'We're so pleased to meet you, Eden. I'm Greg. This is Jerry. Jay Jay has told us a lot about you, both from here and back in New Orleans,' and, to Eden's surprise, the man leant forward and gently kissed her on the cheek.

The meal proceeded pleasantly, with bright and witty conversation on many topics, ranging from art and books to travel in Europe. Greg, in particular seemed knowledgeable about contemporary art, and he was delighted that Eden had confirmed his opinion about Jay Jay's recent purchases from Paris. He said, 'Eden, I didn't know how to tell Jay Jay what I thought of those corny sculptures without hurting his feelings, but you just came right out and said it. And this new artist, Mac-Kenzie, do you think we could get some of his work here? Did I understand you to say that it was very erotic?'

'I'd like you all to come to the gallery opening next week,' responded Eden, smiling across the table. 'You'll see his work there and you can decide for yourselves, but in my opinion it's some of the very best figurative sculpture available at the moment. It's really sexy! And,' she added, 'we can get you a good price for it. But now, Jay Jay, just what is the problem this evening that's so urgent?'

Her host was suddenly hesitant. 'Um, well, you see, Eden, a ... er ... a very special person is coming to dinner tomorrow night. He's someone very important in business, and someone also who ... um ... I hope to make very important in my life.' Jay Jay poured Eden another glass of wine, crisp and cold. But his hand shook. His voice seemed more high-pitched than usual. Something was surely up, thought Eden, and she noticed that Greg and Jerry exchanged deep, knowing glances.

'I'm not satisfied, darling Eden,' Jay Jay continued, without explaining anything.

Neither was she, Eden sighed to herself, though probably for different reasons. She fidgeted restlessly on the dining chair. But as Greg passed around the coffee, Eden's mind fluttered back to the present reality, and to Jay Jay, who continued, 'I simply must have a new painting over the mantel in the master suite! It must be bigger and softer!' He frowned. 'The one upstairs just has too many hard edges!'

Eden was relieved. '*No problemo*!' she cried enthusiastically. 'Let's go up and see! I'm sure we've got something in the gallery that will suit.' On the way upstairs, Eden smiled to herself. Jay Jay's agenda was so transparent: dinner downstairs and then sex upstairs afterwards. She wondered who the lucky man was.

The master suite was opulent in the extreme, with hand-stuccoed plaster walls textured in the latest deep umber and soft Tuscan red faux finishes. Over the mantel was a large canvas by Martin Bulgaria, one of the gallery's best painters and whom Eden had just recently left at Raton's cocktail party.

'It's just not right for the mood I want,' imparted Jay Jay. Greg and Jerry nodded in solemn agreement.

Eden suppressed a giggle at her vision of Jay Jay and his new lover astride each other on the bed, gazing in mutual dissatisfaction at the geometric, hard-edged abstract expressionist work. She asked, all professionalism on the outside, 'Do you think something more representational would be better, Jay Jay?' When he nodded, she continued, 'We do have some new large figurative pieces, based on fragments of Italian frescoes. Annalee Barrett, one of our new artists, returned recently from Italy. She's crazy about Piero della Francesca, and went on the famous art trail, you know, going from Sansovino to Arezzo and Urbino. She's doing some lovely work now, incorporating versions of Piero's fresco fragments into compositions that are layered with landscapes and some abstract motifs. I can think of at least two canvasses that would fit here; they're both sensual in a gentle sort of way, and their colour palette would complement your furnishings.'

Jay Jay was nodding eagerly, and Eden continued, 'I'll get our delivery man to bring them around in the morning for you to make your choice. He can hang a piece and bring the Bulgaria painting back with him. If you like it, we'll trade it out and give you a fair price on the new work.'

Her client nodded his enthusiastic agreement, and said happily, 'Thank you, Eden! I knew you'd be able to solve it!' And he bent to kiss her hand in a delightfully old-world gesture.

She made mental notes about colours and textures and they descended again to the ground floor. The three handsome gay men expressed to Eden their appreciation in fulsome terms. Eden noticed that they *all* seemed to have an interest in the decor, and she wondered if they were planning an orgy with Jay Jay, some sort of human sex chain. Greg and Jerry seemed as relieved as her client over the matter of the painting, and both promised to be there in the morning to help when they were delivered.

As Jay Jay and his friends toasted Eden in the dining room, she found her mind exploring possible scenarios, aided by the sight of a surreptitious kiss by Greg on his lover's lips, and a responding caress by Jerry, whose hand gently passed over his companion's crotch. Eden grinned; there was a definite sexual charge in the air, and she liked imagining these men's naked bodies. These homo-erotic images soon melted into her recent memory of Fineman bringing off Angela in the storeroom. Eden closed her eyes and pictured the critic's pleasuring of her secretary, how she had watched enviously as the supple blonde had flexed over, taking all of Fineman's long penis inside her pussy.

Drifting into a wine-sparked fantasy, Eden suddenly pictured curly-haired Claire and the languid blonde Lola teaming up to seduce MacKenzie, their naked bodies coiled around his, their hands wrapped around his phallus while their agile tongues licked the first of his come as it spurted from his long hard cock. My God! thought Eden, putting down her wine glass abruptly. This was getting bad. It was time she was going!

Taking her leave as quickly as politeness permitted, Eden excused herself from her client-friend's company, promising once more to send Justin round with the new work in the morning. All three men escorted Eden to her car, and offered to drive her.

'Are you sure you're sober enough to drive, darling?' asked Jay Jay, solicitously.

Greg said, 'Eden, it would be no trouble at all for Jerry and me to whisk you back to your place. It's over in Virginia Highlands, isn't it? Jay Jay will keep things warm for us here while we're gone!'

For a moment Eden was tempted, and considered hidden possibilities. If these two handsome men took her home in her recently aroused state would their attentions stop at her door? What if she invited them in for a nightcap? Realising they could be bisexual, Eden tantalised herself with fresh sexual wonderings.

Determinedly, Eden pushed these thoughts aside. She was just imagining this, she told herself. Just because these guys were charming and attentive, and far more courteous than most heterosexual men she knew, didn't imply that they could all jump into bed with each other and act out her fantasies!

Declining all their invitations, Eden satisfied herself with a firm kiss on the lips of each man, extending her touch just a tad longer than normal between friends, and feeling a frisson of delight as she sensed each man's ambiguous response to her tease. As they helped her into her car, Jay Jay playfully ruffled her hair and released himself from her kiss, while Greg and Jerry each stiffened slightly at her touch and squeezed her hand in reply.

45

Briskly, Eden started up her little red Miata, backed out of Jay Jay's driveway, and drove south through the city. It was late, but she was still aroused by her fantasies, her own private viewing of Winston and Angela, and even by the faux-flirting with the gay men at Jay Jay's. From behind the wheel, Eden confronted her recurrent thoughts of Michael MacKenzie, and let her mind run free with images of this man she had known for only a few hours.

Once home she quickly stripped naked, showered for the third time that day and covered her body with fragrant essential oils. As she slid into bed, she couldn't get the image of MacKenzie's naked body out of her mind. With a sigh, she lay back on her pillows, and massaged her clitoris with a sweet blend of cocoa butter and scented cream, the silky texture adding substance to her sexual musings. Her desire to feel MacKenzie's body next to hers was palpable, and the last thing she remembered before drifting into sleep was a sharp pang of jealousy at the thought of Claire and Lola making love to her new artist.

Chapter Five
While the Cat's Away

While Eden dreamed in her bedroom, the reality happening back at Galerie Raton did indeed involve the now naked Claire and Lola writhing with pleasure, each rapidly approaching orgasm. But unlike their roles in Eden's imagination, the young women's sexual contortions were not taking place under the guiding hands of their would-be sexual master, Michael MacKenzie. Instead, Claire's spread-eagled ecstasy was under the thumb of Paul, while Lola was fully occupied with Justin, who knelt as if in a trance, caressing the blonde girl between his thighs.

When the party in the gallery broke up, Justin and Paul had watched in startled surprise as their boss, Alexander Raton and his new artist quit the little gathering, leaving behind a crestfallen pair of young women. The delivery men looked at each other, the same sexy thoughts racing through their minds, an identical spark of lust in their eyes.

'My God, Paul,' remarked Justin, 'if I'd been that new guy or Raton I wouldn't have passed up Claire and Lola! They've been begging for it all afternoon!'

'Yeah, man!' Paul agreed, remembering how flimsy

and transparent the girls' clothing had seemed earlier in the day. 'When they came out of that meeting in the conference room, you could see it all, man! Breasts, nipples; they were flaunting everything! And I don't think Claire was wearing any panties!' His eyes shone with excitement at the memory.

'I've fancied Claire since she started working here,' admitted Justin. 'What do you say we try our luck tonight? The main men have left and these other bozos will be leaving soon. If I go with Claire, will you go with Lola?'

Paul nodded avidly, and the two young men watched eagerly as the last visitors departed, leaving them alone with the girls.

A sudden electric tension descended on the room as the foursome of Claire, Lola, Justin and Paul made desultory efforts at cleaning up the bottles and glasses, each nervous to acknowledge what was on all their minds, and nobody willing to make the first move. There were several bottles of wine opened but not finished, and Paul found some clean glasses and poured each a generous portion. The quartet raised their glasses in a silent toast, smiling slyly at each other. Justin's smile was rather more of a smirk as he imagined what the evening would bring.

'Let's go next door,' suggested Claire. 'That smaller sitting room that Eden and Raton use for their private client meetings is much more cozy than this stuffy place. It's got a sofa, armchairs and a CD player! And a bunch of mirrors! It's pretty cool!' She looked quickly at her friend Lola, who nodded imperceptibly.

'I'll bring the wine,' affirmed Justin, who hastened to gather up the various opened bottles that they had stacked together on the big table.

The foursome roved around the inner sanctum together, their movements reflected in large mirrors hanging along two opposite walls of the smaller chamber. Art hung on the other walls; in the middle of the room, a sofa and upholstered chairs clustered around a sleek low coffee table. To one side, on a bureau, was a miniature audio system and a collection of CDs.

It was a cozy and secluded den, and Justin and Paul were especially impressed by the way the two girls made themselves at home, drinking the boss's wine, making light conversation and now, draping themselves over the furniture, displaying their bodies in ways that left little to the men's sexual imagination.

As he had told his partner, Justin had lusted after the little curly-headed brunette since both women had come to work part-time at Galerie Raton earlier in the year. He had even contrived to be seen naked, showering in the staff bathroom, allowing the door to swing open when Claire was walking by. He knew the girl had admired his tumescent cock, for she had lingered just long enough at the open door to run her eyes over his trim body, and give him a seductive little smile before closing the door and going about her errands.

And now it was his turn to feast his eyes on Claire's body, as she sprawled across the sofa, yet still pert and elegant. As she smiled back conspiratorially, Claire remembered how surprised she had been to see Justin's penis that day in the shower. It was big! Even at half-mast it had been an impressive sight, bigger than most of her previous boyfriends' cocks. She wondered what it would be like fully hard. What would it feel like inside her, hot and filled with come? If Raton hadn't been working in his office down the hall that day, she might have done a lot more than just look.

As the brunette looked at him seductively, Justin followed her gaze as it dropped to his genitals; and while she watched, he rubbed his fingers slowly along the outline of his penis, visible through the denim of his jeans. As his eyes flitted between Claire and Lola, Justin's fondling became more flagrant. At his side he felt Paul's body tense with desire. He looked over briefly at his friend; Paul's hand was also resting between his legs, fondling the length of his hardening rod. Justin could see the shape of it in his friend's trousers.

Lola was watching Paul with rapt attention. Indeed, both female gallery assistants liked Justin and Paul, too, and found their uncomplicated, lusty approach to sex rather fun. They were, thought Lola, rather cute, like over-sexed teenagers. But what would they be like as lovers? Justin, in particular, clearly fancied himself as a slick Romeo. Lola considered both men now, feeling the lips of her vulva grow moist with desire, but still not convinced of their sexual sophistication. She whispered her doubts to Claire, 'They're cute, but compared with Michael MacKenzie, they're like little boys.'

Claire disagreed in a soft voice, saying. 'I think Justin's really sexy! He and Paul are probably as good a fuck as that Scottish sculptor anyway! I know you had the hots for him! Don't deny it!'

'Yeah, but he's not here now,' retorted Lola. 'I fancy both these guys. Which one do you want first?'

'I want to save Justin for last,' admitted Claire. 'He showed me his penis "by accident" in the shower room the other day. It's a beauty! Why don't you take him first, and leave Paul to me?'

The women sat watching Justin as he crossed the room, returning with a wine bottle to refill their glasses. Both wriggled with expectation and as they lounged on the sofa, Claire lay back against her friend and whispered, 'Let's really turn them on!'

Lola smiled her understanding, and reaching towards her friend's lap, slowly and seductively she ran her fingers over Claire's knee and along the golden skin of her thigh, raising the hem of her friend's dress a few inches, and a few inches more, exposing Claire's tanned flesh for the men's appraisal. The startled Justin sipped his wine, trying to look casual, as if this happened every day. Paul was adjusting the CD player, programming some more music, and unaware of the girls' ploy, but Justin couldn't take his eyes off Claire's thigh as Lola slowly rolled the hem of her friend's dress ever higher, until the curve of her buttocks lay exposed. Paul's earlier guess had been right: Claire indeed wore no panties, and the dark curls of her pubic bush peeped out beneath the folds of fabric now creased across the tops of her thighs.

Justin sat on the very edge of his seat opposite Claire. When the sexy little brunette looked up at him with her big brown eyes, he felt his cock go rigid, and his own eyes were filled with transparent lust.

As Claire reclined languidly against the cushions, she parted her legs slightly. To Justin's amazement, Lola leant forward and gently brushed her friend's pubic hair with her fingers. Then she lay back against the cushions herself and looked at him.

Moving his eyes from Claire's loins to meet Lola's eyes, he felt as if his cock would burst out of his jeans. Lola's gaze dropped to his crotch, and he recovered some of his poise, and said in his sassy way, 'I sure like that thin dress; it makes me feel real horny.' He saw a provocative view of her creamy, voluptuous breasts through her transparent garment, and he rubbed his penis through his jeans in slow masturbation.

Amused by Justin's attention, Lola smiled, pulling her loose top lower to reveal the deep cleavage between her breasts. She looked lazily up at him, licking her lips like a knowing cat. As k. d. lang was replaced by Melissa Etheridge, Paul's new choice of music pulsed loudly across the room. Lola pulled Justin to his feet, and began to dance slowly, sinuously and seductively in front of him.

'Dance with me, Justin,' she invited. 'Hold me tight!'

As Justin and Lola writhed in unison to the music, warming each other's lust, Claire's hunger smouldered in her eyes as she sprawled comfortably on the sofa.

Sipping the last of her Cabernet, she watched Lola and Justin. She knew Justin wanted to fuck *her*; he had all but stated so. When he had staged that theatrical set-up in the shower to show off his dick she knew he was trying to get her to suck him off for starters. Now she was about ready to do it, and she'd give his lovely penis a treat to remember! She was already wet. Reaching under her raised skirt, she nestled her right hand in her pubic hair and extended two fingers inside her labia.

Ready now for an appetiser before her main course, Claire glanced across the room for Paul, but he was nowhere to be seen. Recognising that he was unlikely to be gone for long with so much sex on offer, Claire continued to masturbate gently, spreading her legs to give the others a better view, feeling a delicious wantonness spread through her loins.

But, momentarily, her companions were completely absorbed in each other's bodies. As Lola swayed to the music, she pressed her breasts against Justin's torso, her nipples jutting like beacons from her mounds of creamy-ripe flesh. She felt Justin quicken as she rubbed her hand across the clear outline of his erection beneath his tight jeans. 'God! You're a hard one!' she breathed excitedly.

Muttering, Justin pulled her closer. He was panting as his own pulse accelerated, and he slipped one hand inside Lola's dress, dislodging it from her shoulder as he reached hungrily for her breast.

Unable to resist the persistent throbbing intensity of her nipples any longer, Lola begged him, 'Touch me, Justin; suck my nipples!'

Justin drew back a little to stare at Lola's body and as he did so, he slowly pulled her dress down to her waist, revealing the full ripe beauty of her breasts, and then bent forward to take first one and then the other teat between his lips.

Lola felt lustier and lustier as Justin sucked and caressed her. She pressed her pubic bone along his hard-muscled thigh, and shuddered at the contact of her body against his swollen penis. She murmured, 'Justin, pull it off! Now!' She was writhing against him. Her skin tingled as he breathed upon her naked shoulder, and she felt ready to come on the spot. 'I want you!'

Lifting his mouth from her tits, Justin began peeling the dress from Lola's body. Stripping it over her hips, he let it fall to her feet and she stood naked before him save for her tiny panties.

'I want you!' she repeated lustily.

Justin caressed her bottom and gently slid the silk garment to Lola's ankles. Standing again, he cradled her breasts in his hands and murmured, 'I know, babe. Let's do it. Take out my dick.'

She slid her hand to his groin, quickly pulling the zipper down, and reached inside to ease his rigid member free from its confines. Holding it now in her palm, she gently rubbed his shaft and teased his balls with her fingertips. As she looked down, Lola had to admit Justin's penis was one of the grandest she had ever seen: long and thick in the shaft, with a large purple glans swelling like a ripe plum, already moist where some juice had seeped out of its little slit. No wonder Justin considered himself a great Romeo! This was a truly impressive tower of flesh, she marvelled, but she wondered slyly, did he know how to use it like a real lover?

Still dancing in time to the pulsing music, Lola massaged Justin's shaft and using his penis like a tiller, she steered her partner round to face Claire. Lola felt Justin's body go rigid as he saw with a shock that the other girl had pulled her skirt all the way up, had spread her legs wantonly, and was gently masturbating amidst the soft shadows of the sofa.

'Look at Claire!' he gasped.

Lola, who had already been watching her friend with amusement for a few minutes, nodded. 'Yeah, I know. She's over there playing with herself; I bet her little clit is

53

sticking up like a button! It's for Paul's benefit, I'm sure. She'll take care of you later, but right now I get the first taste of your beautiful cock!'

As Justin felt his dick respond to Lola's expert tongue, he still couldn't take his eyes off Claire. As she lay with her legs parted wide, she tilted her pelvis upward to expose the flesh of her ruby lips. As he watched, she masturbated her labia for him, her small tight arsehole winking, her slim buttocks rocking in rhythmical motion in time to the music. From the corner of his eye he saw Paul return to the room carrying a bottle of champagne liberated from Raton's refrigerator. The young man stopped in his tracks, totally transfixed by this unfolding panoply of sex.

Shaking himself from his trance, Paul moved lithely to Claire's side and knelt between her legs, gazing in rapture at the girl's hand as she caressed her clitoris and explored her vagina, her sexy dew evident on her fingers as she moved them languidly in and out.

Claire smiled at Paul, a lazy smile of invitation.

'Man, oh man!' Paul murmured, almost a groan, and his hand went to his zipper to release his own hungry cock as he feasted his eyes on the woman. 'You look like a Greek goddess,' he said, thinking she was as beautiful as a statue, and more sexy than any picture he'd glimpsed in the gallery's collection of erotic prints.

'I'm so hot,' Claire exclaimed, and stopped playing with herself long enough to divest herself completely of her wispy dress, revealing her nubile breasts. 'That's me, Paul,' she breathed. 'Now it's your turn to get naked!'

Paul needed no further invitation. Standing to step out of his boots, he dropped his jeans and underwear, flicking them from his legs with practised ease. The hem of his short white T-shirt stopped well above his chunky penis, which now stood rampant in front of him, angling upward towards his belly.

This was Claire's chance to feast her eyes. Paul's cock

wasn't as huge as Justin's, as she glanced in comparison at that member now rearing so happily in Lola's mobile hands, but it was long and broad, with a beautiful tip that looked already moist.

As Paul displayed his own erect manhood, he sneaked a sideways glance at Lola's expert manipulation of Justin's engorged penis. He had heard Justin boast of his size, and Paul ruefully acknowledged that his friend hadn't been exaggerating, but any fleeting inadequacies he might have felt were instantly displaced by the velvet caress of Claire's lips on his own cock. Bending over to nuzzle her hair, he murmured, 'I want to get you off!'

'That's fine with me,' said Claire, laughing. 'First you and then your friend!' She took the whole length of Paul's succulent member in her mouth, sliding her tongue up and down the full length of his shaft. She pulled Paul on to the sofa, guiding his hand deftly to her vulva. Probing her moist channel, Paul took his cue from Claire's liquid rhythm on his penis, and plied his fingers skillfully within the girl's vagina, feeling her juices flow and her sex muscles contract. With his thumb he fondled her clitoris, and in return felt Claire's fingers probe the tight bud of his anus. Her first orgasm came quickly, and she clenched her thighs together, holding Paul's hand trapped in her sex as she spasmed.

Within moments, Claire shuddered again, and abandoning Paul's still partially hard cock, reached for the unopened bottle of champagne. Standing up, she walked over to Lola and Justin, who by this time were both naked, too. Lola, who squatted between her lover's thighs, was following her girlfriend's example, and having difficulty taking all of Justin's impressive manhood in her mouth. She complained happily, 'This prick is too big!'

Claire's mouth watered at the sight of the rampant rod vibrating under Lola's tender care. Shaking the champagne and uncorking it with a loud pop, she knelt and held the open bottle to Lola's face.

'Drink this instead!' she invited. 'It's going to fizz out the end! Swallow the champagne, Lola, and leave Justin's dick for me!' As the bubbly frothed over Lola's face, she released Justin's penis from her greedy lips and Claire kissed her friend deeply, tasting the Brüt champagne mixed with Justin's musk on Lola's tongue.

Claire sprinkled sparkling drops of the liquid first over Justin's tumescent cock, and then, pushing Lola back on to the cushions, poured a second portion over the woman's breasts and dribbled it down her belly to tease her sex. Claire dipped her head down and lapped at the heady mixture of champagne and love juices between Lola's thighs.

While the blonde girl panted and writhed, Claire laid aside the half-empty bottle of Chandon, and focused on her friend's sex, teasing her clitoris with her tongue and sliding her agile fingers deep inside Lola's drenched vagina. At the same time, Claire reared her bum in the air, offering Justin a wordless invitation.

With champagne dripping from his rigid penis, Justin strode forward, and with a low whistle of appreciation he knelt to plunge his towering flesh into Claire, burying it to the hilt in her quim. Claire could not restrain a gasp as his member filled her like none other. She gasped and writhed as Justin rode her, his finger gathering juices from her vagina lips and tracing a moist trail to the tight pucker of her bum-hole.

'Have you had it both at once, pretty lady?' he grunted, all veneer of sophistication gone and replaced by an animal lust. Claire moaned an indecipherable reply, and Justin eased one slick finger between her sphincter, mimicking the rhythm and thrust of his cock inside her vagina. Claire's body went rigid with compounding sensations, and with a howl of passion went down again on Lola with a renewed frenzy.

The three young bodies rocked in shared ecstasy, enveloped in sensual lust, and Paul moved quickly to fill the most obvious void in the composition of writhing flesh. Grabbing the remaining champagne, he poured it into a glass, and dipped his dick, once more fully erect, into the bubbling liquid, feeling the tingle of alcohol on his sensitive glans. Straddling Lola's face on his knees, he pushed his springing cock downward into her eager mouth.

'You can take all of this one, sweetheart,' grinned Paul, as he fed his member into her mouth, inch by inch. Indeed this was a cock that Lola could more easily manage, and she drank in thirstily the tasty vestiges of wine mixed deliciously with Paul's male musk. While Claire's expert tongue and fingers were bringing her rapidly to her climax, she squeezed Paul's balls gently to foster his eruption. Her orgasm flooded over her; her body arched in joy and her love juices gushed out of her vagina.

Paul withdrew his thick phallus from Lola's mouth, and moved quickly round to take Claire's place between Lola's spread thighs. As Melissa Etheridge's raunchy lyrics throbbed in their ears, he plunged his penis deep inside the blonde girl, stemming her flow, but raising her sensitive flesh to a new peak of excruciating ecstasy.

'Oh. Lola, Lola!' crooned Paul, as he moved his hardness within her. They rocked in a mad rhythm. Lola thrashed in the exquisite torment of her second crashing orgasm in as many minutes.

As Paul and Lola subsided before Claire in an exhausted knot of limbs, Justin chortled, 'Oh, man oh man, what a show! I've never seen anything like that! Now Claire baby, get ready! My cock is bursting!' Quivering with the desire to come, held briefly in check while he absorbed the writhing tableau in front of him, Justin turned sideways to admire his reflection in one of the room's mirrors.

He watched himself driving his mighty manhood deep into Claire's pussy, and he eased his finger from her anus to clasp both hands around her heaving hips. As he ground his groin against her bum, he saw Claire's reflection in the mirror watching him in rapt enjoyment, a smile of utter wantonness on her lips.

'I'm going to fuck you good, pretty lady . . .' Justin gritted his teeth, his jaw clenching with emotion as he drove himself and his partner to climax.

Shaking with the pleasure of her rippling orgasm and the sight of herself being so rampantly taken, Claire fell limp with satiation across the cushions, her own juices and Justin's come flowing across the fabric. Justin felt good, too. He stroked her breasts and teased her nipples for a few moments when she rolled over and smiled up at him.'I fucked you good,' he said.

Claire smiled and closed her eyes, and softly murmured, 'Yes, you did.'

Suddenly voluble, Justin continued, 'Oh, boy! I've wanted to fuck you ever since you started to work here. I guess you knew that when I waved my cock at you in the shower! I know some women would have run to the boss man and complained. I'd have been out of a job, I guess, but I somehow knew you wouldn't mind. You just radiate sex, you and Lola both. God, when she began to touch you, and when you went down on her, it was the sexiest thing I've ever seen! You and she have done that before, haven't you?'

He looked into Claire's eyes as she lay next to him. Her sleepy smile spread to her eyes, as she whispered, 'Yes, sometimes, just for fun, but your cock is the best thing I've ever felt!' and she reached over to trace the length of it with her fingers. 'And this funny little tattoo,' she said, lazily fondling his buttock, 'I haven't seen one of those before. Is that what we look like?'

'It doesn't do you justice, babe,' replied Justin.

* * *

Justin spread one discarded dress over the soon sleeping girl and the other over the recumbent forms of Lola and Paul, by now breathing deeply, wrapped in each other's arms. Justin couldn't imagine sleeping; he was so high with excitement. He moved quietly around their temporary sex parlour and the conference room next door, tidying up the glasses, plates and empty bottles; and turned off the lights. Moving the furniture to the edges of the room, he arranged the cushions on the floor, easing Claire into a more comfortable position. As he lay down beside her and trailed his hand once more between her legs, his new lover moaned softly and stirred without waking. Justin smiled and let his mind replay their sexy scenes. He saw himself taking the woman boldly from behind, his proud dick once more sinking full length into her vagina.

But when the woman turned towards him, the face he saw was Eden Sinclair's.

Chapter Six
The Morning After

*E*den awoke alone at daybreak, in a tumult of sexual yearning. Her first thoughts were of Michael Mac-Kenzie, her dreams having featured the Scotsman, always in a variety of sexy scenarios, sometimes with Claire and Lola, but increasingly starring just herself.

With a lustful yearning, Eden lay in bed for a few extra moments, instinctively caressing herself, desiring nothing more than to give into her bodily need and masturbate to her recurring visions of this artist who was beginning to obsess her. Admonishing herself disdainfully for being in danger of evolving into just another art groupie, Eden's stern sense of self-possession gained control, propelling her into her morning routine.

She tossed aside the short T-shirt she slept in, crossed to the window and raised the wooden Venetian blind. Despite the onset of summer, a front had passed in the night and the day had dawned damp and grey. There was even a slight chill from the window that sent goose bumps across her naked flesh. At this hour there were no neighbours to observe the sight of a nude Eden standing in front of her window, and she felt a momentary pang of regret that no one was there to revel in the sight of her body.

Her brain effortlessly computed that it had been one year, one month, two weeks and three days since she and her last lover had parted in a welter of recrimination and pain. And she hadn't had a man in all that time. It had been her own choice, she reminded herself, not wanting to enter the battleground of love again until her vivid anger and hurt at that betrayal had soothed. No new relationship stood a chance in the mood she had been in these last few months!

But now all that was in the past; no wonder she was so frustrated! Her only amorous adventures recently had involved getting a little stoned and succumbing to the gentle advances of two old girlfriends. Very pleasant, she admitted to herself, but no matter how agile the tongue, how deft the fingers or how elongated the dildo, the experience for her was never quite as satisfying as a man, hot and hard inside her.

And this morning there was no doubt that she was hot for one guy in particular. She caught her breath as a vivid picture of MacKenzie shot to the surface of her mind. Naked, as always now in her thoughts, his penis stood proudly on his flat stomach, rising out of a dark nest of pubic curls. At this point in her fantasy, Eden's visual imagination failed her. She had never made love to a redhead, man or woman.

Idly wondering whether the pubic hair around MacKenzie's genitals would be as bright as the red hair on his head, Eden couldn't suppress a giggle at her schoolgirl level of *naïveté*. As young teenagers, she and her girlfriends used to speculate about their male classmates, imagining the details of the male member before any of them had ever touched one. And here she was now, twenty years later, doing exactly the same thing with MacKenzie and his unknown penis!

Leaving her window, Eden crossed to the closet and

quickly donned her running clothes, black sports bra and Spandex shorts, thick white ankle socks and Reebok trainers. She added a baggy Atlanta Braves' sweatshirt and cap for the cool temperatures outside and headed for the door.

As Eden jogged purposefully towards Piedmont Park, just two blocks from her bungalow, she set out on her regular three-mile route. Pushing herself harder than normal, she sought an alternative bodily release from the tensions that churned inside her.

Thirty minutes later, after her run and a series of much needed stretches, she stood beneath the pulsing shower, letting the hot water and steam flush the residual stress from her mind and body.

On her way to work, Eden detoured briefly for a breakfast of wholewheat pancakes and the *New York Times* at her favourite café on McLendon Avenue. By seven o'clock she was at her desk, long before any of the other gallery staff arrived, with few traces visible from her restless night of lusty and tumultuous dreams. Only the delicate blue shadows around her eyes betrayed her.

Having occupied herself with the selection of two paintings to go to Jay Jay's house as promised, Eden was perplexed by the fact that her thoughts continually strayed to MacKenzie. These meanderings were soon cut short by the ringing of the telephone. It was well before gallery opening time. Eden wondered if this could be MacKenzie calling her.

As Eden picked up the instrument, her hand shook. But the voice on the other end was a woman's, that of her long-time best friend, Belgique du Pont. Eden felt her heart sink a little in her chest with disappointment that it was not MacKenzie calling.

'Oh, I'm so glad you're there, Eden!' came the cheery voice on the other end. 'I must see you! May I come over right away, *ma cherie*?'

'Hi, Belgique,' Eden said flatly. Her friend sounded as dramatic as usual, thought Eden, what was it this time?

There was a pause before Belgique blithely continued, 'I want to hear all about Michael MacKenzie! Eden, are you all right? You sound a little strange.'

'How do you know about MacKenzie?' asked Eden, brusquely, ignoring her friend's question. Odd that she was trying to get the sculptor out of her mind, and now her friend was calling up asking about him!

'Your esteemed employer called me last night, Eden,' replied Belgique, 'and then rushed over to see me! He was positively gushing about his new find, and "the wonderful eroticism of his sculptures". That's a quote, dear; I've rarely seen Alexander so excited about an artist. He told me to be sure to call you today, and said you'd tell me all about him. By the tone in your voice, I'd say there was a lot to tell!'

'I've hardly met MacKenzie!' retorted Eden, thinking hotly again about Raton's deliberate exclusion of her from the artist selection process. 'I saw him for the first time yesterday and hardly spoke to him all the time he was here.'

'Oh, Eden!' scolded Belgique. 'Don't play the innocent with me! Alexander told me that MacKenzie and you were like tongue-tied teenagers all afternoon in the gallery!'

'We were not!' exclaimed Eden, suddenly mortified that her emotions had been so transparent to her boss. She changed the subject and asked Belgique, 'How come Raton visited your place? I didn't think you knew him that well. Do you two have a history I don't know about?'

'Oh, Alexander sold me some pieces before you came up to Atlanta,' answered Belgique offhandedly. 'He can be witty and amusing at times, but he's always at his best when he lets his dick do the talking! It's the most eloquent part of him!'

Eden gasped. She had no idea that Belgique and her

boss were lovers! But Belgique's appetite for men, and women come to that, was insatiable, so it really was no surprise that she had made it with Raton. Eden pondered that he was quite dishy, in a way. The image of her boss naked and supine beneath her friend's body made her smile. Eden felt her mood elevate as a vivid picture of Belgique, riding up and down on Raton's swollen penis, slick with her love juices, came to mind. Aloud, Eden laughed, 'Belle, you're shocking! That's a relationship where you would always be on top, or calling the shots!'

Her friend tittered softly at Eden's remark, but repeated her request about seeing Eden.

'Of course, Belgique,' Eden responded, 'I'm here all on my own right now; come on over and I'll show you some of MacKenzie's work here in the gallery. I'm sure you'll find it sexy as hell; I sure do! I get excited just looking at it!'

'Wow! I'll be there in ten minutes!' said her friend. 'Don't do anything without me!' and she rang off.

Eden walked downstairs into the main gallery where MacKenzie's sculptures had spent the night, frozen in space just where Justin and Paul had placed them the day before. She turned on the lights and drank in their heady sensuality. She ran her hands lightly over the bronzes, and their surfaces winked back at her with a dull sheen.

Even in the chill of a dull grey morning, Eden felt a warmth spreading over her loins as she gazed upon the bronze flesh, rampant and pliable in equal measure. As she rested her fingers on the tumescent penis of the Greek lover Thetis, she noticed how MacKenzie had captured even the roll of foreskin withdrawing over the rising flesh.

She wondered whether MacKenzie was circumcised. Almost all American men were, at least every one she had been to bed with, but in Britain it might be more common the other way round. She wondered what it would be like to suck a penis that carried that extra layer of skin. Would she like it? Would she get the chance?

Eden laughed at her preoccupation with the man's genitalia, but comprehended just how much she wanted to have sex with MacKenzie. And to hell with her policy of professional detachment! If Raton could read her desires so well yesterday, and if MacKenzie was in the same state, then maybe the Scotsman was thinking about her right now! But the memory of Claire and Lola fawning over him the previous night clouded Eden's optimism, and she frowned as she released Thetis from her caress and went into the conference suite to make some coffee.

The first thing Eden noticed when she entered the empty conference suite was an unmistakable musky odour. When she moved into the sitting room and went to pick up the cushions still on the floor, she saw the fabric was stained, certainly with wine and probably with semen too, if her examination was accurate. Her immediate reactions were of annoyance, humour and jealousy, each following hard on the heels of the other. Even though the room was generally tidy, there were overt signs of a hurried departure. As Eden wondered if this was where MacKenzie and those damn girls had had sex all night long, a strong arrow of anguish pierced her core. She switched the air-conditioning fan to high to clear the room of its scent of spilled sex and wine, pulled around the furniture to its more conventional arrangement, and threw the cushions into the closet to be sent to the dry cleaners later.

As she fussed and busied herself, the buzzer at the gallery front door abruptly claimed her attention. That must be Belgique, she thought. Looking at her watch, she saw it was only eight o'clock; the rest of the staff wouldn't be in for an hour yet. Eden regained her composure and walked across the exhibition area to verify Belgique's presence through the security grill across the door. She opened up quickly, shutting the bolts back in place after her friend had entered.

Belgique shook her black curls and hugged Eden, who welcomed her visitor. 'Come in, Belgique; here they are. We'll be undisturbed for nearly an hour, so feast your eyes!'

'Eden, these are marvellous!' cried Belgique. Throwing off her jacket and running her hands over all the critical parts of the sculptures, she murmured, 'Ummm! What lovely details! I can see why you get excited just having them here to look at. God, they're sexy! But what's MacKenzie like? Is he just as delicious as his characters?' She pretended to masturbate one stiffened rod with her small hand.

Eden smiled at her incorrigible friend and observed, 'If Raton recognised my state of arousal yesterday, it's unlikely I can fool you, Belgique!'

Belgique laughed and nodded her head. 'And why bother? We have very few secrets from each other.'

'Yet I didn't know about you and Raton,' Eden reminded her.

Belgique took her friend's arm but remained silent for a while, sensing that Eden was troubled about her dalliance with Alexander Raton.

Eden looked at Belgique. Beautiful as always, the sexy dark-haired woman in her mid 30s, was endowed with the kind of body and manner that turned men's heads. It was hardly surprising that Raton had fallen for her, like so many others.

'Well now you do know,' Belgique rejoined pertly. But she didn't elaborate. 'So tell me about MacKenzie,' she ordered in a playful tone, changing the subject.

Eden came clean. 'He's gorgeous, Belgique. I can't get him out of my mind! I get hot just thinking of him! All we uttered were a few words and some professional stuff, but something about him really got to me. I think it's time I stopped abstaining from men and went after him!'

She squirmed at the thought of a love affair with the handsome sculptor, feeling a warm moistness between her legs as she stood next to his vibrantly sexy sculptures.

Belgique smiled lasciviously and purred, 'I know you too well, Eden. I can tell just how aroused you are! It would give Raton a hard-on if he knew! Perhaps he does?' She ran her hand around Eden's waist and kissed her, saying, 'I think you're right; it is time to break your fast and go after MacKenzie!'

Eden had to agree.

Returning to the statues, Belgique raved on. 'MacKenzie's sculptures are *so* exciting! I must have one of them delivered this morning! I thought I'd ask the artist to bring it round himself, but as you're so horny for him, maybe I'll content myself with your young stud, Justin. He's a hunk!'

'He's no stud of mine,' disclaimed Eden, blushing nevertheless at the memory of her earlier fantasies about the delivery man. Smiling, she admitted, 'Yes, he is a hunk. Trust you to get right to the heart of the matter! Fuck them first and ask questions afterwards! It would be a sight to see how young Mr Romeo handles himself with someone like you, Belgique!' Eden thought it would be fun to watch Belgique seducing Justin, and prophesied, 'I bet you chew Justin up into small pieces, and spit him out!'

As Belgique grinned in acknowledgement of the possibility, Eden added, 'I'll see to it right away,' and hugged her friend, inhaling an expensive Parisian perfume.

Eden received an answering hug from Belgique, who nibbled daintily at her ear, and then gave her a delicate kiss on the lips. The two woman clasped each other for a moment, gazing tenderly into each other's eyes, hands barely touching each other in light caresses.

Breaking their sensual silent embrace, Eden spoke as they pulled apart. 'I have Justin signed up to take something over to Jay Jay Ritchie's place, but Paul can do that, and Justin can take one of these round to your apartment when he arrives this morning. Which one do you want? I've tagged three for the next show, so you can't have those, and of course it has to be something that Justin can handle on his own once he gets to your apartment.'

'Oh, I don't know about that,' demurred Belgique, striking a mock weight-lifter's pose.

Eden remembered seeing her friend at the gym working out with some pretty impressive weights, and advised half-seriously, 'Just be careful, Belgique! Our insurance doesn't cover clients injuring themselves while they move the art!'

Placing her hands upon the statue of a couple locked in embrace, she suggested, 'Look, how about this piece? MacKenzie's *Daphnis and Chloë* would go very well with that suite of prints that you bought last month.' Very hot indeed, Eden realised, as she recalled Belgique's selection from the gallery's 'Private Viewing Only Collection': classy erotica derived from some of Picasso's near-pornographic sketches.

Daphnis and Chloë depicted a sexy duo lounging unclothed on some sort of antique couch, the woman's head resting in the man's naked lap. His legs were spread wide; her hand was nestled around his tumescent penis. Belgique caressed the inner thigh of the male figure, and breathed, 'Oh, yes,' as she gazed at the image of excited pleasure that was visible in every contour of the bronze figures.

'I can't put this in the show,' explained Eden. 'It's just too raunchy for the good burghers of Atlanta. Most of MacKenzie's work has a softer overtone, of love, maybe, rather than raw sex. It takes the edge off the work to a degree that we can show it here. But this one's just lust, pure and simple.'

'Yes,' said Belgique, 'She's just about to swallow him in her mouth. All they're thinking about is coming!'

'She's certainly fixated,' Eden conceded.

'Yes,' said Belgique, 'and isn't it just lovely!'

Both women laughed, sharing their own sexual bond.

As Belgique kissed her friend goodbye, she lightly brushed Eden's cheek with her fingers and murmured seductively, 'Your skin is so soft, darling!' But then she became more brisk. 'Send it over with Justin; and let's meet later this morning, say 11.30, at the health club and lunch afterwards at La Splendour. My treat! I'll report on Justin's performance if you'll promise to let me know everything that happens with Mr MacKenzie!'

She blew Eden another vivacious kiss, turned happily on her heel and sauntered away, her supple hips swinging sensuously in her snugly tailored Chanel suit. She disappeared in a cloud of sexy fragrance out the door.

The gallery seemed especially empty to Eden after Belgique's departure. Her friend was very special to her. While Eden was erotically tuned, she always imagined Belgique to be more so. She smiled at her thoughts, recalling many times when Belgique had regaled and shocked her with stories that sent little quivers of delight through her body. Belgique was renowned for her appetite for male company; but fewer knew about Belgique's liberal appetite for women, too.

Eden and Belgique had met several years earlier, when they were both studying at Tulane University in New Orleans, Eden majoring in art and Belgique in theatre. Even then Belgique was rarely short of money, but Eden was initially astonished to discover that much of it came from her friend's evening work in an expensive New Orleans nightclub, where she was billed as an 'exotic dancer' from Europe. Eden's curiosity had overcome her prudishness and some nights she had accompanied her friend, getting a vicarious thrill from watching Belgique's lusty abandonment on stage.

With her striking dark hair, white skin and hourglass

figure displayed sometimes coyly, sometimes flagrantly, Belgique was a favourite with the club's patrons, and occasionally she would spend time with selected clients after-hours. The criteria were always the same: the men had to be handsome and rich.

Just once Eden had participated with her friend as part of an elite quartet in the private suite above the club. During an exotic evening performance at the club, Belgique had sauntered over to the booth where Eden sat writing an essay for her art history class. Belgique, wearing a glittering green-sequined form-fitting dress that matched her eyes, slid in beside Eden.

The action on stage was hot, and for a few moments the college room-mates had watched the seductive performance in silence. During a pause, Eden had returned to the term paper she was writing.

Belgique had said, 'Hey, Eden, put the pen down. I want to ask you a question.'

Eden had pushed aside her paper. The spaghetti straps of Belgique's dress had slipped over her shoulders. Absently, Eden had reached across the table to adjust them, and asked, 'What is it?'

Belgique, who had known that her room-mate was short of money, had said, 'Now listen, there are these two really cool guys who want to have some fun, but what would really turn them on would be having "a party" with two girls! Will you help out? I know they'll be generous! And it's safe; they check out OK.'

Eden remembered looking down at her empty glass, her fourth or fifth White Russian of the evening, wondering how she was going to make her rent payment that month. She had seen the guys with Belgique: both were sexy, cute and well dressed in expensive suits, probably businessmen from up north.

Belgique had continued, 'They're on the lookout for some New Orleans naughtiness. And they'll pay big bucks!'

Eden, who didn't usually drink so much, had muttered, 'Cute sexy guys; why not, just this once? What the hell! Sure! You lead, Belgique, and I'll follow.'

It had been fun while it lasted. The guys were actually quite nice; attending a conference in the city and looking for some high-priced mischievous sex. She recalled herself and Belgique executing a slow striptease, and when all four of them were naked and got down to unadulterated sex, they had assumed normal positions one-on-one. But before long, Belgique's talents for innovation had raised the tempo.

Much of what had followed that evening had become hazy in Eden's mind. While her memory of the two guys' cocks in and out of her vagina and her mouth, and their hands all over her body had blurred, what hadn't faded was the sudden shock of Belgique's tongue on her clitoris, and her friend's fingers sliding into her vagina. She had been sprawled across the bed, with Belgique's face between her thighs, her friend's tongue and fingers giving Eden a kind of pleasure she had not experienced before.

Belgique's curvaceous bottom had reared up in the air, an open invitation for one of the men, who was standing behind Belgique, sliding his long glistening cock into her pussy. From Belgique's rhythmic moans and the sexy sound of the man's balls slapping against Belgique's open vulva, his penis was penetrating Belgique to her very core.

Driven half-wild with lust by Belgique's expert cunnilingus, Eden had reached for the other man's balls and buttocks, stroking and fondling them as he masturbated.

As if on cue, Eden's body had responded to Belgique's increasingly fervent licking and finger-fucking of her vagina, and her own orgasm had coiled up from deep inside her, rippling through her whole body in a delicious flood of feeling. Overcome with her own sensations,

Eden had barely felt the spurt of hot semen as her masturbating partner had creamed over her breasts.

The sex with the men had been quick and hot, as though they had felt furtiveness was a requirement for this sort of naughty sex. When they had left, Eden and Belgique had taken hot showers and fallen into bed. Her last memory that night had been of Belgique cuddling up to her as they fell asleep.

When she awoke, Eden had found Belgique still lying with her arms wrapped around her, one hand resting lightly across Eden's breast. The room was otherwise empty; the two men long gone. Probably back to their wives in Ohio, or Nebraska, or wherever it was they were from, Eden had thought. Moving gently so as not to wake her friend, Eden had eased out of bed, but had been brought up short by the sight of five $100 bills on the bedside table. A shiver of revulsion had passed through her. She had never imagined she would have sex for money, but the wave of self-disgust had been quickly followed by the memory of Belgique's wonderful love-making, and the unmistakable response of her own body to the woman's tongue and fingers.

Filled with a sudden tenderness, Eden had turned back and nuzzled her friend awake, kissing her gently and stroking her in slow lingering caresses. Belgique had responded with a surprisingly deep kiss, her tongue probing right into Eden's mouth with a genuine passion. Without further thought Eden had moved her hands over her friend's body, delighting in the immediate response of Belgique's nipples as they grew hard between her fingers. Stroking her warm flesh and following her hands with her tongue, Eden had moved slowly down Belgique's body until she had reached her luxurious delta of dark curls.

Eden had reversed roles by burying her face between Belgique's open thighs. The lips of her vulva were pink and moist, and she had felt for Belgique's little love bud

72

with her tongue, and heard a satisfied moan from her friend. She had moved her body to straddle Belgique, offering her friend the sight of her own sex and seeking a repeat of last night's sensations. Belgique had not demurred, and once again Eden had felt waves of pleasure as her friend's agile tongue and fingers had renewed their expert exploration of her clitoris and vagina. But this time Eden had felt she wanted to give as good as she got, and had focused on following Belgique's every move. She had doubted if she could match her friend's skilful technique, but her passion had seemed to make up for any clumsiness, as Belgique came first with a long drawn-out moan and shudder that thrilled Eden and triggered her own orgasm, not as shattering as the night before, but full of satisfaction, as much about her friend's pleasure as her own.

'Well, Eden,' Belgique had observed after a moment of delicious relaxation in each other's arms, 'I didn't know you had that in you! That was as great a tongue-fucking as I've ever had!'

Eden had smiled ruefully. 'It was new to me, too,' she had replied, still a little dazed at what she had done, now that her conscious mind had taken over from the primal lusts that had driven her to such peaks of satisfaction. But a thought had startled her upright. 'What about the money? Belgique, those guys paid us to have sex with them! There's $500 on the table. That makes me a whore!'

'Oh, Eden, don't be such a prude! What did you expect? I do this sort of thing quite often, but only with guys who are checked out by the manager downstairs. He keeps away all the creeps and the kooks. He takes $100 and we split the rest. Those guys last night just needed some good uncomplicated sex. We did them a favour they'll remember for a long time! I know I've got a good body and I like to show it off. And you're as cute and sexy as hell!' Then she had asked more softly, 'Have you made it with a woman before?'

73

Eden had blushed, suddenly very self-conscious, 'No,' she had said, 'never. Does this mean I'm a lesbian?'

Belgique had guffawed delicately, a gleam of genuine amusement in her eye. 'If you could have seen yourself riding that guy's dick last night, you wouldn't ask that question! God, you must be horny! You're no more gay than I am, and even if you were, so what? You're a very sexy lady, Eden, and if you enjoy women as well as men, then that can be double the pleasure! Here, take your $200!'

Eden shook herself awake from her daydream. That had been ten years ago, but the memories were fresher than she had realised, and the same flush rose to her cheeks as she replayed her contrasting and conflicted emotions.

She had never had sex for money again, but her relationship with Belgique had endured, despite her friend's profligate habits. Belgique had enjoyed no end of sexual partners, and Eden wondered how she could remember them all. But Belgique's enjoyment of sex was so full of fun and openness that Eden could never bring herself to censure her friend. One just had to accept Belgique and enjoy her company!

These thoughts were broken by the sound of a key in the rear door. Eden turned to see Paul, who appeared shocked to find her there already in the gallery. Nervously, he glanced sideways into the conference suite and paled when he saw the rearranged furniture.

'Um, hi, Eden, er . . . Miss Sinclair,' he stuttered, now blushing in contrast to his pallor of moments ago. 'I just thought I would get in early, just in case . . . um . . . er, in case anything needed, like . . . um . . . tidying up.'

'Tidying up after what?' demanded Eden, with a sharp edge to her voice. After those wanton hussies had seduced MacKenzie, that's what! she thought.

'Well . . .' muttered Paul, who, desperately shy in front of Eden, blushed deeply. After all she *was* the gallery director, and while it seemed a lot of fun to make sexy remarks about her when Justin was around, now he was on his own he didn't feel half as bold. And he could tell that she had put two and two together about last night. Stammering slightly, Paul continued, 'Justin and me and the girls ... er ... had a sort of party last night after everybody else had gone.'

'You and the girls?' queried Eden, suddenly urgent. 'You, Justin, Claire and Lola? Is that what you're telling me?'

'Well, yes,' muttered Paul, not understanding the thrust of Eden's breathless questioning.

'The four of you had sex, right here in the gallery?' she queried.

'Well, er, yes,' repeated Paul, still in a low voice, avoiding Eden's unblinking stare. 'It did get a little wild, but everybody was cool about it.'

Eden softened when he looked up and said, 'I mean the girls were all for it! I mean, like, we didn't like rape them or anything! We woke up at about 4.30 this morning and went home for breakfast. Claire and Lola are fine, I'm sure!'

Thinking he looked rather like a chastened puppy, Eden kept her face stern, but inside she was buoyant, her spirits bubbling over. So MacKenzie didn't spend last night having raunchy sex with the two nymphets on the cushions! Oh, joy! She was suddenly so happy that she could hardly keep a straight face talking to the red-faced delivery boy. 'I'm going to check with Claire and Lola when I see them,' she said, 'just to verify their version of events. If it all really was cool, then we'll say no more about it.'

Looking somewhat relieved, the young man nodded dolefully, his cheeks aflame with embarrassment mixed with arousal at telling the beautiful woman before him about his evening's activities.

But Eden had more instructions. 'Right now, you go

through the suite with a fine-tooth comb, and make sure everything is properly arranged before Mr Raton arrives!' Eden wondered irritably when Raton *would* return. One day he was under her feet, poking his nose into every-thing and asking fatuous questions; the next he was nowhere to be seen. 'Out with clients!' was his usual line. Eden snorted in annoyance and brought her mind back to the present.

Paul was still watching her anxiously.

'Go on, Paul!' Eden snapped. 'And when you've checked through the rooms, I need you to take a couple of new pieces by Annalee Barrett over to Jay Jay Ritchie's house in Buckhead. I've set them aside in the storeroom. Get his approval on one, hang it for him, and bring the Bulgaria back from his master suite. And keep your mind on the job!'

'Yes, ma'am, er ... Miss Sinclair,' said Paul, wishing fervently that Justin was there to help him out. But gosh, Eden did look lovely when she was angry! Despite himself he felt a nudge of desire between his legs, and he turned away to hide his arousal. He went rigid though when, a moment later, he felt Eden's hand on his arm. She turned him round to face her. He was surprised by the gleam in her eye, which didn't seem fierce any more; now it spoke of excitement and relief.

'Is that really what happened here last night, Paul? You and Justin and Claire and Lola went at it in the conference suite?' She spoke more softly.

Dumbfoundedly, Paul just nodded.

'And no one else was with you? It was just you four?'

Again Paul nodded mutely, and was surprised by a big smile that spread over his boss's face. And he was even more surprised when she took him in her arms and gave him a big kiss on the mouth.

'You're not angry any more, Miss Sinclair?' asked the bemused young man, taken aback by her dramatic change in mood.

'Oh, no, Paul,' replied Eden, unable to keep her delight from her voice. 'I'm thrilled!' And she turned away, climbing the spiral stair to her office with a jaunty bound. Paul busied himself in the conference suite. He thought he wouldn't say anything about this to the others. At least, not until he understood what was going on!

Why did she care so much, Eden wondered, that the revels did not include MacKenzie? And then she answered herself. Because she wanted him. And she didn't want someone else getting him before she did!

Chapter Seven
The Delivery

No sooner had Paul left to install a painting in Jay Jay's boudoir, than Justin arrived for work at the gallery, looking pleased with himself despite his lack of sleep.

Hearing him arrive, Eden ran downstairs and button-holed him as he crossed the threshold. Keeping a straight face, she said crisply, 'Good morning, Justin!' He nodded. Looking him boldly in the eye, Eden asked, 'Do you have any energy left for work today after last night?'

Justin coloured and tried to read Eden's face, looking for clues, but her expression was deadpan.

'You needn't stare, Justin. I know what happened here last night. I'm not going to do anything about it this time, unless I hear complaints from Claire or Lola. But while you work on these premises,' Eden said, 'keep your jeans zipped!' Hypocrite! she scolded herself as her eyes drifted to take in the body of the sexy young man. Wasn't it just yesterday she had harboured lewd thoughts about him? Her eyes dropped inadvertently to Justin's crotch, imagining for a moment his extended penis; when she looked up again and caught his eye, he had regained his cocksure manner.

'Oh, I don't think either of the girls will complain about last night, Miss Sinclair,' he boasted with a leer. 'I think they were very satisfied. Paul and I performed heroic service. Standing in for the Scotsman, you might say!' He grinned at Eden.

Cocky bastard, she thought, wondering how he would feel when Belgique had finished with him. But all she said was, 'Just keep your mind on the job, Justin. Claire and Lola are off today, so there'll be no more opportunities for group sex in the gallery!' She paused for emphasis, but Justin showed no sign of embarrassment. She ploughed on, growing more irritated, 'Paul's already at work; he's taken the small van up to Buckhead and I've got another delivery for you right away. I want you to take that smaller bronze to a client, Belgique du Pont. It's not far, but you need to go at once.'

At the mention of Belgique's name, Justin paid more attention. Everyone in the gallery knew of Belgique, and what they didn't know about her, they invented.

'Which piece is it, Miss Sinclair? That one over there where the girl is sucking the guy's cock?'

Two could play at this game, decided Eden. Showing no reaction to Justin's deliberately crude language, she answered, 'Yes, Justin. Exactly. MacKenzie's companion piece will have a man licking a woman's cunt.' She paused again, this time pleased to notice the shock on Justin's face. 'Now stop trying to be clever, and get to work!' she added vehemently.

For all his braggadocio, Justin retained some common hypocritical attitudes. He thought it quite all right for men to use explicit language in or out of the bedroom, but he was still shocked by a woman doing the same in the workaday world of the office, and especially using the 'c' word. His blush and startled expression revealed his prejudice, and Eden knew she had scored a point.

'Load the sculpture in the large van. And here's the address,' she commanded, handing Justin a note with

79

directions. 'As soon as Angela comes in, I'm off to a client meeting. I won't be back till after lunch.' Turning on her heel, she walked back upstairs to her office, giving him no opportunity for further conversation.

Justin scowled at her retreating figure, and then angrily busied himself with the task of preparing the sculpture. He gathered sheets and blankets from the storeroom to wrap it, before manœuvering the bronze gently on to the hand cart. It was nearly too heavy for him, but he was damned if he was going to ask Eden for help.

Once outside, Justin used the mechanical hoist over the rear bumper to raise the statue into the bed of the truck. Taking care, despite his bad mood, he tied the statue carefully against the racks along the side. He looked at the post-it note with Belgique's address. It wasn't far, only a mile south in an old apartment building on the corner of Peachtree Street and Ponce de Leon Avenue. Justin vaguely recalled, from his high school history class, the story of Juan Ponce de Leon, the Spanish explorer who discovered Florida and then travelled north in search of the mythical fountain of eternal youth. He also remembered the building; it had just been renovated, and now boasted doormen and butler service. 'Reinventing the Glamour of the Nineteen Twenties!' read the estate agent's billboard outside the entrance. He passed it occasionally on the way to one of his favourite topless bars behind the old Fox Theatre.

Before he drove off, Justin sauntered across the street to get a bagel and a coffee from the new Caribou Coffee House. Despite the pleasures of the previous night, he now felt some unfocused resentment at women in general; his conversation with Eden hadn't gone the way he had intended. He didn't like coming off second best. Even the sexy smile of the new girl behind the counter in the coffee shop did little to raise his mood.

It was only when he was heading south on Peachtree in the truck, sipping his French roast, that he allowed himself to reminisce fully about the sweetness and raunchiness of the two women the night before. He would enjoy seeing them again; indeed, a repeat performance would be very exciting. He wanted to talk to them and, picking up the mobile phone, started to call the gallery to get their numbers. He stopped short when he realised that it might be Eden who answered the phone; he could hardly ask for the girls' home numbers after what she had just expressed. Instead, he called Paul. Just as well he had remembered to recharge the mobile phone overnight after messing up yesterday. The Scottish guy, MacKenzie, had become really irritated when they couldn't call from the road.

After only two rings, Paul answered. 'Hey man, what's going on?' he added when he recognised Justin. 'How's your dick this morning?' he guffawed. 'God, what a night that was! Hey,' he added, more subdued, 'Eden's really mad.'

'Yeah, I know,' said Justin, 'She's probably just wishing she was there, too!'

They both laughed, and Paul asked, 'Hey, where are you? What are you doing? Man, I'm really wasted.'

'I'm delivering art this morning, you dope, just like you.' When Paul seemed unimpressed with this witty repartée, Justin continued, 'I'm taking one of Monsieur MacKenzie's sculptures to that stacked lady, you know, La Belgique; the one who screws everything in sight.'

'Yeah, I know, Miss du Pont! La Belgique!' Paul's voice seemed to gain energy as he repeated her name. 'You've got a better deal that I have,' he said enviously. 'I'm up in Buckhead on my way to that gay guy's mansion, with a couple of those funny fake fresco things. Last time I was up here, the guy came on to me. I'm going to keep my hands over my cock this time!'

Justin, waiting at an interminable red light, held the steering wheel steady with his knees and took a slug of the hot coffee using one hand. With the other he held the mobile phone and advised, 'Yeah, buddy. Hang on to it tight. You want to save yourself for the next time we get together with Claire and Lola. Man, when Claire was masturbating herself, I thought I'd come on the spot. Those are two hot and horny women!' He set his cup aside and rubbed his balls, '*Mio cojones!* They got squeezed dry.'

Pausing, Justin put one hand back on the wheel as the light turned green, and then continued as Paul chuckled in the background. 'Anyway, I've got my hands full with this big bronze. It's that one where the girl is sucking the man's dick. Just like Lola and me!' He chortled. 'Hey, maybe Miss Belgique will suck mine. Wouldn't that be cool? You get rich old Jay Jay to nibble your prick and I get this rich bitch to suck me off! Take the phone with you; we could compare notes! Hey, hold on,' he continued, 'I'm here,' and laying the phone down, Justin turned the truck into the curved entrance drive of the Ponce de Leon Apartments. A fountain burbled in the forecourt.

'You still there, Paul?' queried Justin after he pulled to a stop. 'You should be here; this fucking thing's heavy.'

'Yeah,' agreed Paul, 'it's heavy, all right, but Miss du Pont has all these guys hanging around her apartment, butlers and stuff. If it's too heavy, just get one of those dudes to help you. Besides, you've got the trolley.'

'Butlers, huh?' asked Justin. 'All dressed up in tuxedos and stuff?'

'Nah. Well, some are. But they dress mostly in work-out clothes, like judo instructors and stuff.'

'Oh,' said Justin. 'Have you been here before? What's the latest you've heard about this woman?'

'Man, she's rich and she's beautiful and she's got great tits.'

Justin laughed, 'Always on about tits, you are. I'm still thinking about those two cute girls we laid last night!'

Paul whistled on the other end of the phone, 'Man,

don't I know it! Those little ladies are sure something else!' In a muffled voice, he added, 'But you ain't met Miss du Pont yet!'

'Yeah? Well, while you might like tits; I love a cute arse.'

Justin heard Paul mutter an expletive under his breath. 'Oh, shit, here's Jay Jay and a couple of his buddies. They look as if they've been expecting me.' There was a muffled pause and then Justin heard Paul exclaim, 'Sure, I remember you, Jay Jay! Yes, nice to see you, too. Hi, . . . er . . . Greg; hi, Jerry!' Then louder, 'Hey, Justin, I'll talk to you later; I've got my hands full right now!'

The phone went dead.

Justin laughed at Paul's evident predicament and muttered under his breath into the silent phone, 'Rather you than me, pal! I've got the better end of this deal!'

He stopped the truck and turned off the motor. No sooner had he opened the door and jumped down than one of the 'work-out judo types' described by Paul materialised from the junipers flanking the entrance to the building. A tall man, dressed all in black, this stranger was a Steven Seagal clone who looked even more like Steven Seagal than the actor himself.

At the man's sudden appearance, Justin started but then intuitively relaxed. He knew how to handle these guys. Giving the security guard a silly grin, he announced, as politely and fearlessly as he could muster, 'I have an appointment with Miss du Pont to deliver a statue. It's in the truck.'

At first the Hollywood-type said nothing, merely stared at Justin, seeming to examine his earring. Finally, without moving, he flicked his eyes towards the front door. 'She's expecting you. Ring the bell.' Before turning to go, the man cracked and popped his knuckles.

Justin sloped up the flagstone path towards the grand front porch with its columns and funny animals guarding the door, and followed instructions. Nothing happened.

God, when was the stupid butler coming to the door? he wondered, and raised his hand to press the buzzer again. Just then the heavy door was opened by a cute, dark-haired maid, wearing a loose black tunic and silk trousers, wrapped round with a broad white sash.

His hand was still raised, and a goofy smirk returned to his face as he looked into big, dark-lashed green eyes. He declared, stupidly, 'You're not a butler.' As his eyes dropped to the pretty woman's low-cut neckline, he suddenly felt horny again as he stared at several inches of creamy flesh revealed by the slinky black tunic.

The woman looked inquisitively at his upraised hand, now redundantly ready to ring the bell. She opened her full lips to say, 'You can put it down now,' and blithely examined the visible evidence of a budding erection through his twill trousers.

All Justin could think of saying was, 'I've got this art for Miss du Pont.'

'I know. I've come to help you.' The woman flicked the lock to hold it open and strode out to the truck.

Justin followed the cute, curvaceous brunette. Her black uniform looked like a martial arts outfit in reverse. 'Are you a karate teacher?' he asked.

The woman turned. She burst out laughing. 'Me? A karate instructor? Heavens, no, my dear. I just take lessons. But you'd be surprised at what I can do.' She smiled enigmatically, and watched expectantly as Justin opened the doors of the truck, untied the sculpture and lowered it carefully to the ground on the rear hoist.

'I can get this inside on the handcart,' he said, affecting an effortless pose, but when he tried moving it alone, he found he was struggling, his muscles straining with the effort. After his sexual exertions of the previous night and a consequent lack of sleep, he was, he now realised to his chagrin, a little under par this morning. He would need help to get the piece upstairs.

The woman read his mind. 'Here, let me help you,' she

offered, and Justin watched, in surprise, as she untied her sash, removed the black jacket and revealed a figure-hugging black Spandex exercise bra. Laughing up into his dazed face, she tossed the tunic and sash inside the truck. 'Now I can get to grips with this,' she explained, and lightly licked her lips.

The young man blinked, his eyes darting across her upper body. She was really beautiful, he thought excitedly. The exercise bra hardly looked chaste on this strange woman, as her cleavage was accentuated and her nipples clearly outlined through the fabric. But for the moment she was concentrating on the task at hand, and she demonstrated surprising strength in hefting the sculpture in tandem with Justin. He caught a waft of delicate perfume as they worked closely together, and soon the large bronze and its pedestal were safely inside the house, ensconced in the small freight elevator.

Justin's new helper lifted the wrappings from the statue to reveal the sexual tableau, and with a smile stroked the tip of the figure's aroused penis, rigid in his lover's bronze clasp. '*C'est magnifique, n'est ce pas?*' She raised an enquiring eyebrow, and leant forward to lightly kiss the metallic member.

Justin's cock felt as hard as bronze in his pants. He couldn't take his eyes off his unusual companion, who was clearly enjoying his arousal. Both of them were sweating with the effort, for the temperature was rising fast after the cool start to the day, and the woman's bra clung to her breasts damply, outlining every curve and pucker. She watched Justin's eyes fixate on her bosom and grinning up at him, slowly and deliberately cupped both her hands under her breasts, bouncing them in her palms in front of his face. She asked seductively, 'Do you like them?'

Her blatancy undid his composure. 'Jeez!' was all he could say in exclamation, as his mind raced and his erect penis tested the fabric of his lightweight trousers. He was spared further conversation by the gong of the elevator as the doors opened at the penthouse floor.

'We are here, *mon cheri*!' chirped his guide and walked over to unlock a pair of heavy oak doors across the small lobby.

Together they eased MacKenzie's masterpiece inside the apartment. Justin looked around the decorated interior for Belgique du Pont, but she was nowhere to be seen. 'Where does Ms du Pont want the sculpture?' he asked.

'Upstairs, in the bedroom,' replied the woman, with a sexy twinkle in her eye. 'Don't you think that's appropriate?' But Justin groaned as he saw an elegant but small staircase leading up to a large balcony level.

'Come now, young man, we can manage this! It's not far,' taunted his companion, as she stepped close to him, running her hand over his biceps and squeezing the muscles between her fingers in a strong grip. 'If we get sweaty, we can take a shower, *non*?' And she giggled in a way that set Justin's manhood throbbing again.

'OK, lady,' he conceded. 'If that's where it's going, let's do it. You take the top, and I'll take the weight on the bottom.' Together they struggled up the stairs and through a door into an expansive space that held, in contrast to the riot of objects below, only a queen-size bed and an overstuffed sofa in matching bleached off-white fabrics. All was lit by a large palladian window facing over the city centre, where towers sparkled as the sun broke through the morning's clouds. The walls and floor matched a prevailing off-white colour scheme, with the floor reflecting a dull sheen from its polished surface. Was that marble? wondered Justin inconsequently, as he heaved the sculpture over the last step.

As he paused to regain his breath, he noticed several flush doors and cabinets, beautifully detailed into the wall surfaces; they hinted at a menu of hidden delights behind the surprisingly spartan simplicity of the room's furnishings. Then he looked up and gasped. On the ceiling, formed as a gentle concave curve, was rendered a fabulous *trompe l'œil* scene of naked cupids and nymphs, copulating on clouds, their floating bodies intertwined in erotic detail and captured in faultless perspective when viewed from below.

'Jeez!' exclaimed Justin again, before he could school his mouth to a more sophisticated utterance, 'What a riot!'

'Here, Justin!' the woman's voice brought him sharply back to earth. 'Let me show you where I want you to put it.' She looked him directly in the eye, as if to emphasise the deliberate ambiguity of her statement. While she spoke, she lightly caressed herself, softly rubbing her groin, before she clarified, 'The sculpture is to go here.' She pointed to a space in front of a length of unadorned wall, and turned a switch that bathed the area in a soft cone of light from some recessed source.

Together they made one final effort, and a moment later MacKenzie's sculpture was raised in all its explicit glory. The light reflected off the polished bronze, and Justin was admiring the artist's handiwork when he realised the woman had addressed him by name. He drew his eyes up to meet her large green ones, and it suddenly dawned on him that this woman was not the maid.

He straightened up. This clearly was Belgique du Pont herself, the renowned man-eater, and here he was, alone with her in her bedroom. He stood, somewhat awkwardly, as his normally graceful poise deserted him. Justin stuck out his hand and muttered, 'Jeez, er ... madame, I thought you were a personal trainer or something.'

Belgique tittered, 'No matter,' smiling warmly up at him as she placed her small firm hand in his.

When Justin grasped it, he couldn't help his eyes sinking to her chest again, and he proclaimed, 'It's nice to meet you,' rather inanely, as if addressing her magnificent breasts outlined clearly through the sweat-streaked fabric.

Withdrawing her hand, Belgique grinned up at him and quite slowly and deliberately fondled her breasts for the second time in his full view.

'Jeez!' Justin whispered.

'Your vocabulary is rather limited, Justin,' Belgique said, and closed her eyes as she gently squeezed her nipples through the thin fabric.

'Are they . . .?' Justin faltered. Clearly fascinated with the vision of Belgique's bosom, he pointed a shaking finger at one of her breasts.

'Real? Oh, yes.' Belgique laughed, adding, 'Do you want to see them uncovered? And feel them, just to make sure?' She seemed to be taunting him as she fondled her nipples.

'Uh, yes,' Justin responded, in surprise. Here he was, being upstaged in sexual aggression by a hot female again! His voice was husky and low as he suggested, 'Why don't you take it off; let me see! Please?' he added with unusual politeness.

She fluttered her eyelashes at him, and quite blatantly reached inside her black karate trousers and playfully fondled herself there, too. She pulled out the waistband of her trousers. 'And these too?' she asked coyly, and stripped them from her body, so that all she wore was a spartan pair of black bicycle shorts and her black exercise bra.

As she tossed the karate trousers on the couch, Belgique murmured, 'We're all hot and sweaty, aren't we?' She pulled one strap of her black exercise bra over her shoulder. 'Would you like to take a shower?' she asked, lowering her eyes demurely.

'Um, yes,' Justin responded. 'Where is it?'

'Right next door,' Belgique replied in a soft voice as she loosened her other bra strap. Turning away from him, she requested, 'This is pinching me. Will you unfasten it?'

'Sure.' Justin stepped near and unclasped the hooks at the back of Belgique's brassiere.

She arched around to face him and held her bra against her chest. She ordered, 'Before I show you my nipples, you must show me something!'

Understanding her request, and without further ado, Justin unzipped his trousers and slowly pulled out a very large, long and well-shaped penis. He presented it to Belgique who cried with delight. She breathed, admiringly, 'Oh yes! Your vocabulary may be lacking, my dear Justin, but your penis is very eloquent indeed.'

God, he thought, quivering with desire when she discarded her exercise top, she was stacked. As her large breasts bounced freely, she asked him, 'Do you want to play with them?'

'Yes.' His hands reached eagerly for her breasts, his palms tantalising her nipples.

Belgique stepped into Justin's arms and lifted his T-shirt, baring his midriff. Feeling the pressure of his erect cock against her thigh, she deftly undid his belt buckle. Dropping to her knees, she eased his slacks and underpants to the floor, all the time without touching the rampant penis that bobbed in front of her face.

'Do you think you can manage all that, little lady?' asked Justin, with a boastful leer.

Belgique slowly encircled her lips around his shaft, taking the purple glans inside her mouth. She raised her eyes to stare into his face, and briefly released the tip. 'Oh yes, my dear Justin. I can most certainly manage it. You'll be surprised.'

My God, thought Justin, this was like an instant replay! As his own lust surged, his mind raced with images of Lola and Claire, as memories of the previous night competed for his attention with Belgique's ministrations of today. With a touch of panic he felt his come rising, and frantically he sought to calm himself. He didn't want to blow this by spurting after only two minutes!

Belgique released his impressive young manhood from her lips and rose to her feet. Clasping his long member firmly in her hand, she ordered, 'Step out of your pants, dear boy, and follow me.'

He stumbled after her, panting like a dog, and flopped on to the bed as bidden by his new mistress. 'Watch carefully, Justin,' said Belgique, unnecessarily, as Justin followed her every move. She rolled down her Spandex shorts, revealing her luxurious bush of pubic hair. Stripping these over her hips, she stepped out of them, now completely naked before Justin's enraptured stare. She gyrated slowly before him, flaunting her sex just as she used to do on stage.

Justin's penis was standing vertical, a tall mast that was longer than the grip of both Belgique's hands as she came to him and knelt on the bed, taking his cock in a double-fisted grasp. The purple crown blossomed clear of her hands, as she moved them up and down the magnificent shaft, collecting the soft ridge of skin on the upstroke and rolling it halfway over the tip. A small bead of fluid leaked from the slit at the end of Justin's prick, and he moaned with pleasure.

She was nearly drooling at the sight of the distended member as she muttered to him, 'Ah yes, my dear Justin, you like that, don't you?'

Justin nodded dumbly, all his senses now focused on his penis cupped in Belgique's hands.

'But not quite yet,' she teased, running one finger over his balls and down between the cheeks of his bottom, just applying light pressure to his anus.

Justin started with alarm, but Belgique affected not to notice.

'We said we'd shower, and so we shall. Come with me.' And with a bound she was off the bed, pulling her young lover after her through a nearly invisible door set into the bedroom wall.

'Wow!' said Justin, as he saw Belgique's bathroom. The room was nearly as large as the bedroom, with a two-person shower and a sunken bath big enough for a small orgy, and many mirrors. As they stood before one of these many reflections, Justin grasped Belgique around her waist, and let out a low whistle as he contemplated their naked images in the gold-framed glass above the wide basin.

The wall surfaces were covered in murals, depicting a host of nymphs and satyrs, most engaged in a variety of ambitious sexual acts. Justin's quick review suggested that most of the possibilities for love-making he knew about, and several he didn't, were illustrated in the tableau, but his aesthetic critique proceeded no further as Belgique turned on the shower and revolved naked in its fine spray, smiling up at him. She massaged the foam of some scented liquid soap over her breasts and lathered seductively between her legs.

'If I make myself sweet for you to lick, my dear Justin,' she crooned, 'you must do the same for me! It's time to prepare that beautiful penis that's pointing at me.'

Justin needed no further bidding, and he stood under the second shower nozzle.

Belgique passed him the scented soap. 'Here, let me see you wash every inch of it. Slowly, and very thoroughly,' she instructed.

Justin complied with vigour, soaping his genitals under Belgique's strict guidance. She walked behind him. 'And don't let's forget this lovely arse,' she added, rubbing her soapy fingers down the cleft of his bum.

'Hey!' started Justin, dropping the soap in his surprise, but before he could say more, he felt Belgique's hands all over him, fondling his balls and stroking his penis, her mouth reaching up for his in a thirsty kiss. Her tongue probed deeply into his mouth, and they writhed together under the pulsing spray.

Belgique was the first to pull away, and she reached for two plush cotton towels, soft and luxurious on their skin as they rubbed each other dry.

'Ah, Justin,' murmured Belgique as she anointed her breasts with apricot oil, and applied the same sensual lubricant to Justin's ever-rigid penis. 'I think it's time, no?'

Justin was more than ready. He followed Belgique back to the bed with his lust barely under control; his cock was standing forth in all its glory, curling up towards his belly in a self-evident symbol of his desire. He was aching to thrust it into the older woman's pussy, but each time he moved to poise himself, Belgique either rolled or skipped away to a different position, ceaselessly pleasuring his body, but never allowing him to take the initiative.

'Damn it, lady,' growled Justin, 'just keep still so I can fuck you!'

'Ah-ah Justin, you want *me* to keep still?' taunted Belgique as she moved behind him, bringing his hands above his head to fondle her breasts. 'But I want *you* to be still, my dear!' With a deft and sudden movement, she slipped Justin's hands through some silken thongs that hung from the bedposts like ribbons, and tied them off tightly.

'Hey!' yelled Justin trying vainly to move his arms, which were now securely spread behind him. 'What the fuck are you doing?'

'Just that, my little delivery boy,' replied his captor. 'Just that. I'm going to fuck you. But I'm going to do it *my* way, if you please.' In one graceful movement, she slipped off the bed and caught one of Justin's ankles in a grip the strength of which took the young man by surprise. In a trice he was pinned at this third point, with only his right leg remaining free. 'Now Justin,' purred Belgique, 'are we going to make a fuss, or are we going to be a good boy? Give me your other leg.'

'Quit it! Let me go!' hissed Justin, kicking with his free leg.

'Oh, no, dear boy,' murmured a smiling Belgique, as she stood on his left side, and gently masturbated his still rampant penis. 'Look at you, Justin. Your dick is so full of come it's going to burst! See, if I just stroke it here . . .' And she grazed her fingernails down the underside of his shaft and up again to the tip, across the sensitive ridge of flesh, with a touch that sent Justin's body arching into a spasm of desire.

Jeez! he thought, as his flash of antagonism gave way to a bemused blend of worry and desire. This woman was too hot to handle! What the fuck was she going to do next? His question was answered as Belgique's fingers, covered this time in a sensual brew of cocoa butter, smoothed the emollient on his shaft, running down to his balls and into the cleft of his bum, teasing at the little pucker of his anus. His groin pulsed with pleasure under Belgique's expert touch and he never felt, until it was too late, his free leg being tied with silken cords.

Sweet Jesus! he thought. What next?

'Are you ready, darling?' murmured Belgique, as she knelt in front of him, rubbing some more of the cocoa butter over her clitoris and easing a finger inside her vagina. 'I'm ready for you, my big boy!' She lithely straddled Justin's body and eased herself down over his upright penis, burying it in her quim. She squealed with delight as Justin's massive penis penetrated right to her womb. 'Oh, Justin,' she moaned, 'you feel so good in there!' She rode him effortlessly, feeling her juices bathe her captive's prick. Her orgasm built quickly, and she could feel Justin's desire for release. All his resentment was by now submerged in a tide of delicious sensation. She bent forward and kissed him wetly, feeling the angle of his penis change within her vagina, rubbing her walls with an urgent vigour.

'Nearly there, Justin, my sweet,' she whispered in his

ear. 'Just one more little detail!' Feeling beneath the silken pillows, she withdrew a small ebony dildo, smooth as satin to the touch. She rubbed some oil into its grain, bringing a black lustre to its surface. Her lover's eyes flicked to this object with alarm and confusion, a look of concern only compounded as Belgique swivelled her body on the axis of Justin's member, facing now towards his feet. With her hips rocking rhythmically on his proud manhood, and her body poised on the brink, Belgique bent over and gently inserted the slick dildo into Justin's tight anus. 'See how it feels to be fucked, Justin? How do you like it? Do you do this to your girlfriends?'

'Oh, no!' yelled Justin, swamped with a totally new sensation, one in which shame and ecstasy mingled in about equal proportions. His limbs, spread out to the four corners of the bed, tested their bonds as his body bucked under Belgique's body. 'Oh, no! Oh, no!' he cried. And then, 'Oh, yes! Oh, Jeez! That's so good!'

Belgique abandoned herself then, speared on her lover's penis, which was truly one of the biggest she had ever ridden. With Justin completely at her bidding beneath her, she revelled in the rippling crescendo of her release as his cock pistoned within her. She felt him heave inside her, his semen erupting like a volcano under the new stimulus of the dildo sliding in and out of his anus, and his trapped body thrashed like a tethered bronco.

'Oh fuck, oh, fuck, oh fuck,' yelled Justin. 'Oh God, Belgique, oh my sweet Lord! Oh oh oh oh . . .' His groans turned to low inarticulate moans of pleasure, echoed by Belgique as she relaxed on to his thighs, his penis subsiding, yet still firm within her vagina.

'Oh, Justin,' she crooned. 'I fucked you good! Just wait till I tell Eden!'

Justin moaned in resignation. This was just what his boss needed to hear after last night!

Chapter Eight
The Art of Luncheon

*A*n hour after dispensing with Justin's surprise stud service, Belgique was at the health club donning her work-out clothes, readying herself for another kind of exercise.

Eden, having hurried through her office tasks for the remainder of the morning, had grabbed the exercise bag that she always kept in the office, and was finishing a brisk two-block walk to the health club at Fourteenth Street. Still a little early for the lunchtime crowds, the lobby of the new high-rise office building was quiet. Eden's heels echoed as she crossed the broad expanse of the polished marble lobby floor. She had the express elevator all to herself as she rose to the 30th floor of the midtown tower. One could tell the building was new, considered Eden, because everything about it was trying to look old and traditional. But the club was very well equipped, and had a good friendly atmosphere. And today she could look forward to lunch with Belgique.

Lunches with Belgique were so enjoyable that Eden had to be careful to prevent the midday break from extending beyond her self-imposed maximum of two hours. The Latino notion of taking a siesta became overly appealing when in the company of the expensive adventure that was *La Belgique*.

Belgique's independently wealthy status, which she made no attempt to hide, imposed no tight schedule such as Eden's. Belgique's brief, intense and disastrous marriage with an heir to one of Atlanta's great family fortunes, had left her well provided for, courtesy of the divorce settlement. Belgique referred to it coyly as 'hush-money' to prevent her revealing the habits and proclivities of one of Atlanta's favoured sons, but apart from these hints she would never discuss anything about her short-lived state of matrimony.

In recent months, Eden had started to see more of her old friend, as Belgique was developing an interest in art and in artists. Art seemed to supply Belgique with a deeper focus that was previously missing, and she was becoming knowledgeable about contemporary painting and sculpture to a degree that surprised Eden.

As she exited the elevator and entered the club, Eden chuckled to herself. If Belgique's veiled hints about her plans for Justin Scott had been borne out, this new interest and expertise in art was clearly not going to be at the expense of her consuming passion for sex!

Belgique was ready in the dressing room, having changed into a deep green sports bra and bicycle shorts. She wore black Reeboks and thick black socks, which made a sharp contrast with her porcelain skin.

As she donned her exercise outfit, Eden asked her friend, 'How did the installation go?'

'Oh, very well indeed! He's a strong boy, that Justin,' replied Belgique, imparting a none-too-subtle *double entendre* with a coy expression. 'There's plenty to tell! But more of that later, Eden, over lunch.'

Eden's mind was filled with questions, some professional about the sculpture and its arrangement in Belgique's apartment, and others purely personal about her friend's undoubted seduction of young Justin. But

Eden pushed such speculations to the back of her mind and followed Belgique into the work-out room, where both women proceeded to exercise hard on the Nautilus machines for 30 minutes. It wasn't often that Eden exercised twice in one day, but today was different: she craved physical activity as a release from her pent-up emotions. As she sweated through her routine, she noticed that her friend worked every bit as hard as she did herself, going through a punishing round of well-planned exercises.

As they lounged naked together in the sauna, Eden said, 'This is thrilling. Lunch is usually such a hurried affair for me after exercising.'

'Oh, this will be an opulent occasion,' promised Belgique, and added, 'We're dining with Xavier Zachary, and when we dine with Xavier, we all feel we are wealthy, too. But let's go dry off. I want to tell you all about young Justin over lunch! Xavier won't mind!'

Before wrapping herself in a towel, she leant over and kissed Eden lightly on the lips. Belgique brushed her fingertips teasingly across Eden's nipples, sending them into automatic arousal, and whispered, 'Xavier gets very amorous when I tell him what I do with other men. The more I let him know, the more he rewards me!'

Eden watched her friend powder her body. Standing nude before the mirror, Belgique brushed lavender eye shadow on the lids of her green, black-lashed eyes, and added dark rose lipstick to her lips. Then, to Eden's surprise, Belgique painted a touch of pink-tinted make-up on her nipples so that they glowed like ripe cherries, accentuating her smooth, pale skin.

As she put on her lingerie, Eden felt herself growing hot just watching her friend anoint her body. She slid her hand inside her panties and gently rubbed her clitoris with one finger, just teasing the lips of her vulva. She eased one finger inside her vagina, feeling the first flow of juices. She looked up to see Belgique watching her with a grin across her face.

'Oh, Eden, darling!' exclaimed Belgique. 'You'll be even wetter when you hear about this morning! Let's get dressed.'

Belgique liked to make impressive entrances and often wore expensive, lavish clothing to show off her sexy body to full advantage. Today was no exception, as eschewing all underwear, she pulled on a pair of tight-fitting, lavender hip-huggers. Firmly zipped, the thin snug-fitting garment emphasised every contour of her lower anatomy, front and back. The trouser legs flared to wide bell-bottoms at the feet.

After admiring her topless reflection in the mirror for a few moments, Belgique slipped a sheer lavender gauze shirt over her powdered, pink and white torso. She let the whisper of fabric fall open, except for a single pearl button, which she fastened at her waist; the ensemble contrived the simultaneous appearance of clothing and nakedness together. For the middle of the day in mid-town Atlanta, this was a daring outfit, even for Belgique.

She topped the sheer blouse with an open, soft blue velvet jacket and, piling on a lot of jewellery, she added a rosebud to her boutonniere.

Belgique complemented the flaring trumpet pants of her trousers with a pair of delicate sandals in dark purple suede; and in a nonchalant gesture, she bound her neck softly with a velvet-studded collar of blue and purple.

As Eden finished dressing in her simple attire, she appraised her friend's outfitted and adorned physique: a vision in lavenders and blues. Together, the women presented a stunning contrast in beauty: Eden tall, sub-dued and svelte in a proper white linen suit with a cream-coloured silk shirt; Belgique exceedingly curvy and liberally exposed within her panoply of shimmering hues.

* * *

Out on the street, Eden followed the sultry figure of her small, shapely friend and noted, with a detached sense of the inevitable, that Belgique's rear was revealed as explicitly and as enticingly as the front view. Although fully covered by fabric, her trim bottom was outlined in all its well-sculpted form, and Eden could make out a pair of dimples, one on each side of Belgique's swaying, yet taut buttocks.

The two women waited at the traffic light opposite the High Museum, on their way to La Splendour, the smart and opulent Midtown restaurant that currently enjoyed the favour of Belgique's patronage. As Belgique moved, her shirt naturally fluttered open, setting off a magnificent tableau of flesh; a car screeched on its brakes at the provocative display, stopped short of them at the curb and began honking at the women.

'What an idiot!' hissed Belgique. Hailing the noisy and offending vehicle, she strode towards it and, to Eden's horror, proceeded to pull open her jacket and her shirt and show herself. The male driver stared as Belgique flashed her breasts and yelled at him, 'Get an eyeful, OK? Now stop driving with your dick and watch where you're going!'

Alarmed, Eden rushed over and grabbed her friend by the elbow and propelled her quickly across the busy street, amidst the tooting cacophony of horns and shouts. Eden said, 'God, Belgique! You'll get us arrested!'

But they were both laughing as they dashed breathlessly up the steps of La Splendour. Belgique rebuttoned her blouse at the waist, and smiled at the doorman who held the door and ushered them inside the lobby, his glazed eyes following every move. As they swept in, Eden saw dozens of people facing their way and recognised that, once again, Belgique had made a dramatic entrance.

Belgique always attracted attention. She cultivated audiences easily with a stunning combination of dark hair, pale skin and flashing green eyes, and with her curvaceous figure. She enhanced her beauty with remarkable clothing, or, thought Eden wryly, her lack thereof.

But besides being buxom and beautiful, Belgique was also short, and in places like La Splendour, she loved having the opportunity to swagger in, alongside tall and sleek Eden. They made a wonderful contrast as together they traipsed through the lobby to enter the dining room.

As they paused beside the *maitre d'*, all eyes were upon them. Belgique was always in demand among La Splendour's waiters, and the *maitre d'* gestured to a table outside on the patio, beneath a tree. There a handsome young waiter stood poised, enraptured at their approach and delighted at being selected.

The *maitre d'* himself escorted them, and as their waiter held out Eden's chair, she settled in gracefully. Belgique, however, took the opportunity to pause before sitting and flirting with the *maitre d'*, who held her chair. Touching him lightly on the chest with her hand, Belgique skilfully manœuvered herself closer so that her right nipple scraped against his tuxedo shirt front.

The man was stunned by the action, and Eden saw his erection blossom beneath his black trousers. When Belgique finally allowed the flustered gentleman to settle her in her chair, she leant back just for good measure and treated him to a tantalising view of her breasts beneath the opened jacket.

While they had the men's attention, Eden and Belgique gave their orders for cold soup and salad with hot bacon dressing. The waiter and his superior departed reluctantly.

'The wonderful thing about Atlanta is being able to dine on the patio all year round,' remarked Belgique.

Eden nodded agreement and smiled at the way Belgique said 'the patio', as though it were her own, and this restaurant her private dining room. They looked around them. The vibrant spring foliage of dogwood and azaleas had faded, but other pink and white blossoms on the green-vined trellises formed a canopy above their heads.

As the two women finished their vichyssoise, they received a surprise order of champagne and fresh oysters. Belgique clapped her hands together and exclaimed, 'Ahh! This means Xavier's here!'

As they tasted the treats, they greeted Belgique's current beau, Xavier Zachary, who today was dressed in pinstripes. As he bent over Belgique's hand to kiss it, his eyes widened at the sight of the brunette's clearly visible and voluminous breasts through the tulle.

Outwardly sedate and conservative, as Belgique's admirers often were, today's gentleman was positively mannerly, a scion of the Old South. He turned politely towards Eden and kissed her hand, too, stating, 'I am pleased to have the honor of dining with you and Belgique on this occasion.' When he uttered the name 'Belgique', he licked his lips and unconsciously tweaked his moustache.

Eden was acquainted with Xavier slightly from recent weeks, and knew him to be a particularly wealthy admirer of Belgique's. She wondered if Belgique was really going to describe her morning's interlude with Justin for lunchtime entertainment. Was that really what turned Xavier on? Eden had heard of far stranger things than this kind of vicarious titillation, which, she mused, would be like having one's own personal 1-900 number for phone sex. But all she said was, 'The pleasure is all mine, Mr Zachary.'

Shaking his head and wagging his finger at her, he cajoled, 'Eden, my dear, please call me Xavier.'

She nodded accordingly and as he patted his lips with his dinner napkin, he continued, 'Now, tell me about the gallery, my dear.'

Eden did not respond immediately and gladly passed the conversational gambit to Belgique, who admonished, 'Oh Xavier, don't be an old bore! Eden doesn't want to talk about work during lunch! She would rather hear about something else! Something romantic. Something sexy!' She laughed, tossing her black curls, and batting her big, dark-fringed, dusky lavender-shaded green eyes at Xavier. He melted on the spot.

Eden took a sip of the excellent champagne, and sat back to relax and enjoy today's lunch, and silently acknowledged her good fortune that Belgique usually had one or two men friends like Xavier, willing to buy lunch for sexy ladies like them. Or at least sexy like Belgique, she corrected herself, seeing as she, herself, had given up men back in the Stone Age, or so it seemed.

Eden often *felt* sexy, but recently, rarely acted on it. She enjoyed reading about sex and engaging in more and more elaborate and exotic forms of masturbation and fantasy. Her thoughts, increasingly amorous, were jumbled, and sexual images paraded across her consciousness.

Eden wished that she and Belgique could talk alone, in some quiet bistro, rather than with horny Xavier in the noisy, socialite-filled La Splendour; she really wanted to hear about the morning's adventures at Belgique's apartment. She realised with a start that she was just like Xavier, getting off on Belgique's sexy stories! As she watched her friend flirting with her current admirer on the other side of the table, she reminded herself how long she, herself, had been celibate. Currently, all her sex was vicarious, voyeuristic or imaginary! While she wanted to slip away and masturbate, Belgique was pursing very real men for all sorts of real carnal pleasures, considered Eden wistfully. The real thing.

Looking at her watch, Eden pulled herself from her daydream, and returned to the present. She glanced across the table and saw Belgique wink. 'Now for the main course, darlings. I want to tell you all about Justin Scott!'

Clearly wanting both to entertain and arouse her boyfriend and Eden, Belgique launched into an unexpurgated retelling of her dalliance with Justin. Eden was at first shocked into silence and then into fits of giggles as Belgique described the moment when she tied Justin to the bed.

'But is he tanned all over?' Eden wanted to know.

Belgique looked at her friend quizzically. 'Oh, not quite,' she answered. 'His arse is tanned a nice brown, but he's got this very tiny white line around his bum and his dick and his balls are paler. I think he wears a miniature thong and poses in front of sunlamps! Oh, and he's got this funny little tattoo on his right buttock: it's a cartoon of a girl sucking an enormous prick. Just the sort of thing a pretentious young stud like Justin would show off! Mind you, his penis is really lovely; it's no wonder he's proud of it. But I think I gave him an experience he'll never forget! He's not used to women being in charge, that one. Now he's very worried what you'll do to him at work, Eden. He's afraid that his humiliation of being tied up will become common knowledge, or that you'll hold it over him in some way. And he's even more worried by the fact that he enjoyed it!'

As she looked around the expensive restaurant, with potted palms and polite conversation, Eden pondered these new revelations about her colleagues. Everybody was getting laid except her. Belgique was having sex with several guys, even Eden's boss, Alexander Raton! And the desire Eden felt, for one man, Michael Mac-Kenzie, violated her professional policies. She looked across the fine damask tablecloth to see Xavier in a fever of excitement, having followed Belgique's bawdy tale with rapt attention. One hand was in his lap, and a minute twitching of his arm betrayed him playing with himself under the table. What a jerk! Eden thought

103

suddenly. She saw Belgique's hand drift over to keep Xavier's company.

It all seemed so bizarre, watching Xavier surreptitiously masturbate amidst the civilised clatter of bone china and leaded crystal. But Eden recalled her earlier episode with Fineman in her office. Hadn't she been doing the same sort of thing? She had been playing with herself behind her desk, and she probably wouldn't have minded if he'd caught her at it. They might have had sex right there on the floor of her office, leaving her professional ethics in tatters, just for a quickie! Eden began to feel depressed at her imagined behaviour, and lost interest in the remainder of Belgique's chatter. But suddenly the sound of MacKenzie's name being spoken snapped her back to full attention.

Her friend had a familiar twinkle in her emerald-green eyes but Eden was dismayed when she asked, 'Darling, is it possible to arrange for another of MacKenzie's sculptures to be installed, this time with the artist himself present?' Her sparkling eyes teased.

Reluctant to answer, Eden knew full well her friend's appetites. Couldn't Belgique leave this one for her?

But Belgique continued, 'I really want to meet the artist! Young Justin was a pleasant diversion, but he's only twenty-four. He told me so himself. And a real artist would be so much more interesting! Look, I'll buy one of MacKenzie's pieces, the one that Justin brought over, and commission another, something full size.' Belgique paused for Eden to laugh at her little joke, but Eden's lips were set in a firm line. Unfazed, Belgique continued wickedly, 'Those two pieces would be worth about $20,000 to the gallery. Surely that entitles me to a little something on the side, a special customer bonus perhaps?'

Eden's heart sank. There was no doubt in her mind that the 'special customer bonus' would be a personal session in bed with MacKenzie. With a sigh between pleading and anger, she said, 'It's fine for you to screw Justin Scott, but please . . .'

'What, darling?' asked Belgique.

Eden gritted her teeth, 'Belgique, please, not Michael MacKenzie, too!'

Chapter Nine
Sinclair Solo

*B*ack in the gallery, Eden fumed over what she regarded as her best friend's betrayal. Her bad mood was compounded by her inability to do anything about Belgique's behaviour.

As soon as she returned to her desk, she tried to phone MacKenzie, but there was no record of his number at the hotel; and which hotel? She didn't know. It continued to annoy Eden that Raton had brought MacKenzie to the gallery in the first place without consulting her, and now it infuriated her that he had made all the arrangements for the visit himself, without leaving any indication of the details. It was almost as if he were trying to exclude her from the whole deal.

To make matters worse, it was Angela's afternoon off. She must have left at two o'clock on the dot, realised Eden, wishing she herself hadn't dallied so long over lunch. Eden looked around in vain for a note from the receptionist about phone calls, especially hoping for one from MacKenzie, but there was none. Angela was probably off in her little studio somewhere having incredible sex with Fineman, thought Eden, recalling it was not one of Claire or Lola's days to work either. Friday was their day to be in studio at Georgia Tech, as part of their Summer School classes.

Hearing movement in the gallery below, Eden descended to find Paul returning with the large Bulgaria canvas from Jay Jay's. There was no sign of Justin, but that wasn't a surprise. 'Have you just got back?' she asked. 'What took you so long?'

'Sorry, Ms Sinclair. Mr Ritchie and his friends, Greg and Jerry, asked me to stay for lunch. You know, he ended up keeping both the new paintings, one for his master suite and the other for the main guest room. Greg and Jerry helped hang the pieces, and then we had lunch by the pool. It was so hot we had a short swim. They insisted. They really wanted me to stay, and I didn't want to upset them by saying no.' Paul gabbled this long speech, and stood before Eden, blushing and not meeting her questioning gaze.

Eden decided not to press the matter, though she could imagine Greg and Jerry's agenda; Paul was a good-looking sexy young man. However, she couldn't resist teasing him, and she enquired in mock innocence, 'Did you have your swimming trunks with you in the van, Paul?'

Paul's blush deepened as he realised that Eden had put two and two together about his nude swim with Greg and Jerry. It had seemed just good fun at the time, and anyway, nothing really happened, he told himself. But he could imagine what his boss must be thinking! Last night he was having a group sex orgy right here in the gallery, and today he'd been lounging naked around a client's pool with a couple of gay guys! It was as if his fantasies, even the ones he didn't tell anybody about, were all coming true, and it was all very disorientating. His embarrassment was interrupted by Eden's next words.

'We'll talk about this later, Paul. I don't think Justin will be back this afternoon; he's been a little tied up today.' Eden couldn't resist the obvious joke even though

Paul didn't get it. He just looked apprehensively at Eden while she continued, 'Put the Bulgaria away in the racks and update the inventory to record its return, and note the two Barretts at Jay Jay's. Then I want you to man the reception desk for the rest of the afternoon, as I have to go downtown to a meeting. I don't expect to be back today, so you'll need to lock up at six. OK? Oh, if anybody calls for me,' she added, determined not to mention MacKenzie by name, 'just take a message and then call my answering machine at home and leave the details for me there.' God, she hoped he called!

'Sure, Ms Sinclair,' said Paul, relieved that there was to be no further questioning of his sexual adventures in the last eighteen hours. 'You can trust me!' he added, without thinking, until Eden's dark look brought the colour to his cheeks once more.

'Just don't seduce any clients who walk in, Paul. Be polite and take detailed notes of what they want. Tell them I'll call them back first thing in the morning.' With that, Eden skipped back upstairs to her office and sorted her papers for the meeting. She was relieved that Paul was here; it meant that she wouldn't have to close the gallery during business hours. With a shouted goodbye, Eden hurried out the door, and walked the one block over to the transit station to catch the downtown train, descending by the escalator to the underground platform for the southbound service.

A train arrived promptly, and ten minutes later Eden emerged from the Five Points station downtown, from where she walked over to the towering pink granite monolith of the Georgia Power Corporation. In the lobby of this unlikely art venue she paused to admire the large sculpture by Louise Nevelson before entering the downtown branch of the city's High Museum of Art, a little treasure hidden within the body of its unremittently corporate host. But, Eden recognised, it did bring art together with the business world. Some of these corporate types wouldn't drive the two miles to Midtown to go to the parent institution, close to Galerie Raton, but they'd guzzle the wine at the receptions here! But perhaps that was OK if some of them ended up as patrons of art.

The event that brought Eden downtown was the monthly Executive Committee Meeting of 'Art Atlanta', the coordinating body for the visual arts in the metropolitan area. As a reward for giving up their time, the volunteers were reimbursed with a light supper and cocktails. Eden spent an active but entertaining three hours helping to plan the citywide art festival for the following autumn.

Riding the train back to the station nearest the gallery, Eden was one of only a few passengers on this part of the system. All the downtown bankers and stockbrokers had gone home to the outer suburbs. Eden was gratified beyond measure that she didn't have to run her life that way.

Only then did Eden perceive with a start that she hadn't thought about sex or about MacKenzie for several hours. She was rather relieved; she was beginning to obsess about both. But now her mind was back on track, familiar thoughts and images infiltrating her mind, putting her in a renewed state of tension when she arrived at the gallery, now dark and deserted.

Eden hurried inside to check for any messages. There were no notes, but the message light was blinking on Angela's phone. Easing off her suit, Eden undid her blouse and took off her bra with a sigh of relief. She stretched her arms high overhead, making her breasts rise and her nipples jut forward. Relaxing, she punched the button on the phone, and suddenly heard the voice she'd been craving to hear, speaking to her.

'Hi, Ms Sinclair . . . er . . . Eden.' It was MacKenzie. 'I'm very sorry I missed you. I wanted to chat with you about several things.' Including taking her to bed, Eden hoped fervently! 'Maybe we can get together tomorrow,' the digital recording continued. 'I'm just off to see a lady called Belgique du Pont at her apartment. She called me at the hotel to say that she had one of my pieces already installed, and wanted me to come over and see it. She said you helped her pick it out. I'm very grateful to you for moving so fast with my work. Thanks a lot! I'll call again tomorrow.'

Eden stood by the reception desk in a state of surprise, her breasts bare, her bra dangling from one hand. Belgique! Her eyes blazed at the duplicity of her friend. She had promised not to take MacKenzie to her illustrious bed! Eden gritted her teeth at the recent memory, thinking that Belgique had turned right around and phoned him to lure him to her apartment! Justin in the morning; MacKenzie in the evening! Her thoughts racing, Eden had little doubt concerning Belgique's intentions once she got MacKenzie into her erotic domain. But how did Belgique phone MacKenzie at his hotel? How the hell did Belgique du Pont have MacKenzie's number, yet she didn't? Eden nearly screamed with frustration.

Eden moved to the phone, intending to find out just what Belgique and MacKenzie were up to, but with the mouthpiece in her hand and her fingers on the buttons, she froze. What if MacKenzie was there right now in bed with her friend? What would she say? What could she say? 'Belgique, stop fucking MacKenzie right now! He's mine! I want him for myself?' That was what she wanted to say, but she couldn't do it. And she wanted to scream at MacKenzie for being so profligate with his dick. But what would he think of such a jealous outrage? He'd probably turn off in disgust.

Eden knew that deep down she didn't want to believe that MacKenzie was in Belgique's arms, much less in her bed. If she didn't call, then she wouldn't know: that way she couldn't have her worse fears confirmed. She put the

110

phone back in its cradle, and hugged herself as a feeling of misery flooded over her.

She put her blouse back on and stuffed her bra in her briefcase. Leaving by the back door, Eden morosely started the little Miata, flicked on the headlights, and drove out on to Peachtree Street, heading for a bar, preferably one where they didn't know her. She chose a route that avoided Ponce de Leon Avenue and Belgique's apartment building, driving instead east along 10th Street.

Some nameless neon beckoned her, and Eden pulled over and went inside, finding a darkened booth. She ordered a double scotch and soda with a lemon twist from a bored waitress, and sat stiffly, curling her paper napkin between her fingers. She glared a warning at the few single men in the room, and they took the hint, leaving her to fume silently about the untrustworthiness of friends.

However hard she tried, Eden couldn't imagine any scenario other than MacKenzie falling for Belgique's obvious charms and voracious appetite. They were probably in Belgique's bed right now, she reckoned, Belgique on top, riding MacKenzie with her usual wild abandon. Eden could picture it all in her mind: Belgique's movements bringing her partner to an explosive climax that would trigger her own.

Eden writhed in her seat, her vulva growing moist with the intensity of her sexual longing. She looked up to see one of the men at the bar studying her, a quizzical look in his eyes as he watched her squirm on the padded seat. Hurriedly, she paid up, leaving a $5 bill on the table and quickly left the bar. Stepping outdoors, she jumped into her car and fired the motor into life.

She drove aimlessly for several minutes, and then found herself alongside the soccer pitches in Piedmont Park, near the route of her morning runs. Tonight, all the pitches were in use, ablaze with floodlights, as local teams, some men, some women, waged their little athletic battles. Eden liked soccer; ten years ago she had played as a striker for Tulane's successful women's team in the Southern States college competition, but just like her painting, she thought glumly, it had been many years since she was serious about it. Nevertheless, she slowed the car and watched with an informed appraisal as the two men's teams nearest her swept the ball across the pitch with varying degrees of skill.

With mild disappointment, Eden realised they were not really very good, and was about to drive on when a player she hadn't noticed before seized on a loose ball, raced past two defenders and slotted home a low shot into the corner of the net. As Eden studied the goal scorer with new alertness she noticed his thatch of red hair and athletic physique. A shock like an electric charge went through her, before logic took over, and her pulse returned to normal. How could she have imagined even for a moment that this handsome young man was MacKenzie! She didn't even know if the Scotsman played soccer!

But now her attention was held by the red-headed footballer, and Eden pulled to the curb, dimmed her lights, and parked deep in the shadow of the overhanging willow oak trees. As he, by turns, darted and strolled across the pitch, she grew mesmerised by his movements, and settled more deeply into her seat.

Eden turned on the radio to the sound of Simply Red singing 'Never Never Love'. Longing for company, Eden sighed as she leant her head back against the seat. Raising her skirt high over her knees, she stroked her thighs slowly in time to the music, listening to the sexy love song, while observing the athletic grace of the red-haired soccer player.

Reaching for a richer fantasy, she pondered the sexiness of the other redheaded man who dominated her thoughts; she slipped her fingers inside her panties, finding her inner lips slick and slippery. With a wanting, lusty urge she wriggled out of her panties and sat with her legs spread wide apart. Surrendering to thoughts of Michael MacKenzie, Eden reached for the small vibrator she sometimes kept in the glove compartment and turned it on. Playing with it, she slipped the tip of the vibrator inside her pussy lips and felt a series of pulsating, orgasmic rushes. With a thrill, she imagined the dark, dark brown eyes of Michael MacKenzie, pretending that he was watching her masturbate, or masturbating her himself, with his hands, his tongue. Finally! She screamed, under the blare of her stereo speakers. Finally, an orgasm! As the halogen light from the field flickered through the dappled leaves of the great oaks above the car, Eden soared to a satisfying climax.

Relaxed from the intensity of her orgasm, Eden unbuttoned her blouse with one hand as the vibrator continued its gentle pulse inside her vagina. She wasn't wearing a bra, having removed it back at the gallery, and in her reverie, Eden combined her memory of Fineman drawing his endlessly long cock from Angela's mouth with her fantasies of Michael MacKenzie and herself. Slowly and sensuously, Eden imagined rubbing her body against his, swaying, rocking, and as she slowly rubbed one hand across her nipples, with her other she massaged her clitoris, and she softly masturbated herself to another climax.

After she got her breath back Eden opened her eyes and snapped back to reality as she saw through the open car window the young redheaded man dashing towards her! Then she saw the soccer ball that he was chasing as it bounced across the road. Hastily, she lowered her skirt and raised the window, turned on the engine and sat up. She put the car in gear, turned on her dim lights, and eased smoothly and quickly away from the curb, acting a lot more nonchalantly than she felt.

Only two stop lights later did Eden gently slide the

pulsing vibrator from her vagina and place it in her purse on the seat beside her.

Once home in her snug little bungalow on Amsterdam Avenue, Eden did what had become her usual routine when under stress. By habit and training, she fought the blues and chased away her physical frustrations through hard, intensive exercise; and she plunged into a 30 minute session on her exercise bike that stood ready and waiting in the corner of her bedroom.

Her exercise complete, Eden stripped off her work-out bra and bicycle shorts, and cooled down by dancing lazily to the mellow beat of a Keiko Matsui CD. Naked, except for shoes and socks, she walked around her bedroom and stood by the window beside the bed. Rubbing herself gently and rocking in time to the music, Eden glanced out of the window and saw a male body-builder through his window in the apartment building across her back yard. Eden stopped momentarily and stared, at which point the anonymous man picked up on his training routine, pressing weights with practised ease. Could he see her, too? she wondered.

He was far enough away that Eden couldn't make out his face; all she could see was his silhouette in the lighted box of his window. She continued dancing, playing with her nipples, feeling them harden. Seized by a wanton impulse she displayed herself for her anonymous watcher. Plunging her finger deep into her vagina, Eden felt a mounting ecstasy.

Her companion in voyeurism, for surely he watched, too, slowly moved back into his room so that light fell across his body but not on his face, which remained in shadow. He stripped off his T-shirt and exercise shorts, and stood with his burgeoning penis in his hand. He was watching her.

Eden watched his anonymous form slowly masturbate as she performed for him some more, pouring her sexual desires into an explicit dance rubbing her fingers across her breasts and her clitoris. Tilting her hips forward she teased her little bud and eased her fingers inside her vagina, moving in and out with a steady pulse. From her window Eden saw her partner change rhythm, and pump his penis long and hard. She watched him bend at the knees and lean back with one hand cupping his balls, the single light in the room illuminating the full length of his cock, held firm in his right hand. Eden watched his figure undulate, and she imagined his jerky movements meant he was coming in a spout of white. As she continued her fixated gaze he grabbed a towel to wipe his hand and his dick.

They stood still, staring mutely at each other across their anonymous spaces for a brief time. Then the man stepped aside and vanished. A moment later the room went dark.

Eden walked as if in a trance to her bed, and took the vibrator from her purse. She flopped on to the pillows and continued to rub her still throbbing flesh. Her inner lips were distended with desire, and she was feeling wet and pulsing; she pushed the purring phallus into her vagina until she came, wishing, oh, wishing it was MacKenzie's penis she held inside her.

Chapter Ten
Belgique's Bombshell

*E*den lay blissfully still for a moment, as the morning light illuminated her tall white bedroom. But then the emotions and memories of the previous day washed over her, bringing with them mixed feelings of excitement, shame and confusion. In particular, her wanton night-time behaviour was upsetting. Her highly sexual nature was often aroused, but rarely to such heights as public display. Eden winced at her blatant exhibitionism enacted with the anonymous voyeur.

Looking at her alarm clock, she decided that 7 a.m. was too early to call Belgique; MacKenzie might still be there with her. A jealous anger rose in her chest, and she hopped out of bed and plunged under the shower to assuage her tension. Drying herself, she mapped out her wardrobe for the day, selecting a bisque blouse with a double-breasted ivory jacket and a matching slim straight skirt with a kick pleat. Saturdays were always working days in the gallery business. She dressed slowly, trying to focus on her work for the coming day, but unable to banish thoughts of MacKenzie.

The aroma of freshly ground coffee steadied her as she followed the directions on her new cappuccino machine, foaming the milk and spooning it over the dark espresso liquid. She toasted some croissants and ate them with apricot preserve. Showered, dressed and fed, she felt able to face Belgique.

She pressed the speed dial button of her cordless phone for Belgique's number, and paced her living room. Belgique answered on the third ring.

'Belgique, what were you up to with MacKenzie last night?' Eden demanded, without introduction or preamble. 'Don't lie to me, I know he was with you. He left me a message. Is he still there?' Eden screwed her eyes shut as she waited for a reply.

'No, he's not here, Eden. He left hours ago,' answered Belgique, but with a demure coyness that infuriated Eden.

'Hours ago? You mean, like early this morning?'

'Eden,' purred Belgique, 'don't get so upset.' But maddeningly, she didn't answer Eden's question. 'Yes, I saw Michael last night. I invited him over to see his work installed in my bedroom.' Belgique managed to give the location of the sculpture a subtle emphasis. 'And I wanted to discuss commissioning a special new piece. Through the gallery, of course, Eden. You'll get your cut.'

'Screw the commission! And what else did you "invite him over" for?' Angry sarcasm dripped from Eden's voice.

'What do you mean, Eden dear?' Belgique was innocence herself.

'You know very well, Belgique. Don't play dumb with me! We've been friends for too long. Did you take him to bed? Did you fuck him?'

'Don't snarl at me, Eden!' retorted Belgique, some passion rising in her voice. 'If all you can do is shout down the phone, I don't want to talk to you.' There was a pause. 'Anyway,' she continued, suddenly defensive, 'what I do with Michael is my own business!' She was exasperatingly evasive.

The proprietorial way Belgique said 'Michael' annoyed Eden hugely. 'No, it's not just your business!' she snapped back. 'He's my...' Eden stopped abruptly. Exactly what was MacKenzie in her life? Her obsession, she thought. But she wasn't going to admit that to anybody. 'He's my... artist,' she finished lamely.

'Oh, Eden,' murmured Belgique, suddenly contrite. 'Let's not fight. You sound so angry and it makes me upset. I'll treat you to lunch; we can go to La Splendour again. No Xavier this time, just you and me. How about 12 noon? Please say yes. We'll talk more about it then, OK?'

'All right, Belgique,' conceded Eden, flatly. The fire had gone, leaving her depressed. She didn't like arguing, least of all with her friend. 'See you at noon.' She hung up and tossed the phone on to the sofa with a disgruntled gesture. Leaving her breakfast dishes unwashed, Eden picked up her briefcase and keys. She checked the locks on the back door and, stepping into her ivory loafers, marched out of the front door, letting it slam behind her.

Eden drove the three miles from her home to the gallery on automatic pilot. As often was the case, she was the first one there. Being a Saturday, only Angela would be in later, but Eden was in no mood to share her morning with anyone.

Sitting at her desk, she realised that she still didn't have MacKenzie's phone number or hotel address. She had been so angry at Belgique, she'd not even managed to extract that basic information. This little failure served only to depress her morale further.

She made herself some more coffee, trying to lift her mood with caffeine, and was at least able to answer the phone with a modicum of civility when it rang with the first call of the morning. It was Jay Jay.

'Eden!' her old friend exclaimed with genuine pleasure. 'I'm so glad it's you. I'm so *thrilled* with the

118

paintings. Did that gorgeous young man tell you I decided to keep them both?'

Despite her bad mood, Eden found herself smiling at Jay Jay's description of Paul. Well, she conceded, he was pretty handsome. She remembered her fantasies about Paul's tanned and naked body. Now both her delivery men were in demand, she mused. But that brought back thoughts of Belgique, and she shut them off with a snap.

'I'm so glad, Jay Jay,' responded Eden, managing a friendly businesslike tone. 'I'll make up an invoice for you and send it in Monday's mail. Did your ... guest approve as well?' Eden couldn't resist a slight tease at Jay Jay's expense.

'Most certainly,' gushed Jay Jay, not catching Eden's tone. 'Buddy's as delighted as I am. I think we both share the same tastes. It's wonderful!'

Eden was not sure whether her friend was complimenting the art or describing the congruence of their sexual proclivities. She suspected the latter. Buddy? she wondered to herself. Did bankers have names like Buddy, now? Out loud she said, 'I'd love to come over and see the pieces in their new setting some time, Jay Jay, and to meet your friend.'

'Oh, yes, please do, Eden!' rejoined Jay Jay. 'How about one evening next week? And I'd like to meet the artist. Does she live in Atlanta?'

Eden looked in her appointment calendar. 'No, next week is the opening of the new group show. I'll be busy most of the time during the week. Don't forget to come to the reception! How about the following week? And yes, Annalee does live in town. I'll call her and let her know you want to meet her.' With that promise, they agreed a mutually convenient date and Eden hung up the phone feeling a little more cheerful.

The sound of the front door opening downstairs caught Eden's attention, and she looked over her balcony rail to see Angela arrive for work, looking pretty in a short cotton summer dress with a bold flower print, and high-heeled sandals that emphasised her trim calf muscles.

'Hi, Eden,' Angela greeted, looking up as she set down her capacious shoulder bag by her desk. 'I'll grab some coffee, and then I've got a favour to ask you.'

Vaguely wondering what Angela wanted, Eden descended the spiral stair. Her assistant returned bearing two mugs of coffee.

'I brought one for you, too, Eden,' she said, setting them both down on the desk; and reaching into her bag, she brought out a medium-sized black leather portfolio and laid it on her chair. With a start, Angela fished again in the bottom of her holdall, and turned to Eden with a pink telephone message slip in her fingers.

'Oh, Eden,' admitted Angela. 'I forgot to leave this for you yesterday when I left after lunch.' She handed Eden the little piece of paper. 'Michael MacKenzie called while you were out. He asked me to give you this message: something about looking for an apartment this morning. And he said he'd call back.'

'Did he leave a number?' Eden asked sharply. 'Did he say which hotel he's staying at?'

'No, he didn't,' replied Angela, now worried by Eden's tone. 'I'm sorry, Eden,' she added, catching sight of the scowl on her boss's face. 'Was it important?'

'Yes,' replied Eden, the scowl still in place. She turned away, leaving Angela staring at her back in surprise. 'Yes, it was important,' she continued, speaking softly, her voice oddly quavering. 'If you'd given this to me yesterday afternoon instead of now, when it's too late . . .' Eden left the sentence unfinished and felt, much to her chagrin, tears of anger and frustration spilling down her cheeks.

She heard Angela's intake of breath, and felt a nervous but gentle hand around her shoulders. 'Eden . . .' started

Angela, hesitantly. 'What's the matter? Is there anything I can do?'

Instead of shaking off the solicitous gesture, Eden relaxed into Angela's arms with a sigh. 'No, Angela, there isn't. But thanks for asking.' She looked at her receptionist's face and saw a look of genuine concern in her eyes. She blinked away her tears and gave Angela a half-smile. 'It's that old sex thing,' she added, feeling a sudden urge to confide in someone, and Angela certainly looked sympathetic. 'It sure screws you around, doesn't it?'

Angela's face showed fleeting incomprehension, and then light dawned. 'Michael MacKenzie! That's it, isn't it! Oh, Eden, what's happened?'

'Belgique,' replied Eden, in an expressionless voice. 'Need I say more?' she added ironically.

'Oh, I see.' Angela had heard all about Belgique; that lady's sexual prowess and allegedly insatiable appetites were legendary. Angela patted Eden's shoulder softly. 'Have they, like, er . . . um, done it?' she asked.

Eden found the young woman's verbal reticence strange in comparison to her lustful behaviour with Fineman, but it was charming in its own way. 'I don't know,' she admitted. 'But he went over to her apartment yesterday evening, so what do you think? Claire and Lola tried to get him into bed the moment they set eyes on him,' she added scornfully. 'They didn't score, but I doubt if Belgique would be put off so easily.' Eden paused, and then continued in a burst of frankness. 'He's so sexy, I think I'll have to fight half the women in Atlanta to get him for myself!'

Angela smiled shyly. 'Even if you had to do that, you'd probably win,' she said with affection, and gave Eden a hug. 'Don't give up. Even if Belgique has, er, you know, she's probably bored with him by now.'

Eden felt a perverse urge to defend her friend, but reflected that Angela wasn't far from the truth. Maybe

121

she could just wait it out. After all, it hadn't taken Belgique long to dispense with Justin. 'You may be right,' she replied. 'Did you hear what Belgique did to Justin yesterday?'

Angela looked up, an excited sparkle in her eyes. 'No, what happened?' she breathed, questioningly.

Eden couldn't repress a little giggle. 'She tied him to the bed and then she fucked him.' Angela's eyes grew large. 'And she did other things to the poor boy that perhaps are best kept secret.'

'Poor boy, my foot!' snorted Angela. 'He's just a walking phallus waiting for women to fall down and worship him,' she said scornfully. 'It would do him good to be dominated for a change. But what did Belgique do to him?' Angela was very interested; her previous reticence about sex vanished like smoke in the wind.

Eden realised she couldn't edit the story now she had started. Angela had that same eager look on her face that she had had when she was fondling Fineman's penis in the storeroom. Eden thought she certainly shouldn't mention any of that, but instead plunged ahead with Belgique's adventures.

'She had him tied up on the bed, spread-eagled with his hands over his head and his legs tied to each bottom corner. Belgique's pretty strong, you know. Don't let the lace and long eyelashes fool you. Underneath she's a tough lady.' And a formidable adversary, Eden considered warily to herself. 'Have you seen her biceps?' she asked. 'I've seen her in the gym pressing weights that would put some men to shame.'

'But what happened next?' Angela wanted to know.

'The way Belgique told it, she slid a dildo up his anus while she was riding backwards on his cock.' Angela gasped, in shock or delight Eden couldn't tell. 'And, this is the best bit, Belgique said he loved it!'

The two women burst into a mutual fit of laughter at

the image of the macho Justin Scott trussed up and begging for more.

With the retelling of her friend's riotous exploits, some of Eden's animosity fell away. But not all of it. She certainly wasn't going to wait till Belgique tired of MacKenzie; she had to do something positive to influence the situation. Eden felt a little better now, and Angela's friendly support was very welcome. Eden remembered that her assistant had wanted to ask her a favour. 'What was it you needed, before I got started on feeling sorry for myself? That's enough of Belgique for a while. What can I do for you?' she queried.

'Oh,' Angela contrived now to look embarrassed, the sexy sparkle in her eyes suddenly dimmed. 'It's not important. Perhaps some other time . . .' She stared at the patterns on the wooden block floor.

Eden wasn't to be put off. 'No, it's quite all right, Angela.' Her eyes caught sight of the portfolio lying on the receptionist's chair. She pointed at it. 'Is it anything to do with your drawings?'

'Yes, it is, Eden,' Angela admitted. She paused, as if measuring a tall hurdle before starting her run. 'Actually, Eden, I really want to talk to you about my art. I know you've seen some of my sketches, and Winston has looked at them, too. He thinks they're quite good, and you said nice things about them. What I'm wondering is, well, if I showed you some more finished pieces, and you liked them, would you consider showing them in the gallery? Just on consignment, you know. I don't mean for a show; not yet, I mean.' The words tumbled out in a rush. Angela had obviously been rehearsing her little speech.

Eden smiled, feeling on home ground again. This was something she knew how to deal with. 'I'd certainly like to see them, Angela. You're right, I did like the other sketchbook you showed me, especially the drawings of the young man.' She kept her tone neutral, but Angela blushed.

'I brought the wrong book that day,' she admitted with another shy smile. 'I didn't know my drawings of John were in that one.'

'What happened?' asked Eden, suddenly curious, and then cursing herself for being nosy. But Angela understood her question and didn't seem to mind.

'Oh, we just split up,' she replied. 'It was no big deal.' But her expression belied her words. 'He fell in love with someone else, and just upped and moved away, to North Carolina. Charlotte, I think,' she added wistfully.

'I'm sorry,' said Eden. She paused before continuing. 'But I couldn't help noticing that your drawings of John were the best ones in your sketchbook. I mean they were really good. I liked them for their technical qualities, not just because he was . . .' Now it was Eden's turn to stumble over her words. 'You know, not just because . . .'

'Because he has such a lovely dick?' Angela giggled, but her eyes had lost some of their shyness.

'Yes, exactly.' Eden smiled back at her younger companion. 'Was he an artist? Did he ever draw you?'

'Oh, no. He was a computer engineer. What he really liked to do was either mess with his computers, or else go white-water rafting up in the mountains. That was fun. He read a lot, too,' Angela added, as if this was to be regarded as rather strange behaviour.

'Let's have a look at what you've brought,' commented Eden, returning to the matter in hand. Angela unzipped the portfolio and set out several charcoal sketches along with some monoprints for Eden's inspection.

All carried the same theme: a reclining nude or scantily clad man. They were powerful and effective drawings, thought Eden, but they lacked the spark of the earlier ones Angela had made of her ex-lover.

Eden picked up one of the monoprints that her experienced eye had seized upon. 'This work is really promising, Angela. I'd like you to have this piece framed in our standard gallery format, and I'll include it in next week's group show.' She saw the young woman's eyes sparkle with delight. 'And I'd like you to do a new series that we can offer to clients as a suite. Bring another set in when you've done some more variations.'

'Does that mean I'm a gallery artist?' asked Angela, almost breathless with delight.

'Well, not quite yet,' replied Eden with a smile. 'Let's just say it's a trial period. We'll see if the work sells, and we'll see how that next series turns out before I'll think about a contract, but the work is good Angela.' She held the young artist by the shoulders, and looked her in the eye. 'It means that you'll have to get really serious about producing art on a regular basis. It's not a game for your spare time, you know. But you've got the talent. Let's work on it.'

Angela returned Eden's look, matching seriousness for seriousness. 'I'll do it,' she announced. 'Winston offered to help me. Oh, thank you, Eden,' and she flung her arms around Eden in an excited hug, before drawing back in embarrassment. 'Oh, I didn't mean . . .'

'It's fine, Angela. I'm glad you showed me the work. Take care of the framing today, will you? Then the piece will be ready to hang next week.' She gave the girl's hand a squeeze, and picking up her lukewarm coffee from the desk, Eden walked to the small kitchen and microwaved it up to drinking temperature. When she climbed the stairs to her office, Angela was already on the phone to the framer.

Sitting once more at her desk, Eden studied the brief message from MacKenzie. 'Looking for apartment Saturday morning. Will call,' was all it said. Looking for an apartment. The import of these words slowly sank into Eden's consciousness. So he was definitely thinking of staying around. Well, that was good news as far as it went. It meant that he probably didn't have romantic ties back in Savannah. If she could just prise him from

Belgique's clutches! But her train of thought was interrupted by the arrival of some clients, and Eden went downstairs with her professional smile firmly in place.

It was a couple of hours later that Eden managed to take a break from the morning's business, and looked up at the clock to see that it was almost noon. After freshening up in her tiny private bathroom, Eden strode downstairs and announced to Angela, 'I'm going to lunch now with Belgique. Keep an eye on things while I'm gone.' After a moment's consideration, she added, 'Have you seen Mr Raton this morning?'

As if summoned by her words like a genie from a bottle, her employer appeared at that very moment, a spectre in grey.

'Ah, Eden, my dear,' he said. 'Did I hear you say you were just off to see Ms du Pont? How fortuitous! Let me come with you. Now would be the perfect time to clinch the sale of Michael's sculpture!' Without giving her a chance to reply, let alone protest, Raton whisked by her and stood waiting at the front door, holding it open with an exaggerated gesture of politeness.

Eden's heart sank. How on earth could she talk to Belgique about MacKenzie with Raton at their table? She caught Angela's eye and saw there a look of sympathy. She gave a half-smile in return and shrugged her shoulders in resignation. Wondering at her employer's uncharacteristic zeal, she strode briskly out of the door towing Raton in her wake.

Belgique was already seated in La Splendour as Eden and Raton were ushered to her booth in a secluded niche far back in the dining room. Today she was dressed in a cunning tight little Spandex T-shirt with cap sleeves and a turtleneck. It was just as clinging as the black equivalent Sharon Stone had worn at the Academy Awards, mused Eden, but Belgique's was white, and very revealing. It fitted rather like a second, very thin skin over her stunning upper anatomy. It also showed off her sculpted biceps, Eden noticed, having just remarked on them to Angela. The combination was very sexy, Eden admitted, even as she ground her teeth at the thought of those same strong arms holding MacKenzie.

If Belgique was surprised or dismayed to see Raton in the role of unwelcome guest she didn't show it. She was the epitome of Southern charm, and after greeting Eden briefly with a non-committal smile and wary eyes, she offered him her hand and kissed him lightly on the cheek. 'Alexander, what a delightful surprise!' she purred. 'To what do we owe this unexpected pleasure?'

'Well, my dear Belgique,' replied Raton, matching charm with unctuousness, 'I thought I'd just have a little chat with you about dear Michael's darling sculpture.' Eden nearly gagged into her dinner napkin. If Raton noticed, he gave no sign as he continued, 'You know, get the sordid little details out of the way: payments, insurance, you know, things like that.'

Belgique responded casually. 'I'm sure that will all be fine, Alexander, but I certainly don't want to talk business over lunch. Anyway, I'm going to get Michael to do another sculpture, this time for the living room. He and I talked about things yesterday.'

Eden sat bolt upright in her chair, her blue eyes burning into Belgique's green ones. But those emeralds were opaque and lidded; Eden couldn't pick up any clues. She wanted to ask what else she and MacKenzie had talked about, but Belgique's next remarks took the conversation in an unexpected direction.

'Really, Alexander. It really is just too boring to talk business over lunch. You really can be so bourgeois!' But a seductive smile and an obvious squeeze of his thigh robbed her words of their sting. 'We've got much more interesting things to talk about!' As she spoke, Belgique preened herself, stroking her hair and thrusting her breasts forward, so that her nipples jutted towards the startled gallery owner.

Raton gazed in greedy rapture at the contours of Belgique's impressive tits, perfectly outlined beneath the thin translucent Spandex. It was all he could do to keep his hands off those weighty orbs. Indeed, as Raton stared, his hands twitched involuntarily, and when Belgique coyly touched her breasts, highlighting the nipples with her forefingers, Eden saw Raton's knuckles go white.

Despite lapses in concentration brought on by Belgique's increasingly suggestive behaviour, openly caressing herself through the delicate fabric of her clothing, the trio perused the day's tempting specials, but settled only for light salads with Gulf shrimp. Food was not the top item on any of their minds. They all drank unsweetened iced tea.

As Raton gestured to their waiter, Eden looked up and spotted two photographer friends, Liz Angelo and Vivienne Dupree, watching their table from across the room. They waved. They were both photogenic and beautiful and, Eden knew, quite lesbian. She acknowledged their greeting with a smile. She hadn't known the girls were back in town. Last she had heard they were in New York, showing their latest short film at a lesbian feminist film festival.

Belgique followed Eden's gaze, and read her mind. 'They got back from New York a few days ago. I think their little movie won some prize up there. They're certainly very excited about it. Viv was telling me that they're starting a new short feature, set in Atlanta.'

As the waiters fluttered around them, Eden experienced *déjà vu*, wondering if today was a repeat of yesterday, with Raton standing in for Xavier Zachary, or was it merely a variation on an endless theme? It was soon obvious that Belgique and Alexander Raton had become interested only in playing serious footsie, much of it only just below the table, and involving hands instead of feet, rather than having any serious discussion about art matters.

The atmosphere at their table became more and more erotic and arousing as Belgique and Alexander Raton, snug in their secluded booth, rubbed against each other, touching and poking playfully.

Eden was surprised to find herself wondering what Raton's cock would feel like clasped in her hand. Nonchalantly, Eden dropped her serviette on the floor, and as she retrieved it, she lifted the heavy damask tablecloth and checked out the action under the table. Just as she suspected, Belgique's active hand was in Raton's lap, lovingly fondling an impressive, protruding penis, that strained within still buttoned trousers. Eden saw the profile of the bulging, swollen glans outlined by the fabric, as Belgique's fingers caressed his shaft. This man was not the elegant cold fish many had pegged him for.

Eden sat up demurely and sipped her drink, but during that brief peek, the outline of a large handful of male flesh had stimulated a pulsing in her vagina. In further response to the veiled sight of his cock, Eden felt a hot flush travel up her breasts and throat.

Eden swallowed and prettily sipped her water. Conversation was at a lull. Raton had just made some suggestive remark about going to bed when Belgique dropped the bombshell that Eden had been dreading.

'Speaking of bed,' Belgique confided coyly, ignoring the specifics of Raton's suggestion, 'Michael was very pleased with the way his sculpture looked in my bedroom. He said it was well placed in relation to the bed.'

What was that supposed to mean? Eden wondered, flushing angrily. Was this some kind of clever, post-coital art critique? But Belgique was continuing. 'He is just so cute, handsome, and so sexy. After yesterday I decided I'd always call him "my Ginger Root"!'

My Ginger Root? Eden's intuition flashed the not-so-hidden meaning straight to her mind's eye. She imagined

MacKenzie's tumescent penis standing proudly upright from its bed of ginger curls. The image intensified to include the sight of his penis being firmly grasped in Belgique's hand, while the brunette's tongue lapped greedily at its bulbous tip.

Seeing Eden's quizzical expression of alarm, Belgique laughed indulgently and said rather breathlessly, 'I do so like redheads; they're so virile!' Almost as an afterthought she asked Eden, 'You like redheads, too, don't you, darling?'

Eden glared at her friend, only to be met with a guileless stare of winsome innocence. Her patience snapped. 'Excuse me!' she snarled, and stood up suddenly, knocking over her chair with a crash. She continued sarcastically, her voice dripping with venom, '*I've* got work to do; I'm sure the two of you have *plenty* of things you can do without me around!' She tossed her hair, threw a $20 bill on the table and, ignoring her chair on the floor, stormed out across the dining room. All eyes followed her angry departure.

Belgique and Raton ordered coffee.

Chapter Eleven
Humble Pie

Within ten minutes, Eden was back at her bungalow on Amsterdam Avenue, her temper still ablaze. She alternately paced her living room like a captain on his quarterdeck and flung herself into a chair beneath the air-conditioning vent to cool off and relax. But all to no avail. She switched on music; then turned it off. With a long shuddering sigh of despair mixed with anger, she sat slumped on her bed.

Retreating to well-established habits, Eden sublimated her emotions to hard physical exercise. She stripped off her clothes, donning an exercise bra, shorts and running shoes. Slipping her front door key into the pocket of her shorts, Eden hastened from the house and slammed the door behind her.

She doubled her daily run, adding a winding journey through neighbourhood streets in addition to her normal park routine. It was the hottest time of the day; the temperature had soared to 95° and the humidity was close to 100 per cent. Eden was on the verge of exhaustion when she staggered back to her front porch, sweat streaming from her body, every muscle complaining. But with relief she noticed some slight lifting of her mood.

She walked slowly through the house, threw her sopping clothes into the laundry basket, and stood motionless under the streaming water of her shower, letting it cleanse her body and wash away residual depression.

As she emerged from the bathroom wrapped in a towel, Eden heard a knock at her front door. She padded to the door and squinted through the security peephole. To her utter amazement she saw Belgique standing there. Forgetting she was naked under the towel, Eden threw open the door and said, 'What the hell are you doing here? You're the very last person I expected to see.' She studied her friend carefully. Uncharacteristically, Belgique wore no make-up. 'Especially after what you did at lunch!' Eden added accusingly, but her accompanying glare was somewhat compromised by her hasty grab for the towel as it slipped from her body. She just caught the hem of it as it fell from her, managing to wrap it around her loins to cover her sex, but leaving her breasts exposed to the world.

'You'd better invite me in, Eden,' said Belgique, looking appreciatively at this unexpected sight. 'I think you look gorgeous, but the neighbours might be more critical and call the police.' But then she became serious. 'Please Eden, let me in. I want to talk to you. I want to apologise.'

Wordlessly, Eden stood aside to let Belgique enter, and followed her friend to the living room. She and Belgique had been naked together so many times over the years that she didn't bother to cover herself. She simply sat on the sofa with the towel draped across her thighs, her arms along the back of the couch. She waited, unmoving, for her visitor to speak.

Her diminutive friend was obviously having difficulty, for Belgique, by contrast, was looking introspective and did not attempt to compete with Eden's sense of being in charge of the situation. Eden couldn't remember when she had seen her quite so lost for words and uncertain.

But she gave her visitor no help. Eventually Belgique broke the silence.

'Eden,' she said in an uncharacteristically subdued voice, 'I've behaved very badly and I've upset you. I'm very sorry. Let me explain.'

Eden didn't feel like letting her friend off the hook easily. 'You certainly did upset me, Belgique. That's putting it mildly. I was ... *am* furious with you. You knew I fancied MacKenzie! What were you trying to prove? Why the hell did you have to take him to bed?' Eden's voice didn't rise above a conversational level, but Belgique looked startled at the suppressed emotion in her friend's controlled tone.

'But that's just it, Eden. I didn't!' she cried. 'Take him to bed, I mean. I haven't fucked Michael MacKenzie.' She paused. 'It was all an invention,' she added miserably, dropping her eyes. 'Will you forgive me?'

Eden's senses reeled. She sat up straight on the couch, completely unselfconscious in her nakedness. The towel drifted unnoticed from her lap to the floor. This was not what she had expected to hear. In fact she wasn't quite sure she believed it. When was the last time Belgique passed up the opportunity to take a handsome man to bed?

'You'd better tell me all about it, Belgique,' she said sternly. 'I'm not sure I understand what you're saying.' She absently bent over to pick up the towel and held it in her lap.

'Well, once I got rid of Xavier after lunch yesterday, I did call Michael. Alexander gave me his number when he came over to my apartment last Thursday after he'd dropped Michael off at his hotel. I really did want to meet him and for him to see the sculpture in its new home! And I do want to commission him to sculpt another one. All that's true.' She paused, trying to gauge Eden's reaction, but received no flicker of acknowledgement from Eden's face. She rushed on. 'Anyway, he came over about six, and we sat around and chatted for a while. I showed him some of the other pieces in my collection, and then I opened up the erotic portfolio that I bought from Alexander last year. Just looking at those illustrations gets me horny.'

A snort from Eden slowed Belgique's flow momentarily, and she looked up to see a sceptical expression on her friend's face. 'Don't play the innocent with me, Belgique,' she interjected. 'You don't need sexy pictures to get horny!' Eden remembered how aroused she herself had got just standing next to MacKenzie, but now wasn't the time to admit that. 'Go on,' she said.

'Well, I did come on to him a bit, after that,' Belgique admitted. 'I felt I was wrong, because I knew you fancied him, but the man's so sexy I couldn't help myself. You know,' she added, 'one of the most sexy things about your Mr MacKenzie is that he doesn't really know it. He certainly doesn't flaunt it the way that dumb young stud Justin does! *He* thinks he's God's gift to women. All he's got is a big dick; he doesn't know the difference.'

Eden was silent and Belgique continued, 'You know me, Eden. It's not often I fail to take a man to my bed once I've made up my mind to do it. Now I'm both embarrassed for trespassing on your territory and ashamed to admit a failed attempt.' She rolled her eyes. 'I gave him about every hint I could other than taking off my clothes and masturbating or grabbing his cock,' she admitted. 'When I rubbed his back, he almost purred like a cat. He said I had good strong hands. He liked that.'

Eden found herself gripping her thighs, imagining her own hands on MacKenzie's back.

Belgique kept going with her story. 'But then all he did was smile and tousle my hair! He treated me just like a child.' Her voice fell and a blush rose in her pretty throat as she recounted her embarrassment. 'He told me I was cute. Cute!' A sudden concept struck her. 'You don't think he's gay, do you? You know I can usually tell, and I didn't get any such vibes from him at all. But he just didn't seem interested in my body. I thought I must be losing my touch,' she grimaced, but now with a flicker of returning humour.

Eden knew that humble pie was a dish that Belgique couldn't stomach for very long. This apology must be costing her friend. But she wasn't about to release the pressure just yet. And she certainly didn't think Mac-Kenzie was gay. She counted several gay and bisexual men and women amongst her friends, and her gay radar was finely tuned. She said, 'No, Belgique, I'm certain he's not gay. You'd know and so would I. It's not as if it's unknown territory for either of us, is it?' She obliquely acknowledged their sexual forays into exotic tastes.

Belgique managed a weak grin in response.

'Did he say anything about the gallery; about me?' Eden probed.

'He wanted your home number; he said he couldn't find it in the book. I said you were unlisted, but out of some sort of jealous spite, I didn't give it to him. I'm sorry; it was stupid of me, but I was annoyed that I couldn't get him to bed. I'd been looking forward to that.' She smiled ruefully. 'I made up that remark about "my ginger root" to irritate you, because he's definitely more interested in you than in me. I'd been imagining his cock sprouting up from all that red hair. At least I guess it's red. I haven't seen it, honestly, Eden!' Belgique looked anxiously now straight into her friend's eyes. 'I'm sorry I didn't fuck him, but I'm even more sorry I tried. It was a lousy thing to do to a friend, especially someone as special as you.'

She came and sat on the floor and laid her head on Eden's knees, her arms cradling Eden's naked thighs. She gently brushed Eden's skin with her lips. 'Sorry,' she whispered. 'I won't mess up again.'

Eden suddenly became aware again that she was naked save for the towel laid loosely across her lap. She felt no urge to cover herself; instead she recognised a familiar tremor deep in her vagina. 'God, Belgique, you're a trial!' she exclaimed, but with no animosity in her voice. 'If you'd been successful in seducing Mac-Kenzie, I don't know if I could say this so easily, but everything's OK now.' She stroked her friend's dark curly hair, running her fingers through the tresses and applying a firm gentle pressure to the brunette's scalp. Belgique murmured her pleasure at the touch, drifting her fingers to the inside of Eden's thigh.

Belgique's fingers paused in their slow circuit of Eden's muscles. 'Oh. Don't stop, that feels so good!' Eden leant back into the cushions, and Belgique's hand continued its sensual rhythm, tracing a gentle line towards Eden's delta of soft curls.

Eden stirred. She was too fixated on MacKenzie to succumb fully to Belgique's attentions, even though they were part of her apology. She squeezed her friend's hand, unburdened now their bond had survived the drama. 'Come, let's have a glass of wine and I'll get dressed. You can tell me all about what happened with you and Raton this afternoon.' They went together to the kitchen, where Eden opened a bottle of Kendall Jackson Chardonnay, cooled from the fridge, and poured two glasses. 'Come into the bedroom,' directed Eden. 'We can talk while I dress.'

While Eden took her time selecting clothes for the evening, Belgique sat on Eden's bed and scrutinised her favourite friend's naked form. Belgique was filled with relief that their friendship had survived her hedonistic stupidity. She enjoyed the sight of Eden's comfortable display, a vulnerable nakedness that reassured Belgique, in ways that no words could, that things were back on an even keel between them.

'I saw you playing with Raton's dick under the table,' Eden teased, her words capturing Belgique's attention. 'What did you do to the poor man?'

'Oh, Alexander's fun at times,' replied Belgique, 'We just went back to my place. He has some quite particular tastes, but he doesn't like to be tied up!' She grinned slyly at Eden. 'But of course, he saw the sculpture, too; you're about the only person who hasn't!'

Eden turned to her friend and smiled. 'I'd like to come over soon, but I hope to be fully occupied this weekend!'

Belgique grinned. 'I'm sure it'll work out,' she said. 'But you must tell me everything that happens. I want all the intimate details. After all, I may learn something after my conspicuous *faux pas*!'

'I'll certainly report on his pubic hair!' Eden laughed with her friend. 'But I'm not sure I can teach you anything about sex. I've always thought it was the other way around. I'm really going after MacKenzie. This one time I'm ignoring my policy of not pursuing the artist; he's just too good to miss. Who knows where this might go?' she mused.

She studied her body in the mirror, feeling more or less satisfied with her form. All the exercising paid off, she decided. She stroked her breasts, holding the curves of flesh in her hands. They can't compete with Belgique's, she told herself, but those gorgeous tits didn't entice MacKenzie. She tried to feel more confident.

As if reading her thoughts, Belgique came and stood behind her friend, and put her arms around her, easing Eden's hands from her breasts and replacing them with her own. She leant her head against Eden's naked back. 'You've got lovely tits, baby. You look really good. I've been admiring you from the bed. It's a hard job to keep my hands off you!'

'You're not,' said Eden. They both giggled, full friendship restored. 'But we were talking about Raton.' Eden reoriented the conversation and turned to face Belgique, resting her arms around her friends shoulders. 'You haven't really told me anything yet.'

Belgique snuggled into Eden's arms, relishing the

forgiving intimacy of Eden's body, and replied, a little defensively, as if she expected Eden to demure, 'He really is a good lover, you know. Very dexterous. I think it's those lengthy fingers of his; they get everywhere.' She smiled and stepped back to sit on the bed.

As Eden absently selected her underwear, Belgique continued. 'He also knows how to take things slowly, to really pleasure a woman. So many men never manage that.' She snorted dismissively. 'He's good company if only he wouldn't try to be an art scholar!' she continued.

Eden stepped into her panties and paused to brush her hair before the mirror.

'Really, Eden, I've learnt more about art from you in the last year than Alexander knows from a lifetime in the gallery business! He remembers all the names and the jargon, but I don't think he really understands artists. I don't think he'd know which end of a brush to paint with! But boy, oh, boy, is he one good lay!'

Eden turned to look at her, wearing a sceptical expression.

'But you know, something is odd.' Belgique became more serious, and looked at Eden quizzically. 'I've known Alexander for several years on and off; he's always had plenty of money to throw about. I've never known quite where he gets it, but he's never been short of cash. But recently,' she went on, 'he's hardly spent anything. Did you see him order iced tea and a salad at lunch?' Belgique was incredulous. 'Iced tea, for Chrissakes! It's always been champagne here, the best scotch there, expensive clothes, great house, you know, the works.'

Eden nodded.

Belgique queried. 'Have you noticed anything at the gallery?'

Eden shook her head. 'No, our business has been steady; not spectacular, but solid I think. We haven't made any huge sales recently, but, for example, Jay Jay

Ritchie bought a couple of Annalee Barretts just this morning. They're $5,000 each. Why do you ask?'

'Well, it's unlike Alexander,' Belgique replied. 'He's always liked to flash his money around, but not in the last few weeks. Although a friend of mine said she saw him in the casino at that plush topless club on Piedmont Avenue. So he must still have his money; the minimum bets are huge at that place!'

'I wouldn't know,' said Eden dryly. But then a thought struck her. 'Of course, if he's gambling, he could be *losing* money. It has been known,' she added ironically. 'But thanks for the info, Belgique, I'll keep alert and watch out for any funny business.'

'That's enough of Alexander,' said Belgique, abruptly changing the subject. 'I want to know what you're going to do about Mr MacKenzie! Oh, wait a minute.' She went back into the living room and returned with her purse. Opening it, she took out a small piece of paper. 'Here's his hotel, address and phone number. It's north from the gallery, on Peachtree, just over the freeway.'

Eden held her prize in her fingers. Her heart leapt like a teenager's. 'I'm going to call him right now!' she replied excitedly to her friend's question, and strode, dressed only in satin panties, to the telephone.

She dialled the number, and was put on hold for an interminable time. She paced up and down the bedroom, with Belgique watching eagerly from the edge of the bed. Absently, Eden slid her left hand inside her panties and wound tight little spirals in her pubic hair.

'Hello?' The unmistakable Scottish accent shocked Eden into nearly dropping the phone, but she recovered with aplomb.

'Mr MacKenzie, Michael, this is Eden Sinclair.' Was it her imagination, or did MacKenzie catch his breath at the other end? Her manner was crisp and very businesslike, in complete contrast to the vulnerable nudity of her body as she stood in a classical pose like a marble statue in the

139

early evening light. 'I'm so glad I've caught you in,' she continued smoothly. 'There are just a few details about the show I'd like to check with you. Could you come down to the gallery this evening?' She added, 'I'll be working late.'

MacKenzie was all charm in his reply. 'I'd be delighted, Eden. May I call you Eden? It's been a frustrating day and I'd love some intelligent company.' He hesitated. 'Will you be working long?' he queried. 'Perhaps we could have dinner afterwards, or drinks. Could you manage that?'

Eden's face shone with pleasure, animating her features. Placing her hand over the phone, she mouthed a triumphant 'Yes!' to Belgique, who just grinned.

'Told you!' she mouthed back.

Moving her hand and speaking once more into the handset, Eden said, 'That's very nice of you, Michael. Let's see what time I finish.'

'Tease!' hissed Belgique.

'Says you!' whispered Eden, who felt like a schoolgirl planning a first date.

Keeping her business demeanour for MacKenzie, Eden continued, 'Shall we say at the gallery at 7.30? Do you have a rental car? OK, see you then.'

She put the phone down and stared at Belgique. 'Oh, Lord. Let this work out!' She rolled her eyes heavenward and crossed her fingers. 'I'm so nervous.'

Belgique simply hugged her friend. 'Better get some clothes on Eden. Even if it is for only a short time!' she said mischievously. With a deep kiss and a final caress of Eden's breasts she was gone, leaving Eden alone with her wishes coming true.

Chapter Twelve
The Fine Suit

*I*t was 7 p.m. when Eden returned to the gallery. Almost everything nearby was closed for the weekend; only O'Hara's bar and grill across the street was open, a little oasis of merriment in an otherwise austere post-modern landscape.

The idiosyncratic old building that housed Galerie Raton was unlit. Angela had obviously locked up and left at 6.00. MacKenzie was due in half an hour. Eden let herself in and switched on some of the downstairs lights and studied the three bronze sculptures standing ready for the new show. During the next few days, her assistants would put up partitions and hang the paintings she had chosen. Walking up the spiral staircase to her office, she switched on her desk lamp and sat down.

For the meeting, she had donned her sexiest silk lingerie and selected her finest suit from her closet. She had taken special care with her underwear, even though she hoped to divest herself of it before too long. The sensual garments had been selected especially by Antoine himself at Chez Antoine, the most pretentious underwear store in the most pretentious mall in the city: the bra was almost transparent and the bikini panties were merely a thong, with the fabric at the front barely covering her pubic mound, and the single thin band at the rear fitting snugly into her cleft, leaving her buttocks fully displayed in all their trim firmness. She also wore a matching garter belt that made her look, much to her delight, like an elegant sexy model from the Victoria's Secret mail-order catalogue.

Along with the fine suit of taupe linen, Eden wore just the right shoes, the right stockings, and all the other correct accoutrements. Her silk Charmeuse blouse, creamy and lustrous, was the colour of cinnamon and matched her high-heeled pumps. Her chestnut hair was pinned up close to her head.

As she pictured MacKenzie in her mind, her nipples became erect. She enjoyed the feeling as they rubbed against the thin silk of her blouse. She recalled Mac-Kenzie's scent and the apple smell of his hair, imagining the texture of his skin under her fingers. Eden's inner lips moistened as her memories and anticipations grew more intense.

And then, she pictured him naked.

Eden's heartbeat increased as her enriched fantasy depicted the naked MacKenzie, with his 'cock's comb' of red hair, strolling toward her across the carpet of her office. As she visualised him coming closer, the hair on his head and the hair surrounding his genitals, was coloured a bright, bright red.

Restless, Eden stood and flipped on the master light switch against the gathering twilight, flooding her sumptuous office with light. At that very moment the sculptor, Michael MacKenzie himself, sailed up the stairs and stood at the threshold of her domain. She jumped, startled; he was a full fifteen minutes ahead of time.

'How did you get in?' she asked as she faced him, more startled by the feeling he excited within her, than by the simple fact of his being there early. She admired his appearance as he approached her, and felt suddenly weak in the knees.

He looked puzzled for a moment, standing beside the coffee table, a folder of slides in his hand. Then he explained, 'The door was open, so I just came on in. I thought you'd left it open for me. I hope I didn't disturb you.'

Eden shook her head, thinking his voice sounded more husky than she remembered. 'Not at all,' she demurred, extending her hand to greet him. 'I just thought I'd locked it.' Eden was chagrined to realise that in her excitement she had omitted to secure the front door, but as soon as he took her hand in his, her skin again seemed to ignite, just like on the first day, as if a bolt of electricity shot through her. Eden could tell by his eyes, by the way he started, that he, too, was moved by the touch.

'Oh,' she said involuntarily, and closed the distance between them. The sexually charged chemistry that had been hovering in the air for the last 48 hours suddenly grew even stronger.

He moved to her side, and for a quiet moment Eden studied his tall rugged image. He was wearing clean blue jeans and Reeboks, and a crisply laundered white shirt that set off his complexion. For the first time, Eden noticed a light skein of freckles on MacKenzie's cheeks and under his chin. She smoothed her hands carefully down the hips and over the thighs of her suit as she looked at MacKenzie and thought bizarrely, this is a very fine suit. And indeed, the finely woven linen fitted like a dream.

Almost hurting with the desire to touch and be touched, she ran her hands again over the fabric of her skirt, caressing the subtle flair of her hips. It was a fine suit, but what good was it? What good was the fine linen, perfectly suited to her complexion, and contrasting dramatically with her chestnut hair? She had accentuated her wide cheekbones with large, silver gypsy-like earrings. She never wore gold; always sterling silver. Yet, what good was her polished exterior? Eden soberly considered that she had fine clothing and silver jewellery, a few precious stones, but she had no husband, no mate, no steady lover.

Rubbing her finger over the row of tiny diamonds studding the slender inner curve of one earring, she suddenly unthreaded the silver hoop from her ear lobe and held it in the palm of her hand, examining the diamonds. The pair had been a gift from a previous lover. It had been a long time since she had thought of him, she mused, but without regret. Weighing the shiny object like a coin, she tossed it from one hand to the other. MacKenzie was watching her, and impulsively she tossed the earring to him. He caught it. His reflexes were good, she thought.

He smiled quizzically and put down the slides.

MacKenzie examined Eden's earring in his palm. He looked up, his eyes locking on hers, repeating that memorable moment when they had met; and Eden felt that he seemed ready to ask her something she had been hoping he would ask.

But he only pointed at his sheaf of slides on the table. 'I realised that I hadn't shown you these the other day,' he began, but got no further as Eden walked over to him.

'Let's sit,' she suggested, leading him by the hand to the chaise, 'and let's talk. And yes, I'd like to see the slides, too.'

As soon as they were seated the sexual tension between them increased, and as they looked at the images, holding them up to the light, their knees touched accidentally. Eden almost jumped. She pressed her knees together, feeling deliciously wet, thinking how much she wanted him. She asked, 'Do you want a glass of wine?'

'That would be excellent,' he answered and rose to his feet, placing the earring carefully on the table. 'Tell me where it is and I'll fetch it.

'It's in the refrigerator downstairs, in the little kitchen next to the conference room. There are glasses in the cupboard and a corkscrew in the drawer.'

'Be right back,' he said, and briskly descended the staircase. A moment later, a muffled pop and a clinking of glasses heralded his return. His red hair reappeared more slowly above the floor, circling around the spiral treads to reveal his tall frame, smiling and holding the bottle of wine and two glasses.

He poured them each a generous portion, and raised his glass. 'Cheers,' he toasted. 'Here's to a long and fruitful relationship!'

'I'll drink to that,' murmured Eden, tipping her glass to his. The tinkle of the crystal sent a shudder of anticipation tingling down her spine. She took a long swallow of the cool wine, not caring tonight for proper sipping etiquette. She held his gaze steadily and added, 'I'm looking forward to getting to know all about you, MacKenzie. For a start, does anybody call you MacKenzie?'

'No, friends just use Michael or Mike.'

'Can I call you MacKenzie? That's how I think of you in my mind.'

'I'm thrilled to hear that you think of me!' said MacKenzie, with a laugh. 'I'd be honoured if you'd call me MacKenzie. That would be something special between us.'

Eden raised her glass again. 'To something special between us,' she said. MacKenzie's eyes matched her sparkle, and they downed the rest of their glasses.

He reached across to refill Eden's goblet, but to his mortification he misjudged his movement, and tipped the refilled glass from Eden's hand. Frozen, he watched the golden liquid pour over her skirt. Eden leapt to her feet, exclaiming, 'My suit! Quick, a towel. In the bathroom!' She gestured urgently.

As MacKenzie dashed to the office bathroom to comply, Eden stripped off her skirt, which had received a substantial dousing. When MacKenzie turned back, he saw Eden standing partially undressed, incongruously outfitted in only a suit jacket and blouse, tiny jet black panties with garter belt and stockings, and high-heeled shoes. Staring at her speechlessly, MacKenzie handed Eden the towel. The black panties contrasted with her lightly tanned skin. He stood aside, transfixed both by his blunder and by Eden's beauty.

Wiping the wetness from her naked thigh where the wine had soaked through the fabric of her skirt, Eden noticed more splashes on her jacket and blouse. As quickly as she had discarded the bottom half of her fine suit, Eden removed the top half, too.

MacKenzie continued staring, surprised, as before his very eyes, the sexy lady gallery director whisked off her blouse with equal aplomb, revealing to his bulging eyes, a sumptuous view of her trim waist and delicious cleavage framed in a provocative black lace bra.

He couldn't stop his eyes from travelling to her pubic triangle, scantily covered with a mere patch of black silk and framed by the sexy garter belt.

As she stood before him, Eden pondered her rejected clothing lying scattered on the carpet. MacKenzie watched, hugely embarrassed, but smiling none the less, as she gathered the fine suit and silk blouse into a small pile, and opened a closet door, ostensibly to find a change of clothing. As Eden turned to face the closet, he was presented with a brilliant view of her neat bottom, totally naked except for the merest thong between her buttocks.

Eden, intensely aroused by the presence of the man and by her near-nakedness, stood for a long moment, her chest rising and falling, her heart pounding; enjoying the formidable experience of wearing only black lace lingerie in front of MacKenzie. She glanced at MacKenzie's reflection in the full-length mirror beside the cupboard door. It was amusing to see him so completely adrift, and she couldn't suppress a quick giggle at the contrasting emotions of lust and shame coursing across his face.

She turned to face him, and again laughed softly as she appraised the conspicuously increasing size of his dick as it pressed against his jeans. Her laughter did not diminish him, and his erection made a nice tent shape through the denim fabric. She enjoyed her power to make him hard.

'MacKenzie?' she began disingenuously, in a soft, quizzical voice. 'Don't guys always see their colleagues nude? At the locker room and stuff?'

Struggling to appear casual, he shrugged, hands in pockets nonchalantly, and said, 'Why sure, Eden, but . . .' He stopped. 'But that's different.'

She took the opportunity to strut before the mirror in her black bra and panties. Slowly, she unpinned her hair, letting it swing loose at her shoulders.

He asked, 'Eden?'

'Yes, MacKenzie?'

'Oh my God . . . Eden!' he continued, but he got no further as his words dried in his throat.

She laughed again, softly, and asked, 'Why MacKenzie, whatever is the matter?'

MacKenzie had never seen Eden like this, of course: nearly naked in lacy, revealing lingerie; but neither had he imagined the serious young woman strutting and tossing her chestnut hair before his eyes like some beautiful exotic dancer.

Under his breath he whispered, 'God Eden, you're so beautiful, so sexy! I love your breasts, your body!'

In the mirror Eden saw the triangular tuft of her pubic patch showing through the thin fabric. Her mouth was so dry she could not speak and she just stood there staring back at his reflection, smiling. Her eyes travelled down his body and she called him without turning round, saying in a soft voice, 'Come here, MacKenzie.' As he

147

slowly advanced towards her she pretended, 'I don't know what to wear and I'd like your aesthetic opinion.'

Coming close, the tall man stood behind her with only a few inches separating his penis, still projecting tent-like through his jeans, from the curve of her naked buttocks. He brushed against her, ever so softly, murmuring, 'What are we going to do about this?'

She stepped back, another inch closer to him, and pressed her hand over his penis, holding it tightly in her palm; shivering at the sheer nerve of her gesture, relishing the feeling of his body, though clothed, against hers.

Sighing deeply in his throat, MacKenzie seized Eden's shoulders in his hands and pressed her yielding flesh against him, turning her to face him. She ground her pubic mound against his cock, feeling his hardness. Reaching between them, Eden thrust her hands into the waistband of his trousers and unfastened his belt.

Watching their reflections in the mirror as she slowly unzipped his jeans, Eden wiggled and writhed against his body, feeling a flood of desire as she enjoyed the muscular strength of his torso. She reached into his underpants; they felt like silk! She pulled them aside; his huge dick sprang upward!

MacKenzie moaned softly into her hair as he pressed his lips against her temple. As his hands moved over her shoulders and arms, he slid the straps of her black lace brassiere down over her biceps. He bent to lick her neck and felt her strong response to his touch.

Eden arched her back so that her half-naked breasts pressed against his chest and he unfastened her bra. For a second, it dangled from the tips of her breasts for her nipples, eager for his touch, were as hard and erect as berries. As she shook off her bra and her body trembled with desire, she experienced rapid ripples of ecstasy as his warm hands cupped and fondled her breasts, teasing up the nipples into peaks.

Slowly MacKenzie moved his hands down her body

and unclipped her garter belt and stockings, kneeling before her to roll them down to her ankles. Eden stepped out of her pumps. His hands moulded her calves and thighs, and she cried aloud when he reached his fingers inside her panties. He pulled aside the thin silk and kissed her bush of curls, his tongue exploring the new terrain. She felt her clitoris tingle under its fleeting caress.

As they slid to the floor, Eden tore off his clothes until he wore only his underwear, stretched to one side of his gorgeous penis. She slid this remaining item from his legs as, gleefully, he pawed off her tiny panties. Grabbing the cushions from the chaise, they arranged them hastily beneath their entwined bodies. Eden stretched back on the padded pillows and looked at her new lover. She admired his strongly muscled shoulders and chest and laced her fingers in his warm soft body hair. As she moved her caressing hands down his tapering torso the hair gradually became redder, until, clustered in curls around his balls and rigid cock, it was a vivid, gingery red. His penis was circumcised.

'There's the answer to two of my questions,' said Eden, fondling his shaft and masturbating him gently. Mac-Kenzie raised his eyebrows in mute enquiry.

With a slight blush at her carnal speculations, Eden admitted, 'I wondered whether your hair would be red down here. And I've never made love to someone who wasn't an American, and most American men are circumcised. But I'd heard that over in Britain it was different. I've been wondering about your penis.' As if to acknowledge the focus of her attention, Eden bent forward and slowly took his whole glans in her mouth, running her tongue around the purple ridge. She gave a satisfied sigh that was echoed by MacKenzie's own sigh of pleasure.

Lying supine on the cushions, MacKenzie contemplated Eden's nude form bending lithely over his rampant dick. He noted her figure: a slender waist and flat stomach, tanned skin with creamy pale breasts and buttocks. He particularly memorised the contours of her high, finely moulded breasts, with their large areolas and very pointed nipples. A luxurious chestnut thatch of pubic hair in a precise triangular shape between her thighs completed his sensual appraisal. He watched enraptured as Eden paused in her ministrations, and moved to straddle his muscular thighs.

Gushing with juiciness, Eden rubbed against MacKenzie's body with sensuous joy. As they kissed, she pressed hard against his pelvis as his bottom slid off the cushions and rubbed against the fibres of the Persian carpet on the office floor.

But MacKenzie didn't feel the rough surface of the rug. As the slender young woman rode him, all feeling was focused in his penis; it was fully hard and pressing into the warm moist flower of Eden's pussy lips. She reached between her legs and gripped his shaft, easing it into her velvety opening. They were both so slick and eager.

She moaned, 'Oh, MacKenzie!'

To prevent himself from coming in that first instant her vagina sucked him inside, MacKenzie arched his back and squeezed Eden tightly against him, pinning his dick inside her without moving. He cupped her firm buttocks and rocked her slowly. He pressed her clitoris on to his pubic bone, grinding her button against firm flesh. His action brought her off, instantly, explosively. She wailed with that first orgasm as he gripped her in his arms and his powerful kisses covered her face.

The office walls reverberated with their exhilarated screams and shouts, as they rocked, and then he came, too, with an incredible burst of thick, creamy sperm. They collapsed, sweating, to lie in each other's arms, in the middle of the carpeted office, next to a small mound of clothing that had started the evening as a very fine suit.

* * *

'Did you really want to see me about the show, tonight, Eden?' he asked later, lying in her arms after they had made love for the third time.

'No,' she replied. 'I lied. I just wanted to see you naked.'

Chapter Thirteen
Getting Acquainted

*E*den opened her eyes to see the sloping wooden ceiling of her office where her pastel-blue bedroom plaster should be. For a few seconds she lay there confused. The room was strangely quiet, devoid of the myriad of small sounds of morning in her neighbour-hood. There was just the sound of the slow deep breathing of the man slumbering beside her. Her memory flooded back, banishing sleep from her brain, and she turned to snuggle into the Scotsman's firm, warm body.

MacKenzie stirred but didn't wake, and Eden propped herself upon one elbow to survey her new lover. They lay together across sundry cushions from her office furniture, their naked flesh contrasting with the saturated colours and patterns of the fabrics. Her companion was lying on his back with one arm flung out and the other wrapped across his chest. His penis, still looking plump, lay quiescent across his groin, nestled within its bed of startling ginger hairs.

The Sunday morning sunlight was beginning to creep in the office skylight above her desk, and the first line of yellow light painted a stripe across MacKenzie's thighs as if with a thin brush, adding highlights of gold to his short pubic curls. With a shock, Eden realised it must be nearly noon, and then relaxed, for on Sunday the gallery was closed all day. Enjoying this temporary freedom, Eden circled her fingers lazily across the contours of MacKenzie's stomach and hip bones, winding in a slow spiral to his penis. Slowly she stroked the length of the soft member, and around the ridge of his glans just visible above the fringe of pink skin. She enjoyed a thrill of gentle sexual pleasure as she dallied with her lover's penis, cradling it now in her palm, bending over to kiss it and taste the residue of their lust.

Smiling at her memory of the passionate night of love, she felt echoes of that lust gathering deeply in her vagina and she shivered with the memory of MacKenzie's expert touch. But lying next to the handsome man in the warm morning light she acknowledged the beginnings of another and less familiar sensation, the beginnings of a tender passion.

Eden staved off that feeling she had sworn to avoid after Peter broke her heart over a year ago. She had told herself she wasn't ready for the roller-coaster ride of love. Was MacKenzie 'the real thing'? Or was she just over-reacting to the best sex of her life?

Their pent-up desires and their mutual lust sharpened by experience, had certainly taken her to new plateau of pleasure. It was as if every little trick and technique she had learnt from her previous lovers had coalesced last night into a symphony of erotic skill. And MacKenzie had responded in full measure. She wanted to ask him who made love with him before. He certainly knew how to pleasure a woman! Her clitoris tingled with the memory of his tongue and fingers. His love-making had been strong and urgent, but with a gentle undertone that tugged at her heart more than she expected.

'I knew I wanted to make love with you, Mr Mac-Kenzie,' she murmured to herself. 'But I don't know whether I want to fall in love. Not now; not yet.'

The slow sounds of Sunday traffic leaving the Baptist church across the street filtered into the quiet of the gallery. Car doors opened and closed; voices muttered at the threshold of hearing. In the distance a siren wailed, telling of some unknown urgency.

Eden gazed again at MacKenzie's open friendly face. Her cautionary desire to keep some emotional distance between them temporarily dissolved in the warmth that flooded over her. 'Oh, MacKenzie, you gorgeous hunk! I lust after you. I can't help it!' She kissed his warm skin and licked his cock, running her fingers across his balls. She felt a tremor of response as he stiffened slightly in her hand. 'I lust after you, and I want to fuck you again and again and again, forever!'

MacKenzie stirred and opened one sleepy eye. He stared at her in a slightly unfocused way for a moment, and then a boyish grin lit his features awake. 'I was having a dream, Eden,' he said. 'I was in this strange city and a beautiful girl was stroking my body, and murmuring that she wanted to make love to me. And then I woke up before we got to the best bit!'

Eden smiled. 'You haven't missed anything!' she assured him, and kissed his lips, rolling him on to his side and moving astride his thigh so that it lay between her legs. MacKenzie's quadriceps hardened as she ground her pubic bone against his muscles. A familiar moisture spread from her sex and she felt MacKenzie's cock stiffen to a pole in her hand. She pumped him slowly, sensing the shaft quiver under her touch. Her clitoris, riding on MacKenzie's muscle, stood up in unison. Suddenly impatient, Eden pushed her lover flat on his back and straddled him, easing back to let his fully engorged cock slide up inside her.

'This isn't a dream, is it, darling?' she laughed as she rode his wondrous manhood in a rhythmic bucking motion, her hair falling forward to brush his face.

MacKenzie grunted, but his eyes were alight with a

dancing smile. He found his voice between thrusts. 'God, Eden, you're so slick! When your muscles grab me I can hardly stop myself coming on the spot!' His strong hands gripped the cheeks of her bum and held them tight, assisting the rocking motion of her body as Eden squatted over his cock as it slid in and out of her like a well-oiled piston.

'If you move at this angle,' he suggested, 'I won't come so fast. There's not quite so much friction along the back of my shaft!'

Eden moved her body upright and then leant back slightly, balancing her weight on her arms stretched out behind her. She felt the tip of MacKenzie's cock reach up into the very opening of her womb. Her clitoris sprang free from its friction at the base of MacKenzie's tumescent manhood, and she drew his fingers to her greedy love bud. 'Rub me, MacKenzie! Rub me! Make me come!'

Working her rigid button with his thumb, MacKenzie surrendered the initiative and let Eden's movements direct his timing. His eyes fixed on Eden's upthrust breasts as she rode above him. He felt the semen rise up the shaft of his penis; unable now to do anything to control his ejaculation, he cried, 'Oh, Eden! Get ready! I'm going to fill you up! Oh, God, here it comes!' MacKenzie abandoned himself to the torrent of sperm that pulsed from him into Eden's vagina.

In response, Eden felt her orgasm roll up from her core as she enjoyed the warm flush of MacKenzie's come within her, and the persuasive kneading of her clitoris under the sculptor's expert thumb. With a scream of pure lust, Eden felt herself go over the top and collapsed on MacKenzie's chest, her hair covering his face and her harsh breaths falling against his neck. 'Oh, God, MacKenzie! That was so, so good!' she cried, almost sobbing with her release. She felt MacKenzie's hand stroke her hair, and his other arm wrap around her heaving body. She gasped as an aftershock echoed through her groin,

155

and MacKenzie groaned in reply as her vaginal muscles squeezed every last drop of semen from the shaft of his cock.

They lay exhausted for several minutes, not moving save for their combined breathing. Then Eden felt MacKenzie's cock grow limp inside her, and slide out of her vagina, releasing a flow of juices down her thigh. MacKenzie reached with his fingers to touch Eden's come and then wetted them in his own. Raising his fingers to his lips he sampled the salty mixture with evident relish.

'Here, darling,' he said, pressing an unlicked finger to Eden's lips, 'We taste really good together!'

'Yes, we do,' murmured Eden, as she took her lover's finger inside her mouth like a miniature penis, teasing it with her tongue and nipping it gently with her teeth. She couldn't remember experiencing this kind of sexual and personal communion that enveloped her and MacKenzie before; she had no precedent in her memories of sexual partners. As she slid off MacKenzie and lay peacefully at his side once more, she caught him gazing solemnly at her. Her eyes sought his and locked them. 'Yes?' she quizzed, with only an upraised eyebrow, sensing something delicious and frightening in the recesses of her heart.

But after a moment's silence, MacKenzie only grinned. 'I'm hungry,' he declared. 'I think we should tidy up your office, go have brunch at O'Hara's and then go back to your house, if you'll let me in. Then, I think we should make love some more!'

Eden burst out laughing, her tension momentarily relieved.

'OK, sunshine,' she said and jumped up. 'Catch this!' and she threw a cushion at MacKenzie, pulling their clothes into a big bundle before depositing them on her desk. 'Let's get dressed and get out of here!'

* * *

In common with most art galleries, Galerie Raton did not open to the public on Mondays. Sometimes the staff went in, but because Saturday was always a working day, Eden kept flexible hours on Mondays. This was one Monday, she deemed, that wild horses couldn't drag her in!

Turning to this new man who was probably going to shift her world around, she stroked his hair and kissed him a 'good morning' on the lips. MacKenzie smiled his big boyish smile and murmured, 'Good morning, darling. You look wonderful!'

He pulled himself up to kiss her back, his tongue probing deeply into her mouth. 'Hmmmm! You taste and smell wonderful, too! But you deserve breakfast! Let me fix you some bacon and eggs. And I'll put the coffee on!'

Before Eden could protest MacKenzie jumped up from the bed and still naked, walked through to her kitchen.

A momentary pang of alarm quickly subsided in Eden's breast. Why worry if the kitchen was untidy, or some things not properly put away? If she was going to give her body to this man, she thought, the sooner he got to know all about her the better. And her, him, she added to herself. God! What did he feel this morning? A flash of fleeting panic seized her. She couldn't tell a near-stranger the words, 'I want you again and again. I may even love you!' As these unformed emotions brewed within her heart, Eden found it was vital to know what MacKenzie, too, was feeling.

Eden hustled out of bed and wrapped only a short red silk robe loosely around her body. She hurried to the kitchen. MacKenzie met her halfway, coffee pot in his hands, but his eyes frankly drinking in her near-nakedness. She felt her nipples harden under his gaze and her eyes dropped to his crotch. There, sure enough, was his beautiful penis beginning to stir amongst those lovely ginger curls.

But all he said was, 'We're out of milk. For the coffee.'

157

He gestured with the empty pot as if to prove his assertion.

'Oh,' explained Eden, 'I don't take milk. I never have much milk in the house, I'm afraid. I'm not a big milk drinker. Do you . . . er . . . drink much milk?'

MacKenzie laughed by way of reply. 'Actually, yes I do.' He paused. 'This is funny, isn't it?'

'What's funny?'

'Here we are; we've been just about as intimate as two human beings can possibly get, and now we don't know how to talk to each other! Nor do we really know the slightest thing about one another!'

Eden blushed. MacKenzie was right: just about as intimate as it was possible to get. She could still taste him on her lips and smell him all over her body. But she also knew that this was different from any one-night stand; and something told her she should speak her mind.

Bravely, she began, 'MacKenzie, I do have something to say. We made love to each other last night and I feel good about that this morning.' She put her hands on his warm, bare shoulders. She murmured, 'I feel very funny, scared and elated all at the same time. I know I'm totally infatuated with your body, but I think you're pretty cool, as well. I want to know how you feel, because this is really important!' Only when she had made this little speech did Eden realise that her body was shaking with tension. She relaxed her body with a deliberate effort.

'I'm charmed,' MacKenzie said, and then he put the coffee pot on a side table and took her hand, leading her to the sofa in the living room. Standing naked and honest before her, he held her hands for a moment, and caressed her lightly through the silk robe with his fingertips. 'I was just thinking, out there in the kitchen, that I might have dreamt these precious hours.' He paused and smiled deeply, explaining, 'When I saw you at the gallery on that first day, I felt there was something special about you. You looked so cool and so poised, so professional

158

and yet so ... so damned sexy! That's the only way to describe it. Those two young girls, Claire and Lola, were almost begging for sex, but I couldn't take my eyes off you, right up until you had to leave for that damned appointment.'

As if in demonstration of his feelings, MacKenzie's dick continued to rise.

He continued, 'After Raton took me back to my hotel that night, all I did was masturbate and think of you all night!' MacKenzie grabbed his swelling penis and began pumping the thick stalk before Eden's eager eyes.

Eden licked her lips in encouragement, saying, 'Please continue, MacKenzie.' Her voice was low, seductive. Eden stroked MacKenzie's balls and he shuddered. She slid the robe off her shoulders and pressed against him until her nipples were crushed against his chest. She felt his cock go hard in her fingers as her lover's hands moved to caress her body.

'To hell with breakfast!' announced MacKenzie. 'Let's go back to bed!'

MacKenzie woke first from another luxurious lovers' nap and explored Eden's house. The soft lighting from the window shades and the warm white walls were a welcome change after the gallery's ubiquitous cool surfaces and brilliantly lit spaces.

As he wandered from her bedroom into the main living area, he noted that she had made the most of a modest space. A high counter divided the kitchen alcove from a breakfast nook overlooking the garden. Beyond were the main living and dining spaces, high and well lit, lined with books and hung with paintings. Each room had ceiling fans to assist with cooling. He went into the small yet efficient kitchen and took a pair of tumblers from shelves cleverly suspended from the ceiling.

As he padded across the polished oak parquet floor back into the bedroom with two glasses of lemonade,

159

MacKenzie admired the pair of handsome leather Barcelona chairs facing a streamlined sofa, outfitted with ochre cushions.

Eden's interior décor was simple, understated and, MacKenzie realised, in marked contrast to the overly abundant opulence of Belgique's living room. He found the friendship between two such different women puzzling.

Her bedroom was equally elegant, although now in a state of pleasant disarray. On the floor to one side of the bed a small group of teddy bears studied him grumpily, as if blaming him for their abrupt dismissal from Eden's pillows.

Eden woke at his gentle touch and downed her lemonade quickly; and the lovers prepared a simple breakfast in the middle of the afternoon. After filling their stomachs, they began a hesitant show-and-tell.

With MacKenzie's arms around her Eden felt closer to him, sexually and emotionally, than she had to any other man for a long, long time. She found no discomfort in telling her new lover about some past affairs and escapades. Her tales included some descriptively bawdy bisexual relationships. She told him frankly, 'I'd rather tell you about these now, than for you to hear stories from Belgique! There are few secrets where Belgique's concerned!'

MacKenzie asked, 'Did Belgique tell you what happened at her apartment?'

Eden nodded, but failed to keep her emotions from her face.

MacKenzie read them correctly. He stroked her shoulders and said simply, 'She pales in comparison to you!'

Eden's relief was tangible. She leant her head against his shoulder and held him tight.

* * *

MacKenzie was more reticent about his past, and was embarrassed lest his own sexual experiences should fail to match up to Eden's expectations. But Eden was not to be put off.

'I don't need to know about all of your girlfriends,' she told MacKenzie to lighten his task. 'Just let me know about someone important to you, and what she did to this beautiful cock of yours!' With that, she took MacKenzie's shaft deep in her mouth for fully half its length, moistening the glans with her tongue while rubbing the base gently between the forefinger and thumb of her right hand. Eden raised her head and winked at MacKenzie, matching the sparkle in his eyes.

As he enjoyed her ministrations, he felt his reticence about discussing his romantic past slowly drifting away. He put his hands on Eden's shoulders and looked deeply into her eyes. 'The only woman who even comes close to you is Stephanie Pope, my only really serious lover here in America. We broke up six months ago; we'd been together for two years. You could say it was lust at first sight which slowly developed into something more,' he explained, looking at Eden to see if he should continue. She nodded and he proceeded. 'Stephanie and I had sex the very first night we met.'

'We waited three days,' interrupted Eden with a smile. 'Whatever made me so slow?'

'You're plenty fast enough for me, darling,' replied MacKenzie, with his big slow grin, before continuing, 'I was breaking up with another girl, but Steph didn't wait. She literally cornered me at a party. Despite the other people milling around, she started stroking and kissing me, blatantly reaching for my cock. That really got my attention, and before I knew it we were standing on a street corner in Savannah, locked in each other's arms, feeling for each other beneath our clothes. I lived just nearby, and we were half undressed just in the few moments it took to get there.'

Eden felt MacKenzie's penis quiver in her hand as he told the story of Stephanie from Savannah. She planted a kiss on the tip of his long hard cock, smiling her appreciation. As her eyes encouraged MacKenzie with his tale, she said, 'Tell me more about you and Stephanie.' A small bead of pre-come sprouted at the tip of his glans; she licked it off and said, 'Tell me about a specific memory. I want to hear details.'

Breathing harder under Eden's sensual touch, MacKenzie nevertheless managed a smile before he advanced with his tale. 'One of my favourite memories, and typical of Stephanie, was when we visited Atlanta one weekend, and stayed at the Peachtree Plaza, the tall round skyscraper hotel downtown with the glass lifts on the outside. We'd been making love in our room most of the afternoon, and then got dressed to go down to the atrium lobby for a drink. When I came out of our bathroom, Stephanie was already dressed in her fur coat and boots. "It's the air-conditioning," she explained, in response to my surprise at the fur. "They always have it turned up too high."

'We had a couple of gin and tonics at the lobby bar, and then Stephanie suggested we go up to the Pinnacle, the revolving restaurant at the very top, to have a snack and watch the city turn around us. From the atrium level one lift goes directly to the top without stopping at other floors, and so we took that. It's an all-glass compartment that zooms vertically up the outside of the building for 70 stories. It's an experience not for everyone, and there's an emergency stop button in the control panel, just in case.

'Stephanie made sure we were the only ones in the lift and as soon as we started upwards she opened her fur coat, and there she was stark naked in just her high leather boots! I got hard immediately, and seconds later my dick was in Stephanie's mouth as she moistened the shaft and the tip. About halfway up she took off her coat, completely baring her charms in this glass cage visible to the whole city. She turned with her tits to the glass, pressed the emergency stop with one hand, guided my cock into her vagina from behind with the other. There she was, stark naked above Atlanta. There were ranks of office windows only a block away. We could see the lights and people moving around inside.

'Stephanie looked out across the city and said, very calmly, "Fuck me, Michael. I want you to fuck me so all those guys over there can see!"

'And we did just that! Some guys in one of the offices did see us and they went wild! They waved and gestured encouragement. I was getting embarrassed by this time, but Steph just waved back and turned us 90° so the audience could see the whole thing, me pounding into her from the rear while she rubbed her clit to speed her climax. What we lacked in finesse we made up for by the sheer daring of Stephanie's behaviour.

'She came just before I did, and I'd spurted like a fountain moments later when the emergency phone rang! My penis was still stiff inside Stephanie, and I croaked some excuse about vertigo to the anxious hotel operator! I had to place my hand over Stephanie's mouth to stifle her giggles as I reassured the man at the desk that I was fine now, and could make it the rest of the way up. In the few remaining moments of our trip, Stephanie coolly tucked my spent cock neatly back inside my trousers and demurely donned her coat. When we stepped out at the Pinnacle Restaurant only her smile gave any hint of our passion.'

Could she do something like that? wondered Eden, as she felt MacKenzie throb in response to her own vibrant tongue. She recalled her exhibitionist performance for the male body-builder through her bungalow window. That anonymous act didn't really compare, and despite her earlier surety, Eden was pierced by a sudden doubt of her position over Stephanie in MacKenzie's mind. 'Why did you break up?' she asked, suddenly urgent and anxious to know the answer.

'It all had to do with art in the end,' replied MacKenzie, 'not about sex. The special importance of my sculpture to me was something Stephanie found hard to understand. To her it was just what I did, like being a computer programmer, or a stockbroker. We couldn't talk about it with any depth, about art history, about ideas I was exploring, or about the things that I made. She was certainly bright, a public relations expert in fact, but this was a barrier that we couldn't cross with our minds, and even great sex couldn't bridge.'

He smiled with a tinge of sadness. 'The sex kept us going for a long time, but in the end we just gave up. It was my doing really. I was selfish enough to want more, someone who could really share what mattered most of all to me.'

Eden hesitated as a thought struck her, but then took the plunge. 'I have some old drawings of mine in the gallery. I'll show them to you tomorrow if you like.'

MacKenzie's expression took on an extra hunger and look of yearning for Eden. He had been so overwhelmed, he realised, with her sexual and other personal charms, that it hadn't fully registered that his lover might be an accomplished artist in her own right. 'I'd love to see them!' he exclaimed, recognising an important element of this new relationship. 'Do you still have much chance to work in the studio?'

Eden blushed, more embarrassed by her laxity as a serious artist than by the telling of intimate sexual secrets. 'No,' she admitted ruefully. 'I always seem to be too busy.'

MacKenzie smiled again at Eden, this time with only happiness in his eyes. 'Maybe we can change that,' he said softly.

Chapter Fourteen

Double Distrust

On Tuesday morning, a welcome cool breeze found its way through the slats in the pale wood Venetian blinds across Eden's bedroom windows, insinuating itself into the house in the few daylight hours before the outside air was hijacked by the summer heat.

Upon waking, she turned to MacKenzie and snuggled against his body, gently caressing him. As the lovers' bodies intertwined, Eden thought this morning might go down as one of the best of her life, for beside her lay the man who had reignited her lust and was increasingly making a claim for her affections.

The object of her romantic speculation and desire stirred and opened his eyes. 'Good morning, darling,' he murmured. 'What a way to wake up!' he added, becoming conscious of Eden's sexy caresses and his own arousal. As she teased his member into stiffness, he returned the compliment by slipping his hand between his partner's thighs, homing in on her clitoris and fondling it like the expert he had become over their two delicious days in bed. Gently sliding his finger through the lips of her vagina, he discovered Eden was already moist.

Slipping down to kneel between the soft blue sheets, he replaced his finger with his tongue, bringing a purr of satisfaction from his lover. Eden spread her legs wide and raised her pelvis, thrusting to meet his rhythm. She felt her juices flow and heard MacKenzie's sigh of delight as he tasted her.

As ripples of pleasure spread outward from her centre, Eden felt her orgasm growing within her. Raising her hips higher in a series of pelvic lifts worthy of her aerobics class, she urged his tongue deep into her vagina and felt the slight rasp of his two-day old beard across her vulva lips. She trembled with delight. 'Oh, Mac-Kenzie,' she sighed, 'keep doing that! From now on you can shave only every third day!'

MacKenzie's urgency increased to match her own. He moved to bring his penis within reach of Eden's lustful grasp, and rocked back and forth to exaggerate the movements of her hand on his cock. He enjoyed her hands sliding on his shaft in delicious masturbation, her fingers teasing his anus in the way he liked so much. Feeling the sperm rising in his shaft in an unstoppable flow, he focused all his attention on bringing Eden to her climax, but his efforts at restraining himself came to naught as his semen spurted like a white torrent across Eden's breasts, some strands splashing across her chin as his penis reared back and forth.

'Oh, MacKenzie! Keep going!' she begged, almost at the point of no return.

MacKenzie's orgasm did not deflect his desire, as he held his rhythm and returned his tongue to Eden's little bud, now standing up through her pubic hair. Within seconds of plunging two fingers inside her vagina, so slick with juice, he felt her sex muscles contract, gripping his fingers. He circled Eden's thighs with his free arm to press them firmly together against his face, experiencing the full tremors and aftershocks of her orgasm as she climaxed with a long shuddering moan of ecstasy.

Raising his face from Eden's sex moments later, he turned to see her gazing at him with the smile of the proverbial cat who ate the canary. The sight of his lover's eyes and her lips, parted slightly, still carrying traces of his come, moved him to places without words. He eased across the bed to kiss her, long and deep, letting her taste herself on his lips. The flavours of sex were enriched with the unfamiliar tang of his own semen.

'Can we do this every morning?' he asked with a straight face.

'I hope so, darling,' replied Eden, with a large grin. 'And each evening, and at lunchtime, and at coffee break! Hell, let's just do it all day!' Her eyes flicked to the bedside clock. 'Oh, no!' she started up with a note of panic in her voice, 'It's Tuesday! I have to be at work in half an hour!'

They showered together quickly, giggling as they took every excuse to fondle each other, despite their urgency of timing. Dressing quickly, Eden donned one of her standard business outfits of charcoal skirt and white blouse, and applied her make-up with practised speed. MacKenzie, by contrast, wore his days-old crumpled shirt and held his undergarments at arm's length in mock distaste. 'The first place I'm going is back to my hotel and get some clean clothes,' he announced with a grimace.

'You look pretty cute just as you are,' rejoined Eden with a grin, admiring his naked bottom and flaccid penis beneath the tails of his shirt. She reached over and gave it a squeeze. It pulsed in her hand. 'Wow!' she said. 'How does it do that?'

'It's radar-controlled,' replied MacKenzie. 'It's just found the most beautiful and sexy woman in Atlanta!'

Eden blushed. 'Look, I've got to dash,' she said. 'I'll go straight to the gallery; I'll pick up something to eat on the way. If you go back to the hotel to change, I'll see you at the gallery later in the morning. I'll be back before lunch, but first I have to go down south by the airport, to see some new art that's being installed in a library down in Clayton County.'

'Yes, ma'am, certainly ma'am,' replied MacKenzie, touching his forelock in mock servitude.

'Ass!' said Eden. 'Come here so I can kiss you, you gorgeous man!'

MacKenzie took her into his arms and held her for a long slow kiss, breathing the scent of her freshly washed body. 'I'm really falling for you, Eden,' he whispered.

'Me, too, MacKenzie,' she said, reluctantly releasing herself from his grasp and picking up her purse. 'I'll see you at the gallery later. Just pull the front door to as you leave. It locks automatically.' And she was gone, leaving MacKenzie free rein in her own house. The instinctive bond of trust with her new lover pleased her immensely as she drove to work down Amsterdam Avenue.

Eden stopped briefly at the gallery to check on the progress of hanging the new show, and was pleased to see Angela directing Paul and Justin in the final preparations. As she consulted Eden's sketches and diagrams her assistant seemed to have everything under control.

She waved to catch Eden's attention and came over to her side, greeting her. 'Hi, Eden. I've got my piece all framed and ready, but I didn't know where you wanted it in relation to all the others. I had a couple of ideas. See what you think.' She gestured at some notes she had made on Eden's drawings and the two women fell into a detailed discussion of the most appropriate sequence and relationships between the various works of art.

Justin and Paul had already hung several pieces, but their work this morning, although efficient, lacked their usual banter and bonhomie. Eden caught them looking sideways at her a couple of times, and they seemed to be keeping their distance. Justin in particular, looked ill at ease.

Eden raised her voice slightly so that the two men

could hear her remarks to Angela. 'This is all going fine, Angela,' she said, 'but there's still a lot to do; enough in fact to keep Justin tied up all day.' It was a trite joke, but an effective one judging by its victim's beetroot complexion. Angela giggled and Paul looked blank, clearly unaware of Justin's bondage adventures at the hands of Belgique. With a stifled grunt, Justin brushed past his friend and disappeared into the storeroom where he busied himself noisily in the preparation of other paintings. Angela and Eden exchanged quiet grins.

Eden patted her assistant on the shoulder. 'It looks good, Angela; try and get everything up by the end of today. Tomorrow we'll finalise the lighting and do the labels. By the way,' she added, 'MacKenzie will be coming in later, and I'll be back from the library before noon.'

The rise of Angela's eyebrows presaged her question. 'Have you and he . . . er, did you . . .?' She couldn't finish.

Eden laughed. 'Yes we did. And yes we did! Life is looking a lot rosier this morning!' She waved goodbye from the doorway.

'Oh, Eden!' Angela shouted after her. 'Mr Raton said he might be in later. He wants to talk to MacKenzie. Do you have any messages for him?'

'Just tell him I'll see him about noon,' Eden replied over her shoulder as she walked to her car. Angela waved an acknowledgement.

As she headed for the freeway, Eden drove south to the suburban branch library, taking her through downtown. She passed close to the Peachtree Plaza Hotel, thinking of naked Stephanie in the elevator with only a mild frisson of feeling. Was it jealousy or envy? She couldn't decide, but resolved not to let it spoil her day. The morning sun glinted off the gold dome of the Georgia State Capitol as she navigated her way through a maze of freeway ramps and headed for her destination out past Atlanta's Harts-field International airport.

When Eden returned, she found the gallery nearly empty. Angela was manning her post at reception, but Raton was nowhere to be seen and Justin and Paul were presumably on their lunch break. Angela gave her a funny look that she couldn't interpret as she headed for the conference room, where she found MacKenzie seated at the table, glowering at his hands. He didn't look up as she entered.

Her alarm sensors flared, though she knew no reason for MacKenzie's evident black mood. Despite their sexual intimacy, she realised with a shock that she didn't know the man very well. She was at a loss to interpret this dark mood and her words of greeting died on her lips. Instead she asked hesitantly, 'MacKenzie, what's the matter?'

'How could you do it?' was all he said.

His words made no sense. 'Do what?'

'Fuck me around like this, that's what!' MacKenzie was scowling and his colour rose to match his hair. His face was taut with barely restrained emotion, not love or lust this time, but anger, laced with contempt.

'You don't care about your artists, do you?' He began a tirade that rocked Eden back on her heels. 'To you, they're just creatures to do your bidding. You're going to climb to fame on their backs. Alexander told me all about it, how you've hijacked the gallery, breaking his contracts with artists to change all the shows to your own agenda. And your agenda is yourself. You and your ego!

'That's all you care about, isn't it? Getting your name in the magazines, getting your shows reviewed in *Art in America* and those other glossies. And Alexander revealed how you threatened to sue him for trumped-up sexual harassment if he tried to interfere! The poor man's like putty in your paws. But you won't get me like that!'

As MacKenzie's anger boiled over, his normally mild

Scottish accent became more pronounced. Reeling from his unexpected verbal onslaught, Eden thought incongruously with one corner of her spinning mind that it was very attractive. But she couldn't make any sense out of what he was telling her. Without giving her any respite, he was speaking at her again.

'*Do* you have space in your schedule for my one-man show this year? Yes or no!' he demanded.

Eden's mind raced through her carefully planned sequence, all the signed contracts and legal agreements with her new artists. 'Well, no, I don't, but . . .'

His voice rising, MacKenzie interrupted her, riding roughshod over her protestations. 'No bloody buts! You've told me all I needed to know. Alexander was right! He said you'd freeze me out.' He stood up and paced around the room like a caged animal.

Without looking at Eden, MacKenzie launched into another diatribe of frustration. 'I've poured my heart and soul into getting work ready for a one-person show here in America. It's hard to get people to take my kind of work seriously. All they see is the sex, just like that oversexed twit, Belgique du Pont; she just wants to get off on it. What I'm trying to do is so much more profound! I want to take people beyond simple pictures of sex, to see instead the complex human tragedies and comedies behind the lust. I tried in New York and Chicago. I even went to LA and San Francisco, trying galleries there. Nobody was interested; most of them weren't even polite. "Neoclassicism isn't cool," they sneered. "It's not ironical enough." "It's male chauvinist," they said.'

MacKenzie's parody of effete art critics was merciless.

'Well, I say, fuck the lot of them! What do they know?' MacKenzie seemed to be speaking to an empty room as he barely acknowledged Eden's presence. He paced before her, explaining relentlessly, 'So I ended up back in Savannah, teaching at that funny little art school there.

And then I met Alexander when he came to town to speak at the college several weeks ago. He liked my work and promised me a real one-person show with all the trimmings; the starring show of the fall season, he called it. He'd arrange for coverage, *Art Papers*, *Art Forum*, *Art in America*, you name it.'

She was caught in a whirl of strange passion. He continued ranting, 'Raton told me today how he'd agreed it all with you, but then on Friday you told him that you didn't think my work was very good, and anyway there wasn't a time slot for any one-person show.'

'What?' Eden was incredulous.

'And that's not the worst of it,' continued MacKenzie. 'That's when he told me that you threatened him with a lawsuit when he tried to complain and get you to change your mind.'

Eden stared at him, stunned, but MacKenzie didn't notice. He was too wrapped up in his anguish.

'Alexander explained how you and Angela are in it together; how you would claim he sexually assaulted you and she would be the witness. He said you'd ruin him just to get your way! God, Eden Sinclair, you're a real bitch! Alexander admitted he couldn't face you when you got in a temper. He said you frighten him.'

There was no stopping MacKenzie. Eden slumped in a chair, her face buried in her hands.

His angry monologue poured over her. 'You sure had me fooled this weekend! All that loving talk and fancy sex. What were you trying to do? Soften the blow when you told me today? Or were you just using me like you use the rest of your artists? Do you fuck them all; you and your friend Belgique between you?' He paused only for breath. 'You think you can just take over the whole fucking art scene! I'm going back to Savannah, right now!' He stormed out, slamming the door behind him. A moment later Eden heard the echoing slam of the front door and a car engine being roughly gunned out of the parking lot.

Eden sat staring, unable to move.

The conference room door opened again seconds later and she looked up to see Angela standing in the opening, looking aghast. 'What was all that about?' the receptionist asked anxiously. 'I heard him shouting; I heard him mention my name, but I didn't understand what he was saying. Eden, you look awful! What's he done?'

'I don't understand it either,' replied Eden, white-faced and shaking with fright and anger and a deepening sense of despair. 'He said that Raton had told him that I'm hijacking the gallery for my own feminist agenda, and if Raton doesn't go along with it, I'll sue him on a trumped-up charge of sexual harassment. And you'd perjure yourself as a witness.'

Angela's jaw dropped open.

Eden remained in her chair as the receptionist backed out of the doorway and reappeared a moment later with two cups of coffee. 'Here,' she offered, 'drink this. I need it and you probably do, too.' She sat down in a chair next to Eden and instructed, 'Go through this again, more slowly so I can understand. It makes no sense at all! Why would Mr Raton say those things? They're not true, and he must know that.'

Eden sipped her coffee gratefully. The warm liquid helped her concentrate as she replayed MacKenzie's accusations, trying to sort them out in her mind. And just as troubling was the inescapable conclusion that Raton was waging some sort of campaign of misinformation and slander against her. But why?

'It seems that Raton promised MacKenzie a one-man show this fall without ever consulting me or checking the schedule. That was stupid of him, but not necessarily a disaster. I might have been able to work something out. But then,' Eden continued, with a frown of increasing puzzlement on her face, 'MacKenzie started on this litany of lies about me that Raton must have fed him this morning. And about you too,' she added, looking at Angela's worried face.

'Raton apparently said I'm a user of artists; that I'm only interested in advancing my career at the expense of the artists I represent. And then there's all this garbage about you and me blackmailing him by falsifying sexual harassment charges. What the hell is he up to?'

Angela's face was grim when she replied. 'I don't know why, but it's pretty clear that Raton's trying to split you and MacKenzie apart. He left just before you came back, but he must have expected MacKenzie to tell you all this. So Raton will know you'll know he's lying, if you follow my meaning.'

Eden nodded. 'Go on.'

'Well, that means that Raton doesn't care that you know he's told MacKenzie a bunch of lies, which can only indicate that he's deliberately sabotaging that relationship. He wants you out. And me, too, I guess,' Angela added glumly.

Eden pondered the potential wreckage of her career at Galerie Raton. 'That may be what he wants,' she said grimly, 'but I've got a contract, and I'm not going to go quietly! I don't know why he's acting like this but I'm going to try to find out. And then,' she continued, with a firm set to her jaw and fire in her eyes, 'I'm going to get MacKenzie back here and knock some sense into that thick stupid head of his! How the hell could he believe all that nonsense from Raton?'

Eden sighed with a deep disappointment, her bold words masking a feeling of desolation in the pit of her stomach. She had been so close to MacKenzie for two delicious days, and had even toyed with the idea of a long-term relationship with the man. His abrupt and hurtful departure had wrenched her emotions nearly to breaking point. Love! Eden fought tears as she thought about love!

But Raton's actions baffled her. Why would he go to all this trouble to plant this tissue of lies in MacKenzie's mind? Eden suddenly had a thought and looked up at Angela. 'Raton's been seeing a lot of Belgique lately.' She grimaced at her unintended pun. 'I'll call her and see what she's got to say about this.'

Chapter Fifteen

Under the Table

*A*n hour later, Eden turned into the drive of Belgique's building and a young valet opened her door, helped her out and parked her car. As she awaited admittance, she studied once again the pair of bronze creatures, one a sphinx and the other a griffin, flanking the entrance portals of the building. What was their provenance, she wondered. Were they ripped off from some European mansion and brought back to Atlanta by some wealthy magnate?

This train of thought was reinforced as Eden stepped into Belgique's apartment, having been checked out by security and sent up in the elevator. The front door was unlocked and Eden heard her friend's voice from within bid her enter. As she wandered into Belgique's exotic living room, she saw Belgique reclining upon the curved sofa, her body draped with a large antique cashmere throw blanket.

Eden's eyes glanced at the stair to the master suite. She speculated that was where MacKenzie's sculpture must be, but she couldn't raise the enthusiasm to go up and see it for herself. Thinking of the minimal elegance of Belgique's boudoir, Eden marvelled at the contrast with the downstairs rooms. Here her friend had gone almost to the opposite extreme, with ornate furniture and heavily patterned Turkish rugs, especially appropriate for today's pose from the harem.

Mirrors dripped their gilt and multi-branched candlesticks adorned many of the flat surfaces. Heavy swags of velour draped the room's tall windows, tied back with thick ribbons to reveal narrow French doors leading to tiny balconies overlooking the street below. Eden reflected that Belgique's taste in aesthetics was as eclectic as her taste in lovers.

Belgique stretched languorously on the sofa and gestured to her friend, saying 'Come, darling, sit down. I've called the butler. He's new,' she added, and shrugged the cashmere throw to reveal a naked shoulder.

Eden sank on to a sumptuous sofa across from Belgique. She knew that the brunette, who took every opportunity to shed her clothing, probably wore nothing beneath the soft cashmere. She was surprised that Belgique stayed under wraps as her newest butler, a fresh-faced young man introduced as 'Henri', entered the room with a tray of drinks.

The young man blushed as he announced, 'Your mimosa cocktails, Madame.' He was very young, Eden thought, no more than 21, probably a student who was working this job to help himself through college.

Her voluptuary friend slipped the cashmere blanket down her other shoulder as she enquired, 'Henri, darling, do you know Miss Sinclair?'

Turning towards Eden, Henri inclined his head politely and responded, 'I've not met the lady before, Madame. Hello.'

'It's a pleasure to meet you, Henri. Have you worked here long?' asked Eden, from her seat.

'No, Madame,' he answered. 'This is only my second day with Madame du Pont.' He returned his gaze to his employer's naked shoulders.

177

Eden imagined that Belgique expected the butler's service to extend beyond waiting at table. But she had no time for this now and she said urgently, 'Belgique, I *must* talk to you about Raton! I told you what happened at the gallery today on the phone, and I thought you might be able to help me understand what's going on. This is serious!'

Despite her attire, or lack thereof, her friend assumed a dignified air. 'Henri, leave us for a little while, please,' she commanded. 'I will call for you when I'm ready. Then you can bring us some tea.'

The young butler nodded impassively, set the tray on the table between the women and departed, but Eden had already noticed the slight bulge at his crotch. He seemed well aware of his duties, she thought.

After he had left the room, she said, 'Belgique, he's so young! You are incorrigible!'

Belgique glanced appraisingly at her friend as they sipped their mimosa cocktails, but she could tell that Eden was not tasting the champagne. 'I've been thinking about what you said on the phone,' the brunette began, 'and I've decided to tell you everything I know about Alexander Raton. I've been wondering what to do for the last couple of days. It's not a pretty tale but I think it helps make sense of MacKenzie's outburst.'

Eden looked sharply at Belgique. It wasn't often she heard her friend speak with such a deadpan serious tone. And Belgique's next words took her completely off guard. 'I suppose you fucked MacKenzie all weekend?'

'What's that got to do with anything?' Eden asked.

'You'll see,' replied Belgique. 'Anyway,' she continued, 'I'll assume that you did.'

Eden nodded mutely.

'Good. Now listen carefully Eden, I'm not making any of this up. Right?'

Eden nodded once more.

Belgique's calm tone belied the portent of her news as

178

she explained. 'Raton wants to use me as an accessory to cheat the artists in the gallery; and he wants to get you out of the way so that he can run his nasty little scam!' Although her voice was controlled, Belgique's eyes flashed with anger.

For all her friend's extravagant silliness, Eden knew that Belgique's respect for artists, though often of a carnal nature, was genuine.

'While you and MacKenzie were fucking the daylights out of each other during the last two days,' she said with an atypical tartness, 'Raton was here with me for most of Sunday. He wanted to pick up where we left off after lunch at La Splendour, and so we did for a while. He's always been a good lover.' She shifted on the couch, caressing one naked shoulder as if in memory of the man's touch, but continued briskly. 'We'd made love a few times, and were lying in bed, just fondling each other, when out of the blue he made me the most unexpected proposition.' Belgique smiled grimly.

Despite the summer heat, Eden shivered as her friend explained. 'He's cooked up a scheme that will make him a lot of money, and me, too, if I go along with it. Not that I'm going to,' she added quickly in response to Eden's raised eyebrows. 'He wants me to form a bogus company to "buy" work from the gallery at modest prices, which he'll record in the firm's accounts; in reality, the same art would be sold to other unsuspecting private clients "under the table" at much higher prices! That way he'll shortchange the artists on their commission, and he and I would split this extra money. He'd get 75 per cent and I'd take 25.'

Eden felt an angry knot of rage growing inside her, but tried to remain detached. 'Let me see if I understand this right,' she said. 'Say you agree to buy one of Martin Bulgaria's paintings for $2,000. That would be a lot cheaper than normal, but I suppose Raton could convince most artists that there were special circumstances. After

179

all,' she mused ruefully, 'most artists are so pleased to have a sale that they won't quibble too much over the price. With our normal fifty-fifty split between gallery and artist, on paper that would give the gallery $1,000 dollars and the same to the artist.'

'And then,' Belgique took up the tale, 'Raton would sell the same painting to another private client, who knew nothing about my fake purchase, for the full price of $5,000, or higher. After paying the artist $1,000, Raton and I would split the remaining $4,000! His 75 per cent comes out to three grand, so he rakes in an extra $2,000 on the sale over and above what's recorded on the gallery's books.'

Eden realised her mouth had dropped open while her friend was speaking. She snapped it shut, for Belgique continued, 'He skims money off the top, and also reduces his apparent profit and tax liabilities. Meanwhile, I get a $1,000 for doing nothing except lend my name to this fraud. And opening my legs for him,' she added drolly. 'You must admit it has a certain outrageous simplicity!' Belgique smiled wickedly, but there was no humour in her eyes.

But then she proclaimed, 'Eden, Raton has to get rid of you as gallery director, because he knows that you would never have anything to do with such a scheme!'

'But how come he thinks *you* would, Belgique?' queried Eden.

'That's his big error,' replied Belgique. 'Alexander confuses decadence with dishonesty. He can't tell the difference between me bending some of society's morals to suit my own taste, and breaking the law.'

Eden was quiet.

Belgique continued, 'Rather than fire you, which would look suspicious because the gallery is doing so well, I think he wants to engineer your resignation in a way that casts no suspicion on him or his scheme.'

'But why is he doing this?' asked Eden.

'I don't know for sure, but I think it has to do with gambling debts,' responded Belgique. 'I told you I'd seen him in the Platinum Club making big bets. Well, my guess is he's been losing heavily, and he needs the extra cash to feed his habit, or pay off loan sharks.'

'So Raton fed those lies about me to MacKenzie, knowing that MacKenzie would confront me and we'd have a giant row. I'd find out about Raton's lies and then resign in disgust. Is that his plan?'

'Something like that,' Belgique concurred.

'The manipulative bastard!' Eden shook her head. 'Why involve MacKenzie?' she whispered, thinking that now everything could be lost: her man, her job.

'I think that's pretty clear, too, darling Eden,' said Belgique with a sigh. 'Raton's aware of your developing relationship with MacKenzie and he doesn't like it. He doesn't want you getting close to his new artist. So, if he wrecks the relationship, it will make you dislike him even more, and thus more eager to leave.' She paused and added with a sour smirk, 'Raton the Rat.'

'God, Belgique,' Eden said in an awed voice, 'you've got it all worked out, haven't you?'

Belgique nodded her head sorrowfully. 'I'm afraid so, *ma cherie*. But that's not all.' In one swift gesture, Belgique let her blanket fall from both shoulders. As it dropped in a creamy pool, baring her body naked to the waist, Belgique stretched her hand out towards Eden, turning her shoulder so that her upper arm was foremost. She revealed a series of parallel red streaks and purple blotches marking the tender white flesh, and said, 'There is this!' Her voice had changed to a dangerously low growl.

Eden immediately comprehended the cause of the marks. She exclaimed sharply, 'Did Raton do this?'

Belgique nodded.

As she took in the sight of the bruised flesh, Eden

181

imagined Raton's rough grip around the woman's tender arm, and asked, 'Oh, Belgique, how could he?'

'By grabbing my arm!' Belgique replied, demonstrating, 'and by squeezing.' She twisted the white flesh of her other bare upper arm and took her hand away, leaving a row of lighter, red marks, contrasting with her creamy skin. 'He said afterwards that he didn't mean to hurt me. He said he was just carried away with passion. But I know he really enjoyed it. He wanted to hurt me! He's deceptively strong and he frightened me, I admit, so I played along with him.' She paused. 'Eden, what shall we do?'

Eden spread her hands. 'At this point I just don't know. There's so much to think about.' Her mind went on a tangent. 'How could MacKenzie be so dumb to be taken in by all those lies Raton told him?'

'Oh, our Alexander can be wonderfully persuasive when he wants to,' answered Belgique. 'He's been very successful in the gallery business for many years. And just because Michael MacKenzie's a wonderful sculptor doesn't mean he can't be fooled by someone as clever as Raton. But I think you can get him back, Eden, if you play your cards right.'

Belgique looked down at her bared flesh as she spoke, and then with a shrug of remarkable insouciance, she caressed her soft, pretty white breasts, rubbing her nipples amidst the deep cherry pink of her areolas. Dismissing their gloomy conversation, Belgique wrapped the soft cashmere throw around her waist, leaving her torso bare. Brushing aside the unhappy references to Raton and his scheme, she suggested, 'Let us relax now, darling. Perhaps our subconscious minds will tell us what to do.'

Eden wasn't sure this would work; she preferred to take some action. But she had to admit that right this minute she didn't know what that action should be, so she followed the lead of her friend and sank back in the

182

cushions. She wanted to chase after MacKenzie, but she didn't know where he had gone. She wanted to grab Raton by the neck and choke a confession from him, but that didn't seem possible. She watched absently as Belgique summoned Henri to bring long glasses of iced tea, garnished with fresh mint.

'I can see you're preoccupied, Eden, dear,' said Belgique, standing so that her soft blanket slid freely to the floor, revealing her body, completely nude. There was a crash as Henri dropped the now empty tray. 'Stay here and relax as long as you like. I'm just going to take Henri upstairs to discuss his new duties.'

Smirking, Belgique grasped the young butler's arm, leading him stuttering and blushing to the staircase. 'You know where to find us, Eden, if you decide you want some company,' she said over her shoulder. But getting little reaction from her friend, Belgique spoke softly to Henri, and ushered him upstairs to the bedroom.

Left to her own devices, Eden made a decision. She picked up one of the apartment's many phones and called the gallery. Angela answered.

'Is Raton there?' she asked

'No,' said Angela. 'Sorry. There's been no sign of him since he ran out on you at lunchtime. The only person here besides myself is Winston; he's come for his critic's preview of the show, and to write his column for Friday's newspaper. Will you speak to him on the phone? He's got several questions and wants a few quotes.'

The fact that she alternated between lust and despair in her thoughts of MacKenzie did not stop Eden from performing very professionally in her relationship with Fineman. She spoke crisply and concisely about the show and was especially eloquent in her appraisal of the new sculptor's work. She hoped that MacKenzie would read the article; then he would know what she *really* thought of his art.

Fineman spoke from the other end. 'This will be in Friday's art section,' he explained. 'Angela gave me a colour slide of one of MacKenzie's pieces that's a little more reserved than some of the others, so the editor's agreed to run it as a large format illustration. It should make our readers sit up over their cornflakes!'

Despite her black mood, Fineman's words made Eden smile. She heard Fineman make attentive goodbyes to his lover, and then Angela came back on the line speaking hesitantly. 'Eden, I don't want to complicate things even more, but I think I should tell you some gossip that Winston picked up from some other galleries. He told me just before you phoned. He didn't think it was true,' explained Angela sincerely.

Eden braced herself mentally. 'Well, it can't get much worse; what did our esteemed critic hear about me?'

'Some people told him they'd heard that you're having an affair with the boss, and that's why you have such a great office, such great clothes.'

'What?' asked Eden, stunned. 'Raton? Me?' Eden considered her idle fantasies about the man as merely the inconsequential wanderings of a lovelorn mind. She had barely liked him even before this current debacle. The idea that people thought she fucked Raton certainly shook her out of her melancholic reveries. Eden sat bolt upright, her hands gripping the padded arms of Belgique's sofa.

Feeling her cheeks burning, she asked Angela, 'Where did these rumours come from?' But even as she spoke, Eden realised it must be from Alexander Raton himself, dropping hints amongst his gallery cronies. Only he would have any reason to add this slander to his already long list of calumnies! She continued before her assistant could speak, 'Thank you for telling me, Angela. That does it! It's time for me to confront the bastard in person. I bet he's at his villa.'

She hung up and leaning her tall frame back in the

sofa, Eden took a deep breath before punching in Raton's home telephone number. An answering machine came on. Eden left a simple message. 'Mr Raton, I am coming over to ask you some questions. I know you are home. I need to speak to you.'

Raton *was* home, all right, screening his telephone calls and sitting resplendent in the pseudo-baronial grandeur of his leather-bound library. He eagerly awaited the arrival of the lovely Eden, who was, he congratulated himself, acting precisely according to his plan. Women were so predictable, he thought. He anticipated Eden Sinclair's actions with the same surety that told him how to handle Belgique du Pont. He smiled with a movement of his lips that did not touch his eyes, and regarded himself approvingly in the mirror. Specially for the occasion he wore an ostentatious metallic-threaded smoking jacket and he had changed into a pair of heavy silk jacquard lounging pyjamas. He didn't bother with his boxers.

As he smoked a cigar, he listened for the third time to the message his pretty little director had recorded.

'Mr Raton, I am coming ... I know you are home. I need to speak to you.'

As her words spilled over him, Raton studied a book of erotic engravings lying across his lap. Slowly and luxuriously he turned the pages, caressing the fine texture of the handmade paper. He rested his cigar in the ebony ashtray at his elbow when he came to the torture scenes. He liked those the best, and quickly found the one with the image of the young woman who so closely resembled Eden Sinclair.

He felt his erection stirring in his loins beneath the sumptuous silk, and putting aside the book, he reached inside the opening of his trousers and began slowly to masturbate, bringing forth his penis, long and thick, ridged with veins. With his other hand Raton cradled his balls as he lay back in his chair, and closed his eyes.

As he heard his dogs begin to bark, Raton sat up and put his well-primed penis back inside his lounging pajamas. Smoothing the luxurious fabric over his erect and plump member, he realised gleefully that his guest must have arrived.

Eden, too, heard the dogs as she stared up at the gate of Villa Raton, a large house set well back from the road on a five-acre lot in the swanky Roswell neighbourhood. Thoroughly screened from the street by trees and a high brick wall, it was kept secure by a double cast-iron gate set within the wall, which curved to frame a hemispherical forecourt. The entrance was framed between two piers capped with stone and topped by ornamental, though intimidating, dull metal spikes.

She got out of the Miata and approached an entry phone set into one of the brick columns. The sound of her feet crunching on the gravel forecourt was muffled in the hot still air of the summer afternoon.

Eden had visited the Raton estate only once before, for a flamboyant social event filled with shrill female socialites and their vacuous escorts, with many potential and a few real investors. That crowded and superficial experience had not prepared her for this solitary visit, which suddenly seemed fraught with difficulties and even a little danger. She shook her head impatiently. This was going to be awkward enough without her overwrought imagination complicating things further.

As Eden picked up the entry phone, she saw the dogs snuffling and snarling through the bars of the gate. Before she could speak into the mouthpiece, a voice saluted her and a tall man materialised out of the bushes inside the gate.

Although dressed in formal attire, he was clearly a guard. He quieted the dogs. 'Who are you?' he asked, his eyes assessing her as she stood with the instrument in her hand.

'I'm Eden Sinclair. I am here to see Alexander Raton.'

As the man moved closer, she could make out his features. He looked vaguely familiar, and his expression registered recognition at her name. But she couldn't quite place him. Leashing the dogs on an adjacent hook, he reached through and took the phone from her. He spoke crisply but respectfully into it, and she heard Raton's voice, smooth as silk, answering at the other end.

'He seems to be expecting you.' The guard nodded and opened one gate. Closing it behind her, he guided Eden by the arm up the long gravel drive to the house. The extensive landscaped gardens seemed to Eden to need some attention, lacking the pristine rigour evident during her previous visit. She glanced regretfully back at her little sports car, now parked a long way away, and not reachable quickly in the event of a hurried departure. She felt the initiative slipping away from her.

Her escort pushed open the heavy front door set within a deep front porch of giant Ionic columns with smaller Corinthian pilasters flanking the door itself.

Eden and the tall guard paced down the mirrored hallway, her feet making smart, sharp taps on the marble floor, while his rubber-soled dress Rockports made no sound whatsoever. She planned her strategy. She would be serious and firm with Raton, but polite. She would not mess up by jumping the gun and becoming overly emotional. She told herself she would have greater power if she stayed cool and detached.

Most of the doorways they passed were shut, but one was standing slightly open. Eden edged sideways to look in, but felt a firm pressure on her elbow as her companion guided her past, closing the door fully in one swift movement. Eden had the strange impression that the room was totally empty.

They stopped by an open door at the end of the hall,

where the guard announced in a well-modulated tone, 'Mademoiselle Sinclair.' He withdrew unobtrusively.

As she entered the room, Raton stood to greet her. Eden quickly assessed her surroundings, taking in Raton's significant collection of *objets d'art* and vintage photographs in exquisitely gilt frames, all pieces for a proper 'gentleman's study'. The room was filled with dark leather furniture, and many fine leather-bound art books lined two walls in floor-to-ceiling shelves. Only the wild animal heads were missing from the walls of this male emporium, she thought sardonically. But when she looked more closely, there seemed to be several empty spaces, where the lighter colour of the wall fabric betrayed an absence.

As he showed her to her seat, beside a pile of satin cushions in the middle of a spacious sofa, she smelled the usual lavender scent emanating from his skin. His overly attentive manner put Eden more on guard. He hovered at her elbow, smiling or leering, she couldn't determine. 'May I get you a drink?' he asked.

Coolly, she answered, 'Yes, a martini, please.'

Eden had never had a martini in her life.

While he prepared their drinks at an onyx bar folded neatly into a space between two long runs of built-in display cabinets, Eden reviewed her tactics. At this juncture, it was common sense not to reveal her knowledge of his criminal scheme. She would concentrate on the issues of MacKenzie and his show.

Raton put down the silver shaker and returned with her drink in a brilliant ruby-red, long-stemmed crystal glass. Unbeknown to Eden, it was a margarita glass; its size made a very large, very potent martini.

Raton sat upon his majestically proportioned mahogany and leather armchair. He looked across at her and asked, 'Well, my dear, what brings you to Villa Raton?'

She balanced the large martini, and responded boldly,

'I have a question about gallery policy and my role in decision-making.'

Raton made a pretence of looking disappointed. 'Oh, Miss Sinclair, is this a business visit?'

'Of course, I told you on the telephone!' Eden felt her anger rising, and cooled herself by avidly sipping the refreshingly cold drink. She was aware of his eyes following the flesh of her throat down to the low-cut neckline of her stylish blouse. She tried another tactic, 'About Michael MacKenzie . . .'

'Oh dear, you haven't had a spat have you, Miss Sinclair? A lovers' quarrel?' Raton knew he could rile his director with his tone of mocking superiority. He continued, 'It's quite apparent that the two of you have been . . . how shall I say . . .?'

Eden hated his condescending leer and, as she felt the first surge of alcohol hit her bloodstream, she challenged him by completing his thought. 'Fucking?' she suggested bluntly.

'Why, yes,' he asserted, apparently unruffled. He peered at her over the rim of his glass. 'I thought you had a strict policy not to go to bed with our artists,' he added sardonically, mocking her breach of self-imposed ethics.

Before she could guard her tongue, she blurted, 'That's odd, since everyone thinks I'm fucking you!'

But now Raton only raised an eyebrow and commented, 'Goodness, my dear, I'm flattered.'

She turned a deeper crimson. 'It was you who started that rumour!' she accused. She could feel herself getting ready to cross that line where her emotions took control. She took a large sip of her drink.

'Dear Eden,' Raton said archly, 'Don't be angry.'

Eden schooled herself to remain silent.

'And if everyone *thinks* we are fucking, then we may as well be!' Raton's eyes held hers and he winked, his eyelid drooping in a gesture of infinite decadence as his eyes then slid purposefully sideways towards the open door of his adjacent bedroom.

She was aghast. Trying to regain her equilibrium, Eden plunged ahead and abruptly changed the subject. 'Why did you make the decision to bring Michael MacKenzie on board without asking for my input?'

Avoiding a real answer, he chided, 'But, my dear, I knew you would love his work!'

'But Mr Raton!'

'Call me Alexander, my dear. It was a mere oversight . . .'

With her anger barely under control, Eden asked, 'Am I to understand that you consider your promise to MacKenzie of a one-man show without even discussing it with me to be "a mere oversight"?'

Still skirting the issue, Raton taunted, 'But isn't it salient that my choice of bringing in Michael was a brilliant move? I'm sure you appreciate that signing on someone of his abilities, and someone with his speciality in terms of subject matter, was all part of my plan for the future development of the gallery! My gallery, I would remind you.'

Eden realised their argument was like a chess game to Raton, and that she was being led blindfolded through the opening gambits. She quite agreed that MacKenzie was a damn good artist, but she wasn't about to admit that to Raton in this venue. Instead she pressed her point again. 'As your artistic director I should have been in on that decision, Mr Raton, and all the others that follow from it.'

But Raton proceeded to downplay the whole episode, addressing Eden with the full force of his unctuous charm. 'My dear Eden, this is all no more than a little misunderstanding; you know as well as I that schedules can be flexible. I had to lure Michael here before one of our competitors found him. Couldn't you have been a little more flexible in your attitude and your dealing with him?'

My God, thought Eden, he was trying to blame her for the whole sorry shambles! Despite her resolution to the contrary, she felt her anger rise, and said with intensity, 'I didn't have any chance to "be flexible", as you put it. You'd filled MacKenzie's head with so many lies about me that he couldn't think straight.' With a shock, Eden realised that she was defending her recently departed lover.

Her employer only smiled at her, teasingly, 'You are so beautiful when you are angry!'

'I can't believe the sexist crap that's coming out of your mouth!' Eden exclaimed, but Raton persisted, overriding her protestations.

'The way your eyes sparkle when you fight me is most exciting.' His voice dropped to a carnally charged whisper.

When she held up a hand to silence him, he stood and walked over to her. She heard the rustle of his silk pyjamas as he gracefully dipped on one knee at her feet. Astonished, Eden tried to pull her hand free when he grabbed it. He kissed the fingers, his grip like a vice. She remembered the marks on Belgique's arms.

As his eyes rested for a moment on her breasts, Raton murmured, 'My dear, we should get to know each other better, then we wouldn't have these little disagreements. They are so unpleasant!'

Eden found herself fleetingly caught in the power of his disarming but sinister smile. Her senses registered alarm, but her body was slow to respond.

From his supplicating position before her, Raton continued, 'You understand Michael's importance to the gallery. You and I could come to understand each other very well indeed. That shouldn't be too hard, now, should it?' He stroked the flesh of her forearm with his long fingers.

Snapping free from his spell before she was awash in

191

Raton's brew of seduction, alcohol and flattery, Eden put down her glass and broke from his grasp. She pushed him away and stood up, announcing with more firmness than she felt, 'I'm leaving!'

He jumped up and startled her by protesting, 'No, you're not!'

She turned away, her heart pounding.

'Don't play the innocent with me, my sweet,' Raton said to her back. Something in his voice made her stop. 'Turn around, Eden,' he said, putting his hands on her shoulders.

She started at his touch and then whipped angrily around to face him, and opened her mouth to speak. His lustful gaze stopped her.

His eyes were locked on her breasts, and he purred, 'Your nipples reveal your . . . state of arousal.' Maddeningly, he touched her, rubbing the fingers of his left hand against her right nipple as it pressed through the fabric of her blouse and delicate bra. The treacherous nipple stood erect.

Eden fired a hard slap at his face but he grabbed her wrist and with surprising strength held her arm aside as he bent forward to kiss her. He grasped her waistline tightly and moved his strong hands up the sides of her torso, towards her breasts.

Summoning her strength, she struggled from his grasp. She felt sordid, and shuddered more strongly as she looked down at what Raton's hands were doing. He had unleashed his penis. Long and blue-veined, it bobbed as he caressed it.

Adrenalin coursed through her at the sight of his rampantly ready-for-action member. Anger blazed in her eyes as she said, 'Is this another of your "little misunderstandings", Mr Raton?'

She moved quickly then, as he stood in his doorway gazing at her, masturbating his large, moistening dick. Eden turned on her heel, grabbed her purse and ran from the room, hurrying through the hallway. She heard Raton's voice through the open door behind her, calm as though nothing dramatic had transpired.

'Marcus!' he called to the butler-cum-guard. 'Miss Sinclair is just leaving. Please escort her to her car.'

Eden heard the soft click as the door closed. She did not see Raton's smile of satisfaction, nor hear his voice as he murmured, 'Perfect!' With his eyes closed, his hand still around his cock, he chuckled. 'Goodbye, my little Eden. Now off you go to see Belgique.' His warm semen flowed copiously over his fingers and dripped on to his fine imported Axminster carpet.

Eden didn't wait for Marcus. She sprinted down the passage, her skin burning like fire from Raton's touch. Near the main entrance the manservant materialised before her, stepping from some hidden station. He followed her through the grand entrance portico, and into the oppressive summer heat of the late afternoon, escorting her to the front gate.

Eden's skin was gleaming with a thin film of sweat in the harsh afternoon heat before she was halfway along the drive. She hurried to the driver's side and unlocked the door. As Marcus held the door for her, recognition flashed through Eden's mind; this security guard was once a member of Belgique's battalion of butlers. She said, 'You know me; we met at my friend Belgique du Pont's . . .'

'Sure I know you, Ms Sinclair,' acknowledged the man.

Eden seized her opportunity. 'What's with the empty room and the missing pictures on the walls in there?' she enquired with as much casualness as she could muster. 'Has your boss been having a sale recently? I would have liked to have had the opportunity to purchase some things.' She lied convincingly. 'Do you know where they went?'

'I was not consulted, Madam,' he replied. 'All I know

is that we've shipped away a lot of items, furniture, paintings and the like; some of the rooms are closed up now and off-limits to guests. A large truck collected it all about three weeks ago. Where it went I couldn't say.' He offered a minuscule bow. 'Have a nice evening, Ms Sinclair.'

As she roared around the forecourt and on to the public street, Eden cranked the air-conditioning up full. With a burst of acceleration, she propelled the car towards Belgique's apartment. They had things to discuss. The vestiges of a plan were forming in her mind.

Chapter Sixteen
Savannah Sojourn

Michael MacKenzie swung the rental car down the exit ramp from Interstate 16 and on to the forlorn streetscape of Martin Luther King Boulevard, a less than triumphal entry into the city of Savannah, Georgia, his home for the last eighteen months.

But the sculptor was in no mood for aesthetic reflection. The four-and-a-half hour drive from Atlanta across the coastal low country could be boring at the best of times, and today the charmless outskirts of his adopted environment made him homesick for the Scottish borders of his youth. MacKenzie recognised the symptoms of his depression: since stomping out of Galerie Raton that lunchtime, he had found precious little to like about America.

Despite his gloomy mood of introspection, MacKenzie acknowledged, on the positive side, the sexual lustiness of the American women with whom he had shared an intimate acquaintance. Although he had been to bed with several, only one relationship apart from Eden Sinclair had been significant, and that had involved Stephanie Pope, right here in Savannah.

But Eden Sinclair topped the lot in the lust department,

he thought. He had never experienced a lover so exciting and bawdy and tender and tireless, all in just a couple of days! Images of Eden's body arching above his, riding him, as he buried himself deeply inside her, were followed by a multitude of other, fleeting memories of the best sex he had ever had. He saw Eden's chestnut hair flinging around her head with the wild energy of her movements; he remembered how she shuddered when she came, and how she tasted as he lapped her abundant juices, his tongue feasting on her hard little bud. His penis stirred between his thighs, enhancing his recollections.

Just how on earth could he have been so wrong about her, he wondered. He had been so thrilled at being approached by Galerie Raton, certainly one of the most prestigious commercial galleries in the southern states. He recalled his excitement at the promise of his first solo show in the USA; a promise that now lay in tatters, he reminded himself grimly, because of the selfish ambition of this very same Eden Sinclair. He shook his head in renewed disbelief.

MacKenzie pulled away from a traffic light as it turned green and realised he had been driving for several blocks with no destination in mind. On the spur of the moment he turned south on Bull Street, away from the river, and drew to a stop in front of Ye Olde Florin, one of his regular haunts.

As he entered the cozy pub, the barman recognised him. 'Hi, Mike. How are you doing? Long time no see. Been out of town? Your usual?'

MacKenzie nodded. 'I've been over in Atlanta,' he replied, but didn't elaborate. He picked up the pint of MacEwans the bartender placed on the cocktail napkin in front of him, and carried it over to one of the tables. At nearly five o'clock, the place was beginning to fill up with tourists, and he tucked himself away in a small booth near the window.

Sipping his beer, he reflected that this brew was the only reason he kept coming back to this bar. Otherwise its Olde English pretensions irritated him, especially today. He pulled the bar menu towards him. It proudly announced that bangers and mash were the speciality of the day. He tossed it aside in disgust and ordered another pint from the sexy waitress, an older woman who always flirted with him. He thought it must be his accent, as she was always asking him, 'Say something Scottish,' or 'I love to hear you talk.'

'Oh,' she said eagerly, seeing him sitting there, 'I missed you, Michael,' and smiled seductively as she neared his table. Wearing her usual low-cut blouse, Connie – he didn't know her last name – really got into the role of barmaid. 'Is there anything else I can do for you, Michael?' she asked, suggestively, and only half in fun.

'No thanks, bonnie lass,' he replied, trying without much enthusiasm to stay in character. He didn't think he had ever called anybody 'bonnie lass'.

His lack of interest communicated itself to Connie, who shrugged disappointedly, and said, 'Oh, Michael, you don't know what you're missing!' She blew him a kiss, and turned to attend to other customers.

The cold beer, the flirtatious attentions of Connie and the mindless chatter of tourists relaxed MacKenzie after his high-speed drive from Atlanta. He could feel the tension in his neck muscles ease, and began to replay the lunchtime scene in his mind, trying to put it in perspective.

MacKenzie recognised that his anger had been caused by his feelings being hurt and his pride severely dented. He winced with the memory of his outburst, and his sense of betrayal when he had realised that this beautiful new woman in his life had been coldly shafting him professionally while tempestuously fucking him for real in her bed.

Raton had laid out a catalogue of complaints against Eden Sinclair, one by one. MacKenzie remembered just how upset the gallery owner had seemed by his director's duplicity. But if she was that bad, he asked himself, why didn't Raton just fire her?

As he looked back more dispassionately at his abrupt departure, MacKenzie had to admit that he had given Eden Sinclair no chance to explain or even to deny the allegations he had thrown at her, just minutes after hearing them from her boss. All he had done was yell at the woman, the very same person he had just spent two delirious days in bed with! In one corner of his mind, MacKenzie wished he hadn't been so abrupt, that he'd approached the matter differently, and the more he thought about it, the more odd it seemed that Raton had departed so precipitously just before Eden returned from her site visit, leaving him to boil over right on cue. He had the obscure feeling that he had been cleverly manipulated, but to what end he didn't know. He *did* know that he hadn't behaved very maturely. MacKenzie felt a wave of embarrassment and regret wash over him.

But on that hot and sultry summer afternoon MacKenzie's anger had not cooled down completely. He had stormed back to Savannah without a plan of any sort and now, as he left the fake British pub and stood in the street outside, he found himself momentarily at a loss. In his residual bad mood, he didn't want to go back to his little apartment just yet; he couldn't face being in his studio and he certainly wanted to avoid seeing anybody to whom he might have to explain the outcome of his trip to Atlanta. Although the sun hovered lower now in the hazy sky, like a smudgy yellow thumbprint, its heat seemed undiminished. The rivulets of sweat trickling down his torso didn't improve his temper.

Checking the time left on the parking meter, MacKenzie wandered into the adjacent Chippewa Square where the widespread branches of the overhanging live oak trees, festooned with pendant garlands of Spanish moss, screened the lawns and benches of the small park from the heat. In the welcome shade he felt his spirits revive a little. The squares were MacKenzie's favourite places in Savannah; twenty-one of them were laid out like a chequerboard grid in the original historic district, each with a park at its centre. The restored squares were lined with churches, banks and great houses, and connected by streets and alleys of elegant town homes and carriage houses.

Most of the main houses sported large verandas and side porches, built in the days before air-conditioning, and traditionally all the front doors were at first-floor level, reached by a steep stair leading up to a colonnaded entrance portico. These covered entrances in turn were shaded by rows of giant live oaks, grand trees that looked deciduous, yet didn't shed their leaves in the winter. Earlier generations of inhabitants had planted them religiously in rows along all the streets and many had survived, a gracious legacy from the last century.

MacKenzie sat on a shaded bench at the feet of a bronze statue of colonist James Oglethorpe, the English Parliamentarian who had founded the city in 1733. He replayed a history lesson he had learnt from his old girlfriend, Stephanie. She had explained Savannah's rich history to him, taking delight in showing off her native city to her new foreign lover. He thought of her now, and how pleasant their relationship had been; the trouble was it just never seemed to go anywhere. But he had had no complaints about the great sex, he thought ruefully; she had taught him a whole new suite of love games.

MacKenzie accepted that his reluctance to go back to his apartment was bred of a sense of failure. He had hoped that his one-man show at Galerie Raton would be his ticket out of this charming southern backwater, and having to return empty-handed to his modest abode seemed heavily symbolic of his lack of success. And, he told himself angrily, he had thrown away that chance for good. If only it had been just some misunderstanding about the plans for his show; if only he had heard Eden's side of the argument with Raton before departing in high dudgeon. Perhaps the gallery owner had not been completely honest in his recitation of Eden's flaws and failings; perhaps, he thought, she really did like his work after all and did want to exhibit it. But his ill-mannered rage had surely wrecked any possibility of resurrecting the deal. MacKenzie felt very sorry for himself.

As the evening dusk closed in, he rose slowly from his bench and stretched. He had been sitting there for well over an hour, retracing his steps in the same maze of regrets that he had built steadily since the late afternoon. As he walked slowly away, MacKenzie saw a homeless person, whether man or woman he couldn't tell, dash from the trees and claim the slatted wooden seat. He or she had obviously been awaiting his departure. The gnawing poverty of this nameless figure brought MacKenzie to the sobering realisation that at least he had a home to go to. But perhaps just a couple of drinks before going home would ease his gloom. Just a couple, and then he would head back to his apartment. If he walked down to the bars by the river, he convinced himself, then he wouldn't be too far from his flat in a small coach house off Washington Square.

He strolled down Bull Street towards the gold dome of the city hall, and behind that the bars and restaurants that lined the old wharves of the Savannah River, reinhabiting the dignified old cotton warehouses with the froth of contemporary urban nightlife. The tree frogs and cicadas croaked their noisy symphony. The summer nights were never quiet in the south and nature's chorus accompanied him all the way to the Ragin' Cajun down on the waterfront, the most boisterous of Savannah's many drinking establishments.

* * *

MacKenzie woke up the next morning with a feeling of disorientation that persisted for several moments. The numb buzzing in his head didn't help as he slowly pieced together fragments of his inglorious evening.

The drink or two had extended into several, he recalled bitterly, as he had given in to the masochistic pleasure of self-pity. He dimly recalled making an embarrassing pass at one of the waitresses in a bar, and being dismissively rebuffed for his pains. He found he didn't remember much about walking home, but home was definitely where he was, lying half-undressed on his bed. He still wore his T-shirt and white socks, but found himself naked from the waist down. His hand strayed between his thighs and he played softly with himself, stroking his penis slowly to its stiff fullness.

He pictured Eden Sinclair kneeling over him, her tongue nuzzling his dick, her hands cupping his balls. He moved his other hand to fondle his testicles, and increased the manual tempo on his shaft. He imagined Eden's hands gripping his now fully erect cock, and closed his eyes to play the scene from memory. He felt his semen rising, and made no attempt to slow his orgasm. He watched his come shoot from the head of his cock, falling back to mottle his stomach, while the last flow oozed down over his fingers. He shuddered with the physical release of his emotion and frustration.

He showered and shaved himself to a semblance of alertness, and walked naked to the window of his small one-bedroom apartment overlooking the alley. The window sill came only to his knees, and any passer-by who happened to look up would have been surprised to see a tall, naked redheaded man framed unselfconsciously in full frontal view, his flaccid but lengthy penis hanging comfortably with his plump balls below their nest of ginger curls, and its large purple tip just brushing the glass of the window pane. But few tourists came down this alley, so far off the beaten paths highlighted on the official tour maps.

This morning was no exception: the alley was empty. Standing in his window, his hand once more on his stiffening rod, MacKenzie noted his black Chevy pick-up parked next to the dumpster. Something tickled his memory and he remembered with a shock the rental car still waiting patiently outside Ye Olde Florin.

'Damn!' he swore, and hurriedly pulled on his sweat-suit trousers without bothering with underwear, grabbed a shirt and a pair of Reeboks, and remembering his keys just in time, dashed out of the building. He ran fast, trying to remember what time of the morning the traffic cops started giving out tickets. Cutting in a zig-zag pattern through the city grid, MacKenzie jogged past the old Colonial Park cemetery and turned west to reach Chippewa Square. He saw the rental car still there, 50 yards down on Bull Street, and still mercifully without a dreaded cadmium yellow envelope stuck under its windscreen wipers.

Breathing a sigh of relief, he slowed his pace, feeling his chest heave with his exertions. The rising summer heat with its cloying humidity even at the start of the day was MacKenzie's least favourite attribute of the American South. He stood by his rental car, sweat-streaked and panting, and scanned the thin ranks of early bird tourists as they glanced from guide book to building and back again, checking off the items on their historical perambulations. He fumbled momentarily with the unfamiliar key and then slid behind the wheel, starting the engine and turning up the air-conditioning to high. A welcome rush of ice-cold air blew across his face.

MacKenzie drove slowly back to his apartment, wondering what he was going to do with his day. A second shower was the first item of business, and then breakfast. He'd have to eat out, as there was nothing in his refrigerator save a six pack of second-rate beer and a half gallon of week-old milk.

He parked behind his pick-up, ran upstairs to his flat and returned refreshed within ten minutes. The physical exercise had certainly woken him up, and made him hungry. He fancied breakfast at Martha's, a favourite morning meeting place for locals on the corner of Abercorn and Jones Streets. He felt he could even face seeing friends and acquaintances today, although he wasn't sure what he'd tell them about Atlanta if they asked.

A breakfast of French toast and maple syrup put back the calories he had so recently sweated off. As he did most mornings, MacKenzie fished two quarters from his pocket and dropped them in the slot of the newspaper box that held the *Atlanta Democrat*. He opened the door, extracted the last copy and proceeded to read it thoroughly over his coffee. Warming again to his adopted home, MacKenzie enjoyed the endless refills of his mug.

Slowly his mind was coming to grips with useful tasks for the day. There was always work to be done in the studio, and he really should look in at the art college to check his mail. He might even see if the new fitting he had ordered for the small college furnace had arrived. MacKenzie knew he was lucky to have access to good-quality casting equipment in the sculpture department at the Savannah College of Art and Design, known locally as SCAD. But he was constantly frustrated by the limitations of scale placed on his work by the equipment.

There was little in the paper today to hold his attention, and he left it behind on the table with a $5 bill for the food. First of all, he decided, he would get rid of his rental car. The directory in the glove box located the Savannah Hertz depot close by the new suspension bridge that soared like a bird across the river in a single span.

This task accomplished, MacKenzie found himself a

pedestrian once more, but it was only a short walk to the sculpture studios, housed in the old railway sheds off Martin Luther King Boulevard. Back in his familiar setting, he automatically set to work cleaning and tidying, a ritual of his before starting new work. This was a good sign, the first indication that he could put this most recent trauma behind him.

He worked solidly in happy solitude for several hours, stopping only for a mid-afternoon snack. The spring term was over some weeks before, and MacKenzie had the place largely to himself. The comforting ceremonies of preparation eased his mind, and he found he could think again about Eden with less hurt and embarrassment. But, he reminded himself, Eden Sinclair was not likely to welcome him with open arms . . . or open legs.

After the temperature had fallen slightly in the early evening, MacKenzie walked back across town to his apartment, mingling with the last of the day's tourists. He deliberately avoided his favourite bars, and instead started his truck and drove to the grocery store, where he stocked up with a few basics. He drove back through the gathering dusk, eager to get home. He unpacked the groceries, turned on his window air-conditioner, and made a light supper of linguine and red pesto sauce.

Later, after loading his compact dishwasher and setting the dial to economy wash, he lay down on his bed and shuffled the CDs loaded into his CD player with his remote control. He stripped naked and relaxed on his pillows as the sounds of Enya's 'The Memory of Trees' washed over him. He absently fondled himself without bringing himself to climax. The last thing he remembered was just how wonderful it had felt when Eden Sinclair took his penis in her mouth.

Chapter Seventeen

Epiphany

*T*he next morning found MacKenzie back in his Savannah studio, bright and early. None of his half-finished work around the studio interested him; he was anxious to start something new. He began some preparatory sketches of a group of female figures; the classical trio *The Three Graces*, came to mind, or possibly, he thought, *The Judgement of Paris*, rendered in a contemporary setting.

MacKenzie consulted his art history books to make sure he got it right. The goddesses Hera, Aphrodite and Athena each claimed the prize of a golden apple destined for the fairest of women, and Zeus, anxious not to have to choose, delegated the task to a hapless shepherd, Paris, tending his flocks on the earthly slopes below. The handsome young man, unable to escape his fate, chose Aphrodite who then spirited him away to mainland Greece for his own protection from the anger of the two rejected rivals. MacKenzie grinned wryly as he read on. Once at the court of King Menelaus, Paris fell in love with Helen, the King's wife, and the two lovers eloped to Troy, thus precipitating the disastrous Trojan Wars.

Most classical renditions of the theme portrayed Paris,

often nude, lying on the ground admiring the three beautiful women, all similarly unclothed, displaying for him their bodily charms. Using the photocopier, Mac-Kenzie made reproductions of several versions of the event and pinned them to his easel. Taking his pad and a variety of drawing implements, he began a series of studies, reinterpreting the myth. He found himself concentrating on the figure of Aphrodite, truly the fairest of them all, her naked form radiating a sensual energy that overpowered her rivals. As he sketched in some details of the goddess's face, he called to mind Eden Sinclair, the way her hair moved in the light, and the way her eyes shone with lust and sparkled with intelligence.

He enjoyed the rush of sexual pleasure he felt at committing his recent lover to paper. If Eden were to be Aphrodite, he wondered, who would play the roles of the other two women? At that moment the shrill summons of the telephone broke his concentration; he wondered whether to ignore it, but gave in and picked up the receiver. 'Yes. Hello?'

A woman's voice answered. 'Hello Michael?' There was a slight pause. 'This is Stephanie.'

MacKenzie held the phone from his ear, momentarily nonplussed.

'Hello Michael. Are you there?'

'Yes, I'm here,' he replied, trying to keep the shock from his voice. 'How did you know I would be?'

'I saw you in the grocery store last night. I would have spoken to you then, but I was too shy. I was afraid you might not want to speak. This morning I summoned up courage and called your apartment, but got only your answering machine. So I thought you'd be in the studio. It's where you always were.'

If MacKenzie noted a tinge of regret or reproach in his ex-lover's voice, he chose to ignore it. He only said, 'It's good to hear you Steph. Have you been keeping well?'

'Well enough; but I miss you. That's why I called. Can I see you? Do you have plans for lunch today?'

MacKenzie hesitated, unsure of what he wanted. Then, 'OK,' he said, making up his mind. After all, what harm could lunch do? 'Do you want to go to the old place?'

Stephanie's pleasure and relief were evident in her voice at the other end. 'That would be nice. How about one o'clock?'

MacKenzie looked at his watch; just over an hour. He studied his drawing. 'That's fine,' he said. 'See you there.'

When MacKenzie walked into La Scala, a charming little Italian restaurant in an old storefront on Broughton Street, Stephanie was already there. He thought she looked as lovely as ever, five-four, slim, with high pert breasts and well-tanned skin. She wore a conservative business suit that looked good on her trim figure, with a white blouse and flat pumps to complete the office ensemble. The only non-corporate item was a pair of large silver earrings in the form of architectural columns that hung suspended from her ear lobes. Her natural blonde hair, now cut shorter in a retro pageboy, shone with its usual lustre. MacKenzie remembered fondly its scent and texture. She wore a shy smile as he approached the table against the back wall of the restaurant, beneath a large abstract painting that he now recognised as the work of Martin Bulgaria.

She stood up, and reached out to hold him in a light, non-committal embrace. He kissed her lightly on the cheek. 'You look good,' he said with genuine approval in his voice.

Stephanie smiled, obviously pleased at the compliment. 'So do you, Michael; it's been a long time.' Her eyes sought his.

MacKenzie broke the lingering glance by responding to the waiter who materialised at his elbow and deferred to Stephanie, who chose the Caesar salad; he ordered angel hair pasta and garlic shrimp.

'Wine, sir? Madam?' enquired their waiter. MacKenzie raised an eyebrow across the table.

Stephanie nodded. 'Why not? A glass of Chianti, please.'

'The same for me. And we'll share a bottle of San Pellegrino mineral water.' The waiter nodded at MacKenzie's order and hurried away. A silence descended over their small table.

'This is a surprise.' It was MacKenzie who spoke first. 'But a pleasant one.'

'It was a surprise to see you in the grocery store. I heard you'd gone to Atlanta; something about a big show there.' Stephanie paused enquiringly and studied the man seated opposite her. She admired his tall figure and the handsome face ruffled with curly red hair.

'Yes, I took some sculptures over there for a group show; it opens tomorrow.' MacKenzie realised with a shock that he wanted to be at the opening reception.

'Oh, are you going back?' Stephanie's face registered some disappointment.

'I don't know; maybe. I'm not sure. I'm working on some new stuff.' MacKenzie silently scolded himself for his feeble prevarication. He knew full well the real reason he wasn't sure about going was because he was the shy one; he just wasn't sure how to approach Eden again.

Stephanie didn't press the question, and their meal proceeded in a growing ease of companionship. When Stephanie extended her leg beneath the table to brush MacKenzie's calf, he didn't object or move away. And when her shoeless toes climbed a little higher and explored his thigh, he slumped fractionally to bring his groin within range. Stephanie noted the unspoken invitation and gently pressed her foot between his legs. MacKenzie felt his penis harden, and felt from Stephanie's acknowledging pressure that she had sensed it, too. He looked into her sharp grey eyes, seeing there a sparkle of humour and a deliberate invitation.

'I'm free for the rest of the day, Michael,' she said, with simple directness. 'I'd really like to take you to bed. I'm wet just sitting here thinking about it!'

MacKenzie hesitated only fractionally. This was certainly the same old Stephanie, he thought. Was this being unfaithful to Eden? It hardly seemed to qualify, as Eden Sinclair surely felt no claim on him now. 'I'd like that, too,' he replied.

They halved the bill, and leaving the money on the table, hurried outside into the afternoon heat. 'My car's just one block down,' said Stephanie. 'Where's yours?'

'I walked.'

'Let's take mine then; I'll drive.'

Stephanie drove crisply the short distance to her apartment carved out of one of the big mansions overlooking Pulaski Square. She needed only one hand to manoeuvre her sprightly little Honda Civic through the summer traffic; her other hand strayed to MacKenzie's lap, feeling the stiffening outline of his penis through his jeans.

As he followed Stephanie up the beautifully restored staircase to the chic little apartment he remembered so well, MacKenzie ran his fingers over the sensual curve of the wooden handrail. An electric thrill vibrated through him, and his lust brimmed over as he followed this once familiar path to his ex-lover's bed. Watching her lithe body move ahead of him, he felt his dick stretch even tighter against the fabric of his jeans with an urgent erection.

At the top landing, Stephanie searched for her key and slid it into the lock; within seconds they were inside her apartment, laughing and holding each other tight. They undressed quickly and stood naked together in Stephanie's bedroom, on the second floor overlooking the square. MacKenzie enjoyed the familiar setting. There was Stephanie's frameless futon floating on its recessed base and standing against the same pale green walls with dark green window frames and matching wooden Venetian blinds, which today screened the bright sunlight into diagonal stripes. The surfaces and objects and prolific plants in the room were all reflected in the highly polished floorboards, creating the impression of a bottomless and verdant cave. A large brown bear reclined on the woman's bed wearing a faded Scottish tartan bow, with tartan paws to match. 'I see you've still got Angus,' MacKenzie said, with a smile.

'I nearly threw him away when you left,' admitted Stephanie. 'But he's so cute I couldn't do it. Michael,' she added after a slight pause, 'stay here tonight.'

MacKenzie strolled to the window and absorbed the view of lush live oaks and wispy Spanish moss. He turned to face the naked woman who had so eagerly thrust her way back into his life. He tried to read the complex of emotions evident on her face, but couldn't interpret them with any certainty. 'That would be nice, Steph,' he said carefully. 'But just for tonight. Let's see how we feel in the morning before we make any more plans.'

If Stephanie was disappointed with his conditional acceptance, she didn't show it. She joined him at the window and stroked his back and shoulders, raking her nails gently across his skin and leaning her head against his shoulder. MacKenzie felt his flesh respond with shivers of goose bumps across his limbs and torso. He let his lover guide him to her bed, and there they wrapped themselves in each other's arms. Stephanie's eagerness for him seemed undiminished, and her hands and fingers were nimble and dexterous as they caressed MacKenzie's manhood to its statuesque pride.

He parted her labia with his finger, feeling her juices already flowing, and found her hard little bud with his thumb. Stephanie moaned softly as he rubbed her gently, all the while moving his fingers deep inside her passage.

She climbed over him and guided his cock into her. 'Fuck me, Michael. Fuck me! It's been so long,' breathed Stephanie, rearing back to match his thrusts. She gripped MacKenzie's dick with her vaginal muscles and heard him moan in response. He reached for her breasts, and she moved her own hand to her clitoris, rubbing herself in impatient ecstasy.

Even as he came, spewing his sperm in a torrent and feeling Stephanie shudder and scream as she climaxed in accompaniment, MacKenzie's vision behind his tightly shut eyelids was of Eden's face and body. He felt a confused sense of betrayal to both women, but as he lay quietly with Stephanie in the post-coital ease of established lovers, he thought only about Eden, and how she talked to him about art in a way Stephanie would never achieve.

His peaceful body enabled his troubled mind to recall with perfect clarity the first time he had set eyes upon Eden Sinclair. Even then, he realised with hindsight, he had felt something more than lust. Why then, he asked himself, was he lying here, beside this pretty woman, when the one he couldn't shake from his mind was alone in Atlanta? But was she alone, wondered MacKenzie, suddenly rigid with the thought that perhaps Eden Sinclair was this very moment locked in the arms of an alternative lover.

His reverie was interrupted by the telephone by the bed. Stephanie quickly reached across MacKenzie to pick up the phone, her nipples grazing his chest.

'Hello? Oh, hi.' Stephanie's voice faltered slightly. 'No, hold on.' With her hand over the mouthpiece of the phone, Stephanie climbed over MacKenzie and walked next door into the living room, trailing the long extension cord behind her.

Out of politeness MacKenzie tried not to listen, but he

could not avoid hearing a note of urgency in Stephanie's voice, speaking low. Moments later his lover returned, and with a smile on her face, bent to kiss MacKenzie as she climbed into bed beside him.

His eyebrows raised. 'Everything OK?'

'Sure. That was just someone from the office with a silly problem that couldn't wait.' Stephanie's reply was muffled as she curled herself on MacKenzie's thighs, her lips nuzzling the ginger curls around his dick. He couldn't see her face.

They fell asleep in the warmth of the summer evening, naked atop Stephanie's downy futon, but MacKenzie woke several times, always from dreams of Eden, talking to him, touching him, loving him.

Over their early breakfast the next morning an awkward silence descended. Stephanie was already dressed for work in a light summer suit of navy cotton, with a short-sleeved white blouse reminiscent of Laura Ashley. MacKenzie sat in his rumpled clothes from the day before, just drinking coffee. He didn't feel hungry.

'When do you have to leave?' he asked, to break the silence.

'In ten minutes; it only takes an hour and a half to get to Charleston if I take I-95 and cut across on Highway 17. I'd rather go through Beaufort, it's so pretty, but it takes longer.' Stephanie paused in her unnecessarily detailed travelogue. 'Michael, I was . . .'

A pounding on the front door interrupted her. With a startled look, she put down her coffee and walked through the adjoining rooms to the entrance hall, her heels clicking on the polished wood floors. MacKenzie heard her startled exclamation. 'Dwayne!'

Male footfalls approached the kitchen, followed by Stephanie's urgently pattering steps. A worried face beneath a fringe of neatly trimmed brown hair peered round the door. 'Who the hell are you?' asked the face.

The head withdrew and angrily addressed Stephanie, still in the next room. 'Who is he? Why is he here?'

MacKenzie stood up and walked into the living room. He held out his hand. The visitor, who he now saw to be a good-looking young man in his late twenties, dressed like a lawyer in smart suit and conservative tie, ignored it, his normally handsome face marred by a scowl.

Undaunted MacKenzie introduced himself. 'Hello Dwayne. I'm Michael, an old friend of Stephanie's.'

A look of recognition at the name passed over Dwayne's face, to be followed by a mixture of relief and then more worry. He glanced at Stephanie. 'Did you ... Are you ...?' He stuttered to an inarticulate stop, looking between them in evident confusion. 'When I called last night from the road, I thought ...' His speech trailed off again, his colour rising.

If this guy was a lawyer, MacKenzie hoped his courtroom manner was better than this! He took pity upon the newcomer, evidently Stephanie's current boyfriend, and said, 'It's nice to meet you Dwayne, but I can't stop; I was just leaving. I've been out of town for a while and I just dropped by to see Steph; for old times' sake, you might say. She was kind enough to give me breakfast.' He turned to Stephanie, who wouldn't meet his eye. 'Cheerio, Steph. Thanks for the coffee.' He gave her a kiss on the cheek. 'I'll see myself out. I'm sure you want to talk with Dwayne.' With a friendly nod to a blushing Stephanie and her confused boyfriend, MacKenzie walked to the door and down the stairs to the street.

Standing in the square he liked so much, he felt suddenly, breathlessly free. With a spring in his step, he walked the three blocks to Martha's restaurant to buy an Atlanta newspaper and a second breakfast. The newspaper held welcome news.

When MacKenzie picked up the *Atlanta Democrat* to read over his meal, he eagerly sought out the Friday arts section, extricating it from a plethora of ads and sports and local news. In the midst of his country ham omelette and hash browns, his eyes fell upon a half-page, full-colour spread of one of his sculptures. He gasped out loud, turning heads on nearby tables. He smiled back reassuringly, blushing in embarrassment. As he read Fineman's glowing review and Eden's very complimentary quotes about his work, MacKenzie experienced a whirlwind of emotions. He put the paper down and took a deep breath. He started reading again from the beginning.

Eden Sinclair's new group show, 'The Art of Love', opening tonight at Galerie Raton is a masterpiece of curatorial skill, read MacKenzie. *Currently Atlanta's most successful gallery director, Ms Sinclair cleverly blends the work of several artists to express the theme of love and specifically the role of sex in a relationship between two people.*

Outstanding in the show is the work of Scottish sculptor Michael MacKenzie, new to the gallery and to Atlanta. In a rare achievement, his intensely erotic bronzes capture the passion of sex and love without being pornographic. As Eden Sinclair herself says of her new artist, 'I think Michael MacKenzie is one of the best young sculptors working today in the neoclassical style. He captures erotic emotion better than anyone since Rodin.'

There was more in the same vein. Fineman also singled out for special mention a fine new drawing by another artist new to the gallery, Angela St John. MacKenzie frowned; the name was familiar, but he couldn't place it. Then Eden was quoted as 'hoping for a long and fruitful relationship' with her new sculptor.

MacKenzie read and reread that sentence, trying to tease out the full meaning. Was Eden being polite and using formulas, or was there a personal sub-text? Those were the very words he had used in their toast that first night they made love on Eden's office floor. Did she repeat them specifically in the hope that he might get the message that she wanted him back? Was he just being absurdly optimistic? MacKenzie stared at the newsprint, but it refused to reveal any secrets.

Leaving the remains of his breakfast uneaten, MacKenzie hurriedly paid his bill and walked quickly back to his apartment. He packed a small suitcase with clothes for a few days, locked up his apartment, started his truck and headed for the freeway. It was 10.30 on a fine Friday morning.

As the old Eric Burdon and the Animals' song 'Get Back to You' blared from the Classic Oldies Hit Radio Station, he drove Interstate 16 at top speed, daring to apply the meaning of the lyrics to Eden Sinclair. He felt better. He felt good. He felt anxious. He felt sick with nerves. Emotions and moods flashed by as quickly as the signs on the highway.

It was mid-afternoon by the time he reached Atlanta. He drove straight to an Embassy Suites hotel off I-85 near midtown, checked in, freshened up and went out again immediately. He navigated through Friday's early rush-hour traffic as far as Zack's Diner, which gleamed on the corner of Fourteenth Street like some giant 1950s air-stream trailer in chromium and steel.

Now he was so close, he felt foolish and shy. What if he had completely misread Eden's comments? What if there was no special meaning in her words just for him? Not tasting his burger and fries, MacKenzie sat and worried about what to do next. He couldn't decide whether to go directly to the gallery and ask forgiveness of Eden, or just to mingle in the crowds at the reception in a few hours' time and hope she noticed him.

In a morass of indecision, MacKenzie checked his truck in its parking slot, and walked slowly up Peachtree Street to the High Museum of Art, passing only a block from Galerie Raton, but not going in. Once inside the High he wandered around, not paying attention to anything. His perambulation down the building's long curved ramp connecting all its various levels brought him eventually to the basement coffee shop, where he sat till closing time, nursing several cappuccinos and staring through the window at the Rodin sculpture under the trees.

In her office at Galerie Raton, Eden Sinclair's phone rang for the umpteenth time that afternoon. Mostly it had been gallery clients eager for information of the evening opening, having read Winston Fineman's review. 'Hello, Galerie Raton. Eden Sinclair speaking.'

'Eden!' It was Belgique, and Eden heard suppressed excitement in her voice. 'Eden, I just saw Michael Mac-Kenzie! He's back in town! He's wandering round the High Museum in a trance. He didn't see me. I pretended to be studying their giant Frank Stella painting and he walked right by me. I could have reached out and touched him!'

Eden's pulse rate soared, and her breath caught in her throat as she tried to remain calm in response to Belgique's news. Her voice betrayed an excited edge. 'Perhaps he read the article!'

'You were pretty clear, darling,' commented Belgique. '"I look forward to a long and fruitful relationship with Michael MacKenzie!"' She parodied Eden's conversation with Winston Fineman. 'Poor old Winston couldn't quote what you really wanted to say, that you want to fuck his brains out, but the invitation fairly leapt off the page!'

'Oh Belgique,' chided Eden. 'It's more than just sex, you know that!'

'Is there more than sex?' giggled Belgique.

Eden was suddenly businesslike. Checking that no one was within earshot, she spoke softly but urgently into the phone. 'In this instance, yes, there is, and I don't just mean between me and MacKenzie. We've got to get MacKenzie with us for the new gallery!'

'Let's think this through,' replied her friend, catching her serious mood. 'I was going to call you anyway; the

216

news about Michael was just a bonus. Since you came over to my apartment on Wednesday evening, after Raton attacked you,' said Belgique, her voice dripping with venom, 'I've lined up some other sponsors for your new gallery. My friends Hillary James and Cindee Montgomery have agreed to contribute to the low-interest loans you wanted. My attorney is doing the paperwork next week.'

Eden's reply was joyous. 'Oh, Belgique, you're brilliant! I love you! Thank you so much! We're really going to do this!' She smote the air with her raised fist in jubilation.

'Calm down, Eden,' Belgique said, unusually brisk and maternal. 'Now, have you told Angela everything? Is she in with us?'

'Yes, we went to lunch yesterday, and I filled her in on Raton's plan to cheat the artists. She already knew that plenty was wrong between me and Raton, so she wasn't too surprised. She's excited about us starting a completely new gallery and bringing most of our current artists with us. She's been on the phone to many of them, just asking them to come to a meeting tomorrow, and to keep it confidential. We haven't told anybody any details. Angela and I will probably see the rest of the artists at the opening this evening.'

'Good,' approved Belgique. 'I'm glad you've got support there in case Raton tries any more of his tricks. Now, what are you going to do when Michael MacKenzie walks in the gallery?'

'I just don't know,' Eden replied. 'What I would like to do is run across the room and fling my arms around him, and make love to him right there in the gallery! But I don't think the patrons would approve,' she added, regretfully.

'Oh, I don't know, darling,' said Belgique with a laugh. 'We could always say it was performance art! After all, it fits the theme of the show! You love him and you want to have sex with him. What could be more apposite?'

Eden laughed, but then was silent. An anxious Belgique enquired, 'Is everything OK? Did I say something?'

'Yes, you did. You said "you love him".' She paused. 'You're right. I do,' she finished quietly.

Belgique laughed at the other end of the line. 'Oh, my dear Eden, have you only just noticed? It's been obvious for days! Now, I must be going, they're getting ready to close the museum. I'll see you later. Love you. Bye!'

Eden slowly replaced the receiver. It looked as if her plan for a new gallery might just come true after all, and MacKenzie was here in Atlanta.

Eden was already thinking about what to wear.

Chapter Eighteen
The Art of Love

She wore her newest lingerie, especially a new bra with seamless and transparent black lace cups that showed her nipples clearly. She stroked them erect through the patterned lace.

Eden imagined MacKenzie looking at her breasts, running his fingers over the sexy material, fondling her nipples between his finger and thumb. She shivered with anticipation. How would MacKenzie act? Was he still angry? Or would he be pleased to see her? Did he still believe all those lies Raton told him? Would he believe her when she told him the truth? Why was he here, just to see the show or to see her?

Questions tumbled through her mind, as her body ached with desire in anticipation of his touch. She fondled her clitoris as she dressed in front of the mirror, parting her pubic curls to examine the little bud, gently rubbing it between her fingers. She was tempted to reach for one of her vibrators, but resisted the urge to masturbate, preferring to think of MacKenzie's wonderful penis inside her. She eased on the matching bikini thong, as lacy and transparent as the bra, showing off her thatch of hair that once more covered her clitoris, still throbbing between her legs.

She stepped into her short, black, silk sleeveless sheath with thin spaghetti straps. The garment flared to a slight A-line above mid-thigh, showing off her bare legs to perfection, and just covered her breasts in their lacy cups. Struggling for a moment with the zipper up the back, Eden slipped on her high-heeled black sandals, and as a final touch she donned her Mexican silver bracelet, and threaded into her ears companion earrings in an ancient Aztec design. She slung a matching silk jacket over her shoulder in case the night became cool, picked up her dress purse covered in little black sequins and headed out for her car.

Arriving early at the gallery, Eden made one last check of the exhibition and the catering arrangements. The show looked great, even if she did say so herself.

Justin and Paul had installed a series of large movable screen walls into positions that broke the tall exhibition space into three separate but connected 'rooms'. Each was dominated by one of MacKenzie's bronzes. On the white walls hung themed sets of drawings and paintings; the suites of two-dimensional work created clever counterpoints in colour, tone and content with the focal sculpture.

Two buffet tables were set out in the free-flowing spaces that linked each setting, one bearing plates of thinly cut sandwiches, cakes and fruit, while the other was set up as a wine bar, serving a decent Liberty School Cabernet, a Kendall Jackson Sauvignon Blanc and plenty of Perrier, some bottles of which Eden retrieved from the refrigerator, placing them in readiness, along with a cooler of ice.

Angela arrived moments later, looking cute and sexy in lime green and black. Her Italian bouclé cardigan buttoned down the front and her pert breasts moved freely beneath the soft fabric. Her tightly fitting black cotton Spandex leggings hugged her hips, revealing several inches of tanned flat stomach. The ensemble was completed by a pair of high-heeled black penny loafers.

'Wow, you look cute!' said Eden admiringly. 'Mr Fineman is a lucky man!'

Angela reddened. 'No, I think I'm the lucky one,' she demurred. 'But I was just going to say the same about you, Eden. You're looking lovely this evening.'

Eden couldn't hold back her news. 'MacKenzie's back in town. Belgique spotted him in the High Museum just a few hours ago. He must be here for the opening. I'm not going to let him get away this time!' Eden spoke with more confidence than she felt. She quickly changed the subject. 'Now remember, Angela, we've got to get the word about our special meeting tomorrow to all the artists here tonight who don't know, and we've got to do it without Raton suspecting. If I'm occupied with Mac-Kenzie, please make sure you talk to them all privately.'

Angela nodded. 'Leave it to me. You just take care of Michael.' She winked lasciviously at Eden. 'I'll slip the word to everybody as they leave. Raton doesn't usually stay around till the end, anyway. He doesn't like to help with the clean-up!' She broke off as Lola and Claire arrived to assist with the serving arrangements. With smiles at Eden and Angela, they took their places by the bar and buffet. Eden grinned back, leaving Angela to talk to the two students as she retreated upstairs to make one last check of her appearance.

By 6.30, Eden stood near the door as the first patrons began arriving. Winston Fineman came first, clearly eager to be with Angela, who greeted her lover with a deep and lingering kiss. Eden, watching furtively, saw the critic's hands flutter towards Angela's tempting breasts, so easily accessible under her cardigan as she lifted her arms around the tall man's neck. For propriety's sake he dropped his hands around Angela's waist, hugging her to him tightly. Eden's attention was distracted as many more visitors entered, among them Belgique, Jay Jay and others she knew. She greeted them at the door, exchanging pleasantries and chatting informally about the art, outwardly relaxed, despite her inner turmoil about MacKenzie and Raton.

When Alexander Raton arrived, he entered the gallery like some ante-bellum plantation owner, pausing just inside the front door to peruse his domain. Eden froze at the sight of him, despite all her mental preparations for this moment.

Angela and Fineman watched Eden glare fixedly at her boss as he walked slowly towards her and took her by the arm, leading her aside to a quiet space. Drifting silently nearby, Angela and Fineman were shocked by the gallery owner's first words, spoken quietly and meant only for Eden's ears.

'I see that you're wearing your "fuck me pumps",' he said meanly, looking down at Eden's sexy shoes. 'They're just right for an art whore.' His eyes bore into her, issuing a challenge for control of the evening.

'I prefer calling them "fuck *you* shoes",' Eden responded a little too loudly, emphasising the expletive and stamping her foot. 'They make good kicking shoes, too.' She paused, struggling vainly to hold on to her professional reserve. 'Now get out of my face.'

Raton only smiled. 'Don't be angry. Remember, you started it.' He allowed his voice to rise slightly in volume so as to be overheard by a growing circle of interest around them.

'The word "angry" fails to describe my feelings at your loathsome behaviour,' Eden said icily, confounded at his recasting of his attempted seduction of her.

Fineman, Angela and several others eavesdropped with undisguised curiosity, and Raton carefully orchestrated his speech to the listening ears around him.

'You slapped me first,' he reminded her. 'Eden, if you

behave like a little child, you can't complain if you get treated like one.' He spoke loudly enough for a wider group of art viewers to turn their heads in surprise.

'I'm not surprised any more at your sadistic sexist behaviour,' Eden flashed back. But suddenly she comprehended Raton's tactic of using this public gathering to provoke her and to further blacken her name and reputation by clever innuendo. Unsure how to respond to his clever manipulation of the situation, she tried a frontal assault. 'If you insist upon bringing up that evening, you may recall that *you* assaulted *me*. I only slapped you when you ... you touched my breast.' She raised her voice to match his, gathering yet more glances in their direction.

'Eden, my dear,' said Raton, the voice of sweet reason, playing to his audience and wearing a smile that never reached his eyes. 'I'm sure you're overreacting and completely misinterpreting my actions. I was just trying to comfort you and calm you down after your outburst. It was completely innocent; I'm sure you know that. We mustn't let silly personal differences come between us,' he added patronisingly. 'We're such a good team. I so admire your great work in putting together this wonderful show.'

A silence descended over the gallery. Patrons and artists alike were listening, their personal chatter abated. Eden felt Angela's tension next to her; she realised that her next words might determine her professional future in Atlanta. You clever bastard, she thought, looking hard at Raton. You've set me up to appear unstable and erratic in comparison to your reasonableness. If she resigned now, Eden told herself, no one would believe that Raton was at fault.

'Alexander,' she said, putting all the sweetness she could muster into her smile, 'whether I'm overreacting or not to your misbehaviour is a matter for our private discussion. I'm sure the good people here tonight would much rather look at the art, than listen to our squabble.' Ha! Eden thought to herself; it was probably just the opposite! But she continued, 'We have many things to discuss about how this gallery is run.' She focused her blue eyes on his, adding, 'Financially as well as artistically.' Eden put a slight but unmistakable emphasis on the word 'financially', and saw a flicker of fear in Raton's eyes, quickly doused.

She continued to smile at him, and reached to take his arm in hers. He flinched but did not withdraw. 'But all that can wait till next week. Tonight, we have a celebration of these fine talents assembled here. Come.' She steered Raton towards the drinks and offered him a glass of Cabernet. He took it, his eyes watching her as wary as a fox. Eden lifted a glass to his. 'A toast,' she said, her voice carrying across the gallery as she swept the space and the eager crowd with her gaze. 'A toast to "The Art of Love", and to the artists whose works are displayed here tonight!'

'To art! To love!' chorused the assembly in unison, many eyes focusing on MacKenzie's three centerpiece sculptures. 'To sex!' shouted Belgique, her short figure hidden in the throng, and a titter of laughter rippled through the crowd. Eden raised her glass in acknowledgement. 'OK, a toast to sex, too!'

A hubbub of excited conversation broke out again as Eden grinned at her audience. She turned to Raton, whose face was fixed in the hollow vestige of a smile. 'Drink up, Alexander,' she said, dropping the expression of goodwill from her eyes and replacing it with one of loathing, reserved just for him. 'I'm sure you'll enjoy the evening. I'm so looking forward to our little chat next week.' Eden turned on her heel, and replacing the smile on her face strode into the crowd, greeting friends old and new.

Angela caught up with her halfway across the room. 'Good recovery,' she whispered.

Eden's shoulders sagged infinitesimally. 'Thank you, Angela. I nearly lost it there,' she admitted. 'God, I'm shaking like a leaf! I need all the help I can get right now.'

'Will you accept mine?' offered a familiar voice at her elbow. 'It comes with an apology.'

Eden spun round to face MacKenzie who had appeared from nowhere. For a moment she couldn't speak. He looked to her in that instant like a flame-haired figure from a Piero della Francesca fresco, solid, dependable and with the face of an angel. Only his eyes, those melted chocolate eyes, were hesitant, betraying some internal uncertainty. 'Oh, MacKenzie!' cried Eden, 'Thank God you're here.' She slipped her arms around him and relaxed her weight on to his chest.

He stood there like a rock and stroked her hair. 'I only caught the tail end of that little scene,' he said, 'but you seemed to be holding your own pretty well.'

Eden stepped back and looked into his eyes, but she didn't release him from her touch. 'Only just. I've got a lot to tell you about Alexander Raton, if you'll listen.'

MacKenzie smiled. 'I should have listened several days ago,' he said, with a smile that was half a grimace. 'Will you forgive me and let me start over? I think I have a lot to learn.'

Eden felt any vestige of animosity towards the sculptor turn to vapour at his touch. She felt herself growing more aroused by the second, compounded by the firmness of his body beneath her hands and the sexy scent of his skin. She could feel her clitoris press against the silk of her panties beneath her dress.

She realised Angela was talking to her. 'I just saw Raton leave.'

At that moment Fineman came hurrying over. 'He's driven off,' he confirmed. 'I ran to the door just to make sure he wasn't hanging around outside. He looked furious!'

Eden forced herself to be professional. What she really

225

wanted to do was to whisk MacKenzie away and hold him tight to her breasts, to suck his wonderful cock and fuck him till she was sore. But she said, 'Good. We've got work to do.' She looked up at MacKenzie. 'There's a lot of explaining to do,' she told him, 'but first, Angela and I must speak urgently to several of the artists here. Will you let me introduce you to some of our wealthy clients, the ones who might be most interested in buying your work? I'll come back for you within the hour.' She watched anxiously for his acceptance.

Softly he said, 'I was really wrong, wasn't I? I had it all screwed up.'

Eden nodded, a wry smile on her lips.

'Will you forgive me?' he asked.

'Gladly,' she responded. 'Besides, I already have. The moment I saw you.'

'Will you go to dinner with me?' he asked.

'Gladly,' she repeated, as she took his arm, 'anywhere. But in one hour!'

She steered MacKenzie towards a group of well-dressed couples, clustered around the sculpture *Peleus and Thetis*.

Breaking gently into their animated conversation, Eden asked, 'May I introduce Michael MacKenzie?' Just saying his name gave her a shiver of pride and delight. 'He's the sculptor of these wonderful bronzes.' A gasp of excitement went up from the little crowd. 'Mr MacKenzie,' said Eden formally, but with her eyes sparkling at the Scotsman, 'I'll leave you with these good folks, but I'll be back to rescue you in one hour.' She smiled at her clients, spoke briefly to one or two by name, and then turned to find Angela at her side. 'Let's go talk to the artists about the meeting tomorrow.'

By eight o'clock, Eden and Angela between them had engaged in many brisk and businesslike conversations with the artists present. Without giving away any details,

226

they urged each artist to come to 'an important meeting that is vital to the future of the gallery.'

'Will Alexander Raton be there?' asked one. Eden replied directly. 'No, he won't. I can't say any more now, but please come, twelve noon at La Cuba-Libra in Virginia Highlands.'

As together, Angela and Eden studied the thinning crowds, the younger woman said, 'You can leave, Eden. Winston said he would help me and Lola and Claire with the clean-up.'

Eden nodded her thanks, and waving to the two students who had worked hard all night at the bar and buffet, she moved over to extricate MacKenzie from the last group of potential clients. One particularly attractive middle-aged woman, wearing a low-cut black dress and expensive jewellery accentuating her cleavage, had fixed the sculptor with her smoky eyes. Eden heard her ask with more than a hint of suggestiveness in her voice, 'Do you use live models for your sculptures, Michael?'

MacKenzie smiled back, studiously avoiding too blatant a study of the rising flesh of her bosom, clearly helped into prominence by a barely hidden Wonderbra. 'Always, Mrs Hernandez,' he said, widening his smile to include her husband, a small dark-haired Hispanic gentleman in a beautifully tailored white linen suit.

'I'm continually on the look-out for models,' he added, 'and I do personal commissions for portraits, too. When a beautiful lady comes to my studio to sit for me, I always invite her husband or her lover to accompany her. It makes the situation very clear, and often,' he contrived a disarming grin, 'my models do get aroused being naked in the presence of their loved one. That enables me to catch the essence of love and sex more easily.'

MacKenzie noted a flicker of disappointment in the woman's eyes, but saw her husband incline his head minutely and look purposefully into his eyes. It seemed that he had passed some sort of test with that gentleman.

'I would like to talk further on this subject,' said Mr Hernandez softly. 'If I wanted to speak with you next week, how would I find you?'

MacKenzie saw Eden from the corner of his eye. 'All my work is handled by Ms Sinclair,' he said, with the slightest of raised eyebrows in Eden's direction.

Eden took her cue. 'Here is my card, Mr Hernandez,' she said, reaching into her small evening purse she had gathered up in preparation for departure. 'You can reach me on my pager any time. I'm delighted to handle Michael MacKenzie's work. He's definitely one of the best young sculptors working in America today. I would anticipate that he'll have a great one-person show here in the city very soon, after which his prices are bound to rise.'

MacKenzie's eyebrows shot up in startled response, but the husband didn't notice and merely nodded; with a small smile at MacKenzie, he led his wife towards the front door. The woman looked back at the sculptor and blew him a kiss.

Eden grinned at MacKenzie. 'Does that happen often? Am I going to have to fight off all the rich glamorous women in Atlanta to keep you to myself?'

'They won't stand a chance, Eden,' said MacKenzie, and emboldened by her comments, he moved close to kiss her full on the lips, enveloping her in a slow lingering embrace that caught the admiring attention of the few remaining patrons. 'Come on,' he said, 'let's go. Angela and the girls have got everything under control.'

As they left by the rear entrance, Eden saluted Angela.

Her young assistant, holding hands with her own beau, mouthed back, 'Have fun!'

Eden realised she was growing very fond of Angela; and to bring in Winston Fineman on the side of the new gallery would be a major boost.

* * *

Seated at a cozy, candlelit banquette Eden and Mac-Kenzie nibbled at their food, holding hands, and began the process of rebuilding their trust. Eden felt a desire just to surrender to MacKenzie's arms, but she made herself take things slowly, to get some basic misunderstandings cleared away first. MacKenzie helped her.

'I'd like you to tell me everything that's been going on between you and Raton,' he said simply. 'It's pretty clear to me that I allowed myself to be used by Raton that day, and behaved very foolishly into the bargain. I will need to ask your forgiveness several more times before my conscience is clear. I just didn't realise ... I thought it was you who was using me.' He looked into her eyes, anxious to transmit his apology in every way he could.

'Oh, MacKenzie,' said Eden fondly, 'that's in the past now. Let's forget it. I'll probably behave badly and shout and scream at you for no reason one day, and then we'll be equal.' She returned his gaze steadily. 'I'm not always easy to live with, you know.'

'Well,' replied MacKenzie with equal composure, 'let's just say I'm looking forward to finding out. And I'm not going to keep score.' He smiled and stroked her cheek. Eden clasped his hand in hers, and then laid them together on the damask tablecloth.

'I'll summarise the main points about Raton and the mess at the gallery, and bring you up to speed with our plans. Ready?'

MacKenzie nodded. After listening to Eden's tale, he snarled, 'I'll wring his bloody neck! But what's this about a new gallery?'

'That's the most exciting part!' said Eden enthusiastically. 'Angela and I have talked to all the gallery artists, without giving them any details yet, and most of them are coming to a special meeting tomorrow at lunch. I'm going to tell them about Raton's plan to defraud them of their commission, and try to persuade them to join me in opening a completely new gallery here in town. I don't have a location yet, but with financial backers it shouldn't be too hard to find a good space; a warehouse is my favourite idea, something that we can convert into big airy spaces.' She paused. 'It would be ideal for your sculptures,' she added quietly.

'I'd be honoured to be included,' said MacKenzie. 'Thank you for asking. May I kiss you again, to seal our new understanding?'

It was some moments before they spoke further. Eden felt juicy with desire, her clitoris swollen and her nipples erect. She slid over close to MacKenzie so their thighs touched and she let her short hem ride up her legs, revealing a healthy portion of thigh as she snuggled her bum in the upholstery next to him. Without stockings, her firm, well-muscled thighs dragged his gaze down like a magnet, competing with his hungry appreciation of her protruding nipples.

As they talked and finished their drinks, their food now cold and discarded, she leant against his body, allowing her breasts to press blatantly into his arm. Eden was eager for him to lay his hands all over her naked skin; she was ready to wriggle out of her panties, and practically finger-fucking herself under the table.

He noticed the movement of her hand between her legs. 'Shall we go?' he whispered urgently.

'Yes! All I want to do right now is fuck you!'

As MacKenzie pulled her to her feet, she murmured in his ear, 'I'm so hot and juicy I'm leaking through my panties and my nipples are as hard as cherry pits.'

He gasped in response. Holding her wrists in his hands and staring frankly at her perky nipples protruding through her silk sheath, he said, 'Eden, I want you, I want you!' As he helped her into her fitted silk jacket, he delicately rubbed his thumb over one nipple, adding in a low mumble, 'I want to eat you up!' Almost hurting with desire, they called for the bill, paid it somehow and headed for the door.

On the pavement outside the restaurant, they kissed frantically and, locked in an embrace, their hands were suddenly all over each others' bodies. In desperation, she asked, 'Where are we going?'

'My hotel's closer than your bungalow; I can't wait!' With an impromptu decision, MacKenzie hailed a cab and gave the name and address of his hotel to the driver.

Sighing with pleasure, they grappled in the back seat of the taxi as it lurched through the potholed city streets of Midtown. Eden laughed out loud at the image they made: two incredibly horny individuals lusting after each other to the exclusion of all else.

Within a few minutes, Eden's skirt was pulled to her waist and her panties to her ankles. The jerky movement of the cab in and out of traffic made MacKenzie's fondling fingers often miss their target, and suddenly he fell face first into her lap with centrifugal force as the vehicle peeled quickly away from a traffic light.

Eden's laughter was echoed by her lover's muffled cries as he licked her clitoris, stubbornly holding on to her thighs and clamping them around his head. If the cab driver took any notice, she gave no sign; after all, Eden thought, they were probably two of the more normal people she saw in her daily stint on the city's streets. A waft of marijuana drifted through a crack in the armoured glass that separated them from their driver who, Eden saw, was a broad-shouldered blonde-haired woman of about her own age. The two women's eyes met fleetingly in the rear-view mirror; Eden received a deliberate wink, and then the driver's attention returned to the road ahead.

Caught up in their wantonness, Eden shuddered to her first climax right there in the back seat, her vagina tingling with rippling little shocks as MacKenzie's tongue lapped her to distraction. When she relaxed her legs, he sat up and pulled out an elegant handkerchief to wipe his mouth before kissing her lips, but she could still taste her juices in his mouth. He rubbed the insides of her hot naked thighs as she squeezed his dick, prising it out of his trousers and rubbing the shaft with the expertise of long practice. MacKenzie grunted with a combination of lust and ecstasy, but eventually stayed her hand, whispering, 'Not too much! I'm ready to come in your hand right now, but I want to be inside you!'

The cab turned into the entrance of the hotel and stopped. Hurriedly pulling up her panties, Eden stumbled out of the cab on MacKenzie's arm; he had zipped up his flies and was looking considerably calmer and cooler than she. Aware of being stared at under the lights of the porte-cochere, Eden felt as if her naked desire must be imprinted on her face for all the guests to see. As MacKenzie paid for the ride, she turned towards him and pulled him through the wide doors of the hotel.

MacKenzie veered briefly to the desk for his key, passed through the lobby with Eden tight on his arm and stepped into the lift. They both felt people's eyes following them, and then the door slid shut with a firm, automatic sound.

'Thank God, we're alone,' she panted, and as they ascended she reached under her skirt, pulled down her panties and stepped out of them, stuffing them into her purse. MacKenzie stood behind her, watching. His reflection in the mirrored panel of the lift smiled into her reflected eyes, pure lust sparking between them. Eden hiked up her skirt to reveal her naked arse and his eyes widened as he watched her bend forward and reach between her legs, sliding one finger between the lips of her glistening vulva.

MacKenzie eased his own index finger into her slick opening to accompany hers, and slowly masturbated Eden, using her own finger in combination with his.

With a thump, the lift stopped at their floor and the door slid open. Still entangled, they limped to MacKenzie's door and as soon as he had unlocked it, Eden was across the threshold and out of her dress in one step. Wearing nothing but her lacy bra and her pair of 'fuck me' sandals, she surveyed the room calmly, tossing the bundle of discarded clothing into a pile. She unhooked the front clip of her bra, and strolled naked in her high heels across the room to the window and opened the curtains. 'I want to see the city while we fuck, MacKenzie. I want to ride you, feel your dick inside me, and watch all those lights below.' As MacKenzie pulled off his shirt and fought to release himself from his trousers, she heard his moan and the sound of his shoes and belt hitting the floor. She turned and saw his dick, his whole dick and nothing but his dick.

His erection was even bigger than she remembered. Kneeling before him on the downy carpet, Eden caressed his pubic hair; it was beautiful, soft and curly, and so deeply gingery red. She gave herself to worshipping MacKenzie's dick, his great ginger root. Relishing the taste of his flesh, she took as much of his shaft inside her mouth as she could manage. She reached through his legs to play first with his balls and then moved her fingers to the very opening of his anus, stroking back and forth along his most sensitive cleft.

They didn't make it to the bed the first time, but melted to the floor, intertwining their bodies into a 69 position. MacKenzie's mouth was on the burning lips of Eden's vagina, his tongue around her clit, and she came in great spasms before he was even inside her. She cried out in ecstasy, climaxing violently as he performed luxurious oral sex.

When he climbed on top of her, her body was one long ribbon of sensuous delight, glistening with her juices, and his giant member was slick with the first of his come. As MacKenzie entered her, she received him with a fresh spasm of delight, lying on her back and curling her legs so her thighs rested on her breasts, her pelvis thrust upward to receive him, her sex lips spread wide. He came almost immediately as Eden clenched her vaginal muscles and milked a great gush of semen from his pulsing penis.

As he spent himself inside her, MacKenzie looked out from his kneeling position on the carpet through the double-glazed sliding French doors that gave on to his iron-railed balcony. He saw the twinkling lights of the South's greatest metropolis spread as far as the eye could see. Torrents of red and white light swirled along the great ribbons of interstate concrete, eddying round the foot of the hotel. 'I can see all Atlanta, Eden,' he said slowly to his recumbent partner, who was studying him with a languorous smile of satisfaction. 'I can feel my dick inside you, and I can see all over the city.' A tender passion welled up inside him and startled his eyes with little tears of love. Love.

'I love you,' he said. 'I can't help it!'

Despite the turmoil of emotions within her, Eden kept a calm face. She smiled back at this near-stranger who threatened to change her life in the most wonderful way.

'Oh damn!' she exclaimed in mock alarm. 'What the hell do we do now?'

Chapter Nineteen
The Artists' Café

*A*s the two of them sat up in bed together, consuming a room service breakfast of scrambled eggs and sausage patties, with French roast coffee, orange juice and English muffins, Eden leant comfortably against MacKenzie's naked chest and pieced it all together.

'This love thing,' she said, casually. 'It must be catching.'

MacKenzie looked at her quizzically.

'Well, last night you had it,' explained Eden. 'And this morning, I've got it. Do you think it's transmitted orally?'

MacKenzie spluttered toast fragments over the bedclothes. 'Are you telling me what I think you're telling me?' he asked when he recovered.

'Yeah,' nodded Eden. 'I'm saying I love you, too, MacKenzie. And I've got a proposition for you. No!' she added with a laugh, gently removing her lover's hand from between her legs. 'Not that sort of proposition, although that's a really good idea for later. Now sit up and listen!' Eden put the breakfast trays aside and sat cross-legged on the rumpled bedclothes, her breasts swinging free as she gestured with her hands. Her magic triangle of pubic curls peeped out at MacKenzie from behind her heels and calves tucked in against her groin.

'If we love each other, that makes us partners, doesn't it?'

MacKenzie nodded.

'And if I'm going to run a gallery I need a partner, don't I?'

MacKenzie nodded again, and then looked up at Eden, his eyes wide. 'You mean that you want me to be your partner in the gallery?'

Eden smiled. 'Grade A in Logic 101 goes to Mr Michael MacKenzie! Yes,' she added more seriously. 'Yes, I do. I want you as my partner in my bed, in my life and in my business. Boy oh boy!' she looked at the ceiling and rolled her eyes in mock horror. 'If we're going to bomb, we're going to do it royally!'

It was MacKenzie's turn to smile. 'We're not going to bomb,' he said. 'And yes, my love, I accept your offer without any hesitation, but,' he paused theatrically, causing Eden to look at him in expectation, 'with one condition.'

'What's that?'

'That you're my partner in the studio; it's the one important location you left off your list. I want you to start painting again.'

Eden drew in her breath and was silent. 'Will you help me run the gallery so I have the time?' Eden asked quietly, despite her pulse rate jumping with excitement. It would be wonderful to paint again, seriously, and with a great artist who could teach her new skills! She thought of MacKenzie as a great artist.

'Of course I'll help. From now on we're a team.'

Eden flung her arms around MacKenzie's shoulders and pressed against him until her nipples were crushed against his chest. She felt tears coursing down her cheeks as she sobbed into his shoulder, her whole frame racked by her flood of emotion. She felt his cock stiffen against

236

her thigh, rising and probing against her flesh, seeking her mound as if under its own will. She rocked hard against her lover, her emotion now unchecked, matching her desire.

Running her hands over his chest and abdomen, she felt the trails of her tears streaked on his skin. 'MacKenzie, you clever bastard!' she said, between sobs of joy. 'I bet you say that to all your girlfriends!'

'Oh, no,' denied MacKenzie in apparent seriousness. 'Only to the ones who can draw!'

He ducked quickly as a pillow flew at his head, and then Eden was upon him like a demon, panting, her hands scrabbling for all and any parts of his anatomy to suck and fondle. She went down on his dick, teased his anus with her finger, feeling his tight muscle close, and then deep-tongued his mouth before covering his lips with her vulva.

'Eat me, MacKenzie!' she squealed, her knees flanking his head, feeling his tongue flicking her clitoris in little circles. 'Oh God! Make me come!' She rode against his face, feeling the roughness of his day-old beard against her tender sex. She shuddered and shook to another climax, every bit as good as the earlier explosions that had flooded through her in the last twelve hours. Eden lost count of the number of times MacKenzie brought her to the peak of ecstasy. She felt his body jerk beneath her, and warm semen jetted on to her back. She looked over her shoulder to see MacKenzie's magnificent penis release its final load of sperm over his hand, clenched tightly around his swollen shaft.

Eden slid down her lover's body and licked the white fluid from his fingers. Kneeling over him once more, she opened his lips with her tongue, transferring MacKenzie's come to his own mouth. 'Mmmm!' she murmured, tasting his delicious saltiness. 'If we're partners, that means we share . . . everything!'

* * *

'A pick-up truck?' asked Eden incredulously as she followed MacKenzie out of the hotel lobby and over to the huge old black Chevy with its giant V-8 five-litre engine. They were on their way to the lunchtime meeting with the artists. Eden felt nervous, and covered it up with banter. 'A Scotsman driving a pick-up? Are you sure you know how to drive it?' she asked mischievously.

MacKenzie only nodded, but beckoned Eden round to the rear bumper, where proudly displayed was a blue and white cross of Saint Andrew. 'It's a tartan Chevy, my sweet,' he said. 'Special export model.'

MacKenzie followed Eden's directions first to her house, driving swiftly and competently as if to prove his ability to his sceptical passenger. Eden however, was more intent on explaining some further ideas to her new partner.

'I want to work on finding a space right away,' she said, 'and I have pretty good ideas for the first two shows.'

MacKenzie looked interested.

'We'll have to start with a group show, to get everyone involved,' she said. 'If we get a space next week, we could probably get something organised to start within a month to six weeks.'

MacKenzie nodded again. 'I agree. But why wait?'

'I don't want to have just a typical group show of whatever work we've got around,' she replied, animatedly. 'I want to start with something really special; something that will make everybody sit up and take notice. My idea is for a show of wearable art: it can be jewellery, metalwork, fabric; it can be decorative or political. I can just imagine what some of our feminist artists could do with that theme.'

MacKenzie grinned in agreement. 'We'd get some real eye-openers! They'd really strut their stuff!'

'Yes!' cried Eden. 'That's it! We can organise it like a fashion show, hire some models to wear the pieces on a catwalk. We could do some pretty daring things. We'd take the extremes of fashion and push them just a little further; bring all the underlying sexual themes out in the open.' Her eyes glowed with the prospect. 'We could give everybody one month to create specific pieces for the show, and for us to organise it. We can do the invites next week if they'll all agree at lunch. Boy, this could really be a summer sizzler!'

'You also said something about having a second show,' interjected MacKenzie, when Eden paused in her flow of ideas.

'Oh yes,' she replied. 'That's the one that would really start our fall season.' She turned to face MacKenzie. His eyes flicked from the road to her and back again. 'I want to mount a one-person show of your work,' she said simply, 'one that will get you noticed all across the country. I'll call all the critics from the big national magazines personally and get them to come.'

MacKenzie's emotion was betrayed only by a clenching of his fists around the steering wheel. He was silent for a few minutes.

'Well?' Eden asked. 'Will you do it?'

MacKenzie beamed. 'Of course I will, darling. I'm just trying to take it all in. It's not quite the venue I'd anticipated,' he admitted, 'but I think it's a great idea! If it's in the fall, I'll have time to finish some new pieces.' He turned quickly to smile at her. 'If anyone can do a great show for me, I think it's you. There's nothing I'd like better in the whole world!'

'Whoa!' said Eden suddenly. 'We're here.'

MacKenzie came to a quick stop, and backed the truck into Eden's driveway. She led him through to her bedroom, where she laid out a black split-collar polo dress and matching tights. MacKenzie sat on her bed with her troupe of bears and watched her every move. 'It's hard to keep my hands off you,' he said, licking his lips with a music hall leer. 'Come here for just one kiss.'

Eden grinned at her lover. She realised how much she enjoyed just having him around. Wearing only her bikini pants she knelt with him on the bed. 'Shall I wear a bra with this outfit?' She gestured to her sleek stretch velvet dress.

'Not on my account,' said MacKenzie, returning her grin. 'I love knowing that your breasts are naked under your dress. It makes me get really randy.'

'You don't need that excuse!' teased Eden, rolling on the covers with her lover, enjoying his hands over her breasts, his tongue fleetingly on her nipples. 'That's all,' she said after a moment's delicious languor. 'We need to be there in ten minutes. I want to be a little early, before most of the artists get there.'

Taking MacKenzie's advice, she pulled the dress over her naked breasts and stepped into her tights, pulling them snugly round her bottom. Black pumps and a pendant necklace that fitted her cleavage completed her outfit. She studied herself in the mirror. 'Not too formal, not too casual. You think it's OK, darling?'

MacKenzie gave her a lingering kiss as his mark of approval, and they walked the two blocks to Highland Avenue and the row of bars, restaurants and second-hand bookstores clustered there. La Cuba-Libra was housed in a small, single-storey brick building that used to be a neighbourhood general store in the days before supermarkets. It was one of Eden's favourites; cheap and friendly, with huge portions of good food.

At a few minutes to twelve, the restaurant was not yet busy. The nightlife of the area didn't cease until the early hours of the morning, and the bars and restaurants only struggled back to life around midday. Eden had booked the large back room, and when she and MacKenzie arrived, a few artists were already there. Martin Bulgaria stood up as the couple entered.

'Morning Eden, Morning, Mr MacKenzie. We've just ordered some jugs of margarita. Pick up a glass and help yourselves. I assume you're going to tell us what this is all about?' He looked hard at Eden from under his bushy eyebrows.

'Thanks, Martin,' replied Eden, rimming two glasses with salt before filling them with the restaurant's speciality drink. She handed one to MacKenzie. 'Can you be patient with me until we get everybody here? There's a lot I want to say, and it will be easier to say it only once.'

The painter nodded and took his place at one of the large tables set out across the room, with chairs lined on each side. Eden sat where she could speak easily to everybody. MacKenzie took his place on her right, and Eden saved the other seat next to her. 'That's for Belgique,' she explained. 'She'll be joining us shortly.'

By 12.10 the room had filled up, and a buzz of excited conversation filled the air. Angela and Eden had stressed the urgency of the meeting sufficiently to capture the attention of almost all the gallery artists. Eden's quick head count revealed that all but three of the gallery's 50 artists were in attendance. Tapping her glass with her spoon, she got their attention.

'We came to this charming hole-in-the-wall for an important business meeting, but let's do first things first and get lunch organised. I'm afraid I can't afford to pay for you all, but why don't you go ahead and order. They'll separate the bill for us at the end.' Eden beckoned to a small posse of waiters who descended quickly on their customers and efficiently took their orders.

'While we're waiting, I'll give y'all the main outlines of our business here,' continued Eden. 'First of all I want to congratulate all of you for making the show last night such a success.' Her audience munched on tortilla chips and salsa as Eden read extracts from Fineman's newspaper account aloud, pausing for a final quote. 'This is what I really want to draw your attention to,' she said. ' "The stable of artists that Eden Sinclair has attracted to Galerie Raton is as talented a group of painters, sculptors, printmakers, photographers and ceramists as you'll find in all the southern states. This high-powered group certainly represents Atlanta's artistic avant-garde."'

Eden put down the clipping and looked around the room. All eyes were on her, and several artists wore proud expressions. She nodded. 'Yes, you should all be very pleased with your efforts. But I'm here today to tell you that this excellence is being undermined by Alexander Raton! He's trying to force me out and steal your share of sales money to line his own pockets!'

A collective gasp filled the room, followed by shouted questions. 'Why?' 'What do you mean?' 'What's he going to do?' One tall, broad-chested potter from the Georgia hill country spoke slowly through his copious beard. 'The mean little bastard! I never liked the little runt. I say we wring his little neck!' The potter's powerful hands gestured expressively. A nervous ripple of laughter ran through the group.

'Let me explain,' said Eden, tapping her glass loudly again to restore calm. As the waiters efficiently set out the food and more jugs of drinks, Eden proceeded to lay out Raton's scheme in detail, sensing the mood of her audience shift from bewilderment to depression and then to anger at their gallery owner's duplicity. Timing her next announcement for maximum impact, she clapped her hands to still the buzz of conversation.

'I have a solution,' she announced. All eyes fixed on her. 'Alexander Raton is going to get his way.' One or two artists groaned. 'I *am* going to resign as director very soon, but I'll be resigning to start my own gallery here in Atlanta.' She paused as groans were replaced by murmurs of interest and delight. 'And I want to introduce my partner, Scottish sculptor Michael MacKenzie! Some of you met him last night, and most of you saw his fabulous work in the show.' Heads nodded in appreciation round the table; several glasses were lifted in salutation.

MacKenzie smiled and raised his hand in acknowledgement. 'I'm very proud to be associated with all of you,' he said. 'Eden and I hope very much that you'll join us in the new venture. My partner has some very exciting plans.' He looked at Eden for her to continue, his eyes sparkling with love.

She took back the reins of the meeting. 'We propose to open a new gallery to be run by ourselves with the financial backing of a consortium of collectors and investors, headed by Belgique du Pont. As many of you know,' Eden added, 'Belgique's been one of the main supporters of the gallery for quite some time; in fact many of you have works in her extensive private collection. Moreover, we owe it to her for revealing the full scope of Raton's criminal plan.'

As if on her cue, and amid more excited babbling around the table, Belgique walked in and joined the group. After introductions, Belgique confirmed the plot.

'It's all true, unfortunately,' she said. 'Raton and I have been lovers for some time and, I must admit, his timing was superb. He chose his moment, after we'd made love, to lure me gradually into his plans. He made it sound so reasonable; just a little cutting of corners here, just a shaving of profits there. But he's despicable; he's a liar, a cheat, and if you let him do this to you, a common thief! And, he isn't my lover anymore!' she added, to a burst of laughter.

Belgique had the audience's attention in more ways than one. For her performance today she wore only a backless bib-fronted denim overall with a chunky zipper down the front, running from her breasts to her crotch. Its baggy cut fully revealed the luscious sides of her breasts, which continuously threatened to fall clear of the material. Only a designer denim jacket worn loosely off the shoulder kept her from being half-naked in front of them.

Belgique also continued her courtship of the artists by discussing her extensive art collection, and those of her network of wealthy friends. Each and every working artist in the group was attentive to this subject, and Belgique reeled off a virtual 'Who's Who' of significant art patrons in the city and region.

'I can deliver the patronage of these individuals,' promised Belgique. 'I have every confidence in Eden, and Michael,' she paused to blow the Scotsman a kiss, 'to set up a truly outstanding new gallery. I am putting my money behind it. Will you join your talents with us?'

There were enthusiastic cries of assent from around the table. Belgique beamed.

'But what about our contracts with Galerie Raton?' queried Annalee Barrett. Several other artists nodded questioningly.

'That's actually quite easy,' replied Eden, standing up and taking back the floor. 'While I still work there I can invoke the gallery's termination clause to release you all from your contracts without penalty. If I do so quickly, Raton won't be able to do a thing about it as I'm a registered officer of the company. It's in my contract.'

The waiters brought refills for the margaritas.

Eden continued, 'Now, I want a show of hands. Who wants to be a member of the new gallery?' She looked up and down the tables as all hands went up without hesitation; there were no dissenters. She smiled. 'Thank you, one and all! It's unanimous!'

A ragged cheer arose from the assembled artists.

'One more thing,' shouted Eden above the hubbub of excited chatter. 'I have very specific ideas for something that will really grab Atlanta's artistic attention. The first show will be 'wearable art'. We'll call it *Art Vivant*, and it will feature models in a fashion show wearing specially created works of art by all of you.' She gestured around the room. 'Angela St John, my assistant at Galerie Raton, will join us at the new gallery, and together we'll contact you with more details. But count on it happening in about a month's time. The only criterion is that the art must be wearable on a human body in one way or another. You can be as daring as you like!' she challenged them.

One of her younger male artists caught her eye. 'Will the models be dressed or nude?' he asked, a sophomoric grin plastered over his face.

Eden smiled sweetly back. 'It all depends on the art,' she answered, 'but it's OK to raise a few eyebrows.' She turned to face the whole crowd. 'Now, whatever you do, don't mention any of this to Raton! That's very important! I will tell him myself, but only when the time is right. Does everybody understand?'

A chorus of assent greeted her question, and satisfied, Eden said, smiling. 'Thank you all for coming!'

But Martin Bulgaria was shouting from the back of the room. 'Eden, what are you going to call the gallery?'

'Ah,' said Eden, 'good question.' She looked sideways at MacKenzie and then faced the audience. 'It will be called Ginger Root Gallery,' she announced, and gave a big grin and a wink to MacKenzie, who sat there with his mouth open, momentarily nonplussed. Then he assumed an expression of innocence and polite indifference.

There were some polite giggles around the room, especially from Belgique beside her, but most artists just smiled uncomprehendingly. 'It's a private joke,' explained Eden, her grin widening. 'But on to more important things. It's nearly two o'clock and we've all got things to do.'

'Hold on!' shouted a middle-aged artist whose name Eden couldn't remember, although she knew he painted rather attractive cubist-inspired landscapes. 'A toast; we must have a toast to the new gallery!'

'To Ginger Root!' shouted several voices at once, as everyone raised their glasses.

Eden looked straight into MacKenzie's eyes and raised her own glass. 'To *my* Ginger Root!' she said. MacKenzie coloured scarlet to the very roots of his ginger hair.

Chapter Twenty
The Aquarium Qlub

*A*fter the artists had departed, Eden, MacKenzie and Belgique considered the logistics for their new enterprise, sitting alone in the restaurant over dessert and coffee. They knew they needed spaces for the gallery, studios, and perhaps somewhere temporary to hold the special fashion show.

Belgique spoke up. 'Hillary James, one of my friends who's agreed to join my consortium, owns a warehouse complex on the edge of downtown. There's lots of empty space; in fact the only tenant is the Aquarium Qlub.'

Eden knew of the Aquarium Qlub; it was one of the settings her friends Liz Angelo and Vivienne Dupree had used in a hard-hitting and raunchy photographic essay of sex clubs a few months ago. The work had been funded by a State of Georgia artist's grant, but had so outraged the moral conservatives in the State Legislature, that it had never been exhibited publicly. Eden made a mental note that this might be a useful future exhibition. She remembered the place as a cheerful if tawdry, little nightclub with a surprisingly good wine selection and interesting after-hours parties.

Belgique interrupted these reflections by announcing

that she was going home. 'I'm giving a party tonight,' she said, 'and I can't trust Henri to get all the preparations right. I have to supervise his efforts very closely.' She gave the pair a lewd wink.

'I see you're dressed for the part in your work overalls,' quipped MacKenzie drily.

For a moment Belgique didn't catch his meaning, but then beamed at him, toying with the zipper of her denim outfit. 'Oh, Michael! That Scottish humour of yours! Yes, these are most practical. And if I get hot, well this zipper is all I need.' With a quick tug, she unzipped the overalls from her breasts to her pubic mound, letting the garment fall from her shoulders. Her breasts jutted out forward, her nipples erect. MacKenzie gasped, stunned at the vision suddenly unpeeled before his eyes, but Eden only smiled at her friend's unexpected antics. With Belgique around, the unexpected was what you expected, and it usually had to do with sex.

'Oh, Michael,' said Belgique, rolling her eyes with an overly theatrical come-on. 'See what you missed!' She pushed her tits together between her palms. 'But it doesn't matter what I do now that Miss Eden has got her claws in you!' But there was no malice in Belgique's tone, and Eden took no offence. To MacKenzie's delight, Eden checked around to see no waiters were within sight, and quickly leant forward to tweak each of Belgique's nipples in turn.

'Oh, Eden, my dear, you haven't lost your touch!' purred Belgique, as she caressed herself. 'Do you two want to come home and help me with Henri?'

But Eden only smiled as she reached into Belgique's lap and pulled up the zipper, gently but firmly. 'Not today, darling,' she replied with a smile, bending to kiss Belgique gently on the cheek. 'MacKenzie and I have work to do. I want to call Hillary James for keys to those warehouses. I want to visit the Aquarium Qlub, and talk to the models. Maybe we can use it for *Art Vivant*.'

'Leave this to me,' said Belgique, adjusting her overalls. She pulled a portable phone from the zip pocket of her capacious bag and punched a single button. 'Hillary? This is Belgique. Look, I'm with Eden Sinclair and Michael MacKenzie, and I told them about your warehouses. They're interested in them as gallery and studio space; would you lease them out if they fixed them up? Good; I thought you would.' Belgique turned to her friends, and giving them a smile and a nod, whispered, 'Things need to happen fast if we're to scupper Raton the rat!'

She turned back to the phone and asked, 'Hillary, if they wanted to look at them today, could they get a key?' She listened for a moment. 'Oh, that's easy. I'll tell them. Can you phone the club and let them know to expect them within the hour? Fine. Thanks. See you this evening. Henri and I have cooked up a little something special for you! Bye.' She folded the little phone away and palmed it back in her bag.

Belgique smiled at her friends. 'Well, let's regard this as an omen; it's all working out so far. The keys to the buildings are at the Qlub. There's usually someone there during the afternoon setting up for the evening. Hillary's going to call ahead so they'll expect you. And she's willing to lease out some of the space if it's suitable, and if you can arrange to fix it up.'

'We'll do that as soon as the loan is finalised,' replied Eden. 'I have an architect friend who will design it cheaply and quickly if I ask him nicely. And he knows several small contractors who specialise in that sort of work. Thanks a lot, Belgique! That was impressive!'

'Oh, it was nothing,' said Belgique with a shrug and a grin. 'You know I'm more than a pretty face and a big pair of tits!' She giggled. 'Well, if I can't tempt you two into my bed with Henri and Hillary, I'll be on my way. Keep in touch. Bye, y'all!'

Eden and MacKenzie sat closely side by side,

emotionally bobbing in the wake of Belgique's departure. MacKenzie shook his head. 'She's a trip, isn't she?'

Eden grinned. 'She's unique, that's all I can say. I love her and she drives me mad, all at the same time. When I thought she had lured you into bed last week, I was ready to break her neck! How on earth did you fend off her lusty charms?'

MacKenzie blushed and admitted, 'It was very hard; or rather I was very hard.'

Eden reached over and stroked between his legs. 'Ummm, bad joke! Like now, you mean?' she added, feeling his erection rise in her hand.

MacKenzie snuggled closer, allowing Eden to grasp him firmly. She started a slow imperceptible rhythm up and down on his shaft.

'Actually it was the same thought that kept me away from those two little nymphs, Lola and Claire. I was so struck by you when we met, and I felt that you wouldn't want to go out with me if you found out that all I did was follow my dick into various gallery-related beds within 24 hours of arriving in Atlanta! I was on your turf, I knew you'd find out. Besides,' he purred sexily, 'you seemed worth waiting for.' He did not mention Stephanie.

'Do I have my claws into you?' asked Eden, recalling Belgique's phrase of moments before.

'Oh, yes, my lovely Eden, that you do,' replied MacKenzie. 'That you do. And I love it; just as I love you!'

They kissed deeply, enjoying their quiet moment alone. Eden liked the warmth and hardness of MacKenzie's body through his cotton shirt. She enjoyed his hands on her nipples, free beneath the satin lining of her dress. 'Let's make love as soon as we get home,' she said. 'I want to do it now, but first we *must* go check out this warehouse.'

Leaving cash for their portion of the bill, Eden and MacKenzie walked hand in hand up Highland Avenue and turned on to Amsterdam Avenue. Eden's bungalow was the fifth one down on the south side. MacKenzie tossed his keys to Eden. 'You drive, you know where you're going.'

Eden zipped the large vehicle effortlessly out of the driveway, and headed south down Highland Avenue, following the street as it veered west and south to Edgewood Avenue, into the historic black neighbourhood of Auburn, birthplace of Martin Luther King. Edgewood went west under the freeway that swept around downtown, and led to an ambiguous area on the edge of the city centre.

A mere dozen blocks from the spectacular towers of the business district, buildings in this neighbourhood were generally simple brick storefronts and warehouses ripe for gentrification. As yet, nobody had 'discovered' them.

'I like this area,' said MacKenzie, appreciatively. 'It's got lots of potential, and it's near the money!' He gestured at the skyscrapers up ahead.

'Yes, and it's not far from our house,' murmured Eden, concentrating on manœuvring the unfamiliar large vehicle around some parked delivery trucks.

MacKenzie was silent for a few moments as his companion drove slowly around the area, trying to get her bearings and find the right group of buildings. He looked hard at Eden, trying to gauge whether she had meant what she had just said.

'I meant what I said just then,' Eden said in a low calm voice, as if reading his thoughts. 'Our house. Will you move in with me, MacKenzie? I don't want to be away from your side. Ever.'

MacKenzie gasped, but then was serious. 'I presume our partnership would extend to half the rent and utilities, half the housework, half the laundry and half the cooking?'

'You cook?'

'Do you like haggis?' At the startled look on Eden's face, MacKenzie relented his teasing. 'No, don't worry. I don't cook haggis, but I do love to cook. I'm a dab hand at tandoori if I can find the spices. Bit hard in Savannah though sometimes.'

Eden appeared to concentrate hard on her driving.

'But seriously, Eden,' he continued, smiling, 'if you agree to split everything fifty-fifty, I think moving in with you would be the most wonderful thing that's ever happened to me. Boy oh boy!' He laughed out loud. 'This is some week! Do you know the feeling when your whole life seems to be rearranging itself around you?'

Eden nodded.

'Well, that's how I feel now. I'll have to work out what to do about my stuff in Savannah, but if we can find a studio here for us, and I can get in with one of the university art departments, we'll be set up. This is so wonderful! Thank you, thank you, thank you!'

'It's a deal,' said Eden. 'Fifty-fifty. Give me a kiss and it's sealed. Oh, wait a minute; we're here.' She pulled to the curb in front of a large brick warehouse and switched off the motor. 'Now kiss me,' she commanded.

Trembling at the touch of MacKenzie's lips on hers, she put her arms around his neck and pulled him close to her. Her sex lips swelled and moistened, and the urge to mount him right there in the truck was almost irresistible. But from the corner of her eye she glimpsed a flurry of movement as a group of attractive young women walked by and disappeared behind a large steel door. MacKenzie's head was buried in Eden's cleavage, and he saw nothing. Eden eased his face reluctantly from her breasts. 'I bet those were dancers at the club,' she said. 'I reckon they'd make great models for the show; if we have some nudity, they'll be used to it. In fact they'll probably find it rather tame.' She tugged at MacKenzie's hand. 'Come on, let's go!'

The heavy door was unlocked. MacKenzie thumped it

with his fist and heaved it aside, then closed it after them. 'Hello!' called Eden. 'We've come for the keys. Hillary James called you about us. I'm Eden Sinclair.'

They found themselves in the high-tech foyer of a deceptively simple space. In contrast to the rough exterior of the building, the highly polished metallic surfaces on the inside sparkled under the focused shine of miniature halogen lights suspended on wires. Several table areas were thus illuminated, and heftier spotlights defined a long stage area. The shiny surfaces curved and leant at slight angles through the main space. A sensuously curved stainless steel counter separated the foyer space from the main body of the club. Music pulsed at low volume from hidden speakers

'Wow!' said Eden with a low whistle of appreciation. 'This place has changed. It's really gone up-market.'

'Yes, Ms Sinclair, so it has.' Eden and Mackenzie turned to see a pretty brunette in an orange halter top and blue jeans standing by the counter. The skimpy top exposed several inches of trim firm stomach and did only a modest job of covering her ample breasts. She introduced herself, 'I'm Laurana. I manage the Qlub. I was expecting you. Hillary James told me to give you these keys.' She held out a ring with two Yales dangling from it. 'These fit the main doors in the other two buildings across the courtyard.' She gestured at the space around her. 'You like it then?'

Eden and MacKenzie nodded. 'I knew it when it wasn't quite this glamorous,' admitted Eden.

Laurana smiled. 'Yes, we have come up in the world. My boss, the woman who rents this space from Hillary James, reckons that this will be the next part of the city to develop. Smart restaurants and galleries and the like.' She shrugged. 'But the game's the same. We take our clothes off, jiggle our tits and dance for the bankers downtown.' She gestured good naturedly over her shoulder in what Eden guessed was the direction of the

252

city centre. 'They just pay more for it now!' Their hostess laughed. 'What's your interest in this place?'

'We're the smart gallery,' said Eden with a smile. She liked this woman, who looked about her age. 'We hope to have an art gallery and a sculpture studio in this complex. Oh, and a painting studio as well.' She looked at MacKenzie and smiled.

He grinned back and nodded. 'You bet.'

Laurana was impressed. 'Wow! Like cool!'

Eden asked a question that had been forming in her mind for the last few hours, and had crystallised in the last few minutes. 'Do you rent out this space for special occasions?'

Laurana nodded. 'The Qlub? Sure, for the right people, and if the price is right.'

'What about the dancers? For what we have in mind, we need women and men to model fancy jewellery and clothes. Like a fashion show,' Eden explained. 'They might have to be partially nude in some instances.'

The sexy manager considered. 'Well, we've got plenty of girls who'd be fine. We have two or three guys who do some simulated sex on stage with the women for the late show. If you need more men, they probably know some gay clubs that could help out.' Her business instincts took charge. 'This sounds like something we might do you as a package deal: facilities, models and food and drink if you want it.'

Eden nodded. 'I'd like to work something out if we decide this is the place. But we need to see the rest of the complex first.' She held up the keys. 'We'll be back in an hour or so.'

Laurana nodded. 'Go out the side door here.' She gestured to an exit that Eden hadn't noticed. 'It goes right out into the courtyard. Save you time. See y'all later; I've got to get ready myself for tonight.' She turned and disappeared behind one of the curved walls.

As Eden and MacKenzie stepped out into a courtyard,

the feeling of spatial openness took away Eden's breath. They stood, enclosed on three sides by buildings, shaded from the late afternoon sun by inwardly facing façades. Large iron gates provided easy access and an effective barrier from the street. Eden was impressed when Mac-Kenzie drew a small sketchbook from his pocket and instantly began mapping the territory.

Her partner paced briskly about the space, his eyes, his mind and his hands measuring possibilities as yet unseen. Eden watched him with delight. She loved the way his eyes sparkled and his face came alive when he was excited. 'Are you thinking what I'm thinking?' she asked, raising her voice to carry across the space.

'Sculpture court!' shouted back MacKenzie. He gestured to the lifting beams and the large doors on the upper floors of the buildings. 'And access for heavy materials and big pieces!'

Together they explored the interiors of the buildings, looking for a gallery area that would be conveniently accessible from the street, and studio space secluded from the public gaze. The buildings had high ceilings from their previous industrial use, and the one nearer the street had fine oak beams and columns, still with their original cast-iron connectors. North and south light flooded in from tall windows that came down almost to floor level, speaking of a time before the flick of a switch could banish darkness, and when daylight was a precious resource.

'This is it,' said MacKenzie.

'It's fabulous,' agreed Eden. 'I love it here already. We can have the gallery at ground level, opening on to the courtyard, and our studios can be above it.' Her body was quivering with excitement, and she felt her desire mount for MacKenzie in this place that would house their new venture together. 'Come here MacKenzie. It's time I showed you just how much I love you. Let's christen this space. I'm horny and I want you inside me!'

Eden shed her few clothes in record time and stood naked before MacKenzie, who gazed in wonder at his lover's body, painted golden by the setting sun. He felt his cock rise, and he unzipped his fly to release it. Presenting himself, he walked to Eden. 'This is all for you,' he said. 'It's your plaything, to do with what you want.'

Eden cupped her hands around MacKenzie's succulent balls as they dangled, full of come beneath his ginger-haired cock. 'I'll take very good care of it,' she murmured, and lovingly stroked his shaft. 'My wonderful ginger root!'

In a matching moment, he too was naked, and lifting a surprised Eden in his strong arms, he hoisted her to his waist. 'Grab that bar,' he said.

Eden looked up and saw a small beam running between two columns above her head. She reached up and took some of her weight on her arms. MacKenzie supported her gently, and cupping the cheeks of her bum in his hands, stood between her legs. She spread herself wide, her vulva opening like a ripe bud blossoming into flower, her slick lips moist with her juices.

Then MacKenzie was inside her, his penis filling her void to the very tip of her womb, his pubic bone rubbing against her clitoris with every thrust. Eden screamed with delight as spasms of sheer sensuality rippled through her; the unusual angle of MacKenzie's dick stroked her vaginal walls to a tingling frenzy. Her tongue sought his as they rocked together, fusing into one focus of urgent pleasure.

Hanging from her arms, Eden swung herself backward and forward to accentuate the movement of MacKenzie's cock inside her. She retreated to expose all but the tip, the ridge of the glans melding with her vaginal lips, and then slid forward to collide with the base of his shaft, grinding her clitoris against his flesh. She came momentarily before he did, writhing sideways to wrench every nuance of carnal pleasure from their physical union. Corkscrewing her buttocks in his strong grip, she shuddered to a crescendo.

Eden recognised the small changes in MacKenzie's body that told her his orgasm was near: the rhythm of his thrusts, the tension in his muscles. The scent of his lust was tangible.

He climaxed within her in an explosion so forceful that she imagined his semen spraying up into her womb. His bucking ecstasy triggered her aftershocks, and she collapsed with her arms around his neck, gasping for breath amidst his soft auburn hair, biting his neck softly as each little tremor racked her body.

'Oh. God, MacKenzie! How do you do that?' Eden moaned as she held tight to her lover, who bore her weight effortlessly. His dick was still firm inside her as he carried her over to a window overlooking the courtyard.

'I reckon this is our place now,' he said, reverently.

Chapter Twenty-One
Coup d'État

*T*he following morning Eden and MacKenzie went out for breakfast before picking up Eden's little Miata, still parked at Galerie Raton. Midtown was deserted on Sunday mornings, and they drove both vehicles to The New Big Village, a little breakfast place on McLendon Avenue run by a hard-working Greek couple.

From their table, Eden called Hillary James and Belgique on her cordless phone, arranging for them all to meet for a late lunch at the Pewter Rose restaurant in Buckhead, near Hillary James's posh suburban mansion.

Eden had only met Belgique's wealthy friend once before, at the opening of a gallery show. She had a vague memory of a pleasant woman in early middle age, who actually knew something about contemporary art. They had enjoyed a brief conversation about post-modernist painters during which Eden had been surprised by Hillary's grasp of the subject.

With the four of them ensconced in a well-upholstered booth at the Pewter Rose, sipping their mimosa cocktails, Eden came straight to the point.

'Ms James . . .'

'Oh, please call me Hillary.' Hillary James seemed at

pains to put Eden and MacKenzie at their ease. Eden had the distinct impression that the woman had dressed down for their lunch meeting, but the elegance of the Calvin Klein designer-cut of her everyday working outfit of simple white blouse and blue jeans betrayed her ploy to Eden's discerning eye, as did the gold Rolex peeping from her sleeve.

'Thank you.' Eden smiled. 'Hillary, MacKenzie and I visited your warehouse downtown on Edgewood Avenue yesterday. Apart from space for our new gallery, we also need studios for both of us.' She gave MacKenzie's thigh a squeeze under the table. 'We saw some spaces that would work perfectly, and we'd also like to use the courtyard for outdoor sculpture exhibitions.' She stopped to gauge her potential landlady's reaction.

Hillary James smiled. 'I'm so glad you like it,' she said. 'Of course Belgique has told me all about your plans, and you already know I'm very happy to back your venture with some capital of my own. Contemporary art here in Atlanta needs all the help it can get.' She paused, then added, 'In fact, I might be interested in taking some art as partial payment towards the rent. If I had some particular subjects in mind, could we arrange some type of no-fee commission?'

Eden moved to seal the arrangement. 'Certainly,' she said. 'We could agree a monthly cash amount and a commission-in-kind for the first year's rent, and then renegotiate on an annual basis thereafter.'

Hillary and Eden quickly agreed financial terms, and the talk turned to matters of logistics.

'We need to start cleaning things up and organising the space in the next few days,' explained Eden. 'Our architect can make sketch plans for the few things that need altering, and we hope to get a contractor in to do the work by the end of the month. We could have our first show in about six weeks' time if all goes well. Our studio spaces are fine just the way they are; all we need to do is clean them out and fix up some extra lighting.'

'I'll arrange for you to have full access from tomorrow,' said Hillary, 'with the first rent payment due the beginning of next month.'

With the arrival of their food, the lunch devolved into pleasant conversation about the arts in Atlanta, and the gathering broke up in mid-afternoon with a mixture of business handshakes and friendly embraces. With mixed feelings of relief and excitement, Eden and MacKenzie returned to Eden's house to relax before starting on their next week's hectic work schedule.

Once indoors, Eden raced to get naked. MacKenzie had only got as far as removing his shoes and socks.

'Slowcoach!' chided Eden. 'Take off your clothes, MacKenzie. I want to play with that gorgeous dick of yours!'

'Your wish is my command,' he said with a slow smile that lit up his whole face. 'But I think I need some help.'

With a sexy giggle Eden slipped to her knees and unfastened his belt and unzipped his fly. She pulled his jeans from his tight buttocks and slipped her fingers in the waistband of his underwear, rolling both garments together down to his ankles. MacKenzie stepped clear of his clothes and held his rigid penis in his hand, stroking his shaft as Eden gloried at the sight.

'Oh, MacKenzie,' she murmured. 'How many times I dreamed of seeing you just like that! Sometimes I can't believe this is really happening.'

He moved towards her, offering her his dick, and she took him deliciously in her mouth, rocking back and forth and stroking her fingers along the sexy space between his balls and his anus.

'Come to bed,' he whispered. 'I want to do the same to you.'

With a warm glow of delight, Eden straddled her lover

on the bed, offering him her moist sex. MacKenzie lapped her nectar with relish. He plunged his tongue right inside Eden's vagina, sending little shocks of sensation through her as he explored the most sensitive areas of her intimate flesh.

MacKenzie reached for the plastic dispenser of cocoa butter by the bed, and warming a liberal quantity in his hands, he applied the sweet cream to her cleft. Rubbing delicately around her clitoris, he eased three fingers inside her vagina to probe the fullest extent of her channel, and anointed the tight pucker of her anus, gently pushing one finger inside just to the first knuckle.

Before her, MacKenzie's great penis twitched with his passion, and Eden watched as small beads of fluid crested on his purple glans. Afire with her own sensations, she bent forward and cupped his balls in her hands, licking the semen from his tip. She wound her fingers through the dense ginger curls surrounding his shaft, gripping it tightly, and masturbating him in time with his fingers inside her.

'Oh, God, MacKenzie,' she cried, feeling her climax building, 'your fingers feel so good, but I must have your cock inside me!'

Releasing herself from his fingers, she lowered herself directly on to his vertical penis and, placing her hands on his muscled thighs, rocked herself obsessively to orgasm, alternately gripping and releasing his shaft with the muscles in her vagina, completely absorbed this time in her own pleasure. She felt MacKenzie convulse inside her as his semen flooded the hidden walls of her sex, and then her own juices bathed his dick as she came with a shuddering flow of passion.

The next week passed in a blur of activity and tension, as Eden hastened to sort out the myriad details of the new gallery while keeping it secret from Raton. The atmosphere at work between the two of them was frigid in the extreme. Eden steeled herself to ignore her employer's rudeness and plunged ahead with her own preparations. Fortunately, Raton chose to absent himself from work for large periods of time.

Eden signed the papers for the business loans from Belgique's consortium and set up a new bank account. Seeing the words 'Ginger Root' printed on the new chequebooks gave her a frisson of pleasure, as images of MacKenzie's lovely dick rose in her mind.

MacKenzie himself started work on cleaning and fitting out the gallery and studio spaces with the help of the architect friend of Eden's and his brother-in-law, a local contractor. Very little needed to be done other than cosmetic improvements and some rewiring for air-conditioning and new lights. As soon as things were under control, MacKenzie left briefly for Savannah with Paul and the delivery van to load up his portable equipment and materials from his studio, and his clothes and domestic items from his apartment. As much as he liked Savannah, the thought of living with Eden and waking up next to her beautiful naked body each morning filled him with more joy than he could express. He had to be very careful not to reveal any details of their plans to Paul, who, however, seemed preoccupied with his own affairs, and displayed little curiosity.

At Galerie Raton, Eden took advantage of her employer's absence to meet with Angela and Winston Fineman and orchestrate publicity for Ginger Root Gallery's grand opening show. Eden made an offer to Angela that had been on her mind for several days, as she had watched with appreciation the efficiency and energy with which the younger woman threw herself into the new venture.

Angela spent time dealing with the artists, answering a multitude of questions that arose subsequent to the meeting at La Cuba-Libra; she spoke knowledgeably with the solicitor and bank manager about legal and

261

financial details; and she took time out to cuddle with Fineman on his frequent visits to the gallery.

During one of these visits, Eden called the two love-birds into her office. As they came up the stairs, Eden noted with pleasure that Angela's eyes were shining and Fineman had a goofy look on his face. She recognised happily that they were falling in love.

But she was all business when she spoke. 'Angela, I think you're doing a fabulous job, helping with all the work on the new gallery. I want to make you an offer. Would you become Assistant Director?'

Fineman beamed with pride. Angela gasped, 'Really, Eden? You mean it?' Her expression of delight faltered for a brief moment. 'Would I still be able to exhibit?'

Eden smiled. 'Most certainly. I've come to see you as integral to the whole operation, both as administrator and as an artist. Did you see I sold your drawing from the exhibition downstairs?'

'Oh, my God, no, I didn't! I've been so busy I hadn't noticed.'

'Well, congratulations anyway! And Winston,' Eden turned to address the critic by his Christian name for the first time, 'I think you're integral, too. We need a lot of publicity, and we need access to the national magazines. Are you still a contributing regional editor for *Art in America*?'

Fineman nodded. 'Yes, I am,' he said, 'and before you ask, the answer is yes; I will write pieces for them on some of your shows. I'd be delighted. And,' he added, 'I'll speak to my friend who covers the south-east for *Art Forum*, and I think we can get you an interview, locally, in *Art Papers*.'

Eden raised her coffee cup in appreciation. 'It's too early for wine,' she said, 'but here's a toast to a new partnership: the two of you and MacKenzie and me. I have a feeling we're going to be seeing a lot of each other!'

Angela smiled at Eden and blew her a kiss. 'Here's to Ginger Root!'

Eden burst into a fit of giggles.

In the next few days, at Angela's suggestion, the new Director and Assistant Director carefully sounded out Claire and Lola regarding their participation in the new gallery. As usual, Angela's intuition was correct, and the two young students were thrilled at the prospect of working in a more congenial environment. Between them the four women pieced together the final arrangements, anxious, because secrecy from Raton could not be maintained much longer. Their days passed in a flurry of faxes, e-mails and telephone calls to artists, builders, electricians and to City Hall, lining up the required building and business permits.

On the Friday morning of the second week since the opening reception, Eden was confident at last that all was ready. She assembled MacKenzie, Angela and Belgique at the gallery as moral support, but asked them to wait outside Raton's office. 'This is something I need to do by myself,' she said, sounding braver than she felt. 'He's bound to shout and scream at me, but I don't want you to come in unless it sounds dangerous.' MacKenzie looked as if he was about to demur, but checked himself. Eden touched his arm. 'I'll know that you're right outside if I need you.'

Justin was passing by on some errand, and on the spur of the moment, Eden stayed him. 'Justin, can you just wait here with the others? There's something urgent I have to discuss with Mr Raton.'

The delivery man looked puzzled, but nodded. 'Sure thing, Miss Eden.'

MacKenzie held her briefly in his arms and gave her a big kiss. 'We're right here if you need us,' he said. 'Good luck!'

Her heart pounding in her chest, Eden knocked smartly on the door of Raton's office and walked in. Lavender scent wafted to her nostrils.

He was sitting behind his large oak desk in his habitual grey Italian suit. In his well-appointed lair, with its fine antique furniture blending effortlessly with contemporary art on the walls, Raton reminded Eden of an immaculate spider, spinning his invisible webs of deceit over those around him. She felt a flash of repugnance. How could she ever have fantasised about having sex with this man?

Her repulsion must have shown on her face, for Raton said acidly as he looked up, 'Is something wrong with you, Ms Sinclair?'

Eden dropped her bombshell on Raton. She swallowed, and then looked Raton coolly in the eye. 'Here is my resignation,' she said simply, taking a thin sheet of paper from her inside pocket and laying it before him. 'It is effective as of the end of today.'

Raton's eyes gleamed in satisfaction and triumph.

Ignoring his smug look, Eden continued. 'I will be taking all my papers from my office, and,' she paused to relish the moment, 'I will also be taking with me all the works of art in the gallery. The artists are now under contract to me, and have given me their permission to remove their work. After today, Mr Raton, you effectively have no gallery operation here in Atlanta.'

Eden stepped back and waited for the explosion. It came immediately.

'You stupid little bitch!' screamed Raton, his gloating transformed into a look of pure rage. All of a sudden things were not going according to his carefully constructed plan. 'What the hell do you mean, no gallery? All this is mine!' He swept his arm imperiously around the space. 'You can't just walk in here and say you're taking it away! You're out of your feeble little mind! Now just leave; you're fired! You don't need to resign!' He snatched the paper from his desk and tore it into shreds. He flung them at her feet. 'Go!'

Eden stood her ground, her face impassive. 'No, you listen to me, Mr Raton. It has come to my knowledge that you are planning a criminal deception to defraud the artists of their full percentages and line your own pocket,' she stated crisply. Her pulse was racing but her mind was calm now she had the man in front of her.

'I have explained the situation to all the gallery artists.' She spoke slowly and clearly. 'They have unanimously agreed to terminate their relationship with you. Acting on their behalf, I have already annulled their contracts according to the powers given to me under my conditions of employment as Gallery Director.'

Raton barged into her speech. 'You can't do that! That's stealing my artists! I'll have the law onto you. I'll sue you for every miserable cent you've got. I'll ruin you!'

With a massive effort of will, Eden held her temper. 'The only reason you'll need a lawyer is to answer charges of sexual harassment and conspiracy. I have spoken to an attorney about your recent conduct, and I have a witness to your plans who has also made a legal deposition. We will turn these over to the police immediately if you interfere in any way with my operations. I have also talked with a reporter from the *Atlanta Democrat*, who is eager to run the story.' She didn't say that this was only Winston Fineman, the art critic. 'But he has promised not to unless you give me cause.'

The veins stood out on Raton's face. 'I know who your witness is! It's that bitch Belgique du Pont!' he yelled. 'Who would believe her?'

'What does it matter?' said Eden, keeping her voice steady. 'Just think about it; the publicity alone will ruin you here in Atlanta. My advice is to leave town quietly and make a fresh start somewhere else. You've got assets in this building that you could liquidate and start over. If you leave us alone we'll leave you alone. But if you try to mess with us, I've got the papers with our lawyer, and an article ready to give to *Art in America* and *Art & Auction* that will destroy your reputation nationwide.'

Raton's rage boiled over and he stood up suddenly, striding round his desk in a threatening manner. Recoiling with the memory of his bruising of Belgique's arm, Eden stepped back instinctively as Raton advanced towards her, suddenly sinister.

But Belgique stepped through the door and halted him in his tracks. 'I can't stand to be called a bitch, especially by a craven skunk like you,' she said to Raton calmly, and explained patronisingly, 'I've given a very full interview to a local reporter; and I've made a deposition to my lawyer, giving every detail of your proposal to me. He has instructions to go to the police if you make even one move against us.'

'How dare you! I'll fix your miserable little scheme right here and now!' Raton shouted. With a vicious snarl on his face, he moved toward Belgique, his arm drawn back to side-swipe the petite woman.

MacKenzie stepped forward from his position just outside the door, but before he reached Raton, Justin Scott leapt past him and in one swift move froze the gallery owner's arm in mid-air with a strong grip of his left hand. Moving between Raton and Belgique the delivery man slowly but firmly prodded his employer backward.

'Now just hold still there,' he drawled in Raton's ear in his soft Georgia accent. 'Don't you know better than to try hitting a pretty little woman like Ms du Pont here? That just ain't mannerly.' He squeezed Raton's arm, still caught in his fist, bringing a wince of pain to the man's face. 'If I let you go now, are you going to behave yourself like a gentleman?' A further tightening of his vice-like grip brought a squeal from the gallery owner.

Eden stepped forward. 'That's enough, Justin! Let him go, please.' She turned to Raton and said in a silky voice loaded with menace, 'I'm sure Mr Raton knows what's best for him. He'll be quiet and polite now.'

Justin released the ruffled Raton and stepped back, a scowl still on his face, his body tensed for further action. He looked a little disappointed. 'It ain't right to hit a lady,' he said fiercely.

Belgique sidled forward and put her arms around the young man. 'Thank you Justin. You were wonderful!' She squeezed his bicep in a sexy gesture of appreciation.

Raton just scowled at his employee, his mouth still contorted with rage. 'You blundering oaf!' he hissed at Justin. 'How dare you manhandle me! You're fired! Get out of the gallery immediately!'

Justin surprised Eden by simply smiling back at his former boss. 'Well, I guess I'm not surprised about that, mister,' he said. 'But from what I've just heard, I wouldn't want to work for slime like you anyway. Just you keep your hands off Miss Belgique here. If you threaten her again, I'll be back to see you, and Miss Sinclair won't be around to stop me.' His eyes bored into Raton's. 'You get my meaning?'

Raton bristled with anger, but he dropped his stare.

Justin turned to Eden. 'Ms Sinclair, I reckon I'm out of a job, and probably Paul will be too, when he hears about all this. I'd like to work for you and Mr MacKenzie here if you could use me. You know my work,' he blushed slightly and glanced sideways at Belgique, who still held his arm, 'and you know some other things about me, I guess. You can trust me to work hard for y'all.'

Amidst the tension in the room, Eden smiled. 'We're all taking a risk with this new venture,' she said, looking into Justin's eyes carefully. 'I'm grateful for what you did just now.' She looked enquiringly at MacKenzie, whose body had relaxed slightly from its earlier alertness. 'If my partner agrees, you and Paul could start work immediately.'

MacKenzie nodded. 'Fine by me.'

'Right. The first task is to load up all the work here in the gallery and take it to our new premises.' She put a smile of false sweetness on her face as she turned to Raton. 'I'm sure Mr Raton will let us borrow the delivery van just for the rest of the day.'

Despite her outward calm, Raton's expression of pure hatred scared Eden. 'You fucking bitch!' he said softly to Eden, his voice full of menace. 'Don't think you've heard the last of this! You can't do this to me! I'll ruin you!' He swung around to glare at Belgique. 'You're as bad as the rest of them. No one will ever believe the rantings of a rich little whore like you!'

Justin growled and tensed his whole body. He looked as if he would strangle Raton on the spot. But Belgique stroked his arm and whispered, 'Down, boy!'

She turned to face Raton, a smile on her face but loathing in her eyes. 'Oh, Alexander,' she said sweetly. 'Of course they'll believe me. I can be so very convincing.' She almost purred. 'And I have so many rich and powerful friends. Oh, yes, Alexander, everyone will lap it up, you can count on it!'

She closed on Raton and glared right into his face. Justin and MacKenzie stepped in at his sides. 'Your insults don't bother me, darling.' The venom now evident in her voice matched anything that Raton could produce. 'I dragged myself up from the streets of New Orleans; I know a poisonous little rat when I see one. I've got you by the short and curlies on this one, and if you make any move against me, or against Eden, so help me, I'll make you wish you'd never been born, you miserable sonofabitch!'

Eden heard Angela gasp as they felt the force of Belgique's emotion like a physical attack. Raton felt it, too, and stepped back from her tirade, a look of shock replacing his own anger.

MacKenzie gripped Eden's elbow to lend support, and spoke up for the first time. 'Raton, we'll be out of here by

268

the end of the day, with everything that belongs to us and our artists. We won't be back, unless you do something stupid that forces us to take further action against you. Our lawyer is prepared to act immediately if we hear even the slightest whisper of any trouble from you. Is that clear?'

Raton said nothing.

'I said, is that clear?' MacKenzie's voice rose to a pitch of command that Eden had not heard before. She was so glad he was at her side. Despite her tension, she felt a great longing for her new partner and live-in lover.

Raton raised a last flash of anger in his reply. 'Yes, it's clear.' He sneered at the small group surrounding him. 'You think you're all so fucking clever! You think you've beaten me. But you'll see! I'll get even; just you wait. You haven't heard the last of this!'

He stared into MacKenzie's angry eyes, but saw there only hard determination and a will that more than matched his own. With a final snarl, he pushed his way between the assembled group and paused at the door. 'If I see any of you in this building tomorrow, I'll call the police and have you arrested for trespassing! Don't think I won't! I'll get you somehow, you bastards!'

He stormed out of the gallery, and they heard a loud crash as the front door slammed behind him. Eden felt her body go limp with the release of tension. She sat cross-legged on the floor, leant against the wall and closed her eyes. 'That was every bit as bad as I imagined it would be.'

'Yes,' said MacKenzie, 'but I think we won. He may bluster, but he won't give us any trouble. He knows that all the publicity would ruin him. If he's got any sense, he'll sell up and move elsewhere.'

'And feed off some other unfortunate artists, most likely,' said Eden grimly.

'If they let him,' put in Angela with not too much sympathy, and speaking for the first time. 'Anyway, that's not our problem, Eden. We've plenty to do without worrying about anybody else.'

'Right,' said Eden, standing up and bracing herself. 'Let's start. Justin!' She looked around, but couldn't find her new assistant. Angela whispered, 'Belgique took him next door.' She smothered a giggle.

Eden tiptoed to the door and peeked through the crack at the hinge. Sure enough, there was Belgique locked in a kiss with the young man, who had pushed up her blouse and was busily fondling Belgique's wonderful breasts.

'You must come and visit me again, Justin,' purred Belgique, softly.

Justin whispered, 'I'd love that Miss Belgique.' Eden strained to hear as he continued. 'Can you tie me up again? I've been dreaming about that ever since you did it to me!'

It was Eden's turn to suppress a laugh. Before Belgique could reply, she rapped firmly on the door and walked in. Justin moved quickly to take his hands from Belgique's breasts, but the woman clamped his arms in place with hers.

'Don't act like a little boy caught behind the woodshed, Justin,' she said with a wicked little smile on her face. 'Eden's seen it all before. Believe me, it takes a whole lot to shock your new boss!' She let go of his hands, letting her fingers brush Justin's very evident erection. The young man didn't look at Eden, but he didn't start at Belgique's public caress.

'Belgique,' said Eden with mock severity, 'please let Justin go. By all means do whatever you want with him later, but now I need him to earn his new wages.' She caught Justin's eye at last and signalled him to follow her.

Belgique straightened her attire and called after him, 'Call me when you're through, Justin, dear. I'll fix some supper and then we can play all night!' Eden saw the

270

young man's eyes sparkle, but otherwise he was attentive to her instructions.

For the next few hours, Justin, MacKenzie, Angela and Eden loaded art into the gallery's van and shuttled back and forth between Galerie Raton and their new premises. It was dark by the time they had completed the transfer of artwork and papers. Her office empty of all files and personal belongings, Eden felt a twinge of regret at leaving the plush mezzanine, but she pushed the feeling behind her. What lay ahead was more exciting.

She was the last one out the front door. She locked it behind her and pushed her set of keys through the mail slot. She was sure Raton would change the locks anyway. In the darkness of the building, MacKenzie's large new notice stood out clearly, taped to the outside of the heavy doors.

The sign read, GALLERY CLOSED: GOING OUT OF BUSINESS.

Chapter Twenty-Two
Art Vivant!

*A*s Eden and MacKenzie stepped out of their pick-up truck, flashbulbs went off and TV cameras and microphones were thrust in their faces. Shouted questions were barely audible above the chanting of the banner-waving religious fundamentalists penned behind a police cordon opposite the Ginger Root Gallery. Running the gauntlet of the press and crowds of visitors waiting for the gallery to open, they made it to the sculpture courtyard where they were welcomed by a grinning Angela.

'Well,' she said, 'we wanted publicity for the opening of the wearable art show, and now we've got it! I told the press you'd answer some questions here when you're ready.'

'No time like the present,' said Eden, and taking a deep breath she turned to face the reporters.

'Ms Sinclair,' shouted one young woman, 'Channel 15 News. What's your answer to the religious right, who are calling your new show too sexually oriented, anti-family values, and worthy only of Sodom and Gomorrah?'

Eden smiled grimly. 'I think Sodom and Gomorrah got a bad press.' This drew some laughs. 'But seriously,' she continued, 'I think those people over there,' she gestured at the protesters, 'have a very warped sense of values. Our purpose in this show is to celebrate the human body by decorating it with exciting works of art. If you begin from the standpoint that the human body is beautiful, then no fair-minded person can object to this show.'

'Will you be wearing that sexy outfit that was in the paper this morning?'

'Yes,' confirmed Eden. 'I love it!'

'Is it true that your gallery is financed by a coalition of militant lesbians?'

Eden burst out laughing. 'No, of course not! I know who started that rumour, and that unpleasant gentleman isn't to be trusted. Don't believe a word he says!'

MacKenzie cut off further questions with a smile and led Eden inside, closing the door behind them. 'Winston's article and the photographs in the paper certainly did the trick,' he said as they surveyed the gallery, checking for the umpteenth time that everything was ready for the official opening in a few minutes. 'We'll be on the ten o'clock evening news and all over the front page again tomorrow. We should get a good crowd for the next few days.'

Eden picked up the arts section of that day's *Atlanta Democrat*. Taking up most of the front page was a large colour photograph of herself modelling MacKenzie's *pièce de résistance* for the show, a minimal silver body sheath of loosely woven links that draped from high around her neck down to her bare feet, exposing most of her body through the connected rings, except for three denser small areas strategically placed. Winston Fineman had described it well, '... this open mesh has concentrated clusters of silver rings and disks around each nipple, and a triangular focus that cups the wearer's delta of Venus.' The photograph depicted it perfectly.

'The picture looks stunning!' said Angela admiringly.

'Open the doors, Angela,' said Eden. 'We're ready!'

* * *

Within moments of its doors opening, the gallery was filled with the chatter of an excited crowd, as wealthy patrons lured by Eden away from Galerie Raton, mingled with newcomers and the simply curious. Angela, Lola and Claire handed out programmes at the door, while Justin and Paul tended bar. The simple warehouse space had been transformed into a series of smaller enclosures by temporary walls, their surfaces coloured in single bold pigments like giant minimalist paintings. Dark Tuscan reds, deep greens and smoky grey-blues predominated, standing in contrast to the stark white interior walls of the old building.

Each space was inhabited by black and white mannequins, upon which were displayed hand-crafted jewellery and hand-woven clothing, created specially by all the gallery's artists. The bearded potter who had wanted to wring Raton's neck had contributed two matching ceramic pendants attached to nipple rings. More conventional necklaces, rings and earrings adorned some mannequins, but undoubtedly most of the jewellery needed plenty of bare flesh to be best appreciated.

The programmes in the patrons' hands specified the order of the two-part showing; first the static display in the gallery, then a short interval, followed by the fashion show with live models across the courtyard at the Aquarium Qlub.

To provide maximum contrast with her later plans, Eden had dressed modestly for the opening, in a classic black cotton dress, hemmed to mid-thigh and featuring a simple scoop neckline. She wore no stockings and simple wingtip pumps. MacKenzie wore his usual combination of white dress shirt, freshly washed Levis and tan loafers. At Eden's insistence he sported a tie. It depicted rows of teddy bears: Eden felt like hugging him on the spot.

Instead, she concentrated upon working the crowd, greeting old friends and new. Jay Jay and his companions, Greg and Jerry, were there, spending time chatting with Paul at the bar. In addition, Jay Jay sported a handsome mystery man hovering at his elbow.

'How do you like the fresco painting?' Eden innocently asked the newcomer.

The man looked blank for a moment, and then a slow smile spread over his face, lighting his eyes. 'Oh, very well, thank you Ms Sinclair. It's particularly fine in the early morning sunlight!'

Jay Jay gave Eden a pretend slap on the wrist. 'How did you know?' he asked.

Eden stood on tiptoe to kiss her old friend. 'I just looked into your eyes,' she said. 'I can see you're in love.'

Jay Jay returned her appraisal. 'You, too,' he said.

Eden nodded happily, and detached herself to speak with Vivienne and Liz, before moving on to greet Hillary James and Cindee Montgomery. Both women were attended by Xavier Zachary and Eden's curiosity was piqued, but their fledgeling conversation was interrupted by a burst of chatter from the doorway. Eden looked up to trace its cause.

It was Belgique, making her entrance. Dressed in gold.

The sweetheart neckline of Belgique's gown swept across her pectorals, revealing the cap of each shoulder, and diving almost to her navel. The plunging neckline left her breasts free to announce themselves, and as she passed through the crowd, the body-skimming fit of the dress allowed her creamy mounds to tease the audience and occasionally to escape from the silk that brushed against them. Even from several paces away Eden could see that her friend's nipples had been specially made up with gold glitter around each areola. The crowd eddied around her, as men and women alike positioned themselves to catch more than a glimpse of Belgique's stunning breasts. Henri, who had been elevated to the role of personal escort for the evening, walked beside her, a well-composed contrast in formal evening wear, his eyes locked helplessly on his employer's cleavage.

Belgique bore across the room to Eden who felt Belgique's hard nipples press against her as they embraced. 'You look ravishing,' Eden said to her friend, 'but you're not wearing any jewellery!' This was a momentous omission from Belgique's wardrobe.

'Oh, Eden,' she replied with a sigh. 'I couldn't decide what to wear. I just thought I'd buy some new pieces here tonight!'

Eden laughed with her friend. 'You've timed your entrance just right as always,' she said. 'I'm just about to announce the interval and get ready for Part Two next door. You have time to change.'

MacKenzie appeared with a portable microphone which he handed to Eden. She thanked all those present, and invited them to cross the courtyard in fifteen minutes. A buzz of excitement rose from the audience as they headed for Justin and Paul at the bar.

When the more intimate fashion show commenced, it was immediately clear that much of the wearable art amounted to no more than minimal jewellery set upon stripped down bodies. The Qlub had added a fashion catwalk to its normal dance stages, and along its length paraded a series of beautiful men and women, gyrating to the pulse of techno music under the artfully arranged and ever-changing lights. The models wore sleek Spandex and micro-fibre clothing which outlined their bodies like a second skin.

Belgique had arranged with Laurana at the Aquarium Qlub for their dancers to be augmented for the evening by an array of young, unemployed actors. She had personally selected them for the event, telling Eden that they were 'hand-picked'.

Eden had planned the performance to build to a finale, and the second and third round of models featured conspicuously more bare flesh and provocative ornamentation. The emotional temperature in the Qlub rose to new levels as Eden signalled for Belgique and Angela to step together into the lights.

A great gasp went up from the crowd and flashbulbs popped as the two beautiful women paced arm in arm above the guests. They each displayed pieces created by the photographers Liz Angelo and Vivienne Dupree. Angela wore nothing bar a minuscule thong beneath a skin-hugging silk teddy that revealed the cheeks of her bottom and was so finely woven that its transparency barely blurred the outlines of her pubic hair and the profile of her very erect nipples. On to every square inch of the fabric had been painstakingly screenprinted a repetitive series of photographs of Liz in a variety of sexual positions. As Angela sashayed down the walk, the images of the sexy woman rippled in time to her movements. The audience loved it.

Belgique was a stunning contrast. Her shorter figure with her notable breasts and curly dark hair was nearly nude save for small round photographs set in silver frames that dangled from velvet-lined nipple clamps. The photographs illustrated starkly composed black-and-white portraits of Vivienne licking a shiny metallic dildo. But what set the crowd on the edge of their chairs was the completion of the minuscule outfit by a small pair of bikini pants, completely covered with another cropped photographic portrait of Vivienne, this time with her mouth open invitingly. And within the outline of Vivienne's lips, a matching hole had been cut in the bikini to reveal Belgique's dark pubic curls, apparently growing from the woman's mouth.

Applause broke out around the room, but it was stilled by sudden darkness. When light returned it did so in a focused pool of spots that illuminated Eden, alone on the catwalk, sparkling in MacKenzie's creation of the silver-ringed body sheath. Eden walked slowly and seductively under the gaze of a hypnotised audience, her oiled skin glowing in the light. She suddenly stopped and stood motionless. The music ceased, creating a vacuum into which stepped two lithe young dancers, and with flowing grace these attendants divested Eden of her garment. A gasp arose from the audience for Eden wore only a glittering G-string and a necklace across her naked breasts. The necklace comprised a string of sterling silver penises, life-sized and erect, and at the base of each shone clusters of rubies, glowing a bright, bright red!

'Welcome to Ginger Root!' said Eden, and bowed.

Epilogue

The gallery below their studios had been transformed into a cool, minimal space, designed to showcase MacKenzie's erotic sculptures to maximum effect. Proudly displayed in the publicity racks by the desk and the door were glowing reviews of the show from *Art in America*, *Art Papers* and *Art Forum*.

Equally glowing, but not on public view were the bank statements and the sales invoices for the gallery. They told of the sell-out performance of the wearable art show, with repeat orders for many pieces, and of the development of a healthy client list as the Ginger Root Gallery more than filled the vacuum left by the departed Raton. And just this week, MacKenzie had sold two large sculptures that he had finished with the help of the facilities at his new place of part-time employment, Georgia State University, whose campus was only a few blocks from the gallery.

His studio was now filled with highly developed sketches and maquettes for his next piece, *The Judgement of Paris*. Eden, Angela and Belgique had all been cooperative and willing models, separately and together in his studio.

Winston Fineman had needed no erotic stimulations from Angela to write ecstatic reviews of MacKenzie's show, but he received them anyway. The pair had moved into a house together, where she had converted a room into a painting studio. Her work had begun to sell regularly; her only worry was that the duties of Assistant Director in a successful gallery limited her time to paint.

Eden and MacKenzie lay together naked on cushions strewn on the floor in her studio. The soft fall sunlight graced their intertwined bodies, but as they began to make love, Eden raised her head and said, 'MacKenzie, what I really want to do is draw you, to see you as you really are.'

'OK,' agreed MacKenzie, 'but me first. You look so gorgeous I can't wait.'

They gathered together drawing materials, and Eden reclined on the cushions tingling in anticipation, her clitoris as swollen and her vagina as wet as if Mac-Kenzie's fingers were already inside her. Her lover studied her carefully from behind his drawing pad, and with each move of his eyes across her naked body, and with each gesture of his pencil, Eden felt a delicious shudder as if her very core was being stroked and caressed. She watched MacKenzie's cock stiffen like a pole rising from his ginger curls; she eased her hand between her legs, and fondled her clitoris, feeling her juices seep across her fingers.

'Eden,' whispered MacKenzie, 'stay just as you are!'

When it was her turn to draw, Eden posed MacKenzie on his back, propped on one elbow. 'Just play with yourself, darling,' she coaxed, 'but don't come quite yet.' She was so excited at the prospect of MacKenzie before her; all else was blotted out. Looking deeply into her lover's soul, she poured her love into every line on the paper, feeling an intense erotic charge in the pit of her vagina. This time, with this medium, she felt she really possessed him.

As she finished the study, replete with vigorous yet tender lines and crisp black shadows that captured the tense volumes of MacKenzie's body, Eden felt awash with lust and love, and though her hands were occupied with drawing, she experienced a near-orgasm that left her breathless. She dropped the sketch to one side, and leant closer to her lover.

MacKenzie reached to her, his fingers curling inside her vagina, his thumb nestling over her blooming love bud.

Eden could wait no longer. She cried, 'Now, MacKenzie, now! Fuck me, sweetheart. Love me forever!'

A scantily clad Angela trotted upstairs looking for Eden. Wearing only a towel draped around her perspiring body, she was anxious for a shower after work in the small stall Eden had installed in the rear of her studio. Stepping across the threshold, her call of enquiry was stilled on her lips as she saw the two naked bodies sprawling, apparently asleep across the cushions. Eden's hand was still outstretched to hold MacKenzie's soft, plump penis in her fingers; but Angela's attention was also caught by two vibrant sketches abandoned on the floor before the sleeping lovers.

Not wishing to disturb the pair, Angela was nevertheless intrigued by the drawings and she tiptoed to study them. As she bent forward, her towel slid to the floor, unheeded. Standing there naked, she was captivated by MacKenzie's vibrant drawing style, and easily recognised Eden in the sketch. But this Eden was captured in a love-tossed, wild eroticism that explicitly revealed the sexual side of her boss's personality.

What most struck Eden's assistant, however, was the other drawing, clearly of MacKenzie, and thus rendered by Eden herself. It was the most sexy thing Angela had ever seen, demonstrating with a startling clarity the poignant mixture of tenderness and sexual energy that drove MacKenzie in his love and in his art. Angela was spellbound. 'Oh my gosh,' she whispered to herself, 'I didn't have any idea Eden was so good!'

MacKenzie opened a lazy eye and grinned at Angela, unabashed at their mutual nakedness. 'Angela my dear,' he said, 'you don't know the half of it!'